DATE		
		MAY ▮▮ 1992
		OCT '96

THE SEA WITHIN

LOUISE MURPHY

THE *SEA WITHIN*

G. P. PUTNAM'S SONS/NEW YORK

Published simultaneously in Canada by
General Publishing Co. Limited, Toronto.

The text of this book is set in Caledonia.

Library of Congress Cataloging in Publication Data

Murphy, Louise, date.
The sea within.

I. Title.
PS3563.U7446S4   1985   813'.54   84-24767
ISBN 0-399-12998-7

Printed in the United States of America

1   2   3   4   5   6   7   8   9   10

For my mother and father

With thanks to Patricia Myrer,
my agent and friend, for
her criticism and support.

THE OCEAN

People drown in San Francisco Bay every year because of their ignorance of the ocean. To swim out into the bay, halfway across the stretch of water spanned by the Golden Gate Bridge, was no casual undertaking. I had been swimming for a year. It was all in preparation for this moment, for this swim.

There were nine of us in the swimming club, six men and three women, who edged carefully into the icy water on that May morning. The time was correctly planned. The billions of gallons that must flow out through the neck of the bay into the ocean would be almost still when we reached the midsection of the bridge. Then the tide would turn and flow back in, picking up speed gently as we returned to the shore, pressing us along, helping us swim. It had been carefully planned.

We were a mixed group. Three of the men had white hair on their heads and chests. The other three were young—two held hands tenderly as they walked into the cold water; the third was a high school boy. Both of the other women were younger than I, more beautiful, more perfectly shaped. Like so many women, I am cursed with the inability to see another of my kind without instantly checking to see if she is uglier or more beautiful than I. Fatter? Larger-eyed? Thicker of hair? More delicate of nose?

The ocean was cold but I had expected this. We had swum in the bay three times a week for six months getting ready for this hardest swim of all. I caught glimpses of my arms pushing out in front of me, moving through the heavy water, and they shone dark and gray and strong, covered with shining cloth, the muscles almost too large for a woman. It pleased me and I swam faster, feeling the water all around me, the salt against my lips.

My body did not normally please me so much. Like today, for instance, I was once again the ugliest woman of the three women in our group. Definitely the ugliest. My favorite fairy tale as a child was Cinderella, and I had spent a smug adolescence waiting for the magic day when I would rise out of the thick casing of my body and become—become what? Something splendid and delicate and, naturally, beautiful. Sixteen came and went, then twenty, then twenty-five. I was beginning to have my doubts. By thirty, I was feeling definitely cheated.

As I cut through the water, I tried not to think of these past lies and concentrated on my strength, on the smooth flow of my thick torso through the ocean. The water was too dark to see through. It had become unimportant that I was not beautiful.

The swim was going well. The sky was covered with a high mass of fog, but the fog would not come low enough to hurt our visibility. We had checked with the weather stations earlier that morning. The day was safe. We had also double-checked the shipping schedules. Uneasily, I tried to tread water for a second and see over the light waves. I stared out to sea, but saw only a yard or two beyond myself. No ships were due into the bay for hours. We were safe.

I swam hard to stay up with the others. My arms were beautiful. They were almost the color of the water. It had taken me a week of shopping to find my outfit. It was different from the other swimmers in having long sleeves that clung tightly to my arms. I had bought it for the color, a silver gray that veered darkly into black. The suit was one of the shiny fabrics that clung and glimmered, and it pleased me. I had also bought tights that came to the waist in a gray that was only a shade lighter than my swimming suit. From neck to toe I glittered and shimmered a dark gray.

Vanity, you are thinking. More abominable vanity. But you would be wrong. The other swimmers stared for a moment but assumed I was trying to keep my skin temperature up. The last thing you should do in cold water is to kick off all your clothes. Clothes can raise your skin temperature even when they are wet. Everyone thought I was trying to stay warmer.

Warmth. That is something you don't think about when you are in San Francisco Bay. There are no benevolent currents in Northern California to fool you into thinking the ocean is a gentle mother. This was *true* ocean. Not like air and land. Indifferent to human needs, suited only for fish and crabs and seaweed, which drifted in clots of sea lettuce or yellow whips across the surface of the water.

I found my breath getting short already. My head ached from the icy water, and I felt joyous and free. It was going to work. After today I would have conquered a new world, a clean, cold world more vast than all the dusty beaches and cities and suburbs growing like fungus on patches of dirt. The silence and the vastness of the ocean would be my country, my home, my refuge.

I was near the midpoint of the Golden Gate Bridge. The water should have been totally flat and still, but there were heavy swells that had to be fought with every stroke. My tights were loosening in the water and had crept down on my hips. I still liked it. Even as I kicked against the currents and felt the silky cloth moving loose over my feet, it made me feel that I had finally made it. I was in my proper place. I had assumed kinship with the whales.

My fixation with whales had been one of the turning points in my life. It began with a trip to a whaling museum in Hawaii the year before. I had sat home and read book after book about dolphins and sea mammals, but mainly whales. Their size, their grace, their songs, which contain more bits of knowledge in ten minutes than Homer's *Odyssey*, their tenderness to each other, and their ability to live in the silence of the ocean, these things attracted me.

Fighting the ocean, I remembered how exhilarated I had been when it first dawned on me that whales were living a life far superior to my own. They had no house to clean, no laundry to pick up, no bent coat hangers or clogged vacuums or broken exhaust pipes, or yes, even that, no people to talk to. No talk, even. Blissful, blissful. No talk, no conversation, no necessity for talk, no social phone calls, no gossip over lunch. No jobs, no boundaries, no opposable thumb with its nervous demands to pull things apart and clutch everything tight. Freedom. Motion. Reproduction. Feeding. Silence.

I smiled tight-lipped so the saltwater wouldn't get in my mouth. The ocean was beating against me harder now. Was it time to turn and go back to shore? The waves were quicker against me, and every other swell in the water had white froth on the top. The wind was rising.

I flipped onto my back and looked up to my right. The bridge was enormous over me, dark red against the lowering fog. It was impossible to tell how far I had come, so I swam on.

Over the last year I had changed, but whether I had come far enough was impossible to say. My life had the same unmarked quality as the ocean when I swam in it. Endless, gray, every wave like the one before, huge markers that towered over me becoming indecipherable in their awful magnitude.

I had developed a crush on whales. I covered the walls with pictures of them and stood entranced in front of these pictures like an adolescent at the altar of a rock star. And, like an adolescent, I suppose, I began to form secret beliefs about my own similarities to my adored objects. Their mass was as my own. My wide shoulders and heavy torso would glide more smoothly through the water than those of my more curvaceous sisters. My feet, thick and wide, were like to the curving flukes of the whale.

My smallish eyes were set far apart, and my prominent forehead bulged, suddenly whalelike, over my face. Like the gray whales, I knew I would kill for my babies. Like the humpbacks, I had gone to Maui, and like the elegant orca, I never forgot an enemy.

It became clear. I was a displaced whale. A whale soul caught, inarticulate when among humans, clumsy on land, trapped in this ridiculous human body.

I laughed out loud at the remembrance of it and swallowed a salt mouthful of ocean. Choking, I stopped swimming and tried to regain my wind. I treaded water with my back to the waves that were blowing over me now with regularity and peered through the cold spray on all sides.

The bridge still towered over me, but its steel had disappeared in fog. I had no idea if I had gone out in the bay as far as the middle. The saltwater 1 had swallowed made me almost nauseated, so I decided: it was time to go back. The current was beginning to return all the billions of gallons back into the bay through the tight neck of water I was in. It would be a hard swim back, but at least the shore waited at the end. It was colder now and I was chilled. My feeling of joy was gone. Like any miserable land animal I was striking out desperately, hoping to feel the dirt under my feet. Doglike, I began swimming frenziedly back toward shore. I couldn't even know how far it was or where I was. I could only follow the line of the bridge, knowing that it would lead me to land eventually.

But something had gone wrong. I knew it was impossible. The weather report had said the tides would be gentle, the wind low, the fog high. But the wind was whipping the ocean into real waves now, and, glancing uneasily overhead, I saw most of the Golden Gate Bridge disappear into the fog. The fog wasn't supposed to roll in until late afternoon, and yet it was there. I swam strongly, but each time I looked up, another section of the damn bridge was gone.

I realized that it was possible for all the bridge to disappear in the fog and for me to lose my only guide to land. The waves were too high to see over. I slid into troughs and hollows of gray water and fought my way through it, unable to see much of anything.

Paranoia was setting in, and I fought it ineffectually. If the weathermen were so wrong, maybe the shipping reports were also wrong. If the ocean was getting rougher off the coast, why shouldn't an oil tanker or container ship cruise into San Francisco Bay to find calmer water? I knew that if a ship came into the bay it would never be able to see me.

I would be invisible in my gray suit in the water. I kept staring around fearfully, looking for a black ship's hull bearing down on me, cutting me in half or, worse yet, forcing me underneath the hull to be crushed and torn, turned to something like hamburger, pulpy and red, by the barnacles on the ship's bottom.

I swam faster, but my legs were numb. My arms were heavy with cold and I caught myself cheating on the strokes, reaching out less far, beginning to curl inward in exhaustion. It was no good. If I swam hard, I ought to be able to reach land, but my swimming was not as aggressive as when I had begun. Rolling over, I tried to float for a few minutes and regain some strength, but floating was a mistake. The waves broke over my head. I couldn't breathe easily, and my body chilled through as soon as I stopped moving.

Then the first cramp hit my body. It began in the bottom of my calf and moved up the back of my leg. I forced my heel down in the water to pull it out. Another cramp was beginning on my right side, but I ignored it. I had been swimming hard. It was all so damned unfair. I had trained for this for a year, had planned it, had been told that it wouldn't be too difficult, but now, when the day comes, the wind rises, the fog rolls in. I get cramps. Cramps, for God's sake!

I realized that I had gotten turned around. The bridge was no longer to my right. Rolling with the waves, I stared behind me, to the left, but there was no bridge there either. I looked through the heavy fog, swinging my body in circles, ignoring the waves that slopped and broke over me. There was no bridge. Millions of tons of steel and cable made useless to me by a little water vapor in the air.

All I could think of at this point was what my husband would say. He had been opposed to all this swimming in the first place. Supportive of my whim and grateful that it got me out of his hair for a while, but dubious.

His girlfriend was a member of a health spa, and he had suggested that I work out there if I wanted to shape up. After telling me this, his mouth had opened again and then shut suddenly. I knew that in all innocence he was going to say how wonderfully the spa worked for *her*, how hard her little fanny muscles had gotten, how firm her upper arms. I burst into tears, adding more saltwater to that which broke over and surged under me.

He would say it was my lack of reality, my inability to think clearly, that had gotten me out here in the middle of San Francisco Bay in the first place. He hadn't known of my desire to become a whale, but he had been suspicious and raced off to his nonswimming, petite, deeply compassionate and understanding, oh-so-firm-fleshed girlfriend and probably discussed it all with her. She would have said, "Camille must be very unhappy, poor woman. She isn't very stable, but then I won't say anything about her. She is such a nice person. I mean, she tries, and she used to be my friend."

All of this was designed to assure my husband that she was a decent, compassionate woman in an unfortunate arrangement brought about only by True Love, not a sneaky cunt who had slept with the husband of a friend.

Anger flowed physically through my body like a shot of bourbon, but it wasn't long-lasting enough to give me strength. You can go a long way on anger, but only when the anger is fresh and new like a wound with the lips curled back moist and thick-sided. My wound had long since dried over and the edges stuck gluily together in resignation. Even my wound ended up disappointing me.

It was appropriate. Like everything else I had ever tried, nothing ultimately had come of it. My marriage, my job at the nursery school, my desire to get pregnant, my friendships and now my aspiration to be an ocean swimmer, all my carefully laid plans, my training, my visits to doctors' offices and my clumsy attempts to be a good wife and lover, all of it was failure left behind me like piles of dung in the road.

I had done the right things. I had paid my dues. I had even, when really desperate, prayed avidly, greedily, openly, to whatever gods might be, prayers like badly written letters beginning, "Dear God," and ending with "please, please, please," strung out in neat, middle-class gasps.

It had all come to nothing, and now I would drown in San Francisco Bay and, with the tides picking up, not even my body would be found to prove that a life had been lived.

A certain masochistic pleasure was creeping over me and warming the numbness of my flesh. I turned and rocked in the ocean, fighting the waves only enough for an occasional shallow breath of thick, damp air, clinging to my pleasurable feeling of having been misunderstood, sinned against and maligned. I felt myself becoming a tragic figure. A squalid and unimportant tragedy, true, but the best I had been able to produce in thirty-nine years of life. What the hell, I thought, if my death doesn't give me dignity, at least *they* will feel like hell.

That was a lie too, like so many of my thoughts then. They would have been shocked, true, but she would have attended my funeral discreetly, not sitting by him, but exchanging mournful, supportive glances. After a decent interval of three or four weeks they would have been murmuring sadly that "poor Camille had never been happy anyway" and been fucking like rabbits without a care in the world. The idea that anyone will join a monastery if you die or set up a shrine for you where they pour precious oil and light candles for the rest of their life is pure romantic fantasy and wishful thinking. Nobody would have felt like hell for very long.

Weighed down by my sadness, wallowing mentally in it as my body wallowed in the saltwater, I could hardly see for the spray and the chop of the waves. I knew I was going to die, and it wasn't such a terrible idea. Giving up the battle, becoming gentle and compliant in the water seemed such a relief, a luxury almost. Throwing down my stubbornness and my failures and letting other people worry about their careers and their marriages and their goddamn orgasms—what a beautiful idea.

Experimentally, I shut my eyes and let my mouth sag open. The saltwater flowed in along with a piece of seaweed. I gagged immediately. I didn't want any pain. Hadn't I read that people drowning just drifted off dreamily and didn't even feel it? Maybe you had to be unconscious to die like that, or was I confusing drowning and dying in the snow?

The desire came over me to swim to shore, get into my car and drive straight to Tahoe, where I could wade out into the snow and die calmly, painlessly. But the snow might be melted by now in the Sierras, I didn't know, and besides, who the hell knew what it was like to die? Dying in the snow probably wasn't what it was cracked up to be anyway. Another lie to join all those I'd already swallowed like saltwater. Lies being poured into me all my life in spoonfuls, dripped into my ears while I slept, served up three times a day disguised as good meals. No. The snow would be just as bad as anything else. I couldn't get out without pain and suffering.

My arms and legs flailed and thrashed slowly. I wanted to live. I wanted rock under my feet. To hell with the whales. Let the Japanese eat them. I couldn't be one of them. They had rejected me. They didn't want me either.

The ocean got very noisy then, and suddenly I saw a sailboat, bearing down on me, being thrown about by the waves that blew steadily across the bay. As the boat came even with me, I could see three men and hear them shouting, "Catch hold, grab it! Grab it!"

I had no idea what they meant. What could I grab? I watched with some interest as the boat wallowed ten feet from me, sails flapping in the eye of the wind. The men were screaming at me. That was what I'd always hated about life, the screaming, the words going back and forth like clubs or like paper airplanes that always missed the target.

I turned in despair in the water. Another boat was bearing

down from behind me. "Grab it, grab it, you dumb broad!" the man in the first boat screamed again. And then I saw the rope trailing past me in the ocean.

Clutching it, I was tugged and rolled by the waves but my hands held firm. I was hauled in to the sailboat and pulled over the side with a lot of effort and scraping on the part of the three men. I am five-foot-ten and weigh one-seventy, no easy handful on land and half-drowned, an awful lump of flesh.

I lay on the floor of the boat while the men got the sails set for a course to the shore. I vomited twice and lost all their sympathy by complaining that they had been pretty damn rough pulling me in. All I wanted was a warm pat, a kindly word, but I ruined my chances by complaining.

My tights had pulled down and were held on only by the crotch of my swimsuit. They trailed ludicrously from my feet in two wet tails, stretched completely out of shape.

I hated it now. It had been as stupid and romantic as anything else I'd ever done. Sodden and exhausted, my own vomit trickling into my hair, slimy under my cheek, I lay there and bawled. The men ignored me with what was really a certain courtesy. They knew from my howls that plenty of air was getting into my lungs. And that was when I decided to leave. To go away. To give up on all the conventional ways I'd ever had of living and just stop all of it. Not suicide, just a stepping out of life and becoming an observer. No more jealousy or sex or marriage or jobs or friends or anything. Just be. Not like a whale. Being a whale was too strenuous. It was beyond me. I would be like a rock. Camille, that ridiculous, romantic name that my father had cursed me with—it was more inappropriate for me than ever. Camille, a flower that would become a stone.

I don't want you to think that at this point in my life I was some sort of superwoman, an athlete, hard and dedicated and living beyond ordinary human limits. I have always been an ordinary person. All that swimming that I did for a year was just another attempt to put something into my life that was important. Something time-consuming.

Before the swimming had been the horse, and before that I had my job at the nursery school, and before that college. The swimming was just an aberration. When you are a healthy woman in your thirties with no job and no real need to have a job, you wake up every morning with a whole day to fill up.

Don't tell me that I'm too locked-in to the Puritan work ethic. That's what Lacey, my friend who worked at the nursery school, said. Lacey told me to just relax and enjoy the freedom. Easy to say. Lacey has three kids of her own to feed, bathe, and talk to when she gets home. She has an ex-husband who calls her parents and says that the divorce was all Lacey's idea, that he wants to reconcile and be a good daddy again. Then he goes over and threatens to kill the kids if Lacey ever has a lover. Lacey has every second of her day full.

I, on the other hand, have a husband making more money than I ever could who supports me without a murmur and no children at all. My days stretch off before me like a prison sentence. Like a convict, I look forward eagerly to lunch and have to be careful not to eat it at eleven because then the hours until dinner are too many to bear.

Neurotic woman, you are saying, why don't you *do* something? So many women nowadays are going back to school, becoming lawyers, doctors, counselors. All that horde of optimistic, bright-faced divorcées proudly hanging out their shingles as family and marriage counselors. Why can't I just do something like that and be busy?

Because I've never wanted to be those things. Because I wanted to work with children, which I did with Lacey for fifteen years in our nursery school, and then I wanted children of my own and couldn't get pregnant to have them.

Do you know how hard it is to adopt a kid these days? Forget black kids. Black women know about the pill and abortion too. Besides, the old liberal idea that white couples can raise black kids is dead. When I called one adoption agency and suggested that my husband and I would love a black child, the woman asked suspiciously, "Is there some reason for your wanting a *black* child?"

I almost lost my temper and said, "Yeah, we're going to turn him into a Ku Klux Klan member by sixteen," but instead I muttered apologetically, "Oh no, we don't particularly want a *black* child, but we could love a black child as much as a white child."

Instantly I knew saying that was a mistake. By stating that we could love a black child as much as a white, I had implied that the idea had crossed our minds that a black child might not be as lovable as a white child. The rest of the interview was like a game.

"Could you love a black child with some physical problem?" the woman asked me.

"Oh yes," I assured her.

"Could you love a retarded child who is black?"

"Of course," I said doubtfully.

Catching up the doubt like a ball and running with it, the social worker triumphantly described a mythical child, black as the ace of spades, retarded, hunchbacked, a victim of three major incurable diseases. "Could you love a child like that?" she crowed triumphantly.

I had no idea, of course, but in my terror I said, "Oh yes, oh the poor baby. Of course we could," my mind reeling with visions of physical therapy classes, learning to give the child its shots, holdings its crippled body proudly as I carried it everywhere.

"You seem awfully sure of your capabilities," the social worker said. "We couldn't encourage you to take such a child. You have no sense of the reality of such a situation nor of the stresses such a child can cause."

That was the end of our liberal dabbling. I had given the wrong answer. We should have been terribly unsure of our capabilities and then the social worker could have led us step-by-step through an educational process whereby we finally became realistic people, ready to give shots and physical therapy and insist that our little cripples clean up their rooms just like normal children.

◇

Then there was my attempt to adopt a foreign child. My husband was not terribly interested in all this adoption business anyway. "Whatever you want, Camille," he would say.

"But how do *you* feel, Henry?" I'd ask. "Tell me how you honestly feel."

"I think it would be wonderful for you to have a child. You know I'll support both of you. You won't have to work anymore. I make enough money to support two or three children. Just find an agency."

His mind always circled back to money. "But *you*, how do *you* feel?" I repeated.

"I meant what I said," Henry would say soothingly. "We can afford it, and it's something you've wanted for years. Go ahead and contact the agencies."

Soothingly. I think that if anyone ever again speaks to me soothingly I will kill them. It is very depressing to be treated like an old lady who must be cossetted and soothed, told what she wants to hear, babied and pampered while the adults get on with the real business of life.

We were married for sixteen years, Henry and I, and during the last ten I never felt that he gave me an honest opinion on anything except money. We could have a huge argument over some trivial thing and I would end up throwing dishes, screaming, telling him off.

"How do you feel about *that?*" I'd scream, throwing an expensive plate at him.

Dodging the plate easily, he would ignore the crash and say, "You're really upset now. I'm sorry you're so upset." His voice would murmur on, trying to calm me like the hum of a machine, unemotional, unconnected with anything but facts. Half the time this made me feel like a monster. The rest of the time I could calm down, be quieted by his murmured assurances, and wonder what was really happening to our marriage.

It was the same with the adoption idea. Henry said all the correct, sensible things, but I never knew where he stood. Was he for it? Against it? Did he have strong feelings about having children? I never knew. Finally, I gave up trying to peel this rational shell back. I gave up looking for Henry. If he was in there, I didn't know how much it would matter anyway. I just contacted adoption agencies that handled foreign children.

Now this seems easy enough. We all grew up knowing in our cribs how overpopulated India is. There are millions of orphans all over the world in poor countries. Besides, our ever-horny soldiers had been leaving children in Vietnam, Europe, and Korea since before I was born. The supply of foreign children who need homes seems unlimited. I had visions of being sent two or three dark-eyed Indian children and nursing them back to health from a series of exotic skin diseases and semistarvation. I pictured Henry and me, the perfect, slightly aging, American couple. He in his Silver Trumpeter suit, I in my velvet blazer and tweed skirt, picking up the children at San Francisco International Airport. I always saw us walking across the reception room and meeting two women with gray hair who handed us the children. The women wore saris and the children were in a basket. I pictured adopting foreign children as being like receiving a basket of kittens from a grateful friend.

"Thank you, thank you," the women would whisper, backing away. "We'll love them forever!" I would cry magnificently.

And there would be two children curled in the basket. A girl who would become a great ballet star, and on her opening night in *Swan Lake* would throw me her bouquet of roses as she took all her curtain calls directly under our box. My face would go positively awash with tears as I ran through this fantasy.

The boy would be less artistic and have a more normal life. He would be too independent for college, but Henry would stake him one hundred thousand dollars for equipment, and, following an impossible idea, he would make the breakthrough discovery that led to a cure for cancer. Being a modest boy, he would turn the idea over to the scientists older than himself and work under their direction for a couple of years until the vaccine was on the market. Impressed by his brilliance, the scientists would write letters of recommendation for him. He would go to Princeton or Harvard and then give up science because of a deep love of mankind and enter divinity school. He would learn Russian and on a visit to Moscow be imprisoned over a misunderstanding and be sent to Siberia. In Siberia he would gradually Christianize all the convicts and political prisoners and be crucified by the guards as a joke. The CIA would smuggle out a film of our son's crucifixion and show it to Henry and me. We would weep with sorrow and joy as we watched him die for his beliefs on film. All Russia would become Christian as a result of our son's missionary work. The Russians would stop gobbling up little countries and making bombs. The world would be peaceful.

I lived with these fantasies for days after I had written to two organizations about the possibility of adopting a foreign child. Once Henry came home just as I had gotten to the part where the two of us, Henry silver-haired, me elegantly salt-and-pepper, had been shown the film of our son's crucifixion. My face was wet with tears, my expression beatific, when Henry walked in.

"Are you all right?" he asked, staring at me.

It was hard to explain. Henry would never understand that I was reveling in the idea of being the mother of a scientific genius who was crucified for Russia's sins. "I'm fine," I said. "One of the goldfish died."

It was true. One had died. Not by crucifixion, of course. It was probably constipation. I was bored with the goldfish. With enough neglect, maybe they would all die. But saying that I was weeping for a dead goldfish fostered the idea that I was delicate, unable to bear pain of any sort. On the basis of a goldfish's dying, Henry offered to take me out for dinner. "I have a lot of *Wall Street Journals* to catch up on," he said, "but we could go to a movie too if we hurry."

It was a magnanimous gesture. To put my tears before the last little gobbet of news in the *Wall Street Journal*, all those paragraphs about possible mergers and short articles about management changes in computer companies, this for Henry was truly sensitive. We went out to dinner, but I nobly rejected the movie, knowing that Henry was dying to read his newspapers. I was noble only until eleven o'clock, when I refused to make love out of spite and went to sleep with visions of dark-skinned children in my head.

The next day I got the first letter from an adoption agency. There was a long questionnaire to fill out before we could apply for a baby. Shrewdly, I began filling out the first half, planning on leaving the last part for Henry. Seeing two different sets of handwriting, the agency would know that we were both eagerly and equally interested in adoption.

But Henry never got a chance to fill out his half. After the usual set of questions on birthdates, education, and income, the form got to the heart of the issue.

"What church do you attend?" the form asked. "Presbyterian," I wrote. It was true. Two or three times a year, Henry and I went to church.

"Do you attend regularly?" was the next question. Since the letter had said that it took up to eighteen months to actually receive a child, that gave Henry and me a year and a half to become ardent churchgoers.

"Yes," I wrote with a feeling of uneasiness.

"Has Christ come into your life and your marriage?" was the next question.

That slowed me down. True, we had been married in a church, and both of us had been brought up attending Sunday school fairly regularly, but could Henry and I say with any honesty that Christ had come into our lives? Wanting a child too much to quibble over trifles, I wrote, "Yes." After all, it is hard to live in Western civilization and say that Christ has *not* come into your life. We've all been exposed, so to speak.

By this time I was sweating, and when I read the last question I groaned out loud.

"When did Christ come into your life?"

It's not good enough to say, "Yes." They want a time and a date. Two o'clock in the afternoon of August 19, 1973, during a baseball game in the Oakland Coliseum. Oakland was losing, 0–1.

I was afraid to go any further with the form. They might ask for Christ's canceled plane-ticket stub from the Jordan River to our home city, or a snapshot of the three of us sitting on the patio discussing salvation and stuff while the fog rolls in.

Don't get me wrong. If I had to pick one dead historical figure that I would like to have over for dinner, Christ would be very high on my list, if not first. I've never gotten interested in Hitler and all his cult of evil, and who could compete with Hitler except maybe Christ or Buddha? I have a feeling that Hitler would be like a corner shopkeeper anyway, and Buddha probably couldn't eat a thing we have in the kitchen, so it would have to be Christ for Henry and me.

But could I explain this to the adoption agency? Would they understand? I didn't think so. We could make up a date, but the next question was, "Explain what happened when Christ came into your life," and I had no idea how to answer that. I had always figured that if Christ came into *my* life it would be an accident on his part, because God knows I'd never done anything saintly enough to deserve a housecall. And I'm not sure I'd go around telling anyone about it afterward since all that goodness would probably have made me blind, deaf, and totally paralyzed with joy anyway. How could anyone describe something like that?

Henry came home and read the forms and threw them in the trash. It was apparent that religious groups were never going to let two wishy-washy infidels like us adopt one of their orphans. It was sort of crazy when you thought about it. Orphanages in Korea and India bulging with unwanted kids who would be orphans unless Henry and I become faithful Christians.

We ended up putting our name into the county adoption agency on the off-chance that some intelligent, white, healthy young couple would die in a car accident and we could adopt their surviving children who were belted in on the back seat.

Six months after we had separated, my husband and I went on a picnic. "She has a new diet," he said, speaking of his mistress. "She's lost eight pounds already. All her friends are on it. Have you seen it?" I shook my head. "It's on a single sheet of paper." He shaped the corners of the paper in the air with his hands. When he lowered his hands, the paper hung unsubstantially in the air between us, a paper ghost. "I'll get you a copy," he said hopefully.

I smiled at him. He was still so husbandly, so well-intentioned. His mistress and all her friends were becoming thinner, more elegant, more desirable. He wanted this success for me too, although he no longer wanted to live with me. It was endearing.

I don't want you to get the wrong ideas about my marriage. I don't want you to get the wrong idea about my husband either. As a matter of fact, I would like to tell you exactly what he was for me and how our marriage was born, lived, sickened and died, but I don't know any of these things myself. I know how the end of the marriage felt. I know that he can still hurt my feelings or boost my morale faster than anyone. I know that when we die God may line us up and shrug and say that we have to stay married even though we don't *have* a marriage anymore.

But when I try to think about those sixteen years that we were married, all I can see is moments, pieces of time frozen in my memory that have no relation to the next piece. There is no continuity, no flow of buildup and collapse. I will never be able to write my six Volumes of The Rise and Fall of Camille and Henry Anderson's Marriage. If written at all, it would be more like a series of television news spots on the history, decay of politics, and eventual warfare in a distant, small, and unimportant country.

"Good evening, this is Camille Anderson bringing you the news from ———— . The building you see behind me is a home that was torn apart yesterday by sniper fire." The camera would pan in on a stucco wall with large chunks broken off the surface. Then the scene would switch to the New York studios, and everyone would move on to something else.

Telling the story of a marriage in one synchronous flow from beginning to end is perhaps a thing of the past. Tolstoy's *Anna Karenina* cannot be written again with any honesty. The style is not ours anymore.

We are products of film. Seeing life as frames which stand unconnected to anything above or below, unattached to the past or the future, we look at life as an entertainment produced for us. At some of the worst moments of my life, there has always been an invisible camera hovering, dividing each fraction of a second into frozen scenes, panning in, picking out objects, dramatizing and trivializing.

Perhaps the main problem in my marriage was that the film had no end. At Christmas of the sixth year, the camera could have fondled the tree, the decorations, the candles, food, happy guests, the contented, cheerful couple, the feeling of quiet satisfaction. Then the camera would have panned out the door, a long shot moving away from the house in a helicopter, the curtain closing in heavy folds as the credits flash onto the screen.

But life has never caught up with technology. The director that every marriage needs is never there for crucial scenes, and the whole thing just runs on and on like a demented Andy Warhol film.

When I think of the sixteen years of my marriage it is in unconnected pieces with no cause or effect or blame or any way on my part to fix blame or see patterns or get any sense of what it was all about. So, if you ask me, "Why did you leave him?" my answers will be unsatisfactory. Unlike some of my more gifted friends, I cannot sum up sixteen years in a clean paragraph or two with a beginning, middle, and end. I mutter. I tell of instances. I wave my hands. It is most unsatisfactory, I know, but it is the best I can do.

For example, whenever a marriage ends there are always long stories that can be told about the sex problems between the man and woman. Every marriage has its story. The man who suddenly becomes modest and refuses to be seen dressing. The woman who says that she no longer needs sex, she has outgrown it. The man who tries to seduce the babysitters. The woman who suddenly discovers that she is sexy. Every marriage has sex problems, and I don't know if we hear about them when marriages break up because sex is where the anger and alienation are first apparent, or if sex stories are what we will listen to most attentively so it is what we are told about.

My marriage too had sex, and so it naturally had sex problems. The worst problem was that Henry and I thought our sex problems were two different things. I thought the problem was that he ignored me all day, was a workaholic from six in the morning until he had neatly stacked his last *Wall Street Journal* and snapped his briefcase shut at ten o'clock, then wanted exactly thirty minutes of sensual, devoted sex in the same way that he wanted me to pick up the laundry and fix Japanese food once a week. Henry, on the other hand, thought that the problem was that I was frigid and unable to enjoy sex.

Now, when there is a problem in a marriage but it isn't seen in the same way by husband and wife, you naturally get two different solutions. My solution was to try to get Henry to go out more, to have people over, to be more social, to gaze deeply into my eyes over a romantic dinner and make me feel special, beloved, and sexy; to hold my hand in the movies without my taking his hand first.

This never worked. First of all, Henry as usual had logic on his side. He would end most of my plans by simply saying that with the house, our pension savings plan, and our stocks, we couldn't afford to go out often and then it had to be cheap. My attempts usually sounded like the sullen housewife's nagging of her tired husband.

And then the business of hand-holding in the movies. I know. I know. If you want your husband to hold your hand, you should just tell him so. You should give him a typed, single-space, list in triplicate (one copy for his office files, one for his home files, one to read) telling exactly what you want. "Things to Do to Make Me Feel Sexy So We Can Get Laid," it could be titled.

If you don't tell him honestly what you want, then you very likely won't get it, but the solution is as sticky as the problem. If you tell him, "Hold my hand in the movies. It makes me feel sexy and beloved," then he will do it. He will do it faithfully, dutifully. Every time you go to a movie he will clasp your paw and hold on for dear life. When he gets up to pee or get popcorn he will release your hand with a guilty look and pick it up quickly when he returns. He will hold your hand regardless of how sweaty it gets or how hard it is to eat popcorn and drink a soft drink with only one hand available. Then when you get home, he will happily demand his payment because, after all, he was a good boy.

We can't win. None of us. We are trapped in the midst of contradictions. We are doomed to failure.

Then there is always Henry's solution. There is one scene in the footage that I can replay anytime. It stands out clearly from all the debris and chaos.

It is set in our bedroom, a fairly ordinary room with the usual king-size bed, double bureau with a mirror over it, straight-back chairs, and wall-to-wall carpet. There has been some attempt to add a sexy element with a peach-colored, quilted satin bedspread, but it cost so much that it gets folded every night and hung neatly over the straight chair. No one ever sprawls sensually on it for sex. It might spot. The closet is large, with sliding doors. The only moment of real action in the bedroom comes when the doors are slid back too angrily with too much force and fall off their tracks onto the naked or half-dressed husband or wife who then screams in panic and curses appropriately as they both wrestle the door back into the grooves.

The bedspread is folded across the chair. The couple lie on their backs as the camera pans up to the bed. Henry is propped against the headboard. Camille lies on her back, staring at the ceiling. He is smiling and reading aloud to her from a book. She is counting the number of holes in each acoustical tile on the ceiling, then counting the tiles and trying to multiply the two for an exact number which represents the number of holes in their ceiling. When she gets to the multiplication, she always loses count, makes a mistake, and has to go back to the beginning. It is hard for her to remember numbers.

HENRY: My God! This is fascinating!
CAMILLE: Uh huh.
HENRY: There is really a lot in here that I never knew before. More than you'd think.
CAMILLE: Twenty, twenty-one, mumble . . .

HENRY:	I know it's a corny book, but just listen to this. I'll bet you don't know this.
CAMILLE:	(She is silent. Her lips move.)
HENRY:	How long do you think the longest penises in the world are, and what ethnic group has them?
CAMILLE:	I don't know, Henry.
HENRY:	It's the Arabs, and their average size is eight to nine inches.
CAMILLE:	Twenty times seventy-eight—
HENRY:	They aren't as thick as American penises, though. Sort of long and skinny.
CAMILLE:	(She has lost track of the multiplication again. Her forehead wrinkles in annoyance.)
HENRY:	Want to know a neat way to enhance a man's orgasm? You take an ice pack and just as he—

This is one of the scenes I remember. Dear Henry. I don't think I've ever known anyone more American than Henry. He was convinced of the benefits of education. If your wife doesn't want to fuck, just read all of several modern manuals to her out loud in bed. She'll gasp in amazement at some point, fling herself aggressively on you and cover you with caresses gleaned from ethnic groups from Pago Pago to Swaziland.

A little education was Henry's answer to all my neuroses. Just give me the right information and I will lipstick my nipples, stretch plastic wrap around my hips and meet him at the door with a small dog whip in my hand. The only reason in Henry's mind why I wasn't doing these things already was obvious: a simple lack of education and information. Dear Henry. He always tried so hard. He is someone I will always love.

I didn't feel that my whole life flashed before me when I was in the middle of San Francisco Bay and half-drowned, but all of these difficult thoughts went through my head as I lay in the bottom of that sailboat, howling and crying with rage at the unfairness of it all. I had tried, in good faith, to be a happily married woman. Henry had tried, in equal good faith, I believe, to be a happily married man, but we were not happy. Like the spare key to the back door, our marriage was misplaced and lost.

Ignoring all offers of help, I drove alone to my apartment in the city. I lurched into the exquisite neutrality of its three rooms and took off my swimsuit and tights. Dirty and naked, I went from room to room tearing up all signs of my romantic delusions about whales. The books, the posters and photographs, the literature from foundations trying to save the whales, it was all thrown in a pile by the front door.

Not giving a damn about the neighbors, I flung open the door and began ramming the debris down the garbage chute in the hall. It was here, nude and cursing, shoving papers and books and the dripping ends of my wet leotard down the chute, that Henry found me. One of the other swimmers had called him, with that sentimental feeling people have about separated couples, so that he could know about my near-drowning in the bay.

Grinning as he eyed my nudity, Henry tried to be nice. "Swimming has been good for you," he said politely.

I stared at him in his business suit, so neat and successful and unassailable, and included him in my rage. "You don't give a goddamn about my body anymore. You're just like a dog that's peed on the same post for fifteen years. You don't care about the post, it's just that you have to sniff and fake a raised leg whenever you walk by it."

Storming back into my apartment, I was glad the trash was gone. I would have been embarrassed to admit that just yesterday I wanted to become a whale. What an asinine idea. It all seemed in the past now.

"Are you all right?" he asked politely.

"Yes. Sit down if you want. I'm going to shower."

Henry sat and I showered. He was still sitting politely in the same spot when I came out in Levi's and a sweatshirt. Henry had a well-trained modern man's feeling for a woman's right to privacy. Besides, he is just naturally polite, I have to admit, a quality that I have never acquired beyond a surface veneer.

My hands were trembling as I fixed a pot of strong tea and tried to explain to Henry how I stood. It had been a year since I had moved out of our beautiful house in the suburbs and into the city to this unbeautiful but neutral apartment where I could think with relatively few encumbrances of our mutual history as a couple.

"You could have died, you know," Henry said.

KENTUCKY Six rivers slashed through lime and sandstone cliffs to feed the Ohio and water the land. The Big Sandy, Cumberland River, Green River, Licking River, Kentucky River, and all the smaller rivers and creeks, Panther, Barren, Troublesome, Hanging Fork Wolf, Whippoorwill, Silver, Goose, hundreds of streams that flowed clean and cool through that massive wilderness, all of them offering their water for thousands of years before the first white man ever saw them.

The east was mountains, rough and difficult, the dues that had to be paid to enter the sacred land, covered with hardwood forests of trees older than any most men had seen in their life, creeks running over rocks, dark pockets between the trees full of wild lily and mountain flower, dogwood trees blooming like ghosts in the mountain darkness. And always, if a man and woman had time to look up, there were the big trees. Tulip poplar, white oak, chestnut and cherry, walnut, maple, and buckeye. It was a forest of unbelievable richness that was a curse for wagons and teams but a blessing later when the women demanded wooden floors and cradles, buckets, chests, chairs, and a decent cherry bed for Grandma before she dies in this wilderness.

When the first men fought their way out of the mountains they saw a plain sprinkled with massive trees, a rolling land covered with grass which shone blue-green when the wind blew it all in one direction. The topsoil was fifty feet deep in places. A man could scratch a hole and grow anything he liked. It was new land.

And then there was the game. Parties of hunters could kill a thousand deer in two months. The birds and small animals, the possum and coon and rabbit, were easy to catch. A child of ten could hunt and kill enough meat for a family of eight if he was diligent.

Coming through Cumberland Gap in the southeast corner of the state, hardened men wept at the beauty that lay before them and women narrowed their eyes in speculation and began to believe that the hardships of the mountains were going to be justified.

Farther west lay the Barrens, land once covered with brush and trees but burned by the Indians to create a grassland which attracted buffalo and antelope in herds too large to count. This was the hunting land of the Cherokee and Shawnee, who came into Kentucky from south and north to use her riches and then return to their settlements beyond the Ohio River and south into Tennessee.

Above this land was the sky that all men and women expected to see, blue, cloud-filled for warm summer rain, eternally open and hopeful. As they walked over mountain roads, seemingly buried and lost under dark trees, the people raised their eyes to catch sight of a reassuring point of light, a slice of blue that would tell of promises and things pure, untainted by the day-old grease in the iron skillet banging against the side of a horse, or the dark circles under the children's eyes. And when the mountains were at their back, they cried aloud, feeling the weight of shadow falling off them, losing the mountain cold, running out into the rolling plainland where the sun and moon were present from their first rising until their last minutes of setting. Feeling the blue high over them as a release, a promise, an assurance that their intentions were honorable and in concurrence with God's will.

All around them on the land were deep fields and wild game, but another dimension had yet to be discovered by these white and black people who came so nobly across mountains to find a new life. Sick of war with England, men came to carve out a small nation of their own, away from cities and armies and the subtleties of civilization. They brought with them their black slaves, who, being wiser than their owners and more experienced in the ways of life, did not expect anything new or beautiful, the corn mush tasting the same in Virginia as it did in the new land. Appropriately, it was a slave, Stephen Bishop, who was to explore the other dimension of this newfound Eden.

Bishop, so his owner claimed, could see in the dark, his memory was perfect, and he could record with amazing accuracy the land he had merely walked over. Bishop gave to the world the first accurate charts of that other world in Kentucky: the world beneath the ground. For under Kentucky lay a land of darkness and silence and cold more certain than death itself. Stephen Bishop ventured into this land, finding it, perhaps, no darker for his soul than the world of sun on top of the earth.

Carved by cold rivers in the limestone which was the foundation of this new Eden lay the largest caves in the world. Every settler soon had his own cave, which he boarded up so his stock and children would not wander in and be lost forever in the darkness. There were exposed crowns of rock that rang hollow when a man or woman jumped on them, and everyone knew that the rock, lying there in the sunlight, was the top of some vast chamber under the earth, a chamber that no one would ever find through the threadlike windings of underground tunnels, but a place whose invisibility did not make it any less an absolute.

Blue above, fertile land and green plants growing lush everywhere the eye flickered, rivers and creeks moving masses of water through the land, pure springs of it coming up everywhere, it seemed, and beneath it all the dark world of caves and silence and the hollow boom as your boot touched stone, this was Kentucky, the Indian name itself meaning "dark and bloody ground." This was where I had been born. This was where I had to go.

"Henry, I'm going to go home. I'm going back to Kentucky."

Henry nodded slowly. "You're going to stay with your aunt?"

"I may." Best to be evasive about where I was staying. I knew down to the last measured foot of land where I was going to stay, but it was none of Henry's business.

"It might be a good idea for a while." Henry looked at me thoughtfully. "This doesn't mean that we have to rush into a divorce, though. Let's just try this for a while and see how you feel about being there."

"Oh, Henry," I sighed. "We aren't going to get back together with you in San Francisco and me in Kentucky."

"It doesn't hurt to leave things open. You may feel different later. Who knows?"

"Besides," I said, "if you're divorced, she's going to put the screws to you to get married. As long as we're married, you're safe."

Henry protested, but I laughed and he smiled as he protested. We both knew him. To everyone else he had always been a "nice guy." Now that he was having an affair with an ex-friend of mine, his nice guy status was getting a little speculative, but with proper rationalization Henry could keep the banner of nice-guyism flying defiantly if not proudly. It would blow things up if we actually got a divorce. Then he would have to marry or at least live with his lady love. Henry wanted to get laid twice a week with no complications or guilt, but he did not want a woman there every morning and night. He just wanted two nights of fun every week and the *Wall Street Journal* the other five. I was his protection and shield.

"I'm going back to Kentucky. I don't know what I'm going to do, but I'm leaving San Francisco. I'm going to sell out my share in the nursery school to Lacey and use the money to live on."

"I can send you enough to live on every month." Henry had his briefcase open now. He was making notes. He was happy. "I'll send you whatever you need. If you get your own place, I could send half of the things in the house, whatever you want. You might rent somewhere. When are you going?"

"Day after tomorrow," I said. "I have some things to get before I go."

Henry nodded. "I'll have my secretary book you through."

"Oh, Henry," I said. "Who would have thought it would end this way?"

He tried to look surprised. "But it's not ending. We haven't gotten the divorce yet."

I didn't know what to say. Every time I opened my mouth, something trite came out. Trying to explain to Henry would have meant trying for the ten thousandth time to say who I was, and I only knew at this point who I wasn't.

I wasn't his wife. I wasn't a sweet, patient woman who worked all day with other women's children so those women could be fulfilled as vice presidents of insurance companies or whatever they did. I wasn't a mother. I wasn't a swinging, single woman. I wasn't an intrepid swimmer. I wasn't a whale.

And the thought of all these failures on my part reduced my sharp tongue to humility, and I said good-bye to Henry with a certain sweetness. After all, he knew who he was. His days were full. His sex life was neat and orderly in its twice-weekly spasms of romance. He had moments of longing to be Mick Jagger and occasionally examined odd devices in strange shops along Columbus Avenue in San Francisco, but he kept it all in proportion. Had I known exactly who I was, then I might have resented Henry less. I might have been able to love him more or at least to set up my own life and love affairs as practically as he had. I might have been someone.

FATHER

There was probably only one person in the world who thought I was someone. She didn't think of it like that, and would have found the whole question silly, but she knew that I was and always would be someone. After all, I was her brother's grandchild, his only grandchild, and her brother had been the Judge. No one related to the Judge could have possibly been considered nobody. That was the way my great-aunt Nell thought, and everyone in Toms Creek, Kentucky, would have agreed with her.

Unlike my vicious, weak father and my even weaker mother, who survived my birth by only two years, both spent in bed, my grandfather was a man to reckon with. He was a self-made man who had grown up on a small farm and ended up owning the largest farm, most spacious house, and best bay mares in that part of Kentucky. This was enough to make his family count, but he had gone further than that. He had been at separate times during his life Lieutenant Governor, Governor, and then Senator.

Elected by his people, he served with little interest, longing only to return to his bay mares and shady front porch. But he

36

served, and in his austere, naive fashion he did exactly what he thought he had been elected to do: he worked hard, tried to make life better for his people, and never took a bribe or made a nickel off his service. What was so obvious to my grandfather about his ten or fifteen years of political life that he never discussed it with anyone and would allow no talk of it around him was the thing that made us all, all his relatives, somebody. He had astounded the whole state by being an honest man.

As Aunt Nell used to say, "My brother was honest, and God knows he was smart enough to know how to cheat and skim like all of them, but he didn't. He lost money in politics. His tobacco didn't get planted, and he even gave up on his bay horses for those years." She would shake her head in amazement. The only two things that my grandfather had ever been passionate about were his bay horses and his son.

And, all in all, he should have stuck with the horses because the son was no thoroughbred. Following a hardworking father who had always been right about everything, my father stood little chance of being anywhere near good enough or smart enough or hardworking enough to satisfy either my grandfather or the town. After unsuccessfully trying to become first a doctor, then a lawyer, and then doing a short stint as a schoolteacher until he had to be removed for showing too much attention to the more shapely students, my father had married and settled into a life of genteel poverty as my grandfather's tenant farmer.

My father. My father. I can forgive him and even love him for his failures at medicine, law, and teaching. I can sympathize with his foolish marriage and what was probably the more foolish begetting of me, but I cannot forgive my father's genteel alcoholism, which he tried unsuccessfully to hide from his father and the town that watched with interest, and I cannot forgive that he left me his face, feature by feature, which I must see in the mirror every day of my life.

To live from birth with a man who was an alcoholic, with only the visits of Aunt Nell to provide a barrier between my father's rages and my own as I grew up; to live with a weak, sneaky, lying drunk who dressed up every day like a gentleman and was usually lying on one floor or another of the house by night; to live with fear and disgust and later with all the work of the house, that was unforgivable enough. But to brand me with his face, his eyes set far apart, and his habit of staring off into space slack-jawed when thinking, this was my cross to bear. It is a hard thing to see the face of the person you have hated as a child in your own mirror every day. It wasn't his fault, of course. He had no say over what the genes did when mixed with my mother's, but I knew that it pleased him. In this one thing he had been triumphant. When his genes mixed with my silly mother's, his were dominant. A passive victory at best, but my father's only one and cherished accordingly. He used to hold me up on the street for overall-clad farmers, who stood and spat tobacco juice while their wives shopped, to notice the marked similarity of our features.

"See here," he'd say. "She's just a girl, but if she isn't the spit of her old man, I don't know what is." He would press his patchily shaven cheek to mine and laugh his whiskey breath over my face. "Looky here at her," he would demand. And they would look and nod. It was true. We were as alike as twin colts from the same mare, my face more feminine, but just like his.

It was his joke. He had said to me on the day after I left for college, abandoning him against the advice of all the relatives, "Well, you can go wherever the hell you want, Camille. You can leave here and pretend that I'm not your daddy and never have been, but you'll carry me with you till you die."

He had been too drunk when he said this to stand up or to hit me for what I did, so I hadn't said a word, but had gone from one room to another like a crazy person. I threw pictures down off the walls, turned bookcases over, tipped all the food off the refrigerator shelves, wrecked all the nice middle-class respectability of that farmhouse that I had worked for eighteen years to keep respectable and neat.

Picking up my suitcases, I glared at him as he sat there drinking. "I cleaned up your mess for nearly eighteen years!" I screamed. "Now you can live like the hog you want to be. Now everybody can see exactly who you are."

"You look just like me," he slurred. "You're as mean as me, and

38

if you go it's going to kill me." And he wept in that terrible, drunken, self-pitying sorrow that turned me to ice.

"I hope so," I said. And he was right. Without me to get him in and clean him up, he died. The second winter after I left he froze one night, half in the henhouse door, where he had crawled for warmth when he couldn't find the house, his face lying like a child's with the eyes open and a mysterious smile across his mouth. He was found a day later, and although he looked nice at the funeral parlor in his plush-lined coffin with rosy cheeks and a piece of cardboard in his mouth to hold it shut, I always thought of him lying dead with that innocent expression, eyes wide open, his face frozen to the layers of chickenshit under his cheek.

My great-aunt Nell, who had always been simply Aunt Nell to me, took care of the funeral. She was the only relative I had been close to, and it was Aunt Nell who had kept me in touch with what was happening in Toms Creek.

She wrote me every month, and her letters had been the same until about seven months ago. The letters all began with a sentence about the weather, then a page of general gossip about people I had grown up around. Many of these people I remembered only hazily, but Aunt Nell persisted in telling me of every twist and turn in the careers of classmates from high school and who currently owned the farms around town and who had been born or died or was in one of the eternal messes humans find themselves in between birth and death.

Aunt Nell had a sharp tongue, and she usually ended her letters with a reminder that having an alcoholic father had been a burden for me but that my survival had only proved my close kinship to the strength of my grandfather. Therefore, there was no sully on my name because my father died drunk in a chicken-coop, and I should come home to Toms Creek to live.

Her logic was unyielding throughout the years, and I knew she would accept my arrival as the first act of good sense I had committed since graduation from college. I had gone to college only because Aunt Nell had persuaded my grandfather to leave me some money that my father couldn't touch. Everything else was left outright to my father because my grandfather was too proud to admit that his only son was unable to manage the estate.

Pretending that my father was a normal man, of sound mind and ordinary habits, my grandfather left him the huge house, the smaller farmhouse where I had been born, the best farm in the county, and a string of bay horses with bloodlines finer than his own. By ignoring the reality of his son's actions, my grandfather indulged in a weakness that was to kill my father off faster than he would have managed on his own.

For the four years of my high school career and the two afterward until he died, my father was able to drink as much as he wanted.

But it was worse than that. Like most drunks, my father wanted drinking buddies. He wanted to be surrounded by friends who would listen to his excuses and rationalizations and memories of past betrayals. There were only three qualities a man needed to be my father's friend at this time: he had to be unemployed, the better to devote all day to drinking; he had to be able to drink steadily from breakfast until he passed out at night; and he had to assure my father that all the failures of my father's life were caused by his high-handed father, his wife's silly relatives who cut her off after his marriage, his smart-alec child who was a serpent's tooth in her ungratefulness as his daughter, and all the other people who had robbed, cheated, and betrayed him. There must never be any suggestion from my father's friends that his problems began with the first splash of bourbon he put in his morning coffee, and certainly there must never be any suggestion that he sober up. It also seemed part of the service of my father's friends that they all knew how to make a killing if they could only get the capital from someone.

Aunt Nell was perhaps sharper when she suggested that my grandfather left all his estate to my father knowing full well that it would be turned into potable liquids and foolish schemes. The way Aunt Nell tells it, my grandfather figured it out to the penny and knew that as the last scheme fell through, my father would

40

freeze to death in the chickenyard, leaving me free of him for the rest of my life. It was grandfather's way of taking the burden of his son off me, his helpless granddaughter.

"After all," Aunt Nell used to write, "it left you with enough to go to college and start your nursery school. Your grandfather even left you your own cemetery plot so you can come home and be buried with your kin like a decent person. He knew what he was doing."

Aunt Nell harped on this theme in her letters and saw my refusal to come home as a slap at the integrity of her brother, who had so conveniently eliminated my only parent and given me freedom. But recently her letters had become more urgent, more demanding, and it was puzzling to me.

What did Aunt Nell expect me to do? She lived in Toms Creek and I lived in San Francisco. I was sorry that my cousin twice-removed on my father's side had gotten pregnant, but what could I do about it? It seemed like an unfortunate thing, but simple enough to deal with. The girl was only fifteen. She could easily get an abortion.

But the months went on and Aunt Nell still fussed over it. The girl did not have an abortion. She had stubbornly refused in the face of all common sense, and now she must be six or seven months pregnant. I didn't know why she had to run to my Aunt Nell after so many years of no connection. It was true that Aunt Nell was the one member of the family who had always been there when anyone needed nursing or burying or advice or a good chocolate cake to get you through a hard time. But it was ridiculous for this child to latch onto a seventy-eight-year-old woman as the person to live with during an unwanted pregnancy, and I was sure that I would hear more about her pregnancy, about the old farmhouse and how it needed repair, and about the bay mares that existed in the world only waiting for me to clean up the barn and buy them. I didn't care much about pregnant teenagers. She was a girl named Dinah, whom I had never known or heard spoken of as a relative. But I did love horses.

◇

It wasn't bay mares I was going to buy in San Francisco the next morning. If I wanted a bay mare, I wouldn't have known where to go to get one in San Francisco. I drove, ignoring the blue, deceptively warm-looking water that showed in the near distance from the top of every hill. I ignored the beauty of that one-fourth of the city that is so often selected for convention sites by Midwestern dentists and computer programmers.

The store was on a street of small shops off 19th Avenue. The front was two windows with a jumble of goods stacked indifferently against the glass—no pretty display or any sense that anyone cared. A can of white gas served as the base for a box of flashlights, which slid into a T shirt hung droopingly on a hanger over a pile of canteens. The other window held cardboard boxes stacked anonymously with two sleeping bags thrown over them.

The shop was probably one of the best cheap suppliers of camping equipment on the West Coast. Decoration they did not need. They had the real stuff and two bright clerks who didn't have to hustle.

I wandered through the store, selecting a light tent that popped open, providing sleeping space for four, and enough head room to stand comfortably, a summer-weight sleeping bag with a zip-in liner that made it a cold-weather bag, an oil lantern, a set of nested pots and a set of dishes that also packed compactly into one bowl, a spatula, fork and spoon to cook with, a portable chemical toilet, a large flashlight and four duffel-shaped bags for my clean clothes, food, dirty clothes, and kitchenware. I could get a two-burner camp stove and white gas to run it in Kentucky. Maybe I could be really modern and make a solar stove. It was something to think about, but I didn't really care much.

A bearded man packed everything tightly in a large box. I could organize some clothes in a small suitcase and still be close to the fifty-pound limit on the airplane.

"You bought some good stuff. Where are you going?" he asked.

"Kentucky," I answered.

"I hear they have some nice lakes there. Are there any wilderness areas left in that part of the country?" He tied the package with a series of elegant knots while he talked. Like the goods he sold, his motions had no excess.

"Yes," I said. "There's wilderness everywhere. You just have to know where to find it."

"Wilderness is the way to go," he stated.

I nodded. Everything American in me leaped up at the one-sided truth of his statement. To the wilderness was the only way to go, but my wilderness was not going to be the calm, gently rolling Kentucky farmland. My wilderness was the brush and thickets of my failures.

I loaded the box into my car and drove back to the apartment. Tomorrow morning I would fly to the middle of the country, away from the ocean and its whales. I wouldn't keep moving. I'd sit by the trail and watch. The wilderness would grow up over my head and cover me, but I wouldn't care anymore because I would be part of it. Part of the very stones that shape the earth. I would die sitting there, and my bones would lie on the ground and bleach and be covered and there would be no more.

BONES

And so the world began. The oceans surged over the land and covered what we now call Kentucky with a vast sea. The green fields and forests first seen by Indians and later by white and black men were once lying on the bottom of the ocean. Slowly the water receded from the north, and for a few years the Gulf of Mexico touched the earth that became Kentucky. The land was uneasy, shifting, never staying for long in one place, it seemed.

Then came the great cold of the Pleistocene Epoch, the Age of Ice. Glaciers, sometimes as thick as 6000 feet, crept over the northern world and moved as far south as the Ohio River. Grinding boulders to sand in its path, pressing out lakes and valleys, the country was formed by ice, carved by the frozen tons of snow and stone that lay for years on the land.

And the animals fled. They shifted their grazing territory ever southward, trying to find green, living things. They wandered south for hundreds of years, the mammoths, mastodons, peccaries, tapirs like small rhinoceroses. Foxes, bears, horses, and elk all moved southward in front of the ice that followed them like a curse. The great ground sloth came more slowly, dragging its weight over the land, and it joined the other animals in their struggle for survival.

There, in the northern part of what is now called Kentucky, the animals found a huge salt marsh. It was good to rest there. The ice was still on the other side of the Ohio River. The animals gathered at the salt licks and struggled in the bogs and sinkholes to eat the bitter salt they craved. The ocean had left her gift for the animals, and they gathered in great numbers to lap up the mud that tasted so bitter and so desirable.

But life is seldom without its prices. To get the salt, the huge mammals had to chance the bogs and quicksands of the marsh. Unhesitatingly, with heavy step, they sought the salt. They moved toward the salt licks not knowing that many of them would sink in the marsh and die, settling below the water and mud, providing food for the lighter-footed animals. They were huge. Some weighed a ton. They sank in the bitter mud, and, struggling and fighting to get out, they sank deeper until the salt filled their noses and eyes and they died.

Then the ice began to melt. Rivers altered their course. New streams sprang up and old ones vanished. The marshes gradually receded and dried. The old world had vanished, except for the bones. The bones could withstand the sun and rain, the storms and the drive of hail and snow. A bone is something that will endure when the flesh has failed.

The Indians knew of this place and went there to boil salt from the mud, but no white man had seen the area until 1739, when the Indian guides showed it to Charles le Moyne, a French-Canadian officer. Then another man arrived with a party of explorers in 1773.

His name was James Douglas. He was a Scotsman, and he was intrigued by the place called Big Bone Lick. He set up his camp on the place where bones lay visible on top of the ground and used the tusk of a mastodon for his tent pole. Sitting on the backbone of some giant animal, James rested as night fell and watched the bones gleam in the moonlight. They shimmered in the night, ghosts of another world, pearly and pure, licked clean of flesh by time and the elements, and it pleased James Douglas.

44

He slept peacefully under his blankets stretched over the tall tusk and dreamed of jungles and rivers and huge shapes that moved slowly across the earth.

I slept heavily all night. The next morning I took my suitcase and box, called a cab, and went to the airport. Henry had kindly promised to empty the apartment and sell my car. It wasn't a very good car, just an old Volkswagen, but the money might be useful.

The plane was on time, the stewardesses cheerful and clannish like sorority sisters meeting freshmen. I sat belted in and watched the city recede flatly under us as we circled out to sea before heading inland toward the east. Being over the Pacific in a plane reminded me of the last time I had flown, another attempt that failed, another romantic fantasy whose reality was unimpressive.

It was six months after Henry and I had separated. The week before Thanksgiving, Henry told me that he and his mistress and all of her friends were going to rent an old Victorian clubhouse on Mount Tamalpais and have a pot-luck feast. Henry told me apologetically. He knew I had nowhere to go for the holiday.

"Maybe I could fix up a little dish of broccoli or salad and come too," I said.

Henry stared out my apartment window and watched two women walking past the health food store. He watched them with fascination as they checked the apples and oranges in the outdoor bins.

"If I'd known you'd feel that way, I wouldn't have agreed to go," he said. "Now I'll feel bad about your being alone."

"What the hell, Henry. If we ate together it would just be lots of work and then we'd have nothing to say over dinner anyway. You might as well go and have a good time."

Henry cheered up. "I like your view." He gestured to the street outside. "Those bins are sort of nice. They'd make a good photograph, a close-up shot of the wooden packing crates and the vegetables."

Henry was always pointing an imaginary camera at the world

around him. He fancied the softer arts because he could imagine himself doing them. Henry didn't own a camera, though. He didn't think it was worth trying unless you could do it full time, and that was impossible with his job, the house, the stock options, and all his other expenses to keep going. Henry did have good taste. He knew that someday he would manage his time differently and be able to buy a camera. Turning from the window, he got to the real reason why he was visiting me in the city.

"Since I have to go to this thing," he sighed, "I ought to take something."

I nodded solemnly. Henry, who had never cooked more than a scrambled egg while we were married, was the victim of liberation. Nowadays single men had to take their own homemade goodies to parties.

"Can't you just get away with bringing some wine or a loaf of French bread?" I asked.

He shook his head. "Amy asked me to bring a casserole. She suggested that I might cook some sweet potatoes. Everyone likes them a lot."

It was true. All my friends had loved my Southern sweet potatoes with orange juice and butter and melted puffs of marshmallow on top. All the people who would gather for Thanksgiving, all the people I had spent years cultivating, nursing through divorces, babysitting for, all of them had loved my cooking.

"Well, Henry," I smiled, "why don't I just cook it up for you, and you and Amy can pick it up before the party?"

Henry knew better than to take this seriously. "Oh, no. No. You just tell me how to fix them and I'll do it." He lowered his voice. "I don't think Amy would be comfortable coming over here with me."

"Of course," I agreed. Henry was always thoughtful. I gave him the recipe, adding three tablespoons of cayenne pepper just for the hell of it to the usual list of ingredients.

"Isn't that a lot of pepper?" he asked.

"It seems like a lot, Henry, but red pepper is mainly to color up the potatoes, make them a prettier orange. It won't taste strong with all the orange juice and cinnamon," I assured him.

Henry went off with his recipe in hand, and that afternoon I

46

took the credit cards that were still in my name and flew to Hawaii.

The trip to Hawaii had been magnificent at first. To begin with, I had never been there. Henry didn't have time to travel, and his stocks always seemed to do poorly just as Henry had three weeks for vacation. Or, I should say, Henry never traveled except for business. He went to Tokyo, Paris, Rome, New York, and Rio for his company, but they picked up the bills for those trips. I stayed home to take care of the plants, house, dog, and to "keep the home fires burning," as Henry jokingly said.

Thinking back on it, it was amazing that I hadn't poured kerosene all over the house and torched it while Henry was gone. Then, when he had returned with all his stories of how boring it had been, staying in hotels, eating out every night, just one city after another, I could have agreed carefully and, pointing to our smoldering investment, have said brightly, "Just kept the home fires burning more warmly than usual, dear."

But no. We were so upwardly mobile. Henry was providing me with all the security I had never really been able to provide for myself, and he meant so well. It wasn't as if he were spending his money on other women or drinking it away. The only women he knew were my friends, and other than some wine with dinner, neither of us drank much. It seemed ungrateful to complain. Besides, he really did hate to travel.

But standing at the ticket counter that morning, I had suddenly realized how unsophisticated I was. "First class," I said, feeling a thrill go down to my toes. Henry flew first class because his company paid for it, but he had always told me that first class was silly and unnecessary.

"All that champagne and service is just a waste of time," he had said. "There I am, trying to look at reports, and people are playing games and getting drunk. It's ridiculous. I can't imagine why the company bothers with first class."

But Henry had always stoically flown first class, and so I too would fly with the privileged and see what it was like, and I don't think anyone on the airplane had a better time than I did except for the eight-year-old girl who sat across from me.

"Oh, look!" she'd shriek. "Little tiny forks and spoons!"

"They're beautiful," I would agree, and the two of us fingered our cutlery with larceny in our hearts. We both wanted to steal it all, but settled for the tiny salt and pepper shakers and souvenir bottles of crème de menthe.

Then there was the luxury of selecting the music I wanted to hear over the headphones, a full-length movie, more to eat, more to drink, hot moist towels for my hands, orchids in my drinks, more orchids stuck in my pastry, a fruit plate, maps of the islands, and games. Winning a bottle of champagne by correctly guessing the proper year and month when Hawaii became a state brought tears of joy to my eyes. I couldn't imagine why Henry disliked first class.

We landed in Honolulu and I took a small plane to Maui. That was the place to go, everyone said so. I had no idea, but Maui sounded more romantic somehow, more distant, more exotic. Finding a place to stay was my first brush with reality, and I came down quickly from my champagne high.

Maui in November is crowded. Every hotel was full of visitors swilling Mai Tais and peeling their sunburns. I was lucky to find a rental car, and the kid in the rental agency tipped me off: "If you can't find a room around Lahaina, just park in town and walk up on the hill outside the town. Take a blanket and sleep up there. Nobody's going to bother you."

I did what he said for the first night. A blanket was cheaper than a room, and the night was warm. Lying there with my back against the earth and the sky full of stars over me, I felt totally happy. This was what I had left Henry for. Excitement, travel, champagne, and the smell of heavy warm ocean air pouring over me, moist and fragrant with salt and thousands of unknown flowers which opened on Maui that night for me alone.

The next day I got extraordinarily lucky. I found a room with a small balcony overlooking the ocean. It was expensive, but my rage at Henry was still hot enough for that to please me. Let him worry about the bills. He was excellent at managing our affairs. I was merely giving him a chance to demonstrate his expertise.

For four days I wandered around Lahaina, riding the quaint little train to the more elegant Kampali section of the island, eating lunch beside pools in large hotels, watching a young man dive into the sea from a cliff at sunset, wandering through the shops where you could buy jade and pearls and black coral. I thought the black coral was elegant, but knowing that men died sometimes while diving to find it gave the coral a sinister feel that made me shiver when it was around my neck.

The pearls were tempting, but I held one strand next to my skin and flinched. The perfection of those creamy beads made my skin look mottled, my eyes shifty, uncertain. Pearls were only for girls and old women, I decided. Complete innocence or absolute knowledge were necessary for a face to stand up to pearls. Looking in the gilt-edged mirror at my own face, with those beautiful irregular pearls across my throat, I suddenly felt lost. Where was I? On some island in the Pacific, alone, thirty-nine years old with no career or children to show for my life's efforts, I stood there and felt limbo coming down around me.

I handed the pearls gently back to the salesgirl and wandered out onto the street. Those pearls changed my whole trip as instantly as a slap across the face. All of Lahaina looked different then.

The waitresses at dinner wore sleek tubes of silk slit up to one thigh and cut down to show the small of their backs. I ate my mahi-mahi glumly and knew that I would never be a woman who wore dresses like that and made men stare. Most of the other diners sat around with their children laughing and talking. I would never have children either. I chewed the parsley that had garnished the fish and knew the bitterness of reality.

I marched out the next morning to spend Thanksgiving Day on the beach. Heavily oiled and wearing a swimsuit that did the most for me that it could, I was determined to enjoy myself, to regain my pleasure in the novelty of travel. I lay on the beach and drank coconut-flavored drinks that cost more than lunch would in San Francisco.

I wandered through a small museum near my hotel that was dedicated to the history of sailing. Exhibits of harpoons and the knives used to carve blubber hung next to pictures of mother whales lifting their calves gently to the surface with giant fins. Lahaina had been a whaler's port, and the harpooners had drunk and whored all night and killed whales all day. A chill passed down my body as I realized that the air around Maui was wet with blood from the whales. The red had washed up on the sand. Blood had been tracked into the bars at night and was left on the dirty sheets to show brown by morning, smudging the breasts of women like bruises. I bought a book about whales in the museum store and began to read avidly.

The heavy sigh of dying whales filled Lahaina, and the sound set me apart because all the other people seemed oblivious to it. They were happy. They were not alone. Everywhere I saw elegant older couples arm in arm, teenage couples with muscles and minuscule bikinis brushing against each other as they walked, middle-aged couples holding hands. I drank morosely and tried to get up enough courage to move down the beach.

For the first time in Hawaii I was afraid. I knew that I would round a bend in the shoreline and see wedged in the sand of the shallow water a huge wooden boat with a gangplank leading to the deck. Marching up the plank would be a line of happy, tanned, thin couples all smiling and talking to each other.

It was the ark. Everyone was paired off and getting aboard. I would look around desperately for a partner, but to no avail. I was a single creature, a species unto myself. There was no other animal in the world to make a pair with me.

I forced myself to stay on Maui for two more days. The night of the second day I ate a McDonald's Big Mac and drank a Coke on the balcony. My bills were beginning to make me feel guilty as my anger at Henry wore off.

Disillusionment had set in. Where were the beach boys who looked like toasted Greek marble? The ones I saw were pudgy with the fat of late-adolescent blooming. Where were the fascinating sights? I didn't care much about them anymore. It seemed like an effort to get into the car and drive around alone following a map.

I stared at the most glorious sunset in the world and polished off my Big Mac. I should have gotten French fries too, I thought bitterly. To hell with trying to be thin.

Standing against the rail, I threw my napkin and McDonald's sack out in the warm air. To hell with Hawaii. To hell with Maui. To hell with me.

Six stories below there was concrete surrounding the small pool and the neatly stacked lounge chairs. I wanted to jump. The sky was purple and orange, and I knew that even the whites of my eyes were stained red by the sunset. Glaring down, I put my hands on the rail. I wanted to jump so badly that I never could figure out why I didn't. There weren't many temptations that could be answered so easily by a simple leap.

Perhaps I knew that life might get better. Perhaps I thought of Henry and Aunt Nell. Perhaps I hated the romance of the setting. There's no knowing anymore, but mainly I didn't jump because of my father. It seemed like the sort of weak, romantic, silly gesture that he would have made to cause me a lot of trouble and agony. I knew that he would have been vindicated in his poor opinion of me if I had jumped.

"You died drunk with your mouth in chickenshit, but I'm better than you!" I screamed, shaking my fists at the lurid sky. "I'll never do some damn fool thing like that."

Storming inside, I packed and got a reservation for the next day to Honolulu and then on to San Francisco. It was time to go home. I flew home first class, again with no qualms. After all, think what I had saved Henry in funeral expenses.

PEACHES

Going to Hawaii was the start of my fascination with whales, and it led me to swimming, which had nearly left me dead in the middle of San Francisco Bay. There had always been a strong desire on my part to turn into an animal, metamorphose into something more attractive than a human. Just the idea of fur had always pleased me. Think how terrible a bald cat would be. That is how we humans must appear to God, frail and blotchy, our thin membrane unprotected by any glossy pelt.

I remembered my own aberration at the age of ten. It began when my father acquired a new television, a giant console that reigned in our living room with magic power, turning every chair in its direction, rearranging the very tables and lamps until they were all under its subjection. The box that the set came in was even larger, to allow for the packing material and supporting layers of cardboard. My father had thrown the box down the basement stairs, intending to chop up and burn the thing, but it was easy to forget and hard to chop anything when he was drunk, so there it sat for months.

After a particularly miserable day at school, I would always slink down the basement stairs. The basement was safely neutral. There I could escape the questions, "How was school?" "Did you have a good time?" Truthfully, school was ghastly and I always felt I was being condemned to hell as I walked into the dusty building that stank of chalk dust and forgotten lunch bags. But no one would have understood my total lack of popularity with the other kids. It would have puzzled my father. Regardless of his alcoholism, he assumed that I would be normal and well-liked. After all, our family had been one of the groups squatting in that wilderness crossroads who had built first a stable and saloon with rooms upstairs for travelers, then a jail, and finally a dry goods store. Descended from people who had grabbed land and sold dry goods so successfully, how could I possibly be unrecognized in my class as a leader?

But children seldom feel the weight of history, and so I sat for hours in the basement of that farmhouse, staring at the shelves on three walls designed to hold home-canned goods, empty since I was born and my mother had sickened and died. I sat on the steps and imagined rows of string beans and corn, applesauce and rhubarb, filling the shelves with plenitude around me as they had before my birth.

Only four quart jars sat high on one shelf in a corner, forgotten for ten years, filled with peaches, darkened to a blood orange with time, fat and still firm in their sugar syrup. I watched their tender surfaces pressed against the glass and knew they were all the harvest moons hanging near the horizon that my mother had seen before I was born. They were all I had from her. She had never owned jewels, intending for a tablelength of children to crown her life, and all her clothes and books had been given away at her death. Just four jars of fruit proved to me that I had come from a woman who had done womanly things and created sensual smells and tastes and sights in this house.

Sitting there one afternoon, I noticed the box and immediately recognized it for what it was. Unlike the television upstairs, which allowed for no interference, no mistake in submitting to its function, the box was silent and its empty interior was filled with the sweet odor of possibility.

At first I just sat in it. Then I stole a small rug from the upstairs hall and a bedside light and three sofa cushions from the spare bedroom. The box was becoming my home. Looking for me one afternoon, my father peered into the box and drew back, startled by my expression. He hated it that I sat in the basement inside a box when I could have been watching a blurred *Howdy Doody* upstairs. It wasn't normal.

"Down there in the basement like a dog in its kennel," he told his friends. "Sure as God made little green apples, she's going to be like her Aunt Teresa."

To be compared to a dog was not complimentary in my father's opinion, and Aunt Teresa, my mother's sister, had died of cancer at forty-two, to everyone's relief. Otherwise she would have ended up in Saint Catherine's Hospital in Nashville. All the better-off families sent their crazy members to Saint Catherine's. It was run by an order of Catholic nuns who took better care of their crazies than the state hospital would.

In our part of the Bible Belt, Catholics were regarded as idol worshipers who didn't have enough sense of decorum to stop breeding. You had to have children, it was decent to, but rampant breeding with its accompanying poverty was too fetid, too raw and tasteless, for the people of Toms Creek. But they gave their crazies to the nuns. Who else but some women silly enough to wear weird clothes, shave their heads, and become brides of Christ, could be counted on to be kind to crazies?

The only other brush with Catholicism in my childhood was the hushed whispers about a girl who was so wicked that her parents had been forced to send her away to a Catholic girls' boarding school. The school was rumored to be so strict that all the bedroom doors had been taken off the hinges and nuns patrolled the halls like black mastiffs. What the girl had done to deserve such treatment I couldn't figure out till much later, but Toms Creek had great faith in Catholicism for dealing with crazies and oversexed girls. Other than that they couldn't see much point to it.

But my father's calling me a dog in its kennel caught my imagination. I thought about the potential inherent in dogginess. Dogs did not have to go to school or do any jobs at all as far as I could see. They lay in the sun and then trotted off in the afternoon to chase rabbits across the bottomland fields by the river. They got dirty, ate a lot, and never had to know their own mother once they could chew up solid food. As for their father, no dog in the world knows or cares who its father is. This seemed a distinct advantage in itself.

I became more doglike. I even went so far as to try to lap water from a bowl in the privacy of my box. I would curl up for an hour, dozing in a most doglike way, trying to make my mind totally blank. Blankness of mind was a quality that I sought with persistence. All day my teachers tried to beat facts into my head, force me to put two and two together and get something more than two and two, and all afternoon I lay in my box until I was once more reassured that two and two were separate entities which never led to anything at all but floated more and more aimlessly apart the longer I held them in my head.

I don't remember when or how I gave up on being a dog. Something must have happened, but I can't think what. One winter I was in my kennel, the next I had forgotten it. I did not become a dog, but those long empty afternoons, blind to the world in my box, blank-minded and silent, convinced that I didn't have to be human if I didn't want to, stayed with me for life. Part of me is still looking for my kennel.

Until the whale episode I had never again tried to become an animal, but I had done the next best thing. I had bought one. Buying something is not as good as being the thing itself, but what else can we do? If everyone could become what they buy, the population would be depleted as women hurried to turn into houses and antique dish cabinets and fur coats, and the men, of course, would all be silver Porsches and dark-brown Mercedes. But we can't *be* all these things. We are stuck with owning them.

I owned a horse. Why, in this day of inflation and efficiency would any person buy an animal weighing nearly a thousand pounds that does nothing useful except convert expensive fodder to fertilizer? I can't speak for others. I know only my own case.

I bought a horse because my marriage was falling apart, and a horse would create enough of a problem in my life to make the marriage problems insignificant. A horse, unlike my husband, was a large animal that I could understand. The horse would grow to love me because I cared for it so diligently, and we would ride, the two of us moving as one beast, down the trails of life. Besides, horses can be sold or traded when they don't suit you, with no guilt or anxiety over the sale, and they have the decency to die after eighteen years, unlike husbands, who will hang on forever with the proper diet and exercise.

So I bought a horse, and I was right. It did take my mind off my marriage. It took my mind off everything. It nearly exhausted me to the point of forgetting about sex and communication and boredom over the dinner table.

The horse was a gray Arab named Carlita. She was kept at a stable forty minutes from our house. At the stable, it took at least another forty minutes to curry the horseshit off her back and sides that she rolled in when she slept, pick more horseshit and straw from each hoof, and tack her up. Then she had to be ridden for at least an hour or two, round-and-round-and-round-and-

round a gravel ring with occasional jaunts out onto trails as I became more expert at staying on. After the ride there was no way
to go home until she had cooled off, another thirty minutes, and
been curried down and the tack cleaned, another thirty minutes.
Then I could go home.

It bored me after a few months, but it absolutely repulsed
Henry. My dinner conversation became a litany of worm-medi-
cine stories, discussions of pellets versus alfalfa, the dangers of
oats in the diet, meaningful lectures on bloat and colic and
twisted intestines, and then there was all my tack. Our bedroom
chair was upended to become a saddle rack. My hands were
sticky with saddle soap and my hair smelled sweetly of horse
sweat. Henry had no use for any of it.

Hoping to convert him, I took him to the stables twice to ad-
mire my newest piece of madness. Henry sat gingerly in the saddle, with a deathly pale face, as if carved from a piece of stone. It
never dawned on me that he was afraid of the horse, and it never
dawned on Henry that he was afraid either. Only the horse knew
that Henry was terrified. Carlita instantly perceived that I was a
poor rider but was not afraid of her and that Henry was a better
rider but terrified.

She did nothing about this the first Saturday when Henry rode
her. She plodded around the ring in a reassuring manner, lifting
her feet solidly, putting them down solidly, and acting like a safe,
steady mount. Henry was almost cheerful on the way home and
even suggested that he might buy a horse so we could ride together. That Wednesday night we went to a movie in San Francisco, a rerun of *National Velvet,* and both of us sat in the dark
fantasizing how we would take the fences and cardboard walls on
our horses, riding and leaping over the traps of water and brush
and jumping to some new place where we would be happy.

The next Saturday we arrived at the stable early, filled with a
new unity and enthusiasm. Henry announced that he would take
Carlita on a little ride on the trails. I casually agreed. It never
dawned on me that Henry, who flew to Rome without even getting excited, would have any problem with a mere horse.

Henry set off on a trail that ran behind the barn. It curved
around to climb a ridge, disappeared into the woods on the hill,

reappeared on the bald hilltop, and then disappeared again in woods on the other side of the barn. The ride was simple. The only tricky part was a peculiarly steep hill leading down to the horse ring on the other side of the barn. So steep that it had to be negotiated slowly or the horse could slip and break a leg, it had jokingly been named Heart Attack Hill when a horse fell dead halfway up it one hot day in July.

I sat on a fence rail and waved happily as the two of them disappeared into the woods. It was a gray day, and a sprinkle of rain began to fall, not enough to bother me, just enough to make the smell of eucalyptus more pungent.

Henry and Carlita appeared on the other side of the woods. Crossing the top of the hill at a dead run, horse and rider soon leaped into the far side of the woods and began their descent, lost to my sight.

Daydreaming on my fence rail, I watched Heart Attack Hill for the first sign of Carlita carefully picking her way down. Henry's speed across the top of the hill had been pretty to see in a John Wayne sort of way. I was feeling very happy and even sexy as Carlita and Henry broke out of the woods above the riding ring.

At first I was amazed at Henry's courage in riding a horse at full gallop down such a steep hill. He was overdoing it, I thought uneasily, and I would have to warn him later. But as Carlita careened down the rocky slope, I suddenly knew that this was not Henry's idea. Carlita had her neck full out and her eyes flashed white even at that distance. Her every jump was dictated by panic, and she leaped down the slope as if it were red hot and she were being pursued by an irate grizzly.

Henry did not look as interesting as Carlita. He sat rigid on the horse, his body flying up and down, legs flapping, hands locked in a death grip on the saddlehorn. He had lost one stirrup and it banged against the horse's side, pressing her on to greater leaps. I didn't see how Carlita could get down the hill without somersaulting or breaking a leg, and Henry might be killed in either case.

But Carlita had no intention of dying, she just wanted a little run. At the bottom of the hill, where Henry might have regained the reins and his stirrups, she slid to such an abrupt stop that Henry pitched almost over her head. Carlita reared politely to catch him and when he plopped heavily back in the saddle, she turned, danced a step or two, and plunged back on the trail going up Heart Attack Hill with the same panic that sent her down.

Henry still clung to the saddlehorn and refused to fall off, which seemed definitely the best solution. They disappeared, raced across the bare crest of the hill, leaped into the woods, and finally came tearing around the barn.

Seeing me sitting paralyzed on the fence, Carlita slowed to a walk and came over. She was gasping for breath and her foaming saliva flew across my shirt as she shook her head. Nuzzling me affectionately, Carlita became charming. She wanted her sugar.

Henry fell off the horse into the gravel and mud under her. Crawling away on all fours, he was suddenly the town weakling who has been beaten up by the sheriff. He sat panting on the other side of the fence and glared at Carlita and me.

"You knew she would do that," he said.

"My God! She's never acted like that. What did you do to her?"

Henry looked at us with loathing. "I was doing fine until the rain began. She felt the first drop and bolted. The fucking horse is afraid of the rain."

I stared at him. Carlita didn't like lightning and thunder, but fear of a few drops of rain? "You must have spooked her," I said.

Henry said nothing. He gazed at me for a minute and then threw up in the mud. Even then it didn't hit me that Henry was scared. I assumed he had suffered internal damage from the bouncing and it had affected his stomach.

Poor Henry. I never even allowed him to be afraid. He did all the things that I couldn't do, so I imagined he was superhuman. It was the last time we went out to the stable together, and soon I sold Carlita to a fourteen-year-old girl with acne. She had no boyfriends and plenty of spare time to dedicate to her horse.

MONKEYS

I had to fly into Nashville, Tennessee, and transfer to a bus headed north to Toms Creek, which lay just over the state line. I had grown up in the western part of Kentucky, rolling hills and barrens. Everyone in California had thought that Kentucky was all mountains filled with long-bearded men and whiskey stills, feuds, and long-barreled rifles. My part of Kentucky was the land that rolled down toward the Mississippi River, less romantic and violent but equally lovely in a quiet way.

Nashville was not far over the state line to the south. It had been the Big City when I was a child. My Aunt Nell would take me to Nashville every August to buy school clothes and a new winter coat, and we made the trip in February or March to buy summer clothes. Toms Creek had only three small clothing stores, two locally owned and a J. C. Penney's that was fine for sturdy cotton underwear but not good enough in Aunt Nell's mind for my Sunday dresses and coats. So twice a year we made our pilgrimage to Nashville for high fashion.

Nashville was an awesome place to me at six and eight and ten. There were three things I loved and yearned for throughout the year that only Nashville could give me. The first thing was a large cage of monkeys on the third floor of Harvey's Department Store. I had never seen any animals except dogs and cats and farm animals, and the monkeys were like something from a dream, a fantasy animal that no adult would ever approve of if they knew you had invented them.

I would be dragged unwillingly into fitting rooms to try on clothes, agreeing to anything that Aunt Nell wanted just to be free, to get back to the monkeys. I knew that Aunt Nell would take hours with her own wardrobe and might be talked into tea in the tea room if I was insistent enough, and this gave me time to commune with my monkeys.

For they were mine. I stood there longer than any other child, and when I stared at them in trance they would often stop bickering over pieces of fruit and orange peel and stare back at me. Their glittering dark eyes gave me intimations of another world with fallen stone idols, damp jungles, and birds like neon stars clustered in the trees.

The monkeys' lack of courtesy, their lies and tricks, their obscene gestures, put me in an ecstasy. Right here in the midst of my middle-class world were copulating, prying, indecent, dishonorable animals on display for me to study, and just when they were their most nasty, spitting food at each other and screeching for no reason, they would suddenly hold each other tenderly and spend long minutes grooming their mates' fur with such care, such delicate touch. It was the best of all worlds for me at eight: obscenity, motion, unrepressed anger, and tenderness.

My second love in Nashville was the escalator in the department store. There were no escalators in Toms Creek, and I was in a dream state as they floated me up until I had to turn on the fifth floor and float to the basement again. And there was, laid over the magic of going up hundreds of feet in the air, without moving, on a magic carpet of articulated metal, the fear that I felt at the end of each flight. I would stare ahead at the place where the floor ate the steps as they smoothly flattened and disappeared and be paralyzed with terror. What if I slipped? What if I caught a finger in the machinery? I would leap off, goatlike, feeling that I had escaped an ogre, a dark magic spell that would be a cloud around me for life if I tripped. It was thrilling.

My third love was a shop in Nashville that sold maple sugar candy. I ate the molded maple leaves and shells of sugar that turned to smooth paste on my tongue, and I knew the sweetness of life. Nothing felt impossible with a cheek full of maple sugar. I often tried to talk Aunt Nell into going to the candy store first. It was my greatest desire in life to suck on maple sugar candy while riding escalators to and from my monkeys, but she always refused. Candy was my reward for being good in the fitting rooms. She didn't understand that in front of the monkeys I wished only to shed my clothes and be as naked as they, chattering to them, eating fruit with my fingers, shoving pieces of maple sugar through the mesh of their cage, opening the cage so that the whole store, all of Nashville, and the world would be filled with monkeys, all of us swinging from the escalator rails, throwing fruit and chattering, pressing close to one another for gentle touch, for warmth, for love.

There were no monkeys visible in Nashville at the airport and not one could be seen from my taxi window as I went to the bus station. The bus station was like all bus stations: wooden benches, candy machines, metal lockers on the wall, a counter that sold hot dogs and Coke, the floor filthy with spit and spilled coffee and dirt and oil and evidences of the human presence.

"Your bus leaves in just a minute, ma'am," said a lean Tennessee man who took my suitcase and my box of camping equipment.

"Please be sure and get my bags on," I said.

"Don't you worry, ma'am. I'll take 'em out and see they get on personally." He grinned at me as if we had known each other for years, played in the same cribs, gone to the same birthday parties. "I'll do it right now," he assured me.

Southern hospitality. The warmth of it. The courtesy to women and old people. The decency. I had done right to come home, I thought.

The bus was a late-afternoon special that ran workers from their jobs in the city back to their farms and homes outside Nashville. The driver knew every face.

"How're you, Miz Lawson? Your man happy about this weather? It is hot for the end of May, but that don't mean a drought yet. You take care now, y'heah?"

"Been a long day, Honey? Well, you just put your feet up and rest till I set you down at home."

"Hidy, Sam. Haven't seen you for a while. My wife and I sure liked that ham you sent up. Well, I just wanted to let you know that we appreciated it. It's true. Your brother can still cure a ham."

For the first time in my life I sat and listened like an outsider, an eavesdropper. Had I ever talked like that? My accent now was fairly bland and homogeneously American. Nor could my emotions keep up with the effusiveness of the gossip. I felt cynical and old watching the people get off the bus on the highway to walk the dirt roads up to their white frame houses set back from the blacktop, and yet I felt like a child.

The talk was about relatives and crops and the weather, and my strangeness made me shrink again into the body of a child who sat in sleepy silence after dinner while the grown-ups talked over her head. I was too cynical for this world and I was also too young. There was no age in between for me to claim as my own.

The small towns ticked off on the route: Smiths Pass, Hartlinburg, Lucasville, Abbys Corner, until the bus was moving through dusk into darkness and I couldn't see any familiar markers out the window. Fireflies were coming up over fields that would smell pungent with clover and alfalfa and fescue by midsummer, and lights blinked on across stretches of darkness as houses lit up. After the city it seemed so dark, so quiet outside the window. It was, I thought with a new recognition, peaceful.

It was also flat. I was aware that my eye could travel to the far horizon where the sky met the fields with no mountains or buildings interrupting my vision. The trees seemed very small after California's redwoods, and stood like toys at the horizon where the lights of an equally tiny train were moving past in the night. The dark land was empty and moved your eye up to the sky, which was first dark blue, then darker until it was a blue-black, and then the stars all came out.

The bus pulled up at the town square of Toms Creek and I got out almost in tears. It was just the same. The buildings stood in their usual shabby disrepair on four sides, and the equally shabby courthouse sat in the middle surrounded by grass and green benches and some sparsely planted flowerbeds.

I walked across the street and went up a path to the old fountain which still stood in front of the courthouse. The water poured down in a sheet from one ornate platter of stone to the second larger platter to the pool itself, where even in the dark I could see the flick of a goldfish's tail.

They still have goldfish in the fountain, I thought, and it was a sign that somewhere in the world nothing had changed. I raised my eyes and read through the water the plaque fastened to the stone.

> In memory of those men
> who built this building
> and loved their town.

it said, and then the top name on the list.

LIONEL ALLARDS CARPENTER

my great-grandfather, whose idea the plaque had probably been, but a man whose name had been engraved on my personality before I even knew it had been done.

One of the first prosperous townsmen who had come far enough in civilization to want to set up memorials and make buildings instead of drinking and hunting and turning a dollar on travelers, Lionel Carpenter had been a man of affairs who had even sent his wife all the way to Florida for a cure after she had lost a child to diphtheria, a man of vision who talked about river traffic and railroads and Washington and Europe and built ornate fountains to mark his passing.

And perhaps he was right, I thought, walking back to the bus depot. He left his mark with as much grandeur as a saloonkeeper in Toms Creek could have wanted or hoped for. Would I ever have such vision for my times? I doubted it.

I doubted my vision more when I got back to the bus stop and found the bus gone. The clerk was kind and courtly, but his friendliness did not alter the fact that my suitcase and box still sat in Nashville, Tennessee, or God forbid, were on a trip of their own to Memphis or Chattanooga or Augusta, Georgia.

I walked the three blocks to Aunt Nell's house and took no pleasure in the memories they held. Southern charm, I thought bitterly, lots of talk and no efficiency. They'll tell you anything, but your bags aren't there when you need them. The porch light was on at Aunt Nell's. I knew she was waiting for me, but I was no longer sure that I wanted to be here.

THE *RIVER*

THE CEMETERY

The old cemetery in Toms Creek was out the Clemensville road and was bounded on two sides and across the front by a tall fence of wrought iron with leaves and curlicues and tall points at the top. It looked like many spears set in the ground after battle, with the discarded wreaths of victory scattering their leaves and flowers between them. Its purpose was to keep teenagers from parking in the cemetery at night to drink and neck among the tombstones, desecrating the grounds with aluminum cans and the sticky condoms that teenage boys have traditionally used for years in an attempt to slow down life and have a few more years of freedom before the ultimate climb into adulthood.

I had always thought that the fence was correct in design, smacking of ancient battle and an older generation in its construction, but I also believed that the gate should be left open at night. It seemed fitting that one generation should beget its first children by accident while lying on the well-trimmed grass that covered an older generation and would someday cover them and the very children they were forcing back hopefully into the swarming darkness with a piece of rubber.

If the gates were left open, the only people missing from the cemetery at night would have been the parents of the teenagers, and that was appropriate too. The parents were shunned by the children as repressive and criticized by the grandparents for not keeping the world as it should be or had been when they kept it. The children would have sprawled there on summer nights under the warm, moist air and watched the stars while great-grandparents lay under them smiling at all the life above with the certainty that none of it was really as important as the parents and children thought. The parents knew that they were the true masters of reality and that the children were silly and ruining their lives by having no feel for this reality. The children would touch each other and kiss moistly, knowing that all their parents' reality was a lie and had nothing to do with this sweetness which was denied the children because the parents wanted it all for themselves and didn't want the children to have fun anyway.

So, if only the gates could have been left open at night, all the generations would lie down together in their proper places, each feeling alone and different from all the others and sure that only one generation saw life as it really was. But the gates were firmly locked every night by a member of the Funeral Society, leaving the children with only dirt roads and drive-in movies for their fumbling and eventual begetting.

True, they could have walked around past the side fences and entered the cemetery from the back by crawling between the flaccid loops of an old barbed-wire fence, but that would have meant singlemindedly admitting that they wanted to lie on the grass and make love, which was different from just stepping out of the car and sitting on the grass because the cars were too hot in summer. Not many of the girls would have walked that far for privacy and a comfortable stretch of grass. It would have meant that they knew what they were doing and what the boys were planning. As long as they didn't know or thought they didn't know, it was all right.

So the cemetery at night was deserted and silent and the moon marked the white marble slabs and angels and an occasional lamb or cherub which showed a child's grave. It was quiet. It was not connected to any of the life in the town. It was not like any-place I had lived before, and this was part of why I liked it and smiled when I later unpacked my tent and set up my chemical toilet. I was here, and I intended to stay.

Three days later, while an apologetic bus company delivered my missing belongings, Aunt Nell had a fit when I told her that it wasn't my intention to live in one of her spare bedrooms or to rent an apartment or house.

"You cannot do that," she said. "Everyone's going to think you're crazy, and I don't see why you want people to think something about you when it isn't true."

"I don't care anymore what people think," I said. "They used to think I was a respectable, happily married woman, and I was miserable and didn't feel respectable at all, so they're usually wrong anyway, and besides, it seems to me that life is enough to make you crazy if you look at it honestly, so maybe I am crazy, but at least I'm honest."

Aunt Nell shook her head. "Don't be silly," she said as I put my suitcase in the cab. "Of course life can drive you crazy, but you're not supposed to give in like that."

As the cab drove off, Aunt Nell stood on the curb and raised her hand in a desperate gesture. "God doesn't want us to give in like that."

It was the first time I'd heard Aunt Nell use God as an argu-ment against me, and I knew she was upset. I waved good-bye to her and saw her stand there with one arm up in the air, nearly knocking off her straw picture hat which she always wore in summer. The hat was so large and she was so short and thick-waisted that she reminded me of a mushroom growing under the maple tree by the sidewalk. I grinned and was almost in tears. I did love her, but I had to be what I was. Loving someone never had been enough to make me change who I was.

The cab dropped me at the back of the cemetery at the end of a curving gravel path that wandered between the plots. I paid the driver and he drove off. I suppose he was curious, but I hadn't paid much attention. I was too excited. As the cab disappeared, I drew a deep breath and looked around me. Here I was. Here I was going to stay. For the first time in my life I was going to live on my land. My own land. Land that I owned completely with no mortgage, no debt, no other person claiming my right to it.

My land had been created as a part of my grandfather's will. He had left me, my father, and my Aunt Nell pieces of land for our cemetery plots. The will had tied the land up so that even my father couldn't sell his plot for more money to support his alcoholism. My grandfather and his wife were buried at one end. There was an empty space for Aunt Nell. Then my mother and later my father had been buried side by side, and my plot was on the other end, empty like Aunt Nell's until now. I owned it free and clear. It was mine. It was the only piece of land that I owned, and I intended to live there.

Just so you don't think I'm crazy, trying to live on a little twelve-by-eight-foot cemetery plot, let me tell you this. My cemetery plot is one hundred and thirty feet by forty feet. It is large enough to bury all my family and friends and have room for strangers and horses around the edges. The plots owned by Aunt Nell and me and my parents and grandfather are at the very back of the cemetery, sitting across the crest of a little rise in the earth that separates the cemetery from the farm behind it.

Standing on my plot, I could see the cemetery in front of me sloping down through oaks and maples to the far-off iron gate and glimpses of black-topped road beyond. Behind me, the ground also sloped down gently into pastures in front of my plot, a cornfield to the left, tobacco field to the right, beyond the fields a farmhouse, beyond the farmhouse a line of trees, and beyond that, the river.

I had grown up in that farmhouse, which was sold at my father's death to pay his debts. I had played and run through all the fields which ran to Johnsongrass and goldenrod when my father gave up his pretenses of being a farmer and settled into serious drinking. I had learned to swim in Barren River, which ran along the edge of the farm.

When my father died, the whole farm had been sold except for this one strip next to the town's cemetery. My grandfather had stipulated that these four plots of land were to be the family's for their burial. The Cemetery Society had agreed, on the condition that he give the cemetery another strip of the farm to auction off for plots. The society was to take care of my family's plots in exchange for some extra land. It had been a sensible and practical way to ensure that no one in the family had to be buried on strange land.

My grandfather had explained to me about my cemetery plot when I was in eighth grade. Sitting behind his tall, cherrywood desk, he had solemnly handed me the deed. I had gone out the side door of the farmhouse and walked up the hill where I could see the cemetery. Surveyors' stakes marked off the plots of land, and I stood in the center of mine and looked at my land like a kingdom under my feet, marked off with splints of wood with red cloth streamers tacked on the top. I was the only thirteen-year-old girl in town who owned land.

It would have been the big event of my thirteenth summer except for my body interrupting me as I wandered back and forth from the river to the cemetery plot to my dog and the new kittens in the barn. I woke up one morning and discovered as I pulled off the bottoms of my cotton pajamas that I was dying. There didn't seem to be anything for it but to go tell Aunt Nell, so I pulled on my shorts and shirt and walked barefooted to Aunt Nell's house, through the fields and the outlying black section of town to her house on the far side of the hill.

She listened while I told her that I was awful sick, maybe dying, and then she sat down on the porch swing in relief when I told her the symptoms. Fanning herself against the August heat with a paper fan that advertised chicken mash, Aunt Nell explained my body to me.

Peering out from under a black picture hat, she told me that now I was really a woman and could even have babies. Then she fixed me up with a pad and belt, fed me thin cornmeal pancakes with edges crusted like crochetwork, told me not to swim in the cold river water or get too overheated running around at midday, and sent me home.

I entered the farmhouse and walked past my father with scorn.

He thought my cold glance was for his shaking hands, which clutched a half-cup of coffee as he tried to recover from the night before, but he was wrong. I hadn't noticed his condition and it wouldn't have seemed important if I had. My scorn was for his sex, for men in general, for his slight capacity as a father. Men were now in their proper perspective for me, poor creatures with rather uninteresting bodies. My air with him for the rest of the summer was patronizing. How boring to be a man.

And the cemetery plot, a gift to me from my grandfather, another man, shrank in my imagination. It was somehow such a masculine gift. The concern for owning land and worrying about where you'd be after death seemed like all that men could do, I figured at thirteen. They couldn't feel the strangeness of life inside them, so they brooded overmuch about death.

Every time I saw my blood, smelled the heavy scent of my body's possibilities, I felt sorrier and sorrier for my father and grandfather. I became almost tender with my father, and he thought it was the sign of my new womanhood. He was right, of course, but what he didn't know was that my first womanly emotion for men had been simply pity.

When I was eight, we had a summer of drought and heat. In August the thermometer registered 110 by afternoon and barely broke 95 or 100 at night. I suffered terribly from heat rash and was nearly sick with the weeks of unbroken torture, so my Aunt Nell told my father to put a quilt on the grass at night and let me sleep outside the house, whose upstairs bedrooms were still holding the heat of the old day before the new began.

After dinner my father would put several quilts on the grass under the oaks and we would sit there until dark. The heat would become less ovenlike and the chickens would stop their scattered wanderings and roost in the bushes. Bats dipped and wobbled over our heads as the sky darkened, and owls called as they reclaimed the earth we had only borrowed from them during the day.

Watching the light dim and then staring at the course of the moon, I stopped whining and lay exhausted on the quilt. My father gave me the dishes of sherbet and ice cream after dark, and like a night-blooming flower I would revive and eat while he sipped his glass of bourbon and water as he sat propped against a tree.

Living in the cemetery the first two weeks was like sleeping in my front yard when I was eight. The air was hot during the day, so I put my tent in a sycamore tree's shade. The tent was green and blended in with the bushes around the edges of the cemetery, and I stayed there undisturbed and idyllic. If someone had asked me, I would have agreed that November and December were going to follow September and October, but I never thought of that in May and June and lived contentedly, planning to remain there forever on my land.

Aunt Nell left me strictly alone and pretended that I wasn't even in town. I visited her and sat in the dark cavern of her front porch, squinting out at the sun, drinking ginger ale and peering over her pots of coleus, avoiding all topics of conversation that would lead to a discussion of my dead marriage or my current lifestyle. They were not satisfactory visits on either side, and I drifted back to the cemetery with sacks of groceries to sit in peace.

Sitting in peace may not sound too wonderful a way to live at thirty-nine, but after the passions of a broken marriage and the cold worldliness of friends who picked the potential of Henry's fifty thousand a year rather than standing by me and my simple ownership of a cemetery plot, peace was what I needed. It was all I needed, and I lay on the grass getting a tan, smelling more keenly, and eating with more appetite than I had for five years. I needed the rest.

But rest and peace were not going to last for long. In the middle of my third week in Toms Creek cemetery, a long Cadillac pulled up the gravel drive. People came out to the cemetery off and on all the time to put flowers on the graves. It was probably just another relative looking for the grave of a mother or cousin to mourn or to certify once again with subdued triumph that yes, it was true, the son of a bitch was still dead.

I was lying on an old beach towel, listening to the rustle of wind as it blew the long leaves of new corn, hearing the occasional moo of one of the three cows in the field behind me, just enjoying the morning and the thought of the fresh strawberries I would eat for lunch and the new paperback book I had bought.

My favorite reading at this time was fantasy literature, light, amusing, science fiction, mysteries, gothics, but my favorite fantasy books were books that dealt with diet and exercise. There was no more pleasant way to spend a hot afternoon than the way I planned to spend it, lying prone in the shade, dipping a whole quart of strawberries one by one first in sour cream then in powdered sugar, washing them down with white wine which was admittedly warm since I was without a refrigerator, but still was good to drink, while reading a book that showed you how to lose thirty pounds in three months by becoming a long-distance runner.

I looked forward especially to the solemn tones of the question-and-answer section that was always a part of this fantasy genre of literature.

"Can I substitute celery for carrots as my midafternoon snack on day four since carrots make me break out in hives?"

"Yes. You can do this, but remember that the more substitutions you make, the more likely you are to cheat on the diet."

"What should I do when my nipples become chafed after running fifteen miles?"

"You should try one of the new bras designed for athletic women or simply rub a little Vaseline on your nipples before running. A silky shirt sold with shorts in athletic supply stores can be ideal for runners. Some women simply place a Band-Aid over each nipple instead of resorting to bras."

I had my day planned. I was content and drugged with sun and the silence around me when I heard a man's voice.

"Hello, Camille. I haven't seen you since you left town to go away for college."

I opened my eyes and saw a large shape blocking my sun. Sitting up, I tried to place him. He had been thinner the last time I'd seen him, adolescent thin, all collarbones and shoulder blades, feet and ears.

"Tom. Tom Church. How are you?"

He sat down on the grass. "I'm doing just fine. If I keep building shopping centers, and if the new computer plant goes in like it's planned to do, they'll have to name this town Tom Church instead of Toms Creek."

He grinned and ran his eyes slowly over me. He had changed. He was heavily muscled now, and dark tan from working outside. He would have looked like an Indian except that his dark hair had heavy waves in it and his eyes were hazel. The only remnant of the adolescent boy was his quick grin and the nervous way he cracked his knuckles. Tom wasn't taller than I, probably about the same height, but he would have made two of me.

"Like what you see?" He had caught me staring.

"You've changed." I met his eyes and felt my skin get hotter.

"So've you. I never thought you'd pull all that lankiness together. You're built like a model now with those shoulders and your eyes so far apart."

I grinned. Tom had managed to take my two most hated features and make me feel good about them. "Thanks. What're you doing out here at the cemetery?" I asked.

"My sister has been after me to check our mother's grave. Anne hasn't been able to get over here for a few months. God knows what she thinks will happen to it. It won't go anyplace."

I remembered Anne Church too. A pale, blond girl like her mother, she had been a year behind me in school, Tom a year ahead. "How is Anne doing?"

Tom stood up and stared out at the river. "Oh, she's all right. Everybody has their problems, I guess. Have you had lunch?"

I had eaten a few strawberries, but that didn't count.

"Not really. Have you?"

"Nope. I was out checking a foundation we poured yesterday and haven't had a chance yet. Want to join me?"

"Let me put on a dress," I said, going into the tent.

"Sure. We can go over to the Derby House on the highway. It's not as fancy as you're used to, but we like it."

Inside the tent I had to laugh. He was pointedly ignoring my tent and the oddness of my existence. "I don't care about fancy. I'm just hungry."

He opened the Cadillac door for me at the restaurant and placed my hand firmly on his arm. His flesh was heavy and warm. I smelled a faint odor of sweat from him as we got our table and he held my chair for me, a smell that was dark and came from working in the sun. It made my head light and I laughed. He looked at me and smiled back. The way Tom looked at me, I would have sworn that he could read right through to my backbone and count the vertebrae.

Everybody in the restaurant knew Tom. Groups of men called out to him and waved. The waitresses grinned. Tom was known and I felt suddenly foreign and envious. If I had stayed in the town, I would have been there with a group of friends, exchanging hellos. Tom was the one who had stayed. I was the girl who had gone away. I was a foreigner in my own hometown.

"They have great home fries and cheeseburgers," Tom said. "You get whatever you want."

The waitress took our order, brought us each a beer, and Tom leaned over the table to watch me more closely.

"Whatever made you decide to come back here after all these years, Camille? I thought you'd given up on us for the bright lights."

There was an intensity to Tom's hazel eyes when he concentrated on me across the table. I found myself opening up and telling him things that I hadn't been able to tell even Aunt Nell.

"I've never been able to have children, and my marriage seemed to wither away and disappear. I guess I was tired of California and the whole city life sort of thing."

"What are you planning to do now?"

"I don't know. I guess I'll have to think of something. But not yet. It's silly. I feel like I'm sixteen again but without all the worries I had at sixteen."

"You could live with your Aunt Nell, of course."

"I didn't know you knew Aunt Nell. Well, she wants me to, but I don't think I will. Besides, she has a pregnant teenage cousin living with her. Frankly, I think Aunt Nell can deal with that better than I can right now."

Tom nodded. "Teenagers can be hard to understand," he said, and his face darkened. He looked almost angry. "But I think you're right to let her deal with the girl. You have to get on with your own life."

"You don't think I'm being selfish, not moving in with Aunt Nell?"

"You won't do her much good unless you know what you're going to do with yourself. You may even decide to go back to California."

"I don't know. I really don't know."

"Well, I hope not. Now I've got the chance to date you that I missed in high school. Can't understand why I didn't date you back then."

I grinned and Tom grinned and we sat there over plates of home fried potatoes with the warmth and electricity going back and forth as if we were both sixteen.

"Come on out to the construction site with me after lunch. I'll teach you to run a bulldozer."

And I did. I sat by Tom on the bulldozer and he nearly scared me out of my skin deliberately till I would shriek out over the engine's roar and he'd laugh and hang on to me with his hand and shove dirt around and roar up hills.

God, I was jealous. He knew exactly what he was doing every minute. He moved earth and raised buildings and laughed and laughed. I laughed too and we both were covered with a fine powder of red clay in an hour.

Tom stopped the bulldozer hanging on a steep bank of dirt, and he wrapped his arms around me and held me tight. Over the thunder of the motor he deliberately kissed me and then licked my lips slowly until I felt his tongue inside my body like fire rising up.

"That's the way you should be," he murmured. "Kissed and not talking."

I opened my mouth to protest and he kissed me again. "You're covered with dirt," he said. "I think I like you that way. Gets you back to earth where you belong. Dirty girl."

The third kiss left me limp and responsive like a river plant in the current. The bulldozer engine died with a shudder and Tom turned me loose.

"It's going to be a great summer," he said, and I didn't even try to say something sharp and witty to puncture his ego. Tom might be right. He started up the bulldozer again and I was back at my tent before I realized that I hadn't learned to drive a bulldozer at all. I didn't think that I cared.

RUBY CHURCH

She'd never been much of anything. She knew that. Ruby never tried to fool herself about who she was or how people thought about her. Ruby knew that the only chance for her was to be practical.

Her parents hadn't been practical. They'd married at sixteen and had eleven children, eight of them surviving the diet of cornbread and cheap pork to grow up. Five boys and three girls. Two of the boys died in the war. Two were alcoholic and shiftless. One drifted north to Detroit and Ruby never heard from him again.

The girls weren't any better in Ruby's eyes. Both her sisters married young and then followed their husbands from small town to small town, probably producing another series of children who were ill-fed, badly clothed, and doomed to sit slack-jawed for seven or eight years in the public schools. Ruby had no use for her sisters.

Not that Ruby had been so different at first. I was as much a fool as they were, Ruby sometimes thought as she shampooed the hair of a customer. But I got smart and didn't fall in that hole. Ruby would scrub the scalp of her customer till she yelped in pain.

Ruby had sex with one of the first boys she noticed at the age of sixteen. She had gotten pregnant almost immediately and married to give her first child, her only son, a name. And that fool husband wanted to call him Bobby Joe, she thought. But even at sixteen, Ruby knew better. Thomas Patrick Church, Ruby had named him. A proper name. A name unlike the names of her brothers and sisters, that passel of fools named for film stars or given nicknames like they weren't even going to be adults someday.

A year later Ruby had gotten pregnant again and during the second labor she saw the light. Sometimes Ruby squeezed Anne (Anne with an "e" she had told the nurse who registered the birth) tight against her and thanked God for the child.

Second births are supposed to be easier. Everyone told Ruby this was true, but no one bothered to tell Anne Elizabeth. Twenty-four hours of hard labor to get one tiny girl-child into the world, and Ruby changed during those hours.

There are mornings, Ruby thought, when you wake up and think that it's going to be a normal day, just another day with nothing in it to remember, but then something happens that throws your whole life off on a new course like a river suddenly dammed and diverted in a day. Ruby went into labor as one woman, but she came out another.

And thank God for it, she thought often. Thank God for something that gave me some sense. Thank God for a good jolt to wake me up and let me see what life was all about.

Six months after the birth, Ruby divorced her husband for, as her sisters said, no good reason at all.

I have to get rid of him before I stop nursing so I won't get pregnant again, Ruby thought. Besides, she had gotten an application for beautician's school, and she had to have the divorce by July. That would give her two months to find a cheap rooming house and a night job in Nashville. School by day, work as a cocktail waitress at night. The baby was sleeping solidly for eight hours a night now. If the kids wake up, they can just cry a little, she thought.

There was no time for sleep for herself, but Ruby knew it was only for two years. Then she would have her license. She graduated at the top of her class and accepted her diploma with perfectly coiffed and curled blond hair and deep purple shadows under her eyes that she covered with pancake makeup.

Ruby had never cared much about hair and styles before, but she moved back to Toms Creek and became the fastest, nicest, most sweet little hairdresser in town. Ruby was the girl all the old ladies loved to talk to about their husbands' bad digestion and their daughters' poor child-rearing. Ruby was the one that young wives giggled with, and she was the only haircutter in town willing to try crazy new styles for the teenage girls and then talk their mothers into accepting the look. Ruby was everybody's friend.

So the talk began slow and never really picked up. No one could believe that Ruby wasn't happy with her life just as it was. After all, she made the best tips in town. She was only twenty-seven and had her own shop and three other girls working under her. Her kids were nice kids. They made good grades in school and Ruby dressed them up better than any child had a right to expect. Why wasn't Ruby content?

It wasn't like she hadn't had chances to get married again. A couple of nice fellows had courted her. Neither one of them had been rich or even very hardworking for that matter, but a woman nearly thirty with two children should have been grateful for the chance.

"I have two children to raise. I can't take on any more," Ruby said with a grin, and the women grinned back at her and admitted the truth of what she said. Men were like big babies sometimes. Nurtured by women from cradle to grave. Cooked for, listened to, encouraged, cared for. Most of them couldn't find their own socks if they weren't in the sock drawer. Ruby had a point.

But what she did was amazing, even the little bits that drifted back to Toms Creek. Every Saturday afternoon Ruby got on the train and went to Louisville. Saturday night she worked whatever convention was in town and came home Sunday night with money in her purse. On a good weekend Ruby made two or three hundred dollars.

The hotels knew her. If a man wanted a really interesting woman who had lots of ideas for having fun, Ruby was his girl. She had sex in all possible positions, threw baseballs at a nude man while calling him her son, pretended she was a fish, a dog, a nun, a man, a slave trader, a baby, a teacher, a nurse, and once painted herself all over with makeup to look like a black woman.

Ruby wasn't fooled. Everybody wanted her to live alone, work hard, go to church, and never have sex again unless she married some shiftless man and then supported him. Nobody cared if she worked all her life scrubbing dirty heads and got varicose veins and died still scrubbing and talking and aching. Everybody figured that Ruby Church had come just about as far as could be expected when she ran her own beauty shop. Everyone nodded and agreed that, looking at what sort of people the rest of her family were, Ruby had done real well. She had gone as far as the town thought she should.

But Ruby had just begun. She never put pork on her table. Tom and his sister never saw pork till they grew up. Ruby knew that her children had to eat right to be what she intended for them. They would have it all, and that meant she had to have a piece of property.

For fifteen years Ruby had her eye on the old Carlyle house. Mrs. Carlyle lived on and on, alone in the house except for one servant, and Ruby prayed that the old woman would live until Ruby got the money together for the down payment. As Mrs. Carlyle got sicker and frailer, lying in darkened rooms, nearly dying every week with some new symptom of old age, Ruby grew more frenzied. She even spent two weeks with a man who promised her a thousand dollars if she'd stay with him. No taxes would have to be taken out of that thousand.

Then the old lady died and her son flew in from New York to sell the house. A gigantic, red brick place, white columns, oak trees, perfect lawn, a historical home in Toms Creek, the house was sold to Ruby Church.

This was after Tom went off to college and Anne had only another year of high school. What do you want with all that house, Ruby? they all asked her.

She didn't say but just bought it and worked harder to pay for it. Ruby had opened two other beauty shops in nearby towns, and she worked seven days a week now. Anne went off to college. Tom came back and worked with a construction company. Ruby got tired easily, had to slow down. She spent her days lying on a lounge chair, staring up at the sky. For all her love of land and her absolute belief in what land ownership could do for her, Ruby liked the color of the sky best.

When Ruby passed on with cancer, her daughter dyed her shroud sky blue. Tom bought out his sister's half of the house and proceeded to tear it down and put up an apartment building on the land. Then he sold it and didn't even take an apartment for himself.

People were shocked at the destruction of the house. Everyone had taken it for granted that Tom would live in it himself or that his sister and her husband would move back to Toms Creek from where they lived two counties to the east and set up in it with their only child, a boy.

But Tom bought it and Tom tore it down. "Land is a nuisance," he said. "The only land you ought to own is your cemetery plot, and I'm going to be cremated."

Tom's living in an apartment was not unusual. He was, after all, a bachelor. Just wait till he gets married, people said. Some girl will have him buying her a house soon enough. And the people waited, and Tom built houses and apartments and shopping centers, but he never owned any of them for long.

Tom visited his sister every week after she was widowed young, was like a father to his nephew, but he never married, and he had never owned a piece of land so far.

Anne had seen that her mother was buried on a fine plot of land in the cemetery with a rosy marble stone marking her grave. Every Christmas, she put a green wreath on her mother's grave while Tom watched. Then Tom would drive his sister home and drive back to Toms Creek to his own apartment to eat a frozen dinner alone. Ruby had left her mark. Neither Tom nor Anne was known to eat pork.

I didn't think much about Tom Church because I had other things to worry about. If there were no laws to throw me out of the cemetery, then I wouldn't be bothered, apparently. Having had a reputable family for generations and a seventy-eight-year-old great-aunt who had no qualms about going down to the courthouse and straightening out the clerks and judges occasionally, I was relatively safe from harassment, but I was worried.

One worry had been thrown at me by Aunt Nell when I got up for breakfast my first morning in Toms Creek.

"This is Dinah," she had said firmly, and Aunt Nell gave me a sweet smile that was in direct conflict with the riveting glance that she directed at me.

I nodded at the girl who was setting the table. "Hello, Dinah."

"Hi," she said and then went on putting forks and spoons beside the plates.

I looked at Aunt Nell, who was disappearing into the kitchen. Mouthing the words silently toward me too fast for me to catch them, I knew what she wanted. I was to talk to Dinah, to get to know her, to straighten her out eventually.

I watched the girl sadly. It seemed a bit late to straighten her out. What did I have to say to a pregnant girl? I'd never been able to have my own pregnancy after hundreds of dollars spent on tests and doctors and romantic nightgowns. Maybe Dinah knew something that I didn't.

"When is your baby due, Dinah?"

"Middle of August, I guess," she said.

"That must be pretty exciting for you," I added.

Dinah stared at me. She was pregnant the way some farm girls are pregnant: their baby fat and dimples firming up overnight it seems into a huge, heavy body that makes you wonder that there was even a week or two between childhood and this new mass of flesh when the girl was a young woman, a creature who could attract a man. The transition from childhood to motherhood was almost seamless, with no visible stitch, in the form of a man, connecting the two.

But the stitch must have been there, because she was pregnant. Her bones were thick and her hips wide. The ballooning stomach seemed correct, not grotesque the way it would have been on a more slender girl.

And her face matched her body. It was unmemorable except for the dark hair that fell to her shoulders. It was lank and unstyled and gave to her pale skin and dark eyes the look of a mystic or a madwoman. As she stared at me across the breakfast table, I saw in her stare something of that stupidity so powerful that it seems primal, unshakable. Looking into Dinah's eyes was like looking into the eye of a chicken.

"It's not all that exciting," she said. "It's OK, I guess."

"Are you feeling all right?" I asked.

Dinah had to think about this. After a minute she nodded. "Yeah."

The conversation wasn't going to take off. I didn't know what to say to Dinah.

"I'd like to get you something for the baby. Do you want to go shopping some afternoon?"

She shook her head. Turning her back on me to take glasses from the breakfront, she said, "It doesn't matter much. I don't need anything." Turning toward me, she added, "Thank you anyway. I appreciate it," like a well-trained dog. I saw Aunt Nell's fine hand trying to turn this girl into some sort of civilized woman.

"Isn't there anything you want?" I asked, unbelieving.

Dinah stared at the table. Her nose twitched like an animal's with her sudden excitement. "Well"—she glanced sideways at me—"it'd be nice to have some TV at night. Not a big one that'd bother your Aunt Nell. Just one of those little bitty ones that you can watch in bed."

Dinah wanted a tummy-TV. The thought of a white plastic box balanced on the massive curve of her belly as she lay in bed was terrible. The vibrations from one mindless program after another would pass through the patchwork quilt, through the layers of taut skin, disturbing the uterine fluid and eventually forming the very rhythms of her baby as it felt the ripples from canned laughter and gunshots, car accidents, chase scenes, and sexual innuendos.

"Isn't the reception in Toms Creek still pretty poor?" I asked hopefully.

"Oh, that doesn't matter." Dinah smiled. "You can see all right, and you can hear all the talk, all the jokes and stuff."

With no cable or large antenna, Toms Creek's television reception was best described as poor. To watch the programs was like watching moving fuzz at times, and to see this blur of action on a screen no bigger than your hand seemed doubly awful.

"I like the comedy shows," she said.

I nodded. Dinah hadn't had much time since childhood for laughter, I guessed. Lying in the house of a distant relative who had taken her in out of pity when her family turned their backs on her, she wanted to be able to laugh. Canned laughter must sound like the real thing to Dinah.

"All right," I said. "Today we'll go down to the store and get you a little TV."

Aunt Nell came in with steaming plates of eggs and country ham swimming in red-eye gravy and a basket of biscuits hot from the oven. "I hope you two are getting acquainted," she said.

I smiled. "Oh, we are. I'm going to get Dinah a little present this afternoon."

"Something for the baby, I hope?" Aunt Nell was dishing up the plates quickly. She looked sideways at me and I caught a tension in her.

"No. Dinah wants a little TV to keep her company, and if you don't mind, I thought I'd get her one."

Aunt Nell put slices of ham on my plate and two biscuits balanced on the edge. "I don't mind if there's a TV as long as I don't have to watch it, but she needs a baby bed more than a TV."

"We'll get a little bitty one that I can keep in my room," Dinah said. "You won't even hear it."

I was eating my ham with too much relish to pay much attention to Aunt Nell's discomfort. "I hope you won't object to an antenna on your roof," I said. "It's the only way to get any reception at all."

"You might as well," Aunt Nell said. "Dinah must get lonely living here with an old woman like me."

There was no more said at breakfast, and the TV was duly acquired. It wasn't until the next day that Aunt Nell talked to me about the girl. She waited until Dinah had gone, as Aunt Nell said, "to the picture show," and then I got a full dose of anxiety to begin my life in Toms Creek.

◇

85

"It's no good talking to her," Aunt Nell began as we settled down in the summer heat on the porch. At four o'clock the house had heated up until it was no relief to sit inside, and the porch was cooler as the day ended. Aunt Nell sat on a wooden settee that was low enough to let her short legs reach the ground. Under her bottom was a mesh pillow that let air circulate between her and the settee. Later I would water the stone walk to cool it down and the air would be moist and steamy as night set in.

"She doesn't talk about the baby, and she doesn't even seem interested in herself. I never saw a girl so little concerned about her own pregnancy."

Aunt Nell fanned herself vigorously. I lay sated on a lounge chair and watched the sidewalk in a small-town stupor of good home-cooking and neighborliness. I was going to move out to my cemetery plot in a couple of days. Dinah didn't seem that interesting.

"Well, at fifteen she probably doesn't even believe there's going to be a baby. Maybe she'll get interested when she sees it."

Aunt Nell snorted. "That's ridiculous. She's due the middle of August. That baby's moving all the time now. She must feel it. Sometimes her blouse even moves when it kicks, but she never says a word. Now what do you suppose is going on in her mind?"

"You assume that she has a mind. Maybe she doesn't have a mind the way you think of it."

"Well, of course she does! Oh, she watches all that silly stuff on television, but most of the girls her age do that. I'm not talking about any sort of real thinking or anything intellectual. Lots of girls don't ever finish school, but they think about their babies. They get clothes ready and make plans. She hasn't bought so much as a diaper pin." Aunt Nell took a sip of iced tea and her face was gloomy.

"Well, it is odd. Have you taken her shopping? I have some money if you need it, you know."

Aunt Nell smiled. "Well, that's a nice offer, but I have enough to help her out. Thank you, Camille. I took her shopping once. We went all the way to Nashville and I took her to a lovely store.

They had all sorts of beautiful layettes, but she wouldn't buy a thing."

"Naked we are born into this world, and naked Dinah's baby will have to stay." I grinned.

"Certainly not!" Aunt Nell shook her head, and her earrings nearly flew off. Aunt Nell had large, fleshy earlobes and an endless collection of clip-on earrings. I had sent her a pair of jade ones with Chinese ideograms on them for good luck. They were on her ears now and gave an exotic touch to the fine bones of her head. It was a very round head with silver hair pulled back in a bun, and her dark eyes and delicate nose were still beautiful. I'd often wished that I had gotten Aunt Nell's looks and her feminine delicateness.

"I'm going out next month and buy a bed and a layette if Dinah doesn't. She can't just bring a baby home from the hospital and keep it in a drawer like a cat. It just does worry me. She takes no interest."

"She must want it, mustn't she? I mean, well—" I didn't want to offend Aunt Nell. "She didn't have to have it, did she?"

"Well, of course not! Toms Creek is modern too, you know. She could have gotten an abortion like most of the other teenage girls who get pregnant nowadays. She wouldn't do it. She said it was her baby and she wouldn't let anybody kill it for her. But after all that fuss and insisting on having it—well, you'd think that she'd take some interest now."

"How in the world did she come to you?" I asked. "Did she grow up in Toms Creek?"

"No, no. She grew up two counties east of here. You know where I mean. Over by the river bend. All the Malingtons live over there. Your father grew up with Andrew Malington. Don't you remember?" she asked with the irritation of the elderly for those who cannot remember their dead world.

I nodded to keep the peace.

"Her folks are about your third cousins but once or twice removed. They're tenant farmers, not smart or particularly hardworking, but they get by. Dinah was their first. They have four, no, five other children. They aren't bad people, but Dinah was more than they knew what to do with."

"The rebellious teenager," I said.

"Not exactly. She never was loud, and she didn't talk back or be angry with her parents."

"What did she do?"

"Well, they couldn't believe it when it all came out, but Dinah was apparently sleeping with boys since she was eleven or twelve. She was quiet and didn't try to look flashy the way some of these girls do. She didn't wear tight clothes and run around with her front exposed all day." Aunt Nell paused and shook her head.

"I can't see her as the town sexpot," I said.

"Well, she was. That is, she was in a way. She wasn't so much sexy as she just didn't seem to care. She drifted into whatever came next. She is a most irritating child."

I nodded. There had been a girl in my class like that. Sharon Clinton had been available. When a boy was thoroughly frustrated with wrestling at the drive-in movies with his girlfriend, Sharon would relieve his tension in her daddy's barn. Silent and mousy, she had wrecked my illusions about what a sexy woman must be like.

"Sharon Clinton—" I began.

"Oh heavens! Sharon was just like all the Clinton women. They're like cows when they're girls and will do anything with any Tom, Dick, or Harry that comes down the pike, but they settle down and get married. Sharon has three little girls, and she takes such care of them! Once she had children, Sharon changed. She's a pillar of the Baptist Church out at Lucasville, I hear. Sharon just had it in her blood, but Dinah's different. She has no feel for the baby coming."

"How about the father? Is he still seeing her?"

Aunt Nell's face went still. She didn't speak. "That's another story," she finally said. "That's why her parents won't have her at home. They were willing to forgive what happened, but they couldn't accept it that Dinah kept the baby. That's entirely another story."

Getting up suddenly, Aunt Nell went into the house to start supper. I followed her, carrying our iced-tea glasses. Apparently I would get the next installment of Dinah's soap opera later. It didn't worry me. Girls like her had been in every small town in the world since time began. She seemed odd, but anyone who watched television all day would be bound to turn out that way. I doubted that Dinah was much different from the Dinahs I had known in high school.

GOATS

When I was fourteen my father had bought five goats. He intended to sell their milk to the hospital for babies who couldn't tolerate cow's milk formulas. The county hospital had apparently lost its source, and my father saw a way to make a few dollars. I don't think he realized how few the dollars would be from selling milk to the one baby in dozens who might be able to digest goat's milk, but practicality never dampened his enthusiasm.

For a few days my father and two of his friends worked in the barn to make milking stalls for the goats and threw up a pen for the many new kids that would be forthcoming in the next ten years. I watched all this with indifference. My father had already bought dairy cows when dairy cows were high and then sold them low to buy steers, which were then high. The steers were surly beasts and were sold low when beef prices bottomed out, after holding them for months in the hopes that prices would rise. By the time news of a good idea had penetrated my father's alcoholic haze, everyone else had known about it for a year and had moved on.

But he was determined that the goats would succeed and read books on goat husbandry and sent away to the agricultural station for pamphlets and generally threw himself into it.

Unfortunately for my father, goats can't become drinking buddies. If the goats could have just sat around the porch in metal chairs that bounced lightly when they leaned back against the tubular frame, if they could have nodded earnestly as my father pontificated, and if they could have held a bourbon and branch water in their delicate hooves, then all would have been well, but the goats were not suitable for this. They demonstrated a remarkable lack of interest in my father's hangovers and didn't show sympathy when he couldn't work for four days in a row.

Out of pity for the does, I milked them when my father was drunk and then poured the milk out in the river, carrying a pail of milk clumsily across the field, through the trees, wading into the mud to dump the milk. I watched the water around my knees turn white and stood watching the white grow fainter as the green river current picked the milk up and moved it downstream. The warm milk moved around my legs and made them smell faintly of goats. My hands smelled of their wool. My dreams were filled with the gentle nuzzle of their noses and the sudden leaps they took to jump out of their pen.

My father spent the whole summer angry, and our fights escalated into warfare. He couldn't see why I poured the milk into the river rather than processing it for sale. I knew how to use the equipment. I could do it. He even promised me 10 percent of his profits if I would just stop pouring the milk into the river.

I refused. I only milked the goats because I saw no need for them to suffer because of my father. I also saw no reason for my father to make so much as a nickel while he was lying passed out in the porch swing for three and four days at a time. And so it went all summer until my father gave up on me and hired a teenage boy, Harvey Stillman, son of a neighboring tenant farmer, to care for the goats.

Harvey was beady-eyed, weak-chinned, and dumb as a stone, but he was strong and he was male. My father used to have long, solicitous conversations with Harvey about his "future."

Even at fourteen, I knew what Harvey's future would be. If he was lucky his older brother wouldn't want to work the farm and Harvey could work it himself. Every poor decision about crops and stock and equipment would be made by Harvey, and he would manage to lose his job in ten years. During those years, Harvey would have handed his small eyes and weak chin on to four or five or six children, all of them dumb as stones, and they would move away to become part of the faceless urban horde.

But my father was indifferent to all this. He was entranced, enchanted, mesmerized by Harvey's maleness. At dinner my father would command me to put another plate on for "My good friend Harvey," and the two males would sit, talking seldom but always weightily of important things.

"I cain't see no end to this cold snap," Harvey would say slowly.

My father would nod. "What do they say about hog prices, son?"

Harvey would carefully load his fork with mashed potatoes and pot roast and peas in layers from the tip of the tines to a couple of inches up the handle. Pushing the fork in his mouth until you wondered if he would get it out again without inadvertently removing a tonsil, Harvey would chew thoughtfully. After a long silence he would say, "They're running about average." Then there would be another silence.

Harvey's silences were so different from my own quick mouth. Harvey never commented on or seemed to notice my father's drinking. Harvey was slow and strong and dumb, and it occurred to my father as he watched Harvey that it was too bad I had been born a girl.

"If I'd had a son," my father would slur wistfully, "then there'd be some point in taking care of this place. I'd be out there slaving all day if she'd been a boy. I would have worked, by God, Harvey, I'm telling you the truth now, son, I would have worked like a nigger for this place." He would shake his head sadly and Harvey would shake his head equally dolefully. "She can't even carry two of the milk pails when they're full," my father would continue.

And then there was the damning thing about me. Every time Harvey stayed to dinner, my father would gaze in admiration at Harvey's huge hands and say, "She can't even throw a ball."

Harvey would nod and grin. He was the pitcher for the county team and could throw balls like a machine at the county fair that pitched from opening day till the fair was over so kids could practice their batting. Harvey could throw a ball.

"He can't cook pot roast," I had once said. And both men roared with laughter. Why would Harvey want to cook pot roast? Crowds don't gather to applaud pot roast cooking. Besides, Harvey could always get some woman to cook his pot roast.

I was not liberated. I kept on cooking fried chicken with white gravy and rice and upside-down cake and sweet potato pie, hoping that someone would love me for it, but I couldn't be a son for him. There weren't any sex-change operations done in Toms Creek.

THE END OF THE GOATS

Aunt Nell saw the perversity of my father's wanting me to be a boy. It made her come out wholeheartedly on my side. She took me under her wing that winter, had me over to her house, made my father spend more than he wanted to on my clothes, and enrolled me in dancing class.

I was taller and larger than the other girls. My face was not cute but heavy and adult, and I did not look kittenish or beautiful in my first formal dress, camelias fastened to my wrist with a clear plastic clip. But I was female, feminine, unrelievedly on the other side of the fence from the men, with breasts that swelled under the pink tulle and feet shod in silver ballet slippers. I was not a boy.

Aunt Nell had a picture taken of me and put a huge color print of it on the mantel in my father's living room.

"Isn't she beautiful, Jeffrey? She's becoming so womanly. Your poor wife would be so proud."

My father looked at the picture for a long time and then sighed sadly. "Well, I'll have to get a baseball bat to beat the boys off with," he said grinning at me. "I don't want grandsons yet."

It cheered him up considerably, that picture. Aunt Nell relaxed and figured that he was now happy about having a female child. She had worked so hard that I didn't explain to her. He was more content with me not because of his acceptance of my femaleness but because he saw the possibility of grandsons, hulking boys with large hands who could do his work on the farm and throw balls. I had promise after all.

But the necessity of a son became less as the winter went on. One of the goats died of unknown causes. One was unable to kid and was sold, leaving two does and the buck. Both does had kids, but they had them too early. It was February when they were born, and a late snow had fallen.

Now this wouldn't have mattered for a good farmer, but my father's methods were slack. The barn had never been properly insulated, and both were born outside because no one had thought to put them in the barn that night. One snuggled under its mother for warmth, but the other wasn't so lucky. Too weak to wiggle up close to its mother's flanks, the kid lay exhausted on the cold straw.

At least, this was my father's explanation. Whatever the reason, the back legs of the kid were frozen and frostbitten, but he didn't die. He lived but couldn't walk. His back legs were useless. Harvey was going to kill him, when the kid suddenly learned to move around by walking on his two front hooves, his back legs up in the air like a man standing on his hands. He minced around in his pen nimbly and dropped to the ground only to nurse or rest.

This naturally struck my father and his friends as terribly funny and entertaining, and they spent days leaning over the pen, watching the kid and drinking. Word spread in the county that Jeffrey Carpenter had a peculiar goat, and men dropped by to see for themselves. One Saturday there were nine or ten of them in the living room, and my father had brought the kid into the house. The dining-room table was moved aside to let the goat hop more actively. Everyone but the goat was drunk.

Aunt Nell arrived in the middle of this to give me a ride to a Coke party. Fifteen- and sixteen-year-old girls had Coke parties then.

Aunt Nell walked in and a hush fell. My father stepped forward and said, "Why hello, Nell. You must have come to get my little girl?" Turning to his cronies he said, "She hardly stays home with her daddy anymore. She's out the door every time I turn around." They all nodded. The sweet nostalgic sadness of booze hung in the air. Someone belched discreetly.

"I'll be back," Aunt Nell said.

She left me at the Coke party and said nothing except that she'd pick me up at four-thirty. Then she drove back to the farm. Expecting the worst, my father had gotten rid of all but two of the men, and Aunt Nell got rid of them.

"It's time you men got back to town," she said. "Your wives will be looking for you to take them home. They can't spend all day in J. C. Penney's while you look at a goat."

They left and she had a few words with my father. I never knew what she said, but most people in the town made up their own version. When I got home, the men were gone. The dining-room table was back in place. The rug had been sent to the rug cleaners, and my father was passed out on the blue silk sofa, a glass of bourbon cradled against his belly as he lay on his side. Aunt Nell rested her hand on the scrollwork of roses carved in the mahogany of the sofa's back. She looked at my father thoughtfully.

"Get your clothes, Camille," she said. "I can stand his drink-ing, but this sort of perversity is not fit for a child. You'll have to stay with me for a while."

The last three years of high school were a contest between Aunt Nell and my father. When he got too crazy, she removed me from his house. Then he would sober up for a day or two and sit in her living room saying all the things he had to say to get me home so I could clean up the house and cook him a decent meal. I once suggested that he make a tape recording of his excuses and rationalizations and just mail it to Aunt Nell when the house got too dirty.

I never saw the kid again. Aunt Nell had the vet put it down, and it died quietly. My father had to pay the bill for the shot, which didn't please him. Harvey could have knocked the kid in the head for free.

If Aunt Nell decided to, she would keep me for good, and my father fought that until he died. He never praised my good grades or seemed to take any interest in my thoughts, but he was not happy without me. After all, I was his daughter. He had made me, and there wasn't anything else he had done worth pointing to. At heart, he was just a man who was afraid to be alone all night in the house. Even when he passed out, he liked to know that someone else, another heartbeat, another breath less labored than his own, rose and fell under the roof and kept the dark night in its proper place.

Two weeks after putting my tent up, I got my first letter from my husband. Henry was worried about me but happy to have me gone for a while. Without me in San Francisco, he could date and party and be free of guilt. Aunt Nell got into her old blue Chevy and drove out to the cemetery to deliver the letter personally. She was pleased that I had a letter from Henry and left me alone to read it, acting as if she were leaving me with a "beau" who would ask for a kiss once she had gone.

I sat on a folding stool, toweling my hair in the sun. Every morning I swam in the river and washed for the day. The smell of river mud and furred moss, which grew on the roots of trees by the riverbank, clung to my skin. Some people wouldn't have liked it, but I thought it was an exotic scent. By the end of the summer I would smell so like the fields and river that rabbits would sit close to me and river otters ignore me as they played. That was how I figured it, anyway.

The letter was a complication, a perversity of sorts in the cool shade of the cemetery trees, and I didn't like to open it. Henry seemed far away and unimportant compared to the reality of the cows who came over every morning for handouts of salt. Before my swim I would pour a layer of salt on my hands and let the cows lick it off with muscular tongues, their pinkness leaving my hand smooth and relaxed as a massage would.

Henry began his letter by telling me that he had stopped seeing my old friend. "It was just something I fell into while we were breaking up," he wrote. "I didn't really love her, and she deserves a chance to find someone who can care for her more. So I broke up with her," he went on.

Henry's nobility didn't fool me. It was my opinion, cynical though it may sound, that Henry could get no mileage out of a relationship with my ex-friend since I had moved to Kentucky. Without my interest, it just wasn't as exciting. I believed, thinking it over there in the sun by my tent, that most of Henry's passion for her had been his passive way of getting at me.

And I probably deserved it in a way. My misery during the last five years of marriage had been awful to live with. I had all the unhappy-married-woman's symptoms. I had been overweight, angry, nonsexual, and expensive. I did not fool myself that Henry had had an easy life with me, but nonetheless there was a warm glow in my gut and a giggle that would not stay down at the thought of his jilting her. All the hard work of the women I had known—down the drain. All the carefully planned dinner parties and brunches where Henry was prepared for his new marriage. Henry was so very eligible, but he had proved more elusive than they had dreamed. Heartily eating their quiche and spinach salad, Henry had been fattened for the kill and then managed to slip away, leaving the women with dirty dishes and wasted time. God bless him, I thought. He always has been smart.

The letter went on at length, but the gist of his cautious prose was that Henry had become a swinger. He was dating every woman he met and wanted to date those he passed on the street but hadn't met, and it was all terribly exciting and free. Henry was being exposed to a variety of women and swayed back and forth between them. One took him to the symphony. Another was talking him into meditation and vegetable-juice fasts. Yet another wanted Henry to campaign for sewer commissioner.

"I have changed a lot since you left," he wrote solemnly. I smiled and watched the corn leaves ripple as a passing breeze touched them. When a marriage ends, it is obvious that the two people failed. The best defense is to assure everyone how radically you have changed since the separation. Such change proves that the marriage was repressive and did not allow you to develop the way you could outside the limiting strictures of the marriage. It also assures you and everyone who meets you that never again will you fail. After all, *you've* changed enormously. You used to be a schoolteacher and now you're making pots on a commune and eating only sprouted seeds. It must follow, everyone thinks hopefully, that that pain of love found, love tolerated, and love lost cannot happen again. Now that Henry was becoming the *real* Henry, he could choose better and therefore live happily ever after. I wished him luck.

Henry ended the letter by telling me that our aged cat was improving daily. The cat had always been everything that cats can be at their worst. It was surly, unaffectionate, had expensive allergies, and managed to position its backside over the rim of its litter box instead of hitting the granulated clay we had provided.

"I met a woman, Tanya, who is very into alternative healing systems," Henry wrote. "We tried herbs for a while, and when that didn't work, Tanya suggested a spinal adjustment. I took the cat to a chiropractor in San Francisco who doesn't normally do pets but is willing to try occasionally on cats. It has really been surprising how the cat's disposition has improved since then. I've also got both animals on organic pet food with no chemicals added. I tried to put the dog on brown rice to get rid of his aggressiveness, but he wouldn't eat it," Henry added. "Maybe the organic pet food will help."

I lay on the grass and laughed. Our dog was a beagle who thought he was an attack-trained doberman. Every walk with him was a nightmare of snarling, bristling dogs. God knows how many times we had to have the damned dog stitched up after yet another unsuccessful territorial skirmish. The only fight he'd ever won was a clash with a Great Dane where he'd managed to get under the Dane and bite his balls. If Henry put the dog on brown rice and the dog didn't eat it, his aggression would shortly disappear. Of course, so would the dog, but that would be small loss to Henry or the world.

Lying there in the sun, I reread Henry's letter. I felt affection for him, but I was glad it was just a letter and not Henry himself sitting in front of me. Henry's life seemed very far away and important only the way newspaper events are important. I didn't begrudge him his affairs and his organic pet food. Henry was all right as long as there was half a country between us. I had the river, a cornfield, my tent, and a pregnant cousin. Henry had his stocks, his girlfriends, and a cat that goes to a chiropractor. Who was to say that I should be angry at Henry?

Tom Church and I had had two dates. Both were casual. Both were fun. All the electricity was there, but Tom didn't push for more than a couple of kisses goodnight. The first date we had spent at the county fair, and we had ridden all the rides, admired the pigs and cattle, watched a showing of Tennessee walking horses, and eaten snow-cones to try and keep cool in the summer heat. As night came on, Tom bought snow-cones with no fruit syrup on them, and he poured bourbon over the crushed ice. I got pleasantly drunk, but Tom didn't press his advantage.

The second date was for dinner at Ralph and Barbara Covey's barbecue pit. They ran a restaurant out of their house in the summertime, which was more like a club than a restaurant. There weren't any signs on the road, and only townspeople knew that down a gravel road was the best barbecue in seven states.

We ate on a screened porch at long tables with pitchers of barbecue sauce, white bread, and bowls of cole slaw and potato salad sitting under wire screens to keep the bugs off. You helped yourself at the barbecue pit and sat down with friends and ate enormously and drank beer.

Tom knew most of the people there. We sat with three other couples and Tom spent most of the night talking to the men about the possibility of a new highway going near enough Toms Creek to generate a business boom. Tom kept my plate full and my glass refilled, and I sat and felt oddly womanly while the men talked land and construction and the cost of heavy machinery.

I was spending more time than I had intended thinking about Tom Church. He was so decisive, so sure of his life and his future. It made me doubly insecure and off balance when I was with him. No romantic dreams of being a potter or giving it all up to run an antiques store for Tom.

He arrived for our third date at eight o'clock. He was wearing slacks and a shirt, and I was trying to keep cool in a cotton dress and sandals. He stood looking down the slope at the trees that edged the river. The corn was in full growth, the ears standing out ripe from the stalk and the whole field rustling in the beginnings of twilight.

"They say you can hear corn grow at night," Tom said.

"It's true. It rustles all the time even when there's no wind at all."

"God, it's hot tonight. Do you really want to go to the movies?" he asked.

"I don't care. What do you want to do?"

"I haven't been swimming in the river all summer. Been too busy to think about it. I'd hate to think I was so old that a whole summer could get by me without a swim. Let's go swimming. There's a sandbar right across from here, as I remember."

"It's still there," I said. "Let me get my suit."

"Hey now, Camille." Tom took my hand and then pulled me to him and wrapped his arm around my waist. "You aren't going to embarrass me by wearing a suit when I don't have one, are you?"

So we walked through the cornfield hand-in-hand and then through the trees to the bank, where we took off our clothes and hung them on tree limbs, standing modestly back to back. But when my clothes were off and the dirt of the bank was under my feet, I felt a rush of modesty and couldn't turn around until Tom laughed and turned me himself with his hands on my shoulders. I automatically glanced down at his heavy, muscular body, a little fat at the stomach but the rest hard and smooth with a dark line of hair going down from his chest to his navel and then on down to his groin.

"Not bad for two old folks going into middle age," Tom said, and then he grabbed my hand and pulled me into the river, which was cold on our legs. We waded in and stood hip deep and I felt the oily thickness of river mud under my toes as Tom put his hands over my breasts and kissed me.

"Let's swim to the sandbar," he said. "First one there gets to make the other one do whatever they want." He laughed and pushed out powerfully in the water.

I laughed too. Swimming in the river was nothing compared to my rigorous training in San Francisco Bay. I beat him easily and laughed at his startled face.

"I guess you have to do whatever I say," I said.

"You don't ever win unless you're big enough to make the loser pay off," said Tom, and he threw himself on top of me, laughing, pressing me into the sandbar. "Losing can be fun," he said as he kissed me, and we wrestled laughing in the sand.

"Let's swim upriver. We can swim a mile up and then drift back with the current," he said.

So we did. We swam side by side, the light failing slowly and bats beginning to dip over the river. The cows were somewhere out of sight. There was no sign of a person or a light from a house. The stars came out as we turned and lazily floated back down the river. Dark came on us but the moon was enough light reflected on the water, and we drifted without talking.

Our bodies were used to the water and it was warm until suddenly we would hit a cold spot where some underground spring poured water up into the river from the cold, limestone caverns under the earth. Owls hooted from the shadows of trees, and our feet made no sound as we waded onto the spit of sandbar that stretched out into the river.

Tom's body was cool and fragrant with river water. His nipple in my lips when I bent my head to kiss it rose up like a kernel of new corn, cool and hard. He gently pushed me down onto the sand and stood a moment over me, dark, his features hidden. Then he came down on me, and I heard a fox bark anxiously in the hills and the hounds far away baying as they caught the scent and ran.

BEAUTY

I remembered my grandparents. Their wedding photograph showed a stiff young man and a pretty girl who were both handsome in a clean, untouched way. As he grew older, my grandfather increased in power and dignity. As an old man, he was still admired.

"Look at that," people commented as he walked by. "He's better-looking now than he ever was at thirty."

When I was ten and eleven my grandfather liked to take me out for lunch on Saturday. I would walk across the fields to his house, being careful with the barbed wire so my dress wouldn't tear, and we would ride into town in his old Ford.

The routine never varied. He parked his car in the driveway of a friend's house or on the crest of one of the town's two hills. Then we would walk down the hill, past old houses so he could say hello to people he knew. Everyone knew him. Everyone knew me because I was with him.

In town we circled the square once, talking to the men who stood and squatted around the courthouse.

"Hello there, my friend, how's your tobacco doing?" my grandfather would say, and I would offer my hand over and over. I developed the firmest handshake in the state for a girl of ten in self-defense against the rocklike grip of the farmers. Your bones would crack if you didn't grab harder than they did.

"She has a good, firm hand," the men would say approvingly.

We would always end up on the corner where the Five-and-Dime Store was. They had a lunch counter that was my favorite place to eat. My grandfather liked it because it let him talk to the "common folk" and keep touch with the political gossip and the gossip around the courthouse, but I liked it because of the food.

They served turkey and dressing and cranberry sauce with mashed potatoes and turkey gravy for the Saturday special. I had never eaten turkey except at Thanksgiving and Christmas until I began to eat Saturday lunch with my grandfather.

"Can I get turkey?" I asked him in amazement the first time.

"Well, it's a dollar-fifty, but that's what happens when a man takes a lady out to lunch," my grandfather would always say. I felt as if I were getting away with something eating turkey in the middle of August. The Dime Store was the most exotic experience in dining in my life until I left Toms Creek.

And everyone said how handsome my grandfather was, sitting there on his stool, but I never heard them say that my grandmother was beautiful.

She wouldn't let her picture be taken after she was forty-five. "Now don't point that thing at me," she'd cry. I had no pictures of my grandmother as I knew her, just faded pictures of a young woman I'd never met.

Remembering her gentle face with the hair pulled back in a bun, the year she taught me to play hearts and slapjack and fish and finally, canasta, I think she was beautiful, too. Her eyes were disturbing and strange because one was a light blue and the other brown with a gold ring around the iris. She had had a hard time giving birth to my father and had said to my grandfather as she lay exhausted, holding the baby, "The least you can do is buy me a diamond. I've given you a baby."

He made the trip to Nashville that afternoon and bought her a diamond solitaire, which she wore till her death, which I wear now.

Her hair was lovely, her face loving, her eyes riveting. Why did no one say that she grew more beautiful every year? Why was she not told, "You're more beautiful at sixty than you ever were at twenty-five"?

Is it true that men do not get ugly as they grow older? Is it true that they are handsomer as their faces roughen and wrinkle and develop character? Or do we only love them more than they love us?

Having dinner and sex with Tom Church was filling my fantasy life until I almost forgot about Aunt Nell. I went to the library twice a week and read books about the history of Kentucky and the people who settled there. My mind was filled with Indians and Shakers and slaves and Civil War armies which moved across my thoughts like real people, and the sex with Tom and the thought of Aunt Nell became more the dream, the unreal part of my life.

"What are you thinking about?" Tom whispered as he lay on me, his penis half out of me so he could take his time coming. "It isn't real," I said. "Lying here isn't real. It's something I've read about but none of it is real."

Shoving suddenly into me, he said, "I'll show you what's real."

I gasped and cried out with all the appropriate noises of love-making, and he was gratified, and I was limp and sated, but he was wrong. Lying there on a blanket under the stars in that moist air was not real. All the world of people whose bones lay under me seemed more alive than I did during those weeks.

Aunt Nell didn't know about Tom Church. She knew that I was dating him, but she assumed with the privilege of our relationship and her own customs that dating did not encompass sex. I didn't confess to her, and she was always after me to come and see her, talk to her, talk to Dinah, get to know Dinah.

I drifted through the weeks, with no thought for the next day. When it rained I sat in my tent and watched the water wet the fields and didn't care that I was alone in a cemetery with nothing but my camp equipment. I thought vaguely of writing Henry and asking about my share of our house and stocks, but it didn't seem important in July, and I didn't in my heart believe that anything Henry had belonged to me anyway. Who was I to ask him for anything? The thought of owning more than I could put in my tent was terrifying. It was just stuff to take care of, polish, shine, clean, and be bound by. It was merely a way for other people to judge me. Was my furniture good enough? Was the decoration of my place chic or merely following the current trend, and if I followed the current trend, would I change the decorations when the trend changed, and would I change to the most admired new trend or pick the wrong one? It was exhausting to think about. I didn't want any part of it.

"Dinah has never seen the Hermitage," Aunt Nell said one day.

"Did you drive all the way out here to tell me that Dinah has not been educated properly?" I asked with a grin.

"Now don't get smart, Camille. That child has never been taken anyplace. She hasn't even been to Louisville, and she's never seen any of the nice places around here."

I thought of the Hermitage. I hadn't been there since a school trip during high school, but I supposed that it was still there. "Do you think that going to the Hermitage is going to make Dinah take an interest in her baby?" I asked.

Aunt Nell stared across the field at the cows who were walking toward the river for a drink. The calf dawdled behind the others and then suddenly bolted past his mother and turned and threatened her with his head lowered. The cow ignored her calf and plodded on as if he weren't there.

"Don't try to make me sound silly, Camille. I don't think anything like that will really change Dinah, but it seems a shame that she hasn't been shown anything but drive-in movies and bowling alleys. It couldn't hurt her to go look at something like the Hermitage."

"Well, Andrew Jackson was a man of the people, and God knows Dinah is of the people. I guess you can't be more one of the people than an unmarried pregnant farm girl who watches a TV that sits on her belly." I laughed. "If what you're getting at is that I should drive Dinah down to see the Hermitage, I'll do it. You'll have to let me borrow your car, if you think your car can do it."

Aunt Nell shook her head. "It's a silly idea. My car probably wouldn't make it in this heat. I don't know why I come out here to suggest such things, but I'm worried, Camille. Dinah doesn't talk to me sometimes."

I glanced at Aunt Nell quickly. "Do you think she's crazy?"

"Oh no, no," she said with the querulous irritation of the elderly. "You don't understand. She is just upset about this baby."

"Maybe I should take her to Vanderbilt Hospital to be checked out by the psychiatrists there?" I asked.

"Now you see"—Aunt Nell was angry and she stood up to leave—"that's all you young people think. If a girl is silent just take her and dump her on some doctor who doesn't know her and wouldn't even look at her if you didn't pay him. That's the way all your generation is. Well, I don't think that's what she needs, but I can't seem to give her whatever it is. I just thought you might show some interest instead of sitting out here staring at cows. Those aren't even very good cows," she finished indignantly.

She left and I felt guilty. It wasn't much to ask. One day spent driving to Nashville for lunch and a visit to Andrew Jackson's home. It wasn't a bad idea. I went to the library that afternoon and spent two days reading a biography of Andrew Jackson. I probably would have gone to the Hermitage anyway after reading the book. Taking Dinah along was just incidental. I wanted to see the old place again. I wanted to see if there was anything about it that would tell me something. I wanted magic.

◇

I rented a car with air conditioning and a radio. I couldn't imagine the strain of silence all the sixty miles to the Hermitage if Dinah didn't feel like talking, and the heat was oppressive in July after my years in Northern California. The Wednesday we went to see Jackson's house the temperature was ninety by ten o'clock, which meant it would be over a hundred by two in the afternoon and hang there till it got dark after dinner. The humidity was in the eighties, and I was wet all over and slimy under my arms before I could dress and get to the car-rental agency. The car put out odd clouds of blue smoke when I drove it off, but it was air conditioned, so I didn't pay any attention. All I wanted was a car that would run and that would keep us reasonably cool.

I picked up Dinah, and she actually looked almost pretty. She wore pink slacks and a blouse that looked like a pup tent printed all over with small brown bears. It was appropriate for such a young woman, and her face looked pale but pretty above the swell of motherhood. For the first time I saw how Dinah might have been a pretty girl before she became pregnant.

We drove in silence, the radio playing country music. The highway ran through fields and crossed creeks until we got near Nashville. Then the road disintegrated into urban blight. Filling stations, fast-food joints, all sorts of small businesses housed in flat-roofed, square buildings like card houses and just about that permanent. The only good thing to say about the area was that someone could come by with a bulldozer and knock down about three miles of motel-modern architecture in a day. The lack of permanence in this sort of construction always reassured me. It was not built for the ages.

My mind was wandering and everything was going as planned when there was a grinding sound and it felt like the back half of the car had fallen off. I braked, pulled over onto the edge of the road, and got out. Cars whizzed by unsympathetically, and the road smelled of diesel fuel and hot tar. It wasn't as bad as I had thought. "It's just the damn exhaust pipe," I told Dinah. "It fell off and we're dragging it. I'd better get a mechanic to take a look at it. At least he can pull it off and tell us if the thing's safe to drive."

A gas station sign hovered over the road a few hundred feet ahead, and we drove slowly toward it, dragging our exhaust pipe, and who knows what else, ignominiously behind us like a tail.

Dinah said nothing but had begun twisting and squeezing the front of her blouse in her hands as if she were wringing it out.

"It's OK, Dinah," I said. "We'll either get it pulled off, fixed cheap and fast, or get a cab somewhere and ride the bus home. To hell with this damn car. I told them it looked funny with all that smoke coming out. They would go on and rent it anyway. Anything to make a buck."

Dinah sat stiffly in the car and looked pale. I guessed that opening the doors had made the car too hot for a pregnant girl. I hoped that Dinah wasn't going to be sick at this point. Aunt Nell and her ideas, I thought with irritation.

I talked to a mechanic, who was nice enough about our muffler. He jumped into the car and started it up.

"I'll just drive her onto the lift, ma'am," he said to Dinah. "You won't even have to get out. We'll pull it off in a minute and you ladies can go on. It's just the muffler."

He started the car and was pulling forward when Dinah, white-faced and in a panic, threw open her door and tried to get out. She slipped, nearly fell under her car, and threw herself onto the concrete. By the time I ran to the other side of the car and the young mechanic got the car stopped, Dinah was crawling over the oil-stained concrete like an animal.

"Dinah!" I shouted. "Get up. What are you doing. My God—"

The mechanic stopped the car and got out, watching Dinah in amazement. I forced Dinah to her feet. She was panting and her face twisted in panic.

"I don't want to go in there. I don't want to go in there. Don't make me, Camille, don't. Please, I don't want to go in there."

"It's all right," I murmured, patting her awkwardly. "They're just going to fix the damn car. You don't have to stay in the car. My God, Dinah, you could have gotten killed leaping out of the car that way. You scared me to death."

"I'll rip off this muffler, ma'am," the mechanic said. "Your daughter there is just like my wife. My wife took all sorts of ideas into her head when she was having ours. It's just the way some women are."

"She isn't my daughter," I said automatically.

Dinah faced the highway and was still trying to move away from the filling station. There was a Dairy Queen across the street with a few picnic tables under umbrellas. "Come on, Dinah, let's sit down and get something cold to drink. The heat is making you nearly hysterical. God knows I can't blame you. It's enough to make us all sick today."

"I'm not hysterical. I just don't want to go in that place."

I didn't know what on earth bothered Dinah about the filling station, but the mechanic was calling me to come inspect the car. "You just sit here and drink something," I said, handing her a few dollars. "I'll get the car and pick you up."

The mechanic was so upset about nearly running over Dinah that he pulled the muffler off and charged us nothing for it. I drove over to the Dairy Queen and Dinah still sat with the now sweaty dollar bills in her hand. She looked awful.

"Do you just want to go on back home, Dinah?"

"No. I don't care. I guess we've come this far. I can be all right in a minute."

I bought her a Coke and watched as she politely tried to drink it, but her hands were shaking. We got back into the car and I hoped that the air conditioning would revive her. The Hermitage wasn't far off, down a tree-lined road called Rachel's Lane. The road was gracious. It had all the earmarks of people who cared about life.

$\mathcal{T}$HE WILDERNESS
BELLE

She had been thirteen, tanned and agile as an Indian boy, when her father, the Colonel, had taken her and her ten brothers and sisters and mother down the Ohio River on the flatboat *Adventure*. But then she began to be beautiful, olive-skinned, and dimpled when she smiled, which was often. Her beauty was known and courted for miles around, and at seventeen she married, a good catch, a man from a rich and prominent family, and became Rachel Donelson Robards. She and her mecurial, violent husband lived near Harrodsburg with his mother, and Rachel sat and enchanted the old woman, who nodded over her snuffbox.

Trouble began. Who knows why trouble begins in a marriage? He claimed that Rachel flirted with Peyton Shott and John Overton, two young lawyers who boarded with the Robards. She claimed that he was violent and that his jealous rages would be the death of her. In the traditional way, she went home to her family.

John Overton was sent as a peace emissary and discussed the sad case of Rachel and Lewis Robards with another young man who was boarding with Rachel's mother, the widow Donelson. This young man was an esteemed boarder in these times of Indian uprisings, for he was known for his courage as a fighter and a man already at the age of twenty-one. His name was Andrew Jackson.

Rachel went back to her husband. Then she fled to her mother again. Then she went back to Lewis Robards. Then her family sent a man to bring her home through the wilderness, a man who would protect her from harm on the journey. They sent Andrew Jackson.

Robards talked dirt about this "elopement." Jackson said that he would cut Robards' ears off if the talk and slander did not stop. Robards filed a peace warrant against Jackson and was present when Jackson was taken to the magistrate. Promising to harm no one, Jackson was given back his hunting knife, and he unsheathed the blade slowly. Running his thumb over the blade, Jackson stared at Robards, who fled.

Fearing her husband's violence, Rachel declared that she would go to Natchez and stay with relatives until his anger was past. The route lay over two thousand miles of wilderness by way of the Cumberland, Ohio, and Mississippi rivers, or you could go overland by the Natchez Trace, which was known for twenty years to be the most evil path in the West. Jackson joined the expedition to see Rachel safely in the hands of her family in Natchez. By now he no longer was trying to fool himself or others. He loved Rachel Robards.

Changing his tactics, Lewis Robards did not pursue Rachel, but put to the General Assembly in Richmond, Virginia, a petition for divorce. It was rejected and the Assembly passed a bill which gave Robards the right to go to court and to try to prove his allegations. His allegations were stated in this manner: "that defendant hath deserted the plaintiff, and that she hath lived in adultery with another man since such desertion." The bill was passed on December 20, 1790, twelve days before Kentucky ceased to be a part of Virginia.

Robards rumored untruthfully that he was divorced. Jackson broke the news to Rachel. They thought she was a divorced woman. By assiduous courting, Andrew Jackson persuaded Rachel to marry him, and they were married in August 1791. Their first home was a log house in a clearing on a bluff overlooking the Mississippi. The river trailed below them, reflecting the moon as it traveled over the sky, and the owls hooted for no cause while Jackson held Rachel in his arms. They had found each other. They were twenty-four. They would be happy.

The Hermitage was set in a grove of trees, a stately home with white pillars, shady porches, and the tone of American elegance that Aunt Nell loved so much. Dinah and I made our way through the parking lot, paid admission, and joined a group of tourists like ourselves who lined up obediently and waited their turn to see Jackson's home. A clean-cut young man was acting as docent and lectured us as we waited. Dinah was quiet, but her hands still restlessly plucked at the hem of her blouse.

"Listen to what he's saying, Dinah. We'll all be inside in a minute. I just hope to God it's air conditioned."

I would have gone on, but Dinah was listing slightly. Her lips were slick with sweat and she was almost green she was so white. "Oh my God! Are you going to faint?" I cried.

The young man heard me and came over. "Bring her in here," he said. "It's cooler and she can rest until your turn comes."

No one complained when we went through the broad door to the left of the porch since Dinah was so obviously young and pregnant. It was cooler, and Dinah leaned against the wall and drew gasping breaths. "I'm sorry," she said. "I couldn't attend too well to all that you were saying. I guess Jackson liked big houses. This is the biggest house I've ever been in."

"Sit there till you feel all right," I ordered. "We can see the Hermitage anytime. Let's go home if you feel sick."

I had visions of Dinah having her baby beside the mahogany railing that kept us out of the main part of the dining room. I imagined the long-skirted tour guides bringing hot water in Jackson's silver teapot and tearing up the linen tablecloth for rags. I didn't have much choice. I'd brought her down here at the suggestion of an old woman who believed that a sense of history and a heritage would make a fifteen-year-old girl buck up and be a good mother. Falling in with this scheme, I was now stuck in the dining room of an antebellum mansion with a fainting girl who would sit on Andrew Jackson's porch and rock and watch TV if she were given her choice. I couldn't believe that Dinah and the Hermitage had anything in common.

"I don't really know why your Aunt Nell wanted me to come down here," Dinah said. "It was real sweet of her to want me to see it and all, but I don't really care much for all this history and stuff."

If Dinah had been ten years older, I would have laughed uproariously with her and suggested that we go immediately to the best restaurant we could find and spend the afternoon in icy splendor drinking cold glasses of white wine and soda. But she was only fifteen and eight months' pregnant, and getting drunk and talking wouldn't be very good for her. Besides, what could I possibly talk to Dinah about? I never watch game shows—or any other television for that matter.

"Well, we'll just look at some of it and then go home. We can stop at the Burger Delight if you want and get some dinner."

Dinah brightened. She loved hamburgers with onion and pickles and ketchup. Aunt Nell seldom cooked hamburgers, leaning more toward chicken baked in sherry. The cool air was having an effect. Dinah was not quite so white and she almost smiled.

"Can I get a double order of French fries?" she asked.

I promised all the French fries that Dinah wanted and sat by her on a folding chair while people filed by on the tour of the house. The dining room was the first room visited by the tourists, and Dinah and I sat listening over and over again to the same talk delivered by a pretty girl in a long dress of faintly nineteenth-century style.

The usual meal in Jackson's home consisted of a spicy soup and rice, fish, duck, chicken, ham and pheasant, turnip greens and beans, corn bread and hot biscuits, plum pudding, apple pie, fruit and preserves, claret wine, madeira, sherry, and port. A heavily carved mantel in the room had been made by a soldier who had fought under Jackson's command at the Battle of New Orleans, January 8, 1815. He had carved the mantel of hickory wood, working on it one day of every year, January 8, for twenty-four years until it was finished. Jackson had it installed in the dining room on January 8, 1840.

We sat and listened politely to the talk until Dinah looked better. There was all the rest of the tour and the drive home, but Dinah seemed to be more relaxed. Maybe this trip was a good idea after all.

Dinah had some color in her cheeks now, and she walked out of the dining room of the Hermitage with the grace of advanced pregnancy. Her back swaying from the pull of weight around her front, she moved with the concentration of a woman who knows that she is different and that her every movement is rife with meaning. I watched her with some amusement. The high ceilings and grace of the old house seemed to be drawing Dinah in, sucking her into a way of moving that would not be out of place. Her very body was picking up the impressiveness of the house and the dignity of its heritage. Amazingly enough, I thought, Aunt Nell might be right.

The hallway was spacious and opened at both ends with large doors. You could imagine opening both doors to let the cool air circulate on a hot summer night until it was time to lock up before bed. An uncomfortable-looking Empire sofa with hard curves and black horsehair upholstery stood against the wall. Here it was that Andrew Jackson had sometimes napped after dinner. The sofa looked like the last place imaginable for a nap. Its formality and hardness could have been selected only by a will equally hard and uncompromising. The walls were covered with scenic paper, pictures of vague steps leading to pseudo-Greek temples, towering trees, and figures dressed in rustic clothes.

The young docent was standing on the circular staircase and her lecture caught my ear. "Oh look, Dinah. The wallpaper is about Telemachus. Do you know that story?"

Dinah shook her head.

"He was the son of Odysseus, and when his father didn't come home from the Trojan War for twenty years, Telemachus went out and looked for him. He was a good son who was trying to find his long-lost father."

Dinah nodded. She didn't seem very interested, but I was gripped by the notion. Jackson's father had died before he was born. Jackson was a posthumous child. He lost his mother at fourteen. It seemed sad and appropriate that Jackson cared so much about this wallpaper that, when the original batch was sold accidentally to another man after a steamboat fire that confused the entire shipment of some Nashville merchant, Jackson ordered the same paper again, and when it came, put it on the entrance walls of his home. The search for the father. It had been a very popular theme in wallpaper, and it seemed fitting. All those Americans, wandering, leaving home, dying early and losing relatives. Those frontier people would have understood Telemachus' search more readily than a ten-year war fought over a woman.

I followed Dinah up the stairs, was separated from her by other people, and looked up the stairs to see her turning the curve at the top. The full profile of her body was seen for a moment against the wall at the top of the stairs, and her enormous shape suddenly fascinated me. There was a child in there. She was not one but two people moving up the stairs. The child might be a boy, and then what? What could Dinah tell him about his father? Would he care? Would he accept his loss with unconcern? Would that child walk out into the world someday and look for a father he did not know? It seemed likely to me. I remembered all my hours spent brooding over my own father. I had known him, had been raised by him, but had never been willing to accept him for what he was and seemed to be. I was always pushing, trying to find that man I thought he must be, the man who was my real father.

Dinah stood looking over a mahogany railing into a bedroom. The other tourists moved away, following the guide, but Dinah stood staring blankly into the bedroom.

"You think I'm crazy, the way I acted back there on the road. That mechanic thought I was crazy too."

"No I didn't, I just figured the heat got to you, or you were scared to go up on the lift. Are you afraid of heights, Dinah?"

Dinah wrung her hands, twisting the front of her blouse until it was tight over her belly. I watched her with alarm. She was turning white again, this time almost blue around her mouth.

"Camille, I can't bear going in that place. I can't stand it. That's where they got me pregnant. I can't stand the smell of the oil and stuff."

I was confused. "What do you mean, Dinah?"

"They got me pregnant like that when they made the car lift go up and down. It was like that."

Another group of tourists gathered around us and I stared at Dinah in silence until they moved on.

"Dinah, going in a gas station doesn't get anyone pregnant. What do you mean?"

"We were at the ice cream place on the highway and six of them got in my daddy's car with me. We drove around and it was fun at first."

Dinah was silent. Then she burst out again, clutching the rail that held us outside the bedroom.

"They made me lie down on boards across the car lift and put it up and down. The sheriff said I led them on because I didn't scream, but we were way out on the road at the station near Palmers Corner. There wasn't anybody who'd hear me."

Dinah turned to me and grabbed my arm. "I had done it with boys, that's true, but they all did it at once, and I was tied on the car lift and they put oil cans up in me and said they'd unscrew my breasts. They lay wrenches and stuff on me like I was a machine. I never wanted it. I never wanted it. Do you see? I never meant them to do that."

Dinah's voice was shriller now and more tourists were coming up the stairs. I laid my hand on her arm to try and calm her and waited while the docent explained that the baseboards in the room were not marble but were painted to look like marble. Her sentence kept going around in my head. *They are not really marble but are painted to simulate marble as was the style of the time. They are not really marble but are painted to simulate marble as was the style of the time. . . .*

Dinah was almost twitching with nerves and muttering to herself. The tourists stared and moved on.

"Dinah," I said, "they raped you."

"I knew all those boys. I'd known them all. They said it couldn't be rape if I had known them before. It wasn't funny. They laughed at me, but it wasn't funny. They ran the car lift up and down and joked about getting me in the right position to fuck and they made fun of me like they hated me. Like I was an old car or something. The sheriff said I led them on, but it wasn't my idea. I didn't want to do it. I told them. I said. I don't want to do that. I said."

Dinah was talking faster, her hair flying around as she whipped her head around.

"How could they do that to me? They all said it was my fault, but I never wanted to do it. Don't do it, I said. My mother saw the bruises on my back and the oil and I told her, and they said it wasn't true. It won't happen again. Never. Because I know more now. But there were six of them. I couldn't do anything. They tied me on it. They tied me on it."

"Oh, Dinah."

"And the doctor said, why don't you girls take responsibility for your own life and stop asking me to clean up your messes, and he was right and I will be responsible. I'll take care of it."

"Let's get out of here," I said. "I just didn't know, honey. Aunt Nell tried to tell me, but she didn't. I didn't know. Come on now. We'll find our way out and go home."

Dinah gave a shudder like a horse and her eyes showed less white. She had not cried a single tear while she told me this.

"I'm hungry, Camille. Can we get something to eat?"

"Come on," I said. "Let's get out of here."

$\mathcal{N}$OT DISHONOUR

Andrew Jackson had done it. Born the posthumous son of a poor woman, orphaned and the veteran of a war at fourteen, he had been elected twice by the people to the highest office in the land; and this time, having won the electoral as well as the popular vote, he would serve. Jackson was going to Washington, and a man from North Carolina had volunteered to drive the General and his lady all the way from Nashville to Washington in a coach pulled by six white horses. They would burst out of the wilderness into the slime of Washington's swampy climate like a king and his consort. The people had won.

But Rachel had no interest in coaches and white horses. She and Andrew were quiet folks who often sat for hours reading to each other and smoking their pipes by the fire. She had become more pious and loving as she grew older, and she was now known as "Aunt Rachel" to most of the people in Tennessee. She cared little for fancy things. Her food was simple. Her tastes refined but conservative. She had wanted only two things in all her life and she had gotten one of them. As for the second, they had adopted and supported every orphaned child who came near the Hermitage. Cousins, nephews, and nieces, even an Indian boy picked out of the smoldering remains of a village, were sent to the Hermitage and raised as their children. She had had children. She was loved.

But love was not fashion. Her clothes were not fit for society because she seldom worried about such things at the Hermitage, but Rachel wanted to be a proper first lady. Struggling against ill health and a bad heart, Rachel went to Nashville to order clothes suitable for the President's wife. No one knows for sure what happened on December 15, 1838. That much is clear. What isn't clear is why Rachel Jackson fled home to the Hermitage in such a rush. While being fitted for a dress in a booth, she may have overheard two of the town's more vicious gossips discussing the horror of having a first lady who was an adulteress. After all, she had not been married to Jackson for the first two years she lived with him. They had to have a second ceremony after two years of sleeping under the same blanket because it was revealed that her divorce had not been final. Of course, that's what *they* say. Everyone knows, my dear, that she was scandalously immoral as a young woman. Who knows what may even go on today in that mansion of theirs. I mean, they may live like quality, but you can't hide the smell of hogs with perfume.

Perhaps it was that. Or perhaps it was that she happened into the office of a newspaper editor on an errand and saw a pamphlet which had been carefully hidden from her during what was to become in history the dirtiest campaign for President since the country had been founded. Slipping the pamphlet into her reticule, she read it in her coach and then ordered the driver to take her home immediately. The pamphlet called her a whore and Jackson her pimp. Jackson had done an excellent job of protecting Rachel, but the world was forcing itself into their lives. The first victim was the weakest. Rachel went home and on December 17 she had what was probably a massive heart attack with great pain and irregular heart action.

She was bled twice and for three days she seemed to be mending. Jackson sat continuously by her side, but was finally persuaded to sleep in his own bed on the third night. The doctors went to bed too. She was going to be well in a few days and then could follow Jackson to Washington.

Sitting that night with Hannah, her maid, Rachel smoked her pipe by the fire and said, "I had rather be a doorkeeper in the house of God than to live in that palace." A few minutes later, she fainted into Hannah's arms.

Hannah's screams brought the household, and Jackson himself lifted his wife onto her bed. Seeing the doctor's glances, Andrew Jackson's will was firm. "Bleed her," he cried out. They pricked her arm but no blood flowed. "Try the temple," he commanded in desperation. Only two drops of blood fell from the smooth skin onto her lace cap. Jackson was numb. His will was nothing at the last. She had escaped his protection and all the dueling pistols he owned would not help him now.

"Spread four blankets," he ordered numbly. "If she does come to she will lay hard on that table." They laid her out as he ordered, and except for when she was robed in white for her coffin, he stood by her, not leaving her even in death, stroking her brow and ready to defend her against all things.

Ten thousand people, black and white, rode horseback, carriage, buggy, and wagon to her funeral. They walked miles holding their good shoes in their hands, climbing through fields and over fences. And on the eve of his greatest triumph, Andrew Jackson composed the epitaph that would stand over his beloved Rachel, the wilderness beauty who would dare Indians and danger to be by her husband's side, his heart itself, which he seemed to have buried with her.

Every night as the sun went down, Jackson went to her tomb and sat by the epitaph he had written. He never forgot this ceremony until he died, as he never forgot to wear a locket with her picture painted on it and never forgot to read a chapter from her Bible every night. If there is one word to remember when you hear the name Andrew Jackson, it is the word "will," and the gravestone showed how Jackson's will, even when broken in grief, was going to force the truth upon his fellow men.

THE EPITAPH

This is the epitaph written for Rachel Jackson by her husband, Andrew Jackson. It is carved onto her tombstone and stands over her grave at the Hermitage.

HERE LIE THE REMAINS OF

Mrs. RACHAEL JACKSON
wife of PRESIDENT JACKSON,
who died the 22nd. Dec. 1828.
Age 61

Her face was fair her person pleas
ing, her temper amiable, and her
heart kind; she delighted in reliev
ing the wants of her fellow creature
and cultivated that divine pleas
ure by the most liberal and unpre
tending methods. To the poor she
was a benefactor to the rich an ex
ample to the wretched a comfort
to the prosperous an ornament; her
piety went hand in hand with her
benevolence and she thanked her
creator for being permitted to do
good. A being so gentle and yet so
virtuous, slander might wound but
could not dishonour. Even death,
when he tore her from the armes
of her husband, could but transport
her to the Bosom of her God.

We went through the rest of the mansion quickly. Dinah paused at the doorway of the nursery and looked at the picture over the mantel. It showed two small children in beribboned, puffed-sleeve white dresses and pantaloons standing against a dark background. The children stared out into space like tiny ghosts from some bygone time, holding hands against this flood of people who crowded to see them.

Without even a stop for souvenir postcards, we got into the car. It felt like an oven, but the air conditioner started up and cooled the car as we headed north. We didn't stop until we hit the highway into Toms Creek. I pulled over at a hamburger stand with an air-conditioned patio where you could sit and eat.

I hadn't tried to talk much on the way home. That was probably a mistake, thinking back on it, but I was still in shock over what Dinah had told me. It overwhelmed me. Perhaps it would just make her unhappy to dwell on it, I thought, and so I didn't talk about what had happened to her. Basically, I didn't want to think about it.

"What about your parents, Dinah?" I asked when we sat down. Our trays were laden with double hamburgers and French-fried potatoes, and plates of salad from the salad bar. Most of Dinah's salad was croutons, but a few pieces of green poked through the pinkish dressing.

Dinah took a large bite of her hamburger and chewed thoughtfully. "Well," she said thickly, "they told me that I could either get an abortion or go away. They didn't want me in town with a baby that everybody knew had six fathers and that had been gotten at a filling station. They said that if I loved them, then I would get an abortion and never tell about it. They figured that the story would just die down, and I could deny it. So when they saw that I really wasn't going to have the abortion, then they gave up on me. My mother came in my room and packed up a suitcase and my daddy took me to the bus station over in the next town so nobody would see me leave. He gave me some money and that was that."

I looked at the grease dripping around the edges of my hamburger and knew that I couldn't eat it. "How much money did he give you, Dinah?"

"Oh, he gave me a lot. He gave me three hundred dollars. That's a lot of money for my parents. I've got three younger brothers and a younger sister that they have to think about too. My mother said that it wouldn't be good for them to have me around."

"But how could they just do that? How could they leave you, at your age, sitting by the bus station with three hundred dollars?" I was tired and felt angry. Dinah's passivity made me angrier than her parents did.

"It's all right," Dinah said. "It's my responsibility. I'll take care of it. Someday maybe I can pay them the three hundred back. I don't want them to have to lose money because of me."

Dinah ate her potatoes one at a time with fierce concentration. "Well," she said between bites, "those boys probably didn't mean to hurt me that much. It was weird. They just didn't understand how I felt about it. They didn't feel anything about me. They just started to have fun and sort of forgot about me, and my parents aren't to blame really. It's my responsibility. Don't you think?"

I didn't know what I thought. "Well, it is your responsibility to have the baby now, but you're awfully young. Are you sure you want to keep this baby? You could put it up for adoption and it would get a fine home. Have you thought about that?"

Dinah's face closed as if a door had shut. "I don't want to talk about that. I'll do it. I got pregnant, and I'll take care of things. Really, I will."

We finished our dinner in silence. I picked at the potatoes and the salad and left the hamburger almost untouched. The meat had not been cooked through and it was red and bloody in the middle. The soft, raw meat and the grease were too much after so much heat outside.

Dinah ate her meal with relish and she did look better with food inside of her. She looked quite normal when I dropped her at Aunt Nell's and took the car back to the rental agency. I watched her walk up to the house, her blouse waving loosely in the evening breeze. I supposed that she would be all right. Lots of young girls had babies and managed to raise them. She had Aunt Nell, and I could help out with some money if she needed it. I couldn't think what I should say to Dinah, and I was afraid to talk to her too much for fear of just stirring things up. It made me feel crazy when I thought about Dinah on a car lift at night in a dark filling station.

I had to talk to someone about it. That night I sat by Tom Church in a booth and ate dinner and tried to explain it to him.

"They tied her on the car lift and raped her, Tom. They nearly scared her to death, and then they made fun of her. They laughed at her body."

Tom put his hand over mine. "Easy now, honey. It's all over. It's over now. Dinah's safe with your Aunt Nell."

"I know. I know it, but think how awful for that girl. Think what it must do to her to remember that."

"Had she ever had sex before?"

"She said she had. She'd slept with the boys, but my God, not like that, not like—"

"I just mean it wasn't so awful for her as it would have been if she'd never experienced sex before."

"But, Tom, how awful does it have to be, for God's sake? I mean, I've had sex too, and I'm a lot older than Dinah, but that would scare hell out of me."

"Well, sure it would, but you can't know how it started. It sounds like it went way too far."

"Too far! My God." I was upset, but I listened to Tom as he continued.

"But there's no way of knowing how it started. Damn kids. They think up crazy things to do and then holler when they're in the middle of them and it's not what they expected."

"I don't think Dinah knew they were going to do that."

"Well, they were all local kids, kids she grew up with. It sounds like she got good and scared and none of those boys knew how to deal with it."

"Deal with it? Good God, Tom, what do you mean? They dealt with her all too well, in my mind."

"I'm sorry, Camille. I don't mean to make you angry. Of

course you're upset, but it's over now. Dinah's being cared for. She'll be all right now."

"She'll be all right if you think being an unwed teenage mother with a baby is all right. And her family just abandoned her. They gave her three hundred dollars and left her at a bus stop. That poor girl."

"That is sad. Her parents should have helped her out more."

"I can't believe they just left her sitting there on a bench."

"Now I don't want to get you more upset, Camille, but you have to think about it rationally. After all, there may be a lot more to it."

"What do you mean?"

Our dinner came and we sat in silence while the waitress put down plates and refilled our water glasses. Then Tom went on as he cut his steak.

"Maybe her parents aren't all that bad. Maybe she was glad to run away from home. Lots of teenage girls are just dying to get away from their parents. And then nothing much seemed to happen to the boys. I never saw anything in the paper about it. That makes you wonder."

I ate moodily, paying little attention to my meal. "I don't know about any of that."

"Well, you see? I'm sure that Dinah got scared and it's a shame she didn't get an abortion at her age, but there may be a lot more to it. The point is"—Tom paused and ate some salad— "The point is that Dinah is being cared for. She is healthy, isn't that right?"

"I guess she's healthy enough. She goes to her doctor every month."

"She'll have this baby and then she'll forget all the rest of it. She'll settle down and be just fine. It's too bad it happened, but I hate to see you so upset by it."

"Well, of course I'm upset."

"I know. That trip to the Hermitage must have been hell on you. Dinah getting heat stroke and nearly collapsing like that. It shook you up, but you've got to get your own life together."

"I just feel like I should do something, Tom."

"Of course you do. Everybody feels like that when they hear

about the things kids get themselves mixed up in. But it's over. You have to turn loose of the past, Camille. That's your trouble."

"What do you mean by that?"

"You know it's true." Tom stared at me over his water glass. "You sit out in that damn tent and brood over your marriage. You keep going over and over all the past and your life in California, but sooner or later you have to turn loose of it. You can't keep worrying about the past. It's over."

I knew that Tom had a point, and I was embarrassed. I had talked too much to Tom about my marriage. It was not polite or very flirtatious to talk to one man about another one. God knows, brooding about Henry and the past hadn't done me much good. But I still wasn't completely convinced.

"Dinah's experience isn't like coming out of a bad marriage. She was hurt, Tom. Now she may have gone along with it more than she likes to admit, but she was hurt badly. Maybe she needs to talk about it."

Tom looked thoughtful. "Someday she may want to talk about it, but right now there's the baby to think about. If you go prodding around in that girl's mind, she might get so upset that she even loses the baby. Look how upset she got on your trip today. You don't know how stable she is, Camille."

It was true. I didn't know how shaky Dinah's mental life was, and it scared me when I thought of getting into any more talks with her. What if she did go over the edge? What if digging it up pushed her too far? What if it hurt the baby?

We ate in silence. Tom had pie and coffee and I watched him eat. Tom was probably right. I'd heard only one side of Dinah's story. We went to a movie afterward and Tom made love to me passionately in my tent. He was really trying to make me feel better and I liked him for it.

After he left, I was completely relaxed and would have been happy except for the picture that kept drifting into my mind as I lay half asleep. I kept seeing Dinah crawling across the hot concrete of the filling station, made unwieldy by her pregnancy, scrabbling like a scared and wounded animal. I turned restlessly and shut my eyes. Dinah's life was something that I didn't know how to approach.

Maybe Tom was right. Having the baby and getting through the pregnancy would give the girl something positive to do. Then she would be a mother.

I felt the old flash of jealousy when I thought of Dinah's motherhood. That was something I could never have. It may have been scary for her, but at least she'd get a baby out of it. That was more than I'd ever gotten out of my years with Henry.

The filling station and Dinah scrabbling on the concrete kept coming back into my mind, though. You could go crazy if you think about things like that too much. Sometimes it's just better to forget the past, like Tom said. I fell asleep and vowed to be nicer to Dinah. Thinking about her past would get us nowhere.

COUSIN LIZZIE

The council met at Tuckabatchee, the old Creek capital which stood at the confluence of the Tallapoosa and the Alabama rivers. The Creeks were apprehensive about war with the white men in this year of 1811, and they invited the Cherokee to send delegations to hear the talk of a band of northern Indians led by the great Shawnee chief, Tecumseh. Tecumseh was always welcome among the Creeks because his mother had been a Muskogee, and he had fought with the Creeks in the border wars. It was Tecumseh who was trying to unite the tribes into a confederation, and the possibility of his presence had drawn five thousand Indians to Tuckabatchee.

Tecumseh arrived in a dignified procession accompanied by six Shawnee, two Creeks, six Kickapoos, and six from a faraway tribe, the Sioux. Their hair was plaited, and hawk and eagle feathers decorated their heads. Tecumseh himself wore crane feathers for his hair, one white, one dyed red. Under their eyes semicircles of red flared to their cheekbones, a dot of red stood at each temple, and round smears glowed like fresh blood on their chests. That night they danced the furious Dance of the Lakes, but Tecumseh was silent for several weeks.

Then the time came. Tecumseh was a man of vision, a man who could postpone his pleasures until the moment was ripe. He counseled against war with the whites. First, he insisted, it was necessary to return to the old ways. Give up all the paths of the white men and return to the Indian paths. Form a confederation that would weld all Indian tribes into an animal with but one mind. Live in peace until the confederation was alive and strong. Then the time would come to fight. This, Tecumseh said, was the only way to have success against the whites.

There was skepticism among the Creeks. The Big Warrior, head chief of all the Creek people, thought it was unwise to give up the white man's civilization. The Big Warrior doubted that Tecumseh had been sent by the Great Spirit to this council fire.

Tecumseh rose up in anger and despair and said that since the Big Warrior did not believe that the Great Spirit spoke through Tecumseh, Tecumseh would leave the council for home at once. "When I set foot by my own hearth," Tecumseh said, "then I will stamp my foot on the ground of my forefathers and the earth will answer me. It will shake with my anger and every house in Tuckabatchee will move." He rode off in dignity.

The Cherokee were not superstitious. They refused to associate with Tecumseh the comet that had swept across the sky every night, and they scoffed at his predictions. The thing was hocus-pocus. Tecumseh was a madman or a man trying to gain power over others.

On December 16, an earthquake struck the Tennessee Valley region with great force at half-past two in the morning. No Indians could remember anything like this before in all their lives or the lives of their grandfathers or great-grandfathers or in the time beyond the mist when all men and women lived closer to the Great Spirit and the spirits of the forest. Buildings collapsed, springs clear for thousands of years ran muddy, the water in the Mississippi rose and fell like an ocean tide, and land cracked open in furrows. There were strange sounds of crashing in the night, and the ground felt hot to touch in some places.

But Tecumseh was ignored, and war was fought between the Creeks and the white men. The Cherokee fought with the whites, and the peace was drawn up by General Andrew Jackson. When the Cherokee returned to their homes, they found that the whites had destroyed more of their land and property than the enemy

Creeks. The frontier saying, "The only good Indian is a dead Indian," was not familiar to the Cherokee.

After all, the Cherokee had done what the whites wanted. They had a written language and taught their children to read and write. Many Cherokee had converted to Christianity, and they sent their children to white schools. Unlike the migrant Indians of the Great Plains, the Cherokee were a pastoral people who farmed successfully and quickly picked up the use of machines and tools from the white men. The Cherokee were the "civilized" Indians, and some of their leaders had even won the hearts and hands in marriage of gently raised New England women who were white. The Cherokee were going along with the program.

And that was the thing that galled the whites. Looking at the beautifully cared-for farms of the Cherokee, the well-built houses and the thrifty use of land and animals, looking at their children, who were mannerly and well-schooled and their care of their women and aged, the whites were uneasy and angry. After all, an Indian is an Indian. No amount of book learning could make a savage a human being. They were dirty, nasty, subhuman people who deserved to be wiped out. Besides, they were sitting on some of the finest land in the Carolinas, Alabama, and Tennessee. Why should savages live well on such good land when a white man could barely feed his family on his little patch of ground? The Cherokee land was already cleared, ready for the hand of the farmer. The land lay like temptation in the path of the white migration. How easy to move from Pennsylvania to a farm already cleared, tilled, and planted in corn waist high. How nice to move your family into a cabin already built with the pot still hanging on the irons over the fire. The desire was irresistible.

It is a fact of life that the only sins most people resist committing are the sins that don't tempt them much. The whites were sorely tempted by the Cherokee land and demanded that the government get rid of the Indians and put the land up for homesteading. The government, having its next election to consider and being composed of men who thought the Indians were not much above animals anyway, kindly agreed to dispose of the savages.

126

They had been warned. The Cherokee were told all through 1837 that they must move. They were told and told that there was a place in Oklahoma where they could live. They were told to just pack up their gear and children and old and sick and go away. Oddly enough, only seven hundred of them did this. Indians don't have no sense, was the general consensus, and the settlers demanded action from the government.

On May 8 General Winfield Scott arrived at the agency to replace the milder General Wool. Scott had his orders and planned, like the excellent military man he was, to execute them. He later said that he always felt great sympathy for the Cherokee, but orders are orders. He even lectured his troops on the humane way to remove thousands of people from their homelands by force. He didn't want brutality, rape, pillage, beatings, or foul language. The elderly were to be treated with respect. Lunatics and women in helpless condition would require special attention. Scott wanted a neat, orderly, Christian removal.

It is hard to turn loose a mass of armed soldiers on a civilian population which the soldiers see as something higher than mules, but not that much higher, and expect saintliness. Families were rounded up and driven with whips and kicks like cattle. Strays were hunted down and often shot. If mothers were separated from their children because the children were off getting water at the spring when the soldiers arrived, too bad. They could look for each other in Oklahoma. If women were giving birth as they walked, well, throw them in a wagon or let them have the brat by the side of the trail and then walk on. Indians were strong. They were used to rougher ways than white women.

And so it went. General Scott had kindly built resting places on the trail that led from Cherokee agency in Carolina through Tennessee, north through Kentucky to Golconda on the Ohio River, where the Indians were packed into boats and crossed, then on across Illinois, over the Mississippi, through Missouri and Arkansas to Fort Gibson, Oklahoma. These resting places, twenty-three in number, were stockades made of split logs, sharpened and set in the ground, and they were manned by soldiers.

The Indians were stubborn. They had no desire to leave their land for land in another place which might be worse than their fields. They did not want to leave the country that their ancestors had lived on for thousands of years, where the bones of their past lay in the earth. The march did not begin in full force until it was nearly autumn of 1838. And the weather itself seemed to hate the Cherokee. First there was drought which left the people and animals weak and killed over five hundred when the heat and unsanitary conditions in the camps bred dysentery and other diseases. As was usual in these matters, the elderly, sick, and infants died first.

The detachment started toward Nashville on October 1st. The temporary huts were torched, and the order was given to move on. At the head of the people, astride his favorite horse, was Going Snake, eighty years old and white-haired. As the people moved away from their homeland, the sound of distant thunder boomed.

By early November, the roads were churned by rain and ox-carts into a sea of mud which slipped under the hooves and feet and made forward movement almost impossible for the wagons carrying the sick and dying. Then came snow and hail and sleet, which froze the feet and killed many who had no warm clothes. The army, in its excellent command of logistics, had planned for the cold weather. Every family was issued a single blanket. The Indians didn't seem to appreciate this and callously tore the blankets to pieces, trying to clothe the smallest children in the rags. The food supplies were not consistent, and the food was rough—hominy and cornmeal cooked over a fire, greasy fatback, dirty drinking water. The people sickened and died. They died of measles, chickenpox, dysentery, diarrhea, exposure, fatigue, and mental breakdown. They died of beatings and bullets and humiliation. The army had a job to do and proceeded to do it. It wasn't the army's fault that this was the coldest winter in fifty years or that the ice was so thick on the Mississippi that the boats couldn't get through and the people had to camp in the snow on the banks with little food and no firewood until it thawed some. The army couldn't control the weather or the lust for land that possessed the white colonists.

And this was where my Cousin Lizzie, far-removed, from a

side branch of the family, comes in. She was an ordinary woman as far as I ever heard tell. She kept house, had three children, two miscarriages, and four servants to do the rough work in the house and yard. Her husband was the manager of the bank in Hopkinsville, Kentucky, which was growing out of the wilderness and becoming a thriving town. He too was ordinary. He did ordinary things, and, I assume, felt ordinary, predictable emotions.

Lizzie had never shown any interest in Indians. She kept an immaculate house, and if she had ever thought much about the Indians it was with a disdain for their dirt and untidy habits. They didn't use Irish linen napkins and probably didn't wax their floors twice a year whether they needed it or not. Lizzie was too busy being the banker's wife and mother of three active boys to care much about politics and such.

If her sister hadn't been so sick with typhoid fever, Lizzie might have lived out her life in the town and been totally unmemorable, but her sister lived on a farm outside the town and needed Lizzie to help with the children when the fever was high. It nearly wore Lizzie out, caring for her six nieces and nephews and nursing her sister at the same time. She had taken one of her blacks to help out, but the work was constant and frightening. For a few days, Lizzie thought that her sister was gone for sure, but she rallied. Calf's foot jelly, custards, and warm fires in her bedroom strengthened her when the fever broke, and after two weeks Lizzie started home in the buggy with the black woman at her side.

Lizzie had heard her husband talking about the removal of the Indians, but it had sounded so sensible, so orderly. The Indians were to be taken from one place and sent to another, all under the care and protection of the army. They had blankets and food provided, and even wagons for the elderly. Lizzie had pictured a jolly group of people going off down the road like picnickers. Reality was not something that Lizzie was familiar with outside of sickbeds and birthings.

So it was that she received a shock when she tried to get home on a road crowded with wagons and teams and horses and people walking. It took a while to recognize that most of the people were barefooted because the mud formed such a solid substance on their legs, and it took a while to see that many of the people staggered with fever and exhaustion. But the sound took no time to see, and the smell they created was everywhere around them.

Cursed with diarrhea and sickness, many people couldn't even find a bush to crouch behind before they had defecated on their own bodies, and the smell of their sick hung like a cloud over them. Covering her nose, the black woman watched stoically, but Lizzie was nearly unconscious. It made her faint, the smell and the noise, the constant groaning, wailing, screaming that rose up from the wagons carrying women in labor, people whose minds had cracked with the strain of seeing their children and families die in front of them, and the old people who chanted and sang their songs to try and open the gates of another life to their spirits, although they had no proper rites or burials in store.

"The noise. Can't you stop them from screaming so?" she asked a soldier.

"It's just their way, ma'am." He shrugged. "They ain't like you or me."

But Lizzie knew sickness and dirt when she saw it. She made her way home like a woman demented and ordered the largest wagon the livery stable had. Into the wagon she piled all the bedding in the house, even stripping her own children's beds, as the women of the town said later. Every bit of food in the kitchen was added, and she gave orders for all the chickens to be killed, cooked, and broth made from their bones. She set the servants on their ears and they giggled when they thought what the Master would say when he came home to a house bare and empty of even a single dried pea to eat.

Lizzie sent two wagons of clothes, bedding, and food to the migrating people, who leaped upon the wagons with silent desperation to get food and clothing for their families. "They never said thank you," said the old Irish man who drove one wagon. "They just took it and kept on walking."

Lizzie didn't care. She walked to town and began to charge a huge order on her husband's account. When the order got to $100, the storekeeper thought it only right to tell her husband what his wife was up to. Arriving red-faced at the store, the bank president said that it was all a misunderstanding, that his wife was not herself after nursing her sick sister, that he didn't want the goods to be delivered to his house.

And Lizzie was taken home.

At first he tried to talk sense to her. Her compassion was not unpleasing in a woman and a mother, and he sympathized with the plight of the poor Indians, but it was too much to expect him to foot the bills for feeding and clothing the entire Cherokee nation. Lizzie was meek and wept but said nothing.

The next day he went to work, ignoring the snickering of his clerks, but the day ended at ten o'clock when he had to drive outside of town and bring Lizzie back in his buggy. She was cooking over a huge pot set up by the side of the road and had already distributed his entire collection of fine brandy and madeira to the redskins.

As long as the Indians marched westward on their Trail of Tears, he had to stay with Lizzie, sit by her side, and reassure her that it wasn't as bad as she thought. Then it was over. The roads were frozen. The Indians were gone. Thanking God, he went back to the bank and normal life could resume. But something had happened to Lizzie's mind.

The first day she was left alone, Lizzie drove to the stinking path outside of town and tried to set up a first-aid station. The next week she was found cooking a stew by the side of the road, stirring the wooden spoon round and round in the cast-iron pot which she had somehow managed to erect on a tripod over a flame, singing to herself and smiling. There was nothing at all in the pot. Her charge accounts had been canceled.

It went on into the summer. Summer never seemed to come for Lizzie. Her children went unfed and dirty. The house was dusty and always chaotic for all the servants and money that was spent keeping it tidy. Lizzie was impervious to reason or newspaper reports about how well the Indians fared in their new home. Lizzie spent the hot summer sneaking outside town to distribute food and clothes, leaving them by the road when she was taken home, first gently and then roughly by her husband.

It was too much. She smiled and smiled and just didn't behave like a sane person should, so he locked her up in her room. She tried to climb out, so he had the window barred, and then she would tear her clothes and the sheets and blankets to shreds and throw them out the window between the iron grillwork that filled in the space so decoratively. At last she refused to eat because it would leave "nothing for those poor folks outside of town," and that is when her husband took the only step he could.

Lizzie was sent to an insane hospital back East, where her parents could visit her regularly. Her boys were raised by their father, who had grown bitter about women and their stupidity. "If you cry, I'll whip you till you're raw," he used to tell the boys when they were hurt or missing their mother. He had no use for foolish emotion. It didn't pay in this life to be so sentimental. What had all that fine feeling done for his family? Weren't they victims as much as the damned Indians?

Locked in a darkened room in an attempt to keep her calm, Lizzie died a few years later and became in a sense one of the four or five thousand people who died because of the Trail of Tears. No one knows for sure how many died. No one counts Indians with much interest, but Lizzie used to say before they shipped her back East that everyone had died. Everyone. Everyone dead and no survivors.

There could be no survivors of such genocide, the greatest genocide ever carried out on American soil, which was presided over and planned by that old Indian fighter and land speculator himself, Andrew Jackson. Perhaps when Rachel Jackson was laid out on those four blankets with two drops of blood staining her cap, his heart had constricted and died as surely as hers had.

Aunt Nell was pushing her lawn mower, but the grass wasn't getting any shorter. "I like the way you're flattening the grass, Aunt Nell, but won't it just bounce back up tomorrow?"

"I can't understand what the matter is with this machine." She stooped laboriously and stared at the push mower, which must have been fifty years old.

Reaching down to touch the blades, I laughed. "You wouldn't do any damage to a pound of soft butter if you ran this thing over the top of it. The blades are blunt, Aunt Nell."

I threw the mower into her car and took it down to a tool repair shop. "It'd be cheaper just to buy a new one," the man said sadly. "It'd take me a week to fix this one so it works right. How about one of these new ones? They're aluminum and real light for a lady."

I returned with a shiny aluminum lawn mower which weighed about a tenth of what the old one did. "Won't last three years," Aunt Nell sniffed, but she let me mow her grass and then made a pitcher of iced tea for me. We sat on the porch and watched the postman make his second daily walk up one side of the street and down the other.

"Dinah is over at the high school taking a class in typing," Aunt Nell said. "I made her do it. It isn't good for her to just sit around and stop her education. Typing is something she can use whether she goes back to high school or not."

"I'm glad she isn't here. I wanted to talk to you about her." I stopped. Looking at Aunt Nell, I was struck by how old she had become. Her face was lined and tired this morning, and even her large picture hat couldn't throw enough shade on her face to cover up the aging. I was touched. Technically, I knew that a woman approaching eighty was an old lady, but I had never seen my Aunt Nell that way.

Patting her hand gently, I began, "I can see why this has been so hard for you. Dinah told me how she got pregnant. It's more than I dreamed."

Pulling away, my aunt said sharply, "Good Lord, I've gotten old enough to be patted. Everyone always pats old people just like they do children. Or dogs. Soothing down all our little ruffled feathers, hoping we just shut up and put up. Well, don't be so surprised about Dinah. You know that I've worried. Do you think I'm some old fool who worries about pregnancy or some sort of teenage love affair? That's why I tried to get you to talk to her. If she talks about it, maybe it will help her some. I didn't tell you myself because I think it's her business to tell people if she wants."

"We didn't really talk about it much. I didn't know what to say. My God, it's awful. I was just so stunned when she told me about it. In a filling station, for heaven's sake! It's so ugly."

Aunt Nell fanned herself and poured another glass of tea. It had cinnamon and cloves and lemon and sugar in it, and she drank it like water in the summer. She shook her head. "She doesn't really talk about it. Oh, yes, she tells you the facts, but she doesn't *say* anything. She never sounds"—Aunt Nell gestured with her glass—"she never sounds real."

I drank my tea and we sat watching the postman put a stack of junk mail in the mailbox. "Thank you, Harry," Aunt Nell called, and he tipped his hat and waved.

"She's going to have to change or it could be bad for the baby. I keep thinking that she'll start taking an interest. Come look at this."

There were four bedrooms upstairs. One was Aunt Nell's, one was her sewing and junk room, one was Dinah's room now. I stood in the doorway and stared at the fourth room in amazement. It had been painted pale pink and there were organdy curtains at the window. A new baby bed, white with spools delicately rising up the posts, stood against the wall. A matching dresser was next to it, and an elaborate changing table and diaper holder was against the other wall. A fluffy rug lay on the floor and a rocking chair sat squarely on the rug. It was like a picture from a women's magazine advertisement for baby oil or pabulum.

"Why it's just lovely, Aunt Nell. Dinah must have nearly died when she saw it."

"Personally, I think it's corny. Too frilly for my taste, but I thought that a teenage mother would like it. Isn't it the most desperately middle-class homage to a baby you've ever seen?"

I laughed and watched Aunt Nell with curiosity. Her cynicism wasn't ringing true. She was in love with the room. Her hand was gentle as she smoothed the curtains and lined up a picture of cows in a field that hung on the wall. Aunt Nell had never had a baby. She was taking her chance now to enjoy this one.

"What did Dinah say?" I asked. Aunt Nell was opening drawers and showing me clothes and blankets and stretch outfits that she had ready for the baby.

"She thanked me very, very politely. And she hasn't been in here since." Aunt Nell had tears in her eyes. "I know she's suffered, Camille, but she has to go on. She can't hold it to her forever."

I looked at the picture. Fat cows stood near trees and stared back at me. "She'll be all right. Women always manage to get through these things. When the baby comes she'll change."

Aunt Nell shut the door to the bedroom and led the way downstairs, going slowly, watching every step as if she were afraid she would fall. Turning on the way down, she stared up at me.

"You could be right. She'll get over it. Women have been through more than that and survived, but I wonder what it does to them inside. I just wish she could talk about it."

We chatted for another hour about town gossip, and Aunt Nell informed me that Tom Church and I were going to be talked about if we weren't careful. I told her that I didn't care, and then I trimmed a hedge for her. She couldn't reach that high anymore. I felt guilty that I hadn't thought of helping her this summer. It was little enough to do for a woman who had been so good to me. I couldn't believe that Dinah was in much trouble if she had Aunt Nell on her side. Dinah was in good hands.

I spent more time thinking about Tom Church than about Dinah as I evened and trimmed the hedge. It was gratifying that Tom was so interested in me. He seemed to care more about my attitudes and ideas than any man I'd ever known. Maybe it was because he'd been raised without a father and he was able to talk easily to women.

I'd never known Tom's mother. She died after I left the town, and she hadn't been my beautician. Aunt Nell cut my hair. I had been too young to know what the gossip about Ruby Church meant. Probably any woman living alone in a small town would have been gossiped about.

I finished the hedge and went back to my tent. I needed a swim. Swimming in the river was the best way to avoid the late-afternoon heat.

*L*EAH'S DAUGHTER
Leah the unloved. Leah the rejected, the woman
who was married to a man who thought she was her sister and
spent only one night of love with her. When the early-morning
light of her first day of wifehood revealed her identity, there
were no more nights of love but only couplings. She had not been
the woman he thought he married, and Jacob, unwise and passionate, did not know that this is the fate of all men, so he raged
and cursed and demanded the woman he had loved before his
marriage.

And he got her. And she was beautiful. And she was beloved.
And God saw the grief of Leah and gave Leah four sons and gave
to her sister, the beloved Rachel, none. And Rachel in her shame
at the barrenness of her womb gave Jacob her maid, Bilhah, who
had two sons by Jacob, and then Rachel gave Jacob her other
maid, Zilpah, who also had two sons by Jacob.

And so they lived, all of these first cousins and maids and children and half-brothers and camels and sheep and tents and uncles
and aunts and servants, until the day that one of Leah's sons
found mandrakes in the fields and brought them to Leah. Man-
drake, the branched root spreading out like the body of a man,
was deeply magical and had great power when used in the dark
arts. Rachel, barren of womb, hopeful of the mandrakes' magic,
wanted the plants, and Leah said, "Is it a small thing that you
have taken my husband from me, and now you will take my
mandrakes, too?"

Now Rachel wanted those mandrakes. And she was no fool. So
she did what any smart woman would do: she traded her husband
for some mandrakes. It was a simple arrangement. Leah had
Jacob for a while. Rachel had the mandrakes. So for a few herbs
Jacob was thrown into the arms of his first wife by his second
wife. And Leah had two more sons by Jacob, and at last, after
producing six sons with Leah, two with Bilhah, two sons with
Zilpah, Jacob had a daughter with Leah.

There was Jacob, chivied around from woman to woman, all of

136

them in contest to see who could produce the most sons. He seemed a patient man, perhaps a little cowed by all these hot-tempered, beautiful women who needed his sperm to give them their power. Sleep with her! Now with her! Tonight is my night! No! It's her night tonight! He made his rounds and did what he was told and had twelve sons and a daughter when he died, and what he thought of all this no one knows.

But he did manage to produce one daughter. And they called her name Dinah. And she was beautiful and comely. And her father moved over the land and pitched his tent at the gates of the city of Shalem in the land of Canaan and bought land from Hamor the Hivite prince.

And Dinah went out to meet the other girls of the district and was seen by Shechem, the son of Hamor who was the prince. And his soul clave unto Dinah and he lay with her and defiled her.

Jacob waited for his sons to come in from the fields, and he told them of this, and they were shocked and angry. "Don't be angry," said Prince Hamor. "My son wishes to love Dinah and he wants her in marriage." But Jacob and his sons could not let Dinah marry an uncircumcised man.

Hearing this, Hamor and Shechem and all the men of the city were circumcised so that they could bring these wandering people into their families and city, but on the third day after the circumcisions the rage of Jacob's sons was so great that they rose up and killed all the men in the city and took their women and children and destroyed even the last bowl in their houses.

Jacob said, "You have made me stink among the inhabitants of this land."

But his sons said, "Should he deal with our sister as with a harlot?"

So it was that Dinah was once more with her people. We never hear of her again.

LITTLE ALICE

In 1875 a mummy was found in Salts Cave, Kentucky. It had promise as a tourist attraction, being a small mummy that was sturdy enough to take some wear and tear, but it was found in the wrong cave. That was easily solved. The mummy was taken from Salts Cave in the dark of night and propped up on a ledge in another, more appropriate cave owned by Larkin Proctor.

Then Proctor and Little Alice traveled. She attended the World's Fair in Chicago along with an exhibit of the crystal flowers of gypsum chipped out of the caves. Museums examined her, she was bought and sold, and when her last owner retired to his farm, he took Little Alice with him.

George Morrison, another entrepreneur in Kentucky with an interest in caves, discovered another entrance to the cave and opened his own Mammoth Cave. It was obvious that he needed his own mummy, so he bought Little Alice from her owner or stole her from the farmhouse, no one knows for sure. The fact was, he had the mummy and set her up as "The Lady of the Cave." Morrison told a tale about the mummy and let it be known that this was once a beautiful girl abducted by the Indians and tortured. Morrison claimed that Little Alice had fled to the caves, her blond hair flying in the wind, rather than endure further atrocity. Once inside the cave, she had become lost and perished only to be petrified for the ages.

When the National Park Commission bought Mammoth Cave for a park in 1931, Little Alice was included in the deal. But she was no longer the big attraction. Another mummy, Lost John, had been found and his star was in the ascendant.

Little Alice was placed on the bottom shelf of a bookcase in a museum far from the traffic of tourists. She was shabby. Her skin was ripped and dusty. Her legs had been broken and now dangled ludicrously. Her useful days were over.

But curiosity and scientific inquiry continued. Years later, carbon dating established the fact that Little Alice lived during the first hundred years after the death of Christ. Anthropologists said that Little Alice was actually a male child, about nine years old, who died of unknown causes.

Like all hundred-year periods in the world's history, it was a busy time. London was founded out of a squat hovel of shacks on a riverbank. The Romans learned to use soap. Caligula became Emperor of Rome and entertained himself by pushing people off cliffs. St. Paul was kidnapped, beaten, nearly drowned in shipwrecks, and suffered blisters and sore feet during his travels in which he spread Christianity throughout the known world. Buddhism was introduced into China by Ming-Ti, the Emperor, and Jerusalem was razed to the ground except for one wall of the Third Temple, which stood amid the rubble. Rome burned out from under Nero; Vesuvius erupted and buried Pompeii, including a dog carrying a small loaf of bread in his mouth. Thirty thousand Asian tribespeople went west with forty thousand horses and one hundred thousand cattle to join forces with Iranian tribespeople and Mongols from the dark forests of Siberia. They would become known to the world as Huns, and they would be healthy because they drank mare's milk, which has four times as much ascorbic acid as cow's milk. Paper would be invented by a Chinese eunuch, and, deep in the forests of the American continent, a small group of Indian people walk toward the mouth of a great cave, a great hole in the earth. They carry the body of a boy who had died, a boy not yet initiated into manhood and the proper rites of the tribe. Inside the cave they dig a hole and place the small body, his cap and toys, a cord to bind him to his fate and moccasins to carry him swiftly to his new life. They wailed as they left the great hole in the ground. The mother stumbled and her sister held her arm as they climbed from the cave. Their last reed torch flickered and went out.

There is a fascination we all have for dark places. Hearing Dinah's story, thinking about Andrew Jackson and his love and his cruelty, knowing all these things made me want to hide away in the dark. I wanted to crawl off in a hole and not have to think for a while. Darkness, shadows, absence of light, not being able to see, not seeing. I sat by my tent and shut my eyes. I remembered when another dark story had seized me. Seized me, made manifest by acts, not told with words. Some stories never get put into words but become part of us gradually, slowly, and these are always the stories we want to deny.

At ten I had such a story manifested to me by my father's acts until it held me by the throat. By ten, I knew that my father was seriously different from other fathers, so wholly different that no one even dared to mention it. My father was a drunk. The story of his condition was a simple thing. He drank all day. This made him unemployable, undependable, mawkish, silly, and unlovable.

The full effect of my father's drinking oppressed me for two years until I could talk about it to Aunt Nell and then begin my verbal battles with my father. For two years I didn't know what to do with this story of my father's ruined life, so I hid.

On the farm, set back into a rise of rock, there was a hole in the ground. It was thickly grown over with brush, but nothing is safe from a bored child. The hole was large enough to crawl into easily, and it led to a cave.

The first day I crawled into the cave it was enough to just lie near the entrance in the darkness. Knowing that I was alone and unseen, with the loss of responsibility that darkness gave, I lay silent and half-slept. The cave was safe. It numbed me. I could lie and forget the knowledge too large for me to look at and face.

Then I became bored. In a few weeks I became adept at crawling back farther, feeling my way back into the earth. At the end of a short tunnel which broadened and opened up until I could stand easily, my hands found boards. Someone had come into the cave before me and boarded it up. Who had done it? I wondered.

My grandfather leaned over to kiss me one afternoon and then he pulled my head tightly to his face while he sniffed at my hair.

"Where have you been playing?" he cried.

"Only in an old cave."

"No."

140

"Well, it isn't so dangerous. It's all boarded up back inside. It's all right."

"No."

He went out to the cave with his hired hand and drove posts into the ground beside the entrance. Then he nailed boards onto the posts.

"You will never go in this cave again. I absolutely forbid it," he told me.

"Not much way I can now," I said angrily.

My father got drunk for a week after the cave was boarded up. He drank and called out in his sleep. Standing near his bedroom door, with the moon coming in the hall window, I heard him cry out my mother's name.

"Lillian, Lillian," he muttered and called. It was the only time I had heard my father mention her name, and it frightened me. Her ghost was suddenly alive and free to walk the halls, sit in the chairs, and eat our food. I hid under my quilts and slept uneasily for several nights after that.

Stiff from riding in the car, numb with Dinah's story, I walked the fields and stopped by the entrance to the cave. The boards were rotted now by thirty winters of snow and rain. One had pulled off entirely. I looked at the rotted wood overgrown by weeds and again felt the pull of the darkness, the lure of the cave. I wanted to go in, but I didn't.

The cave was just one more dark and hopeless place. Going inside was too much to ask, too tiring. I went back to my tent and sat staring across the river. Everything around me was quiet as the light slowly failed, the fields went from green to gray to dark, and night began.

THE SEA WITHIN

PEARL

When I was a child, everyone I knew went to church on Sunday, and my grandparents and great-grandparents had been pillars of the Methodist Church. But religion was never anything to discuss. All the relatives went to the Baptist or Methodist churches on Sunday and then didn't think about it till the next Sunday. If anyone had ever expressed curiosity about the Catholics or the Pentecostals, I had never heard it. We were a singularly smug and contented family in our spiritual life. There was the feeling that too much thought about religion wasn't normal and somehow was a sign of "queerness" or "weakness."

But there was one person who quoted Scripture to me from the day I was born, when I was laid in her arms with my hospital identification tag still on my arm. She had a better knowledge of her Bible than any preacher I was to know, and she saw the daily turnings of our family and her friends in the context of Bible verses and the working out of God's will. This was the woman who taught me to walk, toilet-trained me, fed me, scolded me, and set me in corners with a smear of molasses on my fingers and a feather to play with. I would sit, happily transferring the feather from one fat hand to the other for the hour it took her to fix dinner for my father and my ailing mother.

Her name was Pearl, which gave my father a constant joke when her men-friends arrived at the back door, "Don't cast that pearl before swine," my father would say, grinning at her. She would sniff. "Don't you worry none about that, Mr. Carpenter. They none of them any good for a poor woman like me. They just being foolish." Then she'd giggle.

But that, like so many things I heard Pearl tell my father and grandfather, was a lie. She was not a poor woman. She could bake and cook and clean. She made quilts in spiraling, whirling patterns she casually designed as she put scraps of cloth in place. She could knit and do fine embroidery and tend a garden and raise the best chickens in town.

But it was her presence that made her a true pearl for my parents and for me. When Pearl came into the back door and the screen slapped to at seven in the morning, the house settled down and became happy. The chickens clucked with contentment, the dog curled up in the sun for a nap, my father was free to go to town and drink with his friends or pretend to be doing business about the farm. My sick mother must have been soothed by those thin, dark brown hands which could lift so effortlessly the fat softness of me at two years.

It was Pearl who nursed my mother until she died. Pearl closed her eyes and said a prayer over her head while my father boo-hooed and howled and went to town to tell all of his drinking friends about his loss and get drunk for three days. It was Pearl who found my father in a bar and drove him home. It was Pearl who got him into a bath and who shaved him when his hands shook too much to hold the razor. It was Pearl who laid out the clothes and helped him dress and told him to stop being such a fool and stand up by his wife. It was Pearl who was entrusted with the baby I was then, and Pearl who was told by my grandfather to raise me as if I were her own. It was Pearl, who had had a son but never a daughter, who lavished hand-smocked dresses and starched lacy pinafores on me every summer and made me

146

into the most beautifully dressed, best-mannered baby in the town.

I can't remember my mother and her funeral and my drunken father swaying by the side of the red clay hole where my mother was laid. I can't remember anything before my third birthday, but I clearly remember that firm voice saying to me, "Speak up nice now. Here comes Miz Whitley. She was a friend of your mama's. You say your piece nice now and don't go putting your fingers up your nose. You want to do that, you just go out with the chickens and stand there looking like a piece of trash. People like that belong with the chickens, but no chil' of mine is going to do that."

"Chil' of mine." I heard that over and over the first six years of my life. This mythical "chil' of mine" was a figure of perfection and cleanliness and mannerliness and brilliance. She was a child that all the world would stand back and gaze at in respect and awe. She was the ultimate child who would always know right from wrong and do the correct thing by instinct because she was a lady. I didn't care what my grandfather or father would have thought of my living in the cemetery with a tent and chemical toilet and campstove. I didn't care what Aunt Nell said about baths in the river and my total inelegance, but I was glad that Pearl lay buried and I did not have to face her with my untidy life and the peculiar outcome of thirty-nine years of living.

Staring at me with that look of hers, Pearl would have said, "No chil' of mine is going to live out there in the cemetery. It isn't decent. It isn't what anybody but trash would do, and no chil' of mine can do that." And I would have packed up my tent, sold my equipment, and moved to a house more fitting for a child of Pearl's.

Pearl poured her training into me as if I were a pitcher and she the water of life. My manners were perfect by the age of four. My clothes were beautiful and I was changed three or four times a day so that I was always fresh. My tendency to sweat in the summer was a constant irritation to Pearl. It caused the high wings of my white pinafores to droop and lie limply over my shoulders. My hair lay in damp strings over my head. I was not "fit to be seen." So I would be bathed and dressed again.

"Pearl is going to wash that child's skin right off," my grandmother said, but Pearl only smiled and nodded politely and kept on bathing me. Pearl would say anything, agree with any criticism of how she raised me, but then she would go right on raising me as she would have her own daughter.

I was never struck as a child. Until my father fired Pearl in a drunken rage when I was six years old, I had never seen anger or physical violence. Pearl did not condescend to hit me. Staring at me with dark eyes, she would simply say, "You know who you are. My chil' doesn't do that. Now you just straighten up."

I would straighten up. Like many black women in the South, Pearl knew exactly what world she was fitting me for. She knew every kink and loop of my culture's requirements better than I did. She also knew exactly what bad manners and incorrect action would do. They would reduce me to the dread label "poor white trash." For Pearl to stare at me and say, "You are acting just like poor white trash, and if you don't behave, I'm going to put you to bed for the afternoon," was to whip me into immediate order. It was more than manners. It was honor.

"Pearl said that you can never break a promise you give to your blood kin, no matter what. Is that true, Aunt Nell?" I once asked when I was about five.

Aunt Nell stiffened and I can remember her sitting very quiet for a while. Finally she said, "That is true, Camille. Never forget that. Pearl is speaking the absolute truth. Never break a promise to your own flesh and blood."

And Pearl, not trusting in my skimpy, sprinkling baptism at the age of two weeks, made sure that I was baptized correctly before she left my father's house. She had been fired. My father couldn't stand her hostile looks when he was drunk and her tattling to my grandfather when he was not sober for a week. Pearl was not a woman to go easy on a drunk.

But she came back the next Sunday and entered the house as she usually did. "You know you're fired," my father said. "I'm just taking the chil' to church," Pearl said. "You don't want her to be missed by her grandmother at the services, do you?"

It was a threat. My father would hear about it if I did not walk down the aisle to sit by my grandparents after Sunday school. He went into his bedroom and slammed the door.

Pearl dressed me in a dress she took out of brown paper. It was all handmade of the finest light cotton, with lace at all the edges. It was pure white and looked like what I had always thought angels must wear. Pearl must have made it for this day and then taken it home with her. I never was to wear it or see it again.

I was washed almost to death and dressed and polished and brushed as if it were my wedding day. I complained bitterly. "Hush. You don't know anything," Pearl said.

We left the house but didn't get into my father's car for the drive to church. Grabbing my hand, Pearl set off walking through the fields. I was astonished. "Where are we going, Pearl? You said I had to go to church."

Pearl said not a word and we walked until my legs were tired, down through fields in the springtime that had been planted and showed green fuzz over them from the tender tips of clover and corn. We walked until we came to a bend in the river where there was a large sandbar that cut out into the water. The sandbar and the banks were covered with people, and I knew some of them. Fat Tuba, Aunt Alice, Jake and Tommy, and Mr. Williams, the black dentist. They stood with their families and smiled politely to Pearl and me.

"How do, sister. I see you brought the young 'un down here to be taken into the arms of her Savior." "How do, Miss Pearl. That chil' is certainly a compliment to you today." "Hi there, sister." "Sister." "Sister."

I glowed in the attention but had no idea why I was here. I had gone to church with Pearl occasionally and knew the people of her church. It had a long title and was more fun than my grandmother's church, but the rules were more complicated. At my grandmother's church I had to be well brought up. At Pearl's church I had to be more perfect than any child ever yet known to mankind.

The minister began. "Come now, sisters and brothers! Come to me as sinners and be washed free of your sin in the water of salvation." He walked out into the river and I stared in astonishment. I had never seen a grown man just walk into the water and pay no attention to the fact that he was wetting his good clothes. I wondered if he had taken off his shoes and socks. "Pearl," I whispered. "Did he take off his shoes first?"

"Hush," she said. "Don't talk. The Holy Spirit is here."

People walked out into the water. The minister held them in his arms and then suddenly tipped them over backward into the water. I was stunned. All the people had on white robes except for one man who seemed shabby and dirty. As the preacher tipped this ragged man under the water, people cheered and laughed. "Hold him down now, preacher." "That man has too much sin to get rid of with just a little dampness." "Lord God! Look at that sin fighting to hold on to him!" "Don't let go, preacher! Hold him in there." The water churned as the man struggled and then it grew smooth. Half-drowned, the man was helped up onto the bank by laughing friends.

"Now it's your turn," Pearl said. "The Holy Spirit is powerful after saving a sinner like Sam Turner."

I didn't have time to protest. Pearl whipped off my shoes and marched me in my white socks and white dress down to the edge of the water.

"Walk in," she commanded, and there was a kindness in her voice that I seldom heard. "Walk to the preacher. He'll take care of you."

I waded out to the preacher, who came in closer and picked me up.

"Look at the little child in all her prettiness. See the little young one here in my arms. I say to you, you are never too young to lay your sins before your Savior and be washed by the water of life. Then were there brought unto him little children that he should put his hands on them, and pray, and the disciples rebuked them. But Jesus said, Suffer the little children, and forbid them not to come unto me, for of such is the kingdom of heaven."

As he said "heaven," he suddenly tipped me backward into the water. His thumb and forefinger pinched my nose shut and I was held under the green river water with arms as strong as oak rails. I lay still for a second and waited to be lifted up, but it didn't happen. I opened my eyes in astonishment. I had been good. I had spoken politely and not stuck my finger in my nose. I had been washed and brushed and hadn't torn my dress or gotten dirty. I had been good. Why was this preacher going to drown me?

Through the water I could see his dark form above me, the face indistinct and unavailable for appeal. I thrashed and tried to cry out, but the water was everywhere around me and I was held down. The greenness grew heavy and dark, and suddenly I was torn out of the darkness and thrown up into the air. I choked and coughed and couldn't see for the brightness of the sun in my eyes. The preacher held me tenderly. "You have been saved by our Lord Jesus. You are a Christian now, little sister."

I couldn't speak. I was carried back to Pearl's arms and lay limply on the grass. Everything was very bright and I was tired. "Can I take my dress off, Pearl? It's wet and I want to get dry."

"That's the water of life on you. The sun will dry you off soon."

It had been an amazing day. I was allowed to get wet in the most beautiful dress I had ever had on. Then I was allowed to play tag and hide-and-seek with the other children and get filthy dirty and scream and holler and behave in front of Pearl's friends as I never had been allowed to behave before. Then I was allowed to eat all the fried chicken and sweet-potato pie and potato salad and country ham and beaten biscuits that I wanted. I was allowed to eat while I was playing, running with food in my hands like a child with no upbringing at all, and most amazing of all, Pearl had taken me out of the preacher's arms and held me to her and cried, fierce cries that I could feel tearing through my body.

"Pearl, Pearl, I'm all right. He didn't drown me. It's all right."

I lay in her arms and tried to comfort her for I knew not what. It wasn't that she wouldn't see me anymore. Pearl lived not far from my father's farm in a little house with her sister. I could visit her every day if I wanted. I patted her face and felt sobs coming up in me and we stood there at the river's edge crying together in the sunlight.

◇

Tom knew Eli Branch, the man who had bought my father's house and had lived in it since the year after my father's death, twenty years ago. Mr. Branch was a silent old man who pretended that he didn't know I was living in a tent within sight of his front porch. I had often looked down the hill, over the corn and the cows in pasture, and wondered what my home was like now.

"Come on," Tom said when I told him this. "Eli doesn't farm much. He's usually home. Let's go see if he'll give us a tour of the old homestead."

"I'd feel silly, Tom, prying around in his house."

"He won't care. His wife died a few years ago, and he's all alone now. It may be pretty messy."

"Mr. Branch," Tom said as he walked up the porch steps, "this is Camille Anderson. She and her daddy used to live here, and she thought we'd come visit you. See the house and all, if it's all right with you, sir."

Mr. Branch rose up out of the porch swing that hung from the rafters and creaked gently in the afternoon breeze. "I'm real pleased to see you again, Camille. I met you before when you were just a little bitty thing. Out walking around town with your grandfather."

"I'm glad you remember me, sir. I wish I remembered things as well," I said.

Apparently there was no one Tom didn't know. "You running for office?" I whispered to him. "You sure know everybody."

"If you'd lived here all your life, you'd know everybody too," Tom said. He was right. I was a stranger in my own town.

"Feel free to look around," Mr. Branch said. "I've got some ice tea, and you can join me in some if you want. I can't offer you bourbon, Tom," he said, grinning at Tom. "You know I'm a good Baptist. Don't keep that stuff in the house."

"Between you good Baptists and all that bootlegger money coming into town, we're going to be voted dry again if we're not careful." Tom shook Mr. Branch's hand and they smiled at each other.

I walked in nervously, half expecting to hear my father's querulous voice drunkenly demanding his dinner. The house was dim and sparsely furnished, but it looked fairly unchanged.

"You want a surprise, Camille, you come look what my wife had done to the kitchen." Mr. Branch led us down the hall and opened a swinging door from the dining room to the kitchen.

I didn't want to see the kitchen much. It was the one room that gave me bad memories. My father had one of his worst alcoholic breakdowns while in the kitchen. I went through the door hesitantly, and it was beautiful.

Mrs. Branch had ripped out the back wall and had a bank of windows put in like a greenhouse. Under the windows were a table and chairs in one nook and benches with storage under them on the other side. The house was on a ridge of land, protected from floods, and now it had a glorious view of the river and fields and the hill on the other side of the river.

"Oh, Mr. Branch," I said. "It's beautiful. Why, in autumn it must be hard to ever leave this room. You can see all the hills, and the trees must look like they're on fire when the sun hits them."

"That's just what my wife used to say." Mr. Branch smiled. "She got sick before we got all the plumbing done and the new washer and dryer and dishwasher. I made them quit work so she could come lie in here. Put a hospital bed near the window. She loved the countryside. Said it looked different every hour of the day."

I took Mr. Branch's hand. "That's how I feel too. I looked at that view every day out my bedroom window. I had the little room upstairs. I'm sorry I didn't know your wife, Mr. Branch. I'm real glad she lived here, though."

Mr. Branch was pleased. "She did love the country. I'll get the ice tea and see if I don't have some cookies here. Y'all look around and then come on out front."

Tom and I were left standing by the windows. I was so happy. All the depression of the kitchen as I had remembered it had gone.

"God, Tom, look at that. It makes the house so beautiful. I hope nobody ever builds anything on that hill across the river. It looks so wild and natural."

"Well, I hate to be the voice of rational thinking, Camille.

That hill is too steep for farming, but a good restaurant or a set of condominiums could be built there. Overlooking the river, it would be a nice view."

"Don't you dare suggest that," I said. "Leave something unspoiled."

"You aristocrats. You want to own all the land and keep everybody else off. I can't stand that. Fuck the land. Spending your whole life trying to own it when you could have a condominium or an apartment and no problems. What's so wonderful about owning land?"

I didn't know what to say. If Tom couldn't see it or feel it, I didn't know if I could ever make him understand.

"When people don't own some land they don't treat things right. Look how dirty cities are. People don't care about the earth when they feel it isn't theirs and they're all squashed up together with not even a garden or a patio to sit on."

"You're bourgeois, Camille. You'd sit all your life and dig in your little patch of dirt and never have a thought in your head except to keep other bourgeois from taking your patch of dirt away from you."

"It's more than that. It's like we're born into this world and we have to love it."

"I love it. I love taking this world and leveling it and making shopping centers and parking lots and condos. I love making something of it."

"Yeah, I saw your latest effort. The tract houses north of town. You threw those up and managed to cut down one of the prettiest woods left in the county. And for what? Crappy little houses that will fall apart in fifteen years. I bet there isn't a door in those houses that closes right five years from now."

"Well, it's easy for you to complain, but those people have to live somewhere. Not everybody is lucky enough to have a tent and a cemetery plot. The family home that lasts for four generations is dead anyway. Those tract houses will last just fine until they get their divorces in seven years, and then the next set of starry-eyed newlyweds can move in and improve them for their seven years. Nothing lasts, Camille, not land, not those marriages, not all your aristocratic sentiments. You're living in the past."

I moved angrily back through the house and sat on the porch, drinking iced tea. Tom was speaking truth of a sort. You couldn't refuse to have cheap housing for young couples. You couldn't shut everyone out and just let a few people own all the beautiful land. But that wasn't what I meant.

I hated the way everything seemed to have been forgotten except quick profits. I hated the way Tom casually destroyed a beautiful, alive woods because it was cheaper to rip the trees out than to take the time to build around them.

I wouldn't change my mind. I loved the land. The ugliest land on earth in its natural state is more interesting than the parking lot of a shopping center. Lust for land could destroy you, it was true. I remembered Aunt Nell telling me the story of an ancestor of mine named Molly who had married a man with a crazy passion for land. She'd given up on owning land too.

Who was I to talk? I, in my own way, had also given up. I hadn't come home after college and claimed my family's land. I had moved away and done other things. Modern life was like a river that ran at flood all the year, tearing you away from everything you tried to hold on to, everything you could value. I shivered in the shade of the porch. Aunt Nell was right. Living in a cemetery would make me morbid if I kept sitting there all summer.

A THOUSAND YEARS TO LIVE

She hadn't wanted to come to this wilderness. He wanted it, so she packed up her quilts and the baby and they loaded up three mules and a wagon, which was abandoned on a hillside in the mud of April before they could get through the mountains into Kentucky. She walked by his side all the way and didn't say much. "I ain't a thoughty man," he'd said when they were courting, but he wasn't one to speak to her either unless it was necessary.

Raised on a Pennsylvania farm by parents who had lavished all the love of elderly people upon their last child, she had been accustomed to country life, and she knew how to grow a garden, plant and hoe and dry the crop for winter, how to jerk meat and salt down fish and sew and cook and spin and weave. She was ready for the life she chose and went to it expecting Kentucky to be little different from her mother's life in Pennsylvania.

She was not ready for his solitariness. He couldn't stand towns or even the sight of another roof or road running by his place. He grew angry in towns, and he selected a homestead in 1815 that was thirty miles from any town and twenty from a neighbor. That kept him safe. No one could drop by to talk when he was wrestling out the stumps from his fields. No one could comment on the stinginess of the cabin he built, begrudging the hours used to make his dwelling place when he could be clearing more land, and more land after that. No one could see his wife gradually becoming as silent as he was, bearing two more children in the cabin, once in the winter with his help and once during spring plowing when she didn't call him in from the fields for fear of irritating him in his passion to dig up this soil and become—become what?

She didn't know. Sometimes when she worked in the garden she rose up and stood looking toward his shape across the fields if she could see him. Was it rich he wanted to become? The richest farmer in Kentucky? His back was hard and tight as he plowed, and he never talked to the mules but plowed like he was angry with the land. She watched uneasily and dreaded his coming back at night, hoping he was tired. If he was too tired he ignored her and slept with his head by his bowl like a drunkard, but when the work was light he turned to her in the night and moved angrily down on her in silence as he moved over his land.

It wouldn't have been so bad if there had been neighbors or a road near them with travelers stopping for water and a greeting. But she hadn't been prepared for the silence of this place. At times she knew it was too much for her, and she would sing in panic for hours until her throat was hoarse to keep from falling into that leaden silence that drew up around the cabin. If she fell in, there would be no crawling out, she knew that, and then she would go mad as women sometimes did.

And it might have gone on like this for fifty years, moving on farther into the wilderness as the towns crept up on them and the buggies arrived bearing women with loaves of bread and samples of their jam. But he died. It wasn't a sickness or the Indians, who she was sure were going to kill them every spring when the news came of new attacks on lonely cabins. He had just fallen over in the mud for no reason and left the plow to scrape on over the field until the mules stopped at the edge to graze awkwardly around their bits.

Night came and she took a lantern and went out in a light rain to find him. Her bare feet sank in over the ankles in the plowed field. She had known it was too early for him to plow yet, but he couldn't stand waiting in the spring. She had to walk the fields for an hour, crisscrossing the earth, slipping in the furrows on the wet clay until she found him, and then she had to get the mules from the yard, where they had finally come at dark dragging the plow behind them, and put her husband's body in the wagon so the animals wouldn't tear his flesh during the·night.

She buried him herself, and when she went to town for supplies, the word spread. Molly McClure, David McClure's wife, was a widow with three children and was sitting alone out there on what was going to become a promising piece of land in a few years. True, she had three children to worry you, but children grew up fast in Kentucky. The eight-year-old boy would be a man in another four or five years. With a horse and a rifle he could light out West himself at thirteen. Then there'd only be the two girls. Girls marry quick in the wilderness. And that would leave Molly and all that land that her husband had crazily carved out and any other children that you might get on Molly because she was still a pretty thing and young enough to have more.

So they came courting. She wasn't ready the first few times a man rode up into the dirt around the cabin. She greeted them with little interest, offered water for their horses, and invited them to dinner at noon when they showed no signs of leaving. Then she understood. Her husband had left her with something other men wanted. All his tiredness and anger had changed the land until she was suddenly worth something to all these strangers.

It must be admitted, she used to think when she was an old lady, I did enjoy it some at first. She had dressed up every Sunday and waited for the men to come courting. It seemed strange, a woman with three children around her to have men bringing her candy and talking as sweet and melting as the candy was in her mouth. She knew they wanted the land. It bordered a river which promised to become a highway for goods and people, and they looked hungrily past her shoulders at the land lying fallow around the cabin. She wasn't fooled by them, but she enjoyed it just the same for a few months.

Finally it came down to two men. They visited her on alternate Sundays and she was courteous with both. It was so good to be able to talk that she chattered on with both of them, not caring that each week the face changed. They were pretty much the same as far as she could see, and they were willing to sit and listen to her. She was happy until one of the men decided to end this foolishness and claim what he felt was justly his by right of neglecting his own life for months to listen to her talk and to dandle her children by another man on his knee.

He didn't go home after dinner, stayed to supper, and when Molly uneasily put the children to bed he tried to force himself on her. She struggled, not shouting out because there was no one but the children to wake up and they would just be frightened, and finally she let him lie on top of her and do whatever he wanted. All right, she thought, it won't take long anyway. And it hadn't.

The next morning he was silently triumphant and slapped her bottom gaily as she poured his coffee. It was over. He could relax now and get on with his life. "We'll be married in two weeks," he said. "We'll get the preacher to do us up in town." Then he made his only error so far. He left Molly alone and rode off to check the land deeds on her property and figure out where he could expand and creep over into the woods around them. "I'll be back in ten days," he shouted over his shoulder. "We'll be married when I get back."

158

She just sat all that morning and ignored the children when they got hungry. Then she made up her mind. "He didn't even ask me," she said, and that was the last time Molly McClure ever mentioned him to anyone.

By night she was standing on the porch of the Judge's house in town asking if she could bed the children down in his stable loft and then come in and talk to him. The Judge and his wife took her in, and she was never to go back to that cabin. She left it, taking only her quilts and cooking pots and blankets. She left the farm tools and turned the chickens loose in the woods. She never had felt much for the chickens anyway. The cow she tied to the back of the wagon and sold the first day she was in town.

By the time her beau got back with copies of the land deeds, she had sold the land, cabin, and any chickens that anybody could find in the woods and moved on in her wagon. She didn't know where she was going, but it would be toward the East, she told the Judge. The man who had spent the night with her talked a lot of dirt about Molly and how she slept with him, but he quit and moved to Tennessee when the men began teasing him about driving a woman away after only one night of his romancing. He had lost that hand.

Molly didn't know where she was going, but she seemed to recognize it when she got there. The great brick houses rose up around a turn in the bend and Molly drove up to the door of the largest building, with three children looking out from under the blankets like squirrels at all the people and buildings and the tamed land spreading out around them. "Welcome to Pleasant Hill," said a woman to Molly. "You're all pleased to join us at the table."

Molly joined them and listened in fierce concentration for a week. "You have to be what you seem to be; and seem to be what you really are; you can't carry two faces," they said.

Molly stared at the broad floors gleaming with wax, at the white walls with chairs neatly hung on pegs, at the glorious soaring of the twin spiral staircase that went up almost to heaven, it would seem. "Clean your room well, for good spirits will not live where there is dirt," they told her, and she smiled, remembering the filth of her cabin yard and the dirt that lay in clods from her husband's boots as he sprawled across the table snoring.

"Do all your work as if you had a thousand years to live and as if you were to die tomorrow," they told her. It made sense to Molly. She loved the work when there were other women spinning and weaving and cooking by her side. She loved the way she could work alongside the men as she used to work by her brothers in Pennsylvania, and she was one of them. She loved the prayers and order and the way her children had a school and other children to keep them company. She loved her hours away from the children. She loved being listened to. It never gave Molly pause that Negroes ate by her side and danced every Sunday the dances of holy love. They were her brothers and sisters. Besides, she'd never had a slave.

"You must be sure that you can live pure in the eyes of God. You must be able to live a holy life and not desire the fleshly pleasures." And this made Molly smile a smile they saw as the best possession she had carried out of the wilderness. The smile said, "I will live a pure life with my sisters and brothers. I never need the lust of the flesh again if I can find peace in my heart here."

Molly would never again know sex, but the passions of her life seemed too all-encompassing for it to matter. So she became a member of the Shaker fellowship, and she danced in the huge room in line with her sisters, facing her brothers, and lifted her voice up in joy, letting her body tremble and feel the grace of God which had lifted her up from a life of silence and sin in the wilderness and let her live out her days in clean purity and honest labor with her family. "I think that Sister Molly will bear a sound, good cross," said Elder Rebecca.

And so it was. She became expert in weaving silk from the cocoons bred and raised at Pleasant Hill and spent her days gathering leaves, winding the silvery silk thread and weaving broad scarves for the brethren and the sisters. Sitting under the mulberry trees one hot afternoon, she looked up at the turmoil around her of the Civil War and, with a radiant smile, greeted the man who loomed above her.

General John Hunt Morgan looked down from his horse,

"What is that you're doing, ma'am?" he asked the old woman.

Holding up the silk that shone between her fingers, Molly said, "I am putting my hands to work and giving my heart to God, sir. Be welcome."

Looking across at the fields which his raiders were ravaging, General Morgan said, "You never have to tell my men that, ma'am."

And he rode over to the center family dwelling house to eat eggs, sausage, onions, pickles, milk, stewed apples, butter and cornbread, sassafras and sage tea. Drinking the last of his tea, Morgan looked gloomily into the dregs in his cup of what his men called "Jeff Davis Coffee" and shook his head. "The food was enjoyable," he said with Southern courtliness to his Shaker hosts, "but the pleasure would be more if I didn't know that your women would be feeding the very same breakfast tomorrow morning to the Union parties following us." Bowing politely, he leaped into the saddle and rode off, tipping his hat as he rode past to the little woman under a mulberry tree. Her hands raised in reply shone with light from the loose silk threads. It was a light that trailed around her where the sun touched her dress and made him think of things other than war. That silk is nice stuff, Morgan thought. I should have gotten a handkerchief for my wife. But it was too late. They were in the woods already and heading for the Ohio River.

Dinah wanted to go to church. I asked her if she wanted to drive up to her old church and attend services before the baby was born. No. She didn't ever want to see her parents or any of those people again.

"I don't have much to say to them, Camille. But I would like to go to a church on the Pottersville Pike. It's a lot like my old church and I'd like to go out there, maybe this Sunday."

How could I complain? This was the first thing that Dinah had ever stated as a desire except for the tummy TV. She was silent and uncomplaining, and a simple request to be taken to church was small enough. I'd never had a baby. Who knows what fears she's having about going into labor? I thought. Maybe church will make her feel less nervous. I didn't know why Dinah had picked that chapel, but I promised to pick her up at eight and we'd drive out there for the nine-o'clock service.

When I told Tom Church that my Sunday morning was going to be busy, he laughed and said, "Oh my God! I haven't been to a church like that since my uncle used to take me out to the foot-washers by the river. I'll go with you." He nuzzled into my neck and sighed a fake sigh of melancholy. "You wouldn't deny this sinner the chance for redemption, would you?"

I didn't want him to come with us. "You have to be good," I warned. "This is serious for Dinah. She's under enough strain without you mocking or snickering at her. You have to sit there and shut up and be nice about it. I don't want any French rationalist lectures."

Tom solemnly stated that he had never heard of any Frenchman worth reading, rational or otherwise, and that he only wanted to lay his soul at God's feet. I was amused but nervous. I wanted Tom to entertain me, but I didn't want Dinah to be hurt.

Tom picked me and Dinah up in his Cadillac. Dinah was startled to see Tom, but she said hello and climbed quickly into the back seat.

"Have you been to this church before, Dinah?" I asked when we arrived.

Dinah shook her head as she staggered out of the car. "No. I just heard that they were full of the spirit," she said solemnly.

We went into the church, a tiny white clapboard building big enough for about fifty people. We were the first worshipers to arrive. The windows were plain glass, the seats were wooden and hard. There were no pillows or a rug down the aisle or an organ or even an altar. There was just a raised platform—the kind professors stand on in a classroom—and a folding chair on it. Next to the chair was a small table, and that was it.

"I like this," Tom whispered loudly. "No Popish foolishness. Just a group of honest sinners raising their hearts to the Lord." Leaning across me, he asked Dinah, "Are the rattlesnakes here yet, Dinah?"

162

Dinah stared at him. "What snakes? I never heard of snakes in a church."

"Oh," Tom said in mock sadness. "I thought this was the church where they handle rattlesnakes and eat strychnine. Isn't that right?"

I glared at Tom. "You know this isn't one of those churches. Now stop that." Tom was almost as fidgety as Dinah, and I could tell he was upsetting her. She had sat down quickly and kept me between her and Tom.

The church began to fill up. These were poor people, poor farmers and their wives and little children who seldom saw two pairs of shoes in a year, old men and women and a sprinkling of uneasy adolescents and older children who were already struggling to throw off the fear of God and neck at the drive-in movies with guiltless abandon.

The people rustled with anticipation when a lean man walked down the aisle and stood on the stage. He knelt and bent over the folding chair in prayer. His brow furrowed and he was in a passion of worship. A few amens were heard as he knelt, and the woman behind us said, "You can feel the spirit coming down among us." This generated quite a few amens, including a small one from Dinah and a loud and fervent one from Tom Church.

Standing up, the minister pointed his thin finger at us and moved it over all the assembled heads. "The devil is among us night and day, poor sinners that we are. The demons hide in every corner and the light is dim."

"Amen," the people breathed in joy.

"We have all sinned. We are all black-hearted and damned. Yes, all of us. That little child—" He turned and pointed full at a boy about eight who sat gaping in the front row. "That little child is not without stain and blemish." Leaning toward the child, he squinted his dark eyes and said in a whisper, "You will burn in hell and be damned to eternal darkness out of the sight of our Lord for your sins if you don't come to Jesus.

"Let us sing," he demanded.

We all stood and sang "Love Lifted Me." Dinah began in a

163

quavering soprano and Tom Church joined in loudly. The song dragged and faltered until the chorus and then everyone hollered out—

> Love lifted me,
> Love lifted me,
> When nothing else could help
> Love lifted me.

The preacher began to read from his Bible, and I began to wonder if this was such a good idea after all. I just wanted Dinah to have a nice warm feeling after this morning. Then Dinah could go home and have her baby in peace. This preacher was about as warm as a lizard. There was nothing easy about his God. He began to read.

> I am the woman who has seen the afflictions that come from the rod of God's wrath. He has brought me into deepest darkness, shutting out all light. He has turned against me. Day and night his hand is heavy on me. He has made me old and has broken my bones.

I was ready to leave. He read on and on. Dinah was turning pale, and even Tom was silent. It was terrible. I was angry that I had brought Dinah into this. Why should she listen to such doom and gloom?

"It's all right," I whispered to Dinah. "He's just getting carried away."

Dinah shook her head and listened intently to the preacher. He went on and on about sin and damnation and the terrors of life until I felt claustrophobic. Then he moved the chair and table to the back of the platform and held out his arms.

"But I say to you," he said, "we are pressed on every side by troubles, but not crushed and broken. We are perplexed because we don't know why things happen as they do, but we don't give up and quit. We are hunted down, but God never abandons us. We are knocked down, but we get up again. So come now and confess your sins. Witness for Christ and accept him into your heart and into your life."

Dinah stood up at once and moved out of our pew and up the

aisle. She walked slowly and with great firmness. Her face was white, but she looked all right otherwise.

"I am a sinner," she began in a soft voice. "I have gotten pregnant and I'm not married, and I hate them all and I just want to get Christ into my heart."

She said this so straightforwardly that I felt tears in my eyes. I looked over at Tom, but he looked unmoved and almost angry. "My God, she is so pitiful," I whispered to him. "Why are you so angry?"

Tom was silent and then said, "I just hate her upsetting you, honey. You have a lot to figure out without this hysterical girl to bother with."

I was touched by his caring about me. "It's all right," I said.

"Hear this worthless sinner, O Lord," the preacher was saying over Dinah's bowed head. "Forgive her her sins and let Jesus come into her heart."

Dinah rejoined us and other people went up. Dinah was so white that blue shadows showed around her mouth, and she didn't seem happy and relaxed like the sinners who had gone up and witnessed for Christ. They were the most talkative and cheerful of the congregation, fully aware of their courage in going on stage with their sins and ready to relax and enjoy life, but Dinah was still, tense, and silent.

We shook the preacher's hand at the door. He stared at me and I cringed a little. I had not witnessed. His look said as plain as day that he knew I was taking my stinking little sins home to nourish for another week. I moved on outside and Dinah asked him a question.

"Can God forgive sins that you haven't committed?" she asked.

The preacher stared at her and held her hand gently in his as he thought. "God can do anything, sister, but sins that haven't been committed are sins that don't have to be committed. You have witnessed today. In the words of our Lord, go and sin no more." He dropped her hand. "Come on out anytime and talk to me." He felt in his pocket. "Here's my number. You can leave word with my missus. I'm home most nights."

Dinah took the card and hesitated. She seemed about to speak,

leaning toward him and opening her mouth. Tom was close behind her waiting to shake the preacher's hand. Dinah flinched
from Tom and went to the car.

Tom dropped Dinah and me at Aunt Nell's. Aunt Nell was out
to a luncheon, and I didn't want to leave Dinah alone. She was
too overwrought.

"Dinah, we shouldn't have gone," I said as I fixed tuna sandwiches for lunch. "It upset you, all that talk about sin and damnation."

"That wasn't it, Camille. I just felt funny with Mr. Church.
He's Bobby McCarey's uncle, and he's been about the only father
that Bobby ever had, I guess. I just felt funny."

"Bobby. That must be Anne's son. But why should that bother
you? Dinah? I don't understand."

"Bobby was one of those boys. You know. He was one of the
ones who—you know, Camille."

I stared at Dinah. "You mean Tom's nephew is one of the boys
who raped you?"

"Yeah. I felt sort of funny around his uncle."

"My God, Dinah. You didn't tell me. I would never have
brought him if I'd known." I made the sandwiches, but the grad-
ual meaning of what Dinah said took my appetite. Tom knew
more about the rape than he dared let on to me. He probably
knew more about it than anyone other than Dinah and the boys.

"After my mother and father found out," Dinah went on,
"they called the sheriff, and he knew Mr. Church."

"Everyone knows Mr. Church," I said.

"That's right. So Mr. Church came over and talked to everybody. He knows all about it and it's sort of embarrassing."

It was more than embarrassing for me. I remembered the way
Tom had just happened to run into me at the cemetery when he
was checking his mother's grave. I remembered our lovemaking.
I got Dinah settled down for a nap and left. I had to think, and
then I had to talk to Tom. It wasn't a talk I wanted to have. For
all of Tom's neuroses about owning land, I admired him as the
man who stayed, the man who was decisive and a part of the
whole community. I had wanted, I suddenly realized with a pain

that surprised me, for Tom to love me and let me become part of his steadiness, his sureness. I didn't know now if I really knew who Tom Church was.

Tom was going to pick me up for dinner that night. I sat by my tent all afternoon and hadn't dressed or put on any makeup when his blue Cadillac pulled up in the graveyard.

"I'm not dressed, Tom."

"Well, come on. Unless you want hamburgers, throw something on, Camille."

I didn't stand up, and Tom got out of the car. He stood over me and laughed.

"We can just make love now if you want, but I thought a man had to feed a woman first. I always believed that women had this survival instinct to eat before they let a man make love to them. It sort of insures that they'll get fed every couple of days."

"Tom, I have to talk to you. You might as well sit down. I don't even know where to begin."

Tom sat and looked wary. I was miserable. Whatever I said, I doubted that Tom and I would eat dinner afterward and then make love romantically under the stars. One half of me was too angry to care, but the other half stared longingly at Tom's hair, wet from his shower, and wanted to touch him, stroke him, and feel him effortlessly pull me to him and kiss me.

"Tom, you knew all about Dinah. You knew those boys. You knew about the rape and everything that happened to Dinah, but you pretended you didn't. Why?"

Tom sighed and stared at the trees across the field. "I don't know. I don't like to talk about it much myself. Why should I? I guess you talked to Dinah?"

"She told me your nephew was one of the boys."

"That's what she said?"

"Is it true?"

Tom hesitated. "Yes. It's true. He and five other boys had sex with her that night."

"Raped her."

"Now look, Camille—it was a crazy idea, tying her on that car lift, but she agreed to it. I believe that."

"Oh, come on, Tom!" I was angry now. "How can you believe she agreed. My God. Being tied up and then treated like a goddamn machine. Dinah's not crazy."

"But she had had sex with them before. You know that."

"Going out and experimenting with sex doesn't mean a girl wants to be raped."

"They'd all had sex with her before. You can't say she was some innocent little girl." Tom was getting angry now too. His hands were clenched and he stared at me as if he hated me.

"You're looking at me the same way you looked at Dinah. You hate her, don't you," I said.

"Goddamn right I hate her. Bobby never did more than get a couple of speeding tickets, and then I get a call one day that he's accused of rape. Goddamn right I hate her. Bobby toes the line for me. Since Anne was widowed, I nearly raised the kid. He makes good grades. He's going to a better college than my sister or I could afford. He'd never messed up before."

"How the hell can you hate Dinah just because she was the victim? Try hating Bobby instead. He's the rapist."

Tom stood up so quickly that I drew back. Then I stood up. We were of nearly equal height, equally angry.

"She was a slut."

"She was a scared girl who got raped. I'll bet they didn't call her a slut when she had sex with them. Besides, they had sex too. Why call just Dinah names?"

"I raised him. I taught him how to fish and hunt and we took his car apart last summer. He knows everything I do, dammit. He can use a bulldozer almost as well as a grown man."

"Strong, smart, little Bobby. He was probably the leader of the pack."

"No. He wasn't. Another boy was the ringleader. Bobby wasn't the one."

"You mean he just got to her third or fourth? You better go back and teach him a few more lessons, Tom. Real men are always first in, in gang rapes."

"Shut up, Camille."

"I won't shut up. You came out here and dated me to see if I

168

had come to town to rake this up. You chased me just to keep me busy."

"No."

"You don't want anybody interrupting Bobby's perfect career of hunting and fishing and driving hot cars."

"Dinah's a slut. Any woman who'd sleep with all those boys isn't worth ruining the lives of six boys for. I won't have Bobby ruined for some teenage slut with hot pants."

"They raped her. They raped her and they left her pregnant and half crazy. What about *her* life?"

"I care about her life. I went over there at three in the morning and I worked for two days talking my head off to make sure that it wouldn't go to court. Do you have any idea of what a good defense attorney would do to Dinah with her record of sleeping with boys? Do you know what her parents and brothers and sisters would go through? I was trying to help Dinah. For her to leave town and just get it hushed up—goddamn it—it gives her a chance to start again. Nobody has to know unless she tells."

"Unless Bobby tells. Unless those boys brag about what fun they had at a gas station one night."

Tom sat down heavily, his head in his hands. "They won't talk. When I got through with them, they knew they'd better never open their mouths about it. They won't talk."

"So you pulled it off. A gang rape completely hushed up. The girl gotten neatly out of town. Everything taken care of."

"Look, Camille. I did the best I could. Would you put Dinah through a trial? Do you think giving the newspapers something to print is going to help Dinah?"

I didn't know. I didn't know what I would have done. "I just wish you'd been honest with me, Tom. You lied to me."

"I never told you I didn't know about Dinah."

"No. But you let me think you were utterly ignorant about the whole thing. That's as good as a lie."

We sat in silence for a while, and then Tom asked, "Do you want dinner?"

"I'm not hungry. Frankly, I don't think I can eat anything tonight."

"Well, it makes me feel bad too. You barely know Dinah. Bobby is probably the closest I'll ever have to a son. We ought to talk about this some more."

"I guess so. I have to think."

"Well, don't go running off half-cocked. Just think about whether it's going to help Dinah before you do anything."

"I don't know. God knows what I could do at this point anyway. You could have been more honest, dammit."

Tom drove off and I felt like crying. I was partly upset for Dinah, but I had to admit that a lot of my crying would have been for me. I thought Tom and I had something good starting between us. Selfish though it was, it was my loss that I would have cried for most. Tom didn't want to take any responsibility for Dinah, but who did? How responsible can we be for other people's children?

MARIA

She hid in a patch of blackberry bushes all day until it was dark. The first time she escaped, it had been broad daylight when they caught her walking on the road to Marysville. During the day, you get caught. Maria knew. Maria knew she'd be caught and sent back like the other runaway slaves.

The second time she had traveled by night, and that time she found Marysville and the house where her mother worked. She found her mother. The third time it was easy. Her mother had hidden her for two days in the chicken coop before the master's son came and pulled her out.

Two days of having her mother take the thorns out of her feet. Two days of her mother touching her cheek and telling Maria—

Telling me nothing, thought Maria. Telling me that I can't come back. Telling me that she can't do nothing. But she can. She can do something. He is touching me all the time now. He lies on me at night, and he touches me all day under my skirt, and the missus hates me.

Maria tried to keep clean and neat while she walked. Her sunbonnet hid her face, and the basket on her arm was her safety. A nigger girl with a basket and a list (stolen from the kitchen) is a nigger on an errand.

Master was angry. He had run the ad three times now. He was looking silly. The ad was placed again in the *Observer and Reporter*. Everybody in Lexington could read it. December of 1859. Lots of ads and his running with them. A man who can't keep his niggers at home.

> $50 Reward. Ran away from the subscriber, a Negro girl, named Maria. She is of a copper color, between thirteen and fourteen years of age, bareheaded and barefooted. She is small for her age—very sprightly and very likely. She stated she was going to see her mother in Marysville.

Get close behind that fat woman. Slip in. The store is safe if they think you're with some woman. Carrying her basket.

Put an apple, one potato, two potatoes, three potatoes, a twist of herbs into the basket. Steal a little more. Steal a little more. A full basket gets me from here to my mother. Two miles outside town on a busy road. People asking, "Where you going, girl?"

"Been to store for Missy. Been for Missy. Got my list right here."

Full basket. Crackers. Little sack of brown sugar, anything from a low shelf, from behind the skirts of the women. Pretend you're their nigger. Another apple. Carrying their basket. Eyes down. Slack mouth. Look stupid. Another apple. Two eggs. Now out. Go slowly behind a woman. Shuffle foot. Slack jaw. Men blocking the door. Move. Move. Please God, move them. The men talking to the woman.

"Just got here from the hanging. Colonel Lee and J.E.B. Stuart had to be sent in by the President to catch the devil."

"Made him ride on his own coffin. Setting there like Old Nick hisself. My friend John Booth, he got excited. Said Brown was all that's wrong with this country."

"That John Booth from over Henderson County?"

"No. Not John Casey. John Wilkes Booth. In the State Militia, the Richmond Grays. A good man."

"We stood there and watched Brown drop. Got his damn neck stretched, 'scuse me, ma'am."

"Great day for the nation."

"Puts an end to it, by God."

"There may be more where he comes from."

"The hell you say. There'll never be another John Brown in this country."

"Let's hope. Look out, girl. We might string you up like ol' devil Brown."

"Oh, no suh, no suh. I gotta go home to Missy, suh. 'Scuse me, please, suh."

Out. Out of the store. Too many eyes on her. Now the street. Walk slow. Now slower. Don't run. Only two miles. Could run it faster than a springtime mule. Slower. Little nigger girls don't run on errands. Through the bushes. Over the creek. Cross the chickenyard. The back window? No. She's not in the kitchen.

The butter house. Creek cold. Smell of buttermilk cool. Her back to me. Thin and tall. Strong hands.

"Mama."

The woman turned and stared. Without a pause she seized the child to her. Clawed her to her with muscular arms, pulled Maria against her body.

"Mama, he touches me. They hit me. Soony threw hot water on me 'cause Missus was angry. Mama. Mama. Don't send me away. Don't let 'em get me away. Mama."

Night in the corncrib. Corn hard like rock under the shuck.

Rustle.

Rustle.

Rats? Maybe mice. Little mice. Very little mice. They won't bite just a little girl. Rustling mice. Hide for now. Mama. Hide for days under the shucks. Hide for a lifetime eating sweet butter on cornbread. Mama.

"Come out, chil'. Come out. You got to stretch."

"Mama, he lies on me. He's heavy. I feel sick, Mama."

"You know they breed us. There's no fussing about it, Maria. You can't stop them trying to make more money off us. You can't come back here. You can't do that. The third time now."

"Mama, don't make me go back. Mama, I'm scared."

"Now what do you expect? I'm pregnant again, chil'. I can't do nothing. You'll likely be pregnant too, soon. Soon now."

172

"Mama."
"I can't do nothing."
"Mama."
The scream. "Stop it! I can't do nothing."

Lights on in the house now. Lights on.

"Look in the well. I know. I know. I didn't mean to holler at you, Maria. Look in and if you see the moon there you'll get your wish."
"I don't see the moon. There's nothing there, Mama."

The strong hand brings the stone down hard on Maria's head. Arms lift the unconscious child. Hold her tight. Climbing up, stagger. Hold her tight. The swollen belly of the woman pressed to the belly of the child like a lover in her arms.

"Stop her! Jesus Christ, she's gone crazy! Grab her, David. Don't let her jump."

Hold her tight. Hold her. Down into the water. It isn't so far. Hold her. Hold her. I can't do anything. I can't stand it. I can't see her come through the door again. I can't see her come through the door.
"Goddamn the nigger. We'll have to break her arms to bury them."
"To hell with it. Just make a bigger coffin."
"I ain't wasting a coffin on this nigger. Killed one child and another inside her. Not to mention having to clean the well."
"Not to mention."

The moon in the well. Cold white. Promises of wishes to give. Promises. The well carrying the moon on its breast like a child. The moon. Carried. Floating silent. Like a child. The promised moon. The promised child. On the breast. Floating. Like a promise. Child.

◊

173

Tom came out to see me Wednesday, and we walked through the fields until we came to an old stone wall shaded by a walnut tree. The wall was made of slabs of granite and was probably built by slaves. Part of it had fallen apart, but most of the wall stood as it had for over a hundred years, wild lilies like drops of blood blooming against the stone, weeds trying to find a hold in the joints between stones.

"Let's sit here and talk," Tom said. "I'm afraid you got the wrong idea on Sunday."

I sat on top of the wall and rested my hand on a stone where the sun warmed it. There didn't seem to be much to say. I felt beaten and discouraged. Running from one mess in California to a new place, only to find myself caught in a worse mess, I wasn't sure after three days of thinking whether it was even my right to judge Tom and interfere in Dinah's life. Building any sort of relationship was becoming less and less possible, it seemed.

Safety

You cannot step carelessly when building a stone wall. Loose stones can slip and pin your leg or ankle. A fall onto hard stone can cause serious injury. Never put your fingers under a loose slab when you are moving it. Use the curved end of your pinch bar to remove loose gravel from under a stone which is up on blocks. Never carry a stone that is too heavy for you.

"Look, Camille, I tried to do the best thing. If Dinah felt she wanted something else, she never told me about it."

"Did you talk to her parents?"

"Talked to her father. He had suspected that Dinah was out having sex with a lot of boys. He didn't seem surprised that the girl wound up in trouble."

"Tom, we're not talking about the same event. You say Dinah was in trouble, but I think it's the boys who should have been in trouble."

174

"Of course they were. They got their share of trouble. It could have ruined their lives, for God's sake."

"Then you think it's lucky that it only ruined the life of a poor dumb girl. You think it would be more of a loss if some damn kid didn't go to Princeton than it is for Dinah to have this baby?"

"She didn't have to have the baby. Her mother spent a lot of time arguing with her. I don't understand what happened. It was all set up for Dinah to have an abortion, and then she didn't get one. Her parents were determined that she'd have an abortion. I can't figure what happened." Tom took my hand in his.

"Tom, I don't know how I feel about this, but you don't even seem to understand what really happened that night."

How to Split Granite or Limestone

You need good strong tools. You need a grinding chisel with a flattened top, a hammer of about three pounds with two pounding surfaces, a metal rod with a curved tip.

Grasp the chisel and hold it vertically over a marked point. Strike with the hammer. After each blow, turn the chisel clockwise. Cut six holes. Put in each hole two metal shims with a wedge between them. Using a sledgehammer, pound the wedges into the stone. Remove them and insert larger wedges. A crowbar will then split the stone. If two persons are available, a line can be drawn on the stone and one man can move a sledgehammer across the line while the second person hits it with another sledgehammer.

"I think you shouldn't worry so much about it, Camille." Tom played with my fingers as he talked. "I know this is a messy business, but it shouldn't ruin your summer. We've had a good time together, and we can go on having a good time if you'll let us."

"Did you get friendly with me and date me just to try and keep me quiet?" I had to ask even if I hated his answer.

"Of course not. I'm dating you because we have a good time together. That's as good a place as any for a man and a woman to start."

The Foundation

Dig a hole for the foundation stones about three and a half or four feet wide and deep enough to hold at least one layer of heavy stone. Leave small spaces between the first layer of stone and fill the spaces with crushed rock for drainage. Lay flat stones over these rock-filled gaps to prevent the dirt from seeping in.

I couldn't tell if Tom was lying or not. He held my hand and put his other arm around me. His right hand massaged my neck tenderly.

"Listen, honey, there have been Dinahs in the world since time began, and people like us and your Aunt Nell have been stuck with cleaning up their messes. Dinah's going to be all right. She's a healthy girl."

"How in the world could those boys do that? You say you raised your nephew. What did you teach him?"

"Same things everybody teaches their kid. Taught him to ride a bike, put up a tent, tie a diamond hitch. I taught him to hunt and how to catch trout and tie flies. I threw balls with him. I didn't do anything different. There's nothing wrong with that, is there?"

"I guess not. I just wonder what went wrong."

Raising the Wall

The formula for laying the stones is one over two, two over one. This means that you lay two stones over one large stone, and then a single large stone covers those two on the next layer. Every stone must be level and touch every stone around it. As the wall rises, every stone should cast its own shadow. Then the wall will not curve in as it rises. The stones should overlap on each layer, leaving no deep cracks when viewed from above.

"Maybe I spoiled him," Tom said. "Maybe he got things too easy."

"But Tom, all this hunting and fishing stuff, that's not the point. What did you tell him about women and sex and all that?"

"I never told him how babies are made, if that's what you mean. They all get that in school anyway."

"But how could he treat a girl like that?"

"I don't know. I never said anything to him that all men don't say."

Corners

A weak corner can cause the collapse of each adjoining section of wall. Construct your corners carefully. Lay each stone so that it binds the stones on each side as well as those below and above. The largest slabs provide good stones for corners and the finishing stones for the wall's top layer.

"What do you mean, you never said anything that other men don't say?" I asked.

"Well, shit, Camille. Men look at women. They talk about them. You know. Like whistling at a pretty girl, or something. What in the hell's wrong with that?"

Strengthening the Wall

All the stones must be level. This cannot be said too often. The pull of gravity will gradually loosen any stones set at a slant. In winter the water that seeps between the stones will freeze.

*When water freezes it expands by 1/12 its own bulk. This ac-
tion of water will move the stones in a wall. If the stones are
set level, the wall will merely rise slightly. Any slant in the
stones will cause the wall to gradually buckle and fall apart.*

"I don't know if anything's wrong with it."

"You really want men to just sit and not say a word about
women? We're just human. I can't be a saint."

"I don't want you to be a saint. I just want you to be honest."

"It's not a question of honesty. It's a question of reality. I
didn't have a philosophical problem to sit on my butt and deal
with. I had to drive over there at three A.M. and do what I
could."

"You don't see that Dinah was raped and you helped cover it
up?"

"I see that Dinah didn't get dragged through court and humi-
liated. I see that she is being cared for now. If you think it's easy
taking care of something like this, let's see you do any better."

Tools

*It takes a certain number of tools to build a stone wall.
Assembling these before you begin simplifies the building. You
will need:*

1. *A stoneboat for moving the largest stones*
2. *A yardstick*
3. *A strong wooden level*
4. *A pinch bar*
5. *A five-foot crowbar*
6. *Several spades with long and short handles*
7. *A pickax*
8. *A fifteen-pound sledgehammer, a three-pound hammer, two
   bevel-edged hammers*

9. *Six or seven sets of metal wedges and shims*
10. *A stone-dust remover and hand drills*
11. *An old ax blade*
12. *As many wooden blocks as you can gather together and several planks*

◇

"You don't look happy." Aunt Nell stared at me. "You've got that droop at the corners of your mouth like you always got as a child. You can't fool me."

I drank my iced tea and didn't answer. I wasn't sure that Aunt Nell would sympathize with my romantic problems.

"Have you heard from your husband lately?"

"Oh sure. I got a letter last week, as you know good and well since you brought it out to me at the cemetery."

"Well, how is he?"

"He wants to become a jet-setter, and that isn't a black hunting dog, Aunt Nell."

"I know what that means. I read as much as you do, Camille. Why on earth would he want to do that?"

"He just took a new job. He and a friend started a brokerage house of their own, and it has been incredibly lucrative in the last few months. They are apparently pretty good at picking stocks, and Henry has been having lots of elegant lunches with elegant people. They're the ones that have the money to invest, after all. Maybe he wants to hang out with the fast set so they will invest their money with him. I don't know."

"Is that what's worrying you?" Aunt Nell watched me closely.

"Nope. Henry can do whatever he likes for all I care. It's just that I'm upset about Tom Church. I spent yesterday with him, and then I sat out at my tent last night and thought. Don't get upset when I tell you this. I'm not following in my father's footsteps, but I sat there and drank gin until I passed out. I never do that. I haven't been drunk more than three times in my life, but I just needed to pass out last night."

"Did it make you feel any better?"

I shook my head. "No. I feel the same today plus a headache and all the symptoms of booze. In addition to feeling bad, I also look like hell. Liquor and aging women don't mix."

Aunt Nell looked at me sympathetically. "Tom isn't very good for you, it seems."

I nodded unwillingly. "It isn't really his fault."

"Why do women always defend men?" Aunt Nell said to herself. Looking at me, she went on. "You remind me of your grandfather. He once tied on a drunk that lasted for three days."

"When was that?" I asked in amazement. "I thought he was a teetotaler all his life."

"This was before you were born, before your father was born. Your grandfather wasn't so sober-sided then. He ran around with a pretty wild bunch when he was in his twenties. That was when Carry Nation was leading the battle around here to vote for temperance and destroy the saloons."

"She was crazy, wasn't she?"

"Well, you can't hold some queer behavior against Carry. She was of good stock. She was a Moore from over in Garrard County. It isn't Carry's fault if she was odd. Her mother thought she was a lady-in-waiting to Queen Victoria. Then she promoted herself and became the Queen. She sent one black man ahead of her coach with a hunting horn to announce her royal visits when she went out, and she had a little black boy riding on the back in a fancy uniform like a footman. Carry's grandmother lived in one room all her married life and gave birth ten times in that room but wouldn't come out. One of Carry's aunts thought she was a weathervane and they had to go out in all kinds of weather and pull the poor woman off the roof."

"My God."

"True. She certainly had burdens to bear. Her own daughter was crazy and had to be put in a hospital. It must have been terrible for her to see that."

"She was violent on the subject of drinking because her family moved to Kansas. Not that people in Kentucky didn't drink hard enough, but those people who drifted west were a mixed bunch. Some of them were failures who kept trying new places. Sitting out there in sod houses on the plains, lots of men drank themselves to death. Carry's first husband was an alcoholic who died when he was still young."

"I never can understand why the wives didn't just leave the drunks when they were married to them," I said. "I know that divorce was a stigma then, but it must have been preferable to living with a drunk. I always thought my mother got off light when she died so young." I meant this. It had been simpler for my mother than trying to deal with my father.

"It wasn't quite so easy back then. Carry Nation said that she was fighting drink for the sake of women, and it was true. Oh, a woman could get divorced, but she couldn't own property, so the man got everything they had and anything she had brought with her into the marriage. Besides, the husband could take the children away from her if she left him. The woman couldn't go off and leave the children with a drunk who probably took them just to spite the wife.

"Your grandfather and his friends used to drink and hunt and fish and play cards and then they'd write letters to one of Carry's newspapers. She had two of them, one called *The Hatchet* and the other *The Smasher's Mail*. Your grandfather and his cronies would write lots of funny letters about the glories of drink, and Carry just put them with no comment in a special column with the title 'Letters from Hell.'

"Poor Carry. She had a chair broken over her head in Elizabethtown. She called Elizabethtown a 'bad rum town,' and it was for her. They nearly killed her. She got crazier as she got older. There was actually congenital syphilis in the family, but no one knew how to treat it then.

"Your grandfather was a real Kentuckian. He liked his bourbon and his corn likker like all the young men, and he wasn't interested in temperance at all. But then he married your grandmother, and she wouldn't have it. She cleared out his rowdier friends and he settled down."

Aunt Nell was silent and stared over the coleus, which unfolded in the shade of the porch with purple and red and green leaves.

"It's hard to say what happened. They had been married about a year, and your grandfather got drunk. He went out and drank with his old friends for two or three days. I didn't know about this till later, and your grandmother never said a word about it. The town watched, and I heard from the grapevine.

"It seems that he arrived down on the river at one of those floating gambling boats where they kept poker games going. He was drunk when he got there, and he stayed there for three days. When he got back home, she was gone."

"Where'd she go?" I asked. My grandparents had always been sober and dignified and represented everything that my father was not. The thought of my grandfather drunk and my grandmother running away was astounding.

"Let me show you." Aunt Nell went into the back bedroom and came out with a cardboard box. It was full of snapshots, letters, and postcards. She flipped through a stack of pictures and handed me two. One showed a young woman standing in front of a grassy mound of earth. The other showed the same girl on the frail platform of what looked like a viewing stand about fifty feet high. I knew it was my grandmother because of her one blue eye, which showed light, and the dark spot of her brown eye. Her chin was set and determined, but her face was somber. I noticed with pain that her mouth drooped the way mine did when I was sad.

"These were taken up in Ohio, where she went. She packed everything she owned. She took every stitch of clothing and her Bible and all the material she had just bought to make dresses. She packed up and ran off to her older sister's in southern Ohio. She stayed three weeks, and this picture was taken during the visit."

"But why did she go up there? Was she that angry that grandfather was drunk? She must have known that he drank sometimes if he had done it before they were married. I'm surprised that she didn't just stay home and take a stick to him when he staggered in."

Aunt Nell sat looking at the picture. She didn't say anything.

"But what happened?" I persisted.

"Nobody knows that for sure," she said, handing me the picture brusquely. "She had gone to her doctor and found out she was pregnant that afternoon. Then your grandfather got home.

That night he arrived drunk down on the river. She left the next morning early on the train for Louisville, and he stayed drunk for three days. Her sister and her brother-in-law got her and took her up to their place."

"But what on earth is she doing on top of that platform? All those spindly little steps! What on earth was she doing?"

Aunt Nell glanced at the picture. "That is one of the tourist attractions in southern Ohio. That's the platform where you climb up and can look down on the Serpent Mound. You know about that. It's one of the mounds that the Indians built, heaven knows when. It could be two thousand years old. It's huge. The Indians heaped up rocks and covered them with piles of earth five or six feet high. They made the shape of a snake. The thing curls and twists for thousands of feet. The platform was built so you can stand up there and see the whole thing at once.

"The sister took your grandmother out there to entertain her. It's a beautiful place. You drive, or at least you did then, in a buggy up a winding dirt road to the top of a heavily wooded hill where there are grassy meadows and huge trees, some of the most beautiful trees you have ever seen. This great big snake sits on the top of the hill.

"I heard from Ruth, who was sister to Alice who worked for your grandmother, that it was a rainy day when they went to see the Snake Mound. Alice went to Ohio with her mistress. She knew your grandmother was pregnant, and she wouldn't let her go alone. Alice told Ruth that it began to get dark and the wind came up.

"Your grandmother was insistent that she climb up the steps and stand on the highest platform so she could see the whole thing. They couldn't dissuade her. She was determined to be able to see all of the snake at once. She was standing up there, alone, when they took the picture. It began to thunder and then a lightning storm started.

"I don't have to tell you, Camille, what a lightning storm is in this part of the country. A good bolt can split an oak tree in a second. Well, the sky just opened up and you could see the forks of lightning coming from miles up in the sky. Everyone stood on the ground and screamed at your grandmother to come down. The viewing platform is wood, but the steps and railings are all metal. It was a perfect lightning rod. They just knew she'd be killed.

"But she stood on the platform and didn't move. She looked at that big serpent rising out of the earth and coiling in the woods, and she didn't say a word. Finally, Alice ran up the stairs and dragged her down. Alice was a good woman with a lot of sense. She knew that someone had to go up there. No one else was willing to put a foot on those metal stairs while the lightning was coming down.

"The mound is impressive. At the head of it it looks like the jaws are open and it holds a circle of earth like an egg in its mouth. It's a beautiful thing to find rising out of nowhere in the woods."

"You've seen it?" I asked.

"Yes."

"But why did she go up there? What on earth happened between her and my grandfather? Surely he wasn't unhappy to hear that she was pregnant. He always seemed to like children."

Aunt Nell picked up our glasses and put them on a tray. She stacked our plates beside the glasses and lifted the tray. "It doesn't matter. That's old stuff. But your grandfather never drank another drop when your grandmother came home. Not a drop. Ever. Look at you," she went on tartly. "Maybe you should take a page out of his book."

She went into the house and left me sitting there. I couldn't imagine either of my grandparents acting so strangely, but then it's hard to know your own people.

S*HAWNEE* Three hundred years before Christ met the woman at the well, four hundred years before the fall of Jerusalem, a people lived in the forests in the heart of a continent and built mounds for their dead. They made copper replicas of falcons, and pipes carved to represent the animals who danced the dance of life with them.

And they laid their babies on a board and strapped them down firmly to make them straight and to teach them, perhaps, that life is something that you are tied to whether it pleases you or not. And a spot on the back of their heads became flat from the board of their first reality, shaping their very skull bone and giving them a skull that was different from that of the white men and women.

They were not like other Indians. They had no ancestral lands neatly partitioned off for them and their children. They spent the summers in Ohio and built houses of bark and trees which they abandoned casually when winter came. Then they wandered throughout Kentucky and Tennessee and anyplace else they wanted to go. And they were welcomed by Creek, Delaware, Miami, Wyandot, and Cherokee. Living off the land, they were willing to join with these people and be traveling mercenaries. For the right to hunt and live on the land, the Shawnee joined with other tribes to fight mutual enemies. They were warriors.

A more stubborn and difficult group was seldom encountered by the whites. The Shawnee were suspicious of the habit of white people to stay in one place, depending on the crops they grew for their food. It was not correct.

To hunt was the way to be alive in the forests. Feeling the power of the animal, joining in a dance of movement that must end in death, becoming one with the animal until the hunter turned as the animal turned, the hunter turned before the animal knew it was going to turn, and the animal followed the power of the hunter—this was the way for a real people to live.

Hiding in the brushy edges of the river, the Shawnee watched the huge buffalo swim the Ohio, snorting and plunging, great waves of them darkening the green water in the summer sun. The animals staggered ashore and were killed and eaten—the fat humps, the delicate tongue and succulent eyes, tasted and known to the Shawnee people. The hunters watched in the light of dawn as the wrinkled eyelids of wild turkey fluttered and quivered in death and closed upward over the shiny eye. And this was the correct thing to do. Life was also death. The animals danced their dance and died to feed the Shawnee, and the men and women watched their death and felt their own life inside themselves. Seeing the deaths of deer and rabbit and raccoon and fish,

185

the Shawnee knew their own death. They saw the shadow of their death coming closer with every gasp and cry of their prey, and this was as it was meant to be.

They followed the trails through Kentucky. The Great Warriors Path led through the wilderness at the Cumberland Gap and allowed the Indians to squeeze between the mountains into Virginia. The Buffalo Trace led from where the buffalo swam the Ohio River every year to the salt licks southward in the middle of the state. If not these trails, there were paths made by animals, paths on the top of hills which were blown clean of snow and trails in the valleys where the hunting was good.

At night they lay under skins and watched the stars circle and wheel over them. The men embraced their women, who tasted of the sweet syrup of maple sugar which had boiled in kettles all day, or who tasted bitter from the steam of the kettles at the salt licks where the water was boiled out to leave the pale granules of salt. The sweet and the bitter. It was all correct.

But the whites came. They wanted land. They believed that they could own the land. As Davy Crockett said, "I've shot and chopped and drowned the critters. I've fried 'em by the houseful and roasted 'taters in their grease."

The words were all separate. "Grease" and "Shawnee" and "white" were all separate things. It wasn't difficult for the whites to see how easy it was to cut off that one word, Shawnee. It could be separated from the rest of the language, dropped, killed, made a thing apart. Soon the whites would forget the word itself. There was no unity in the English language that made impossible the loss of a word, or the loss of an entire people. Every thing was a separate object. Every man for himself.

So the Shawnee were made to live in Oklahoma. There were no forests. There were no deep rivers and the game was scarce. They refused to give up their language or to adopt the religion of their conquerors.

And at night when they embraced their women, the women tasted no longer of maple sugar or the cutting bitterness of salt. There were no sugar maples or salt licks in Oklahoma. The men loved their women, but it was not the same. The smell in their beds was more likely to be rye whiskey and the dirt of poverty.

The taste in their mouth was defeat and the unnatural life of permanent houses and fences, and the metallic spikes of barbed wire cut their hearts out to dry in the relentless, dusty sun of Oklahoma. The Great Serpent still coiled in the forest of Ohio, but no one knew anymore how to make it dance.

Dear Camille,

I am doing just great in my new business. John and Frank and I are even thinking of hiring a commodities broker to add to our firm, and we are rolling in money. The trucking stocks have done well, and my portfolio is up.

I have been thinking about us a lot. You know, I have dated a lot of women, but they weren't the sort of people who could live the way I can see myself living for the next ten years or so. What I need is a smart woman who can entertain and be able to organize things at home while I am getting rich. Getting rich for both of us, of course.

It has hit me recently that we have been really lucky not to have any children. When I think what most of our friends are going through with their teenagers and drugs and beer parties and smashed-up cars, I think we got lucky. What the hell do kids do for you, anyway? They are expensive and might grow up to be drug dealers or bums as easily as go to Stanford or be interesting adults. How many people do you know who honestly like their kids? Not many. I think we got off light.

And that comes round to what I want to say. I don't want to get hung up with a woman with three kids who is trying to survive with no alimony and little child support. Kids are like stones around your neck. What I want is to live. I just want to do all the things we couldn't afford to do before.

I'll be able to get a condo at Squaw Valley or around Tahoe somewhere by next winter. We could travel in the summer, go to the places where really interesting people hang out. With no kids to worry about, we can give parties, too. There is a real party circuit in San Francisco, and we could be part of it as much as anybody else.

I know we never did stuff like that before, but with the right clothes and a house that is better suited for parties, you could be as good-looking a hostess as any woman I know. You might like it. I handle the money of a few women in San Francisco who live the good life, and they seem to enjoy themselves a lot. (No, I do not sleep with them. I don't sleep with women when I'm managing their money.) They play tennis and go to all those places for lunch where you used to want me to take you. It's a nice life.

How about it? It might as well be you and me, the way I figure it. We've known each other for too many years to let something silly come between us. Granted, I shouldn't have slept with one of your friends, but so what? Things like this happen in every marriage. Why drop the marriage over something that is past and done for. I don't want to run around and sleep with a lot of women. Frankly, I'd rather do a big push and get rich.

I'm coming to Kentucky to talk to you about this. I have to be in Louisville and Nashville to visit some companies. I will land in Nashville July 23 on Eastern flight #67. Can you meet me there about two o'clock?

Hopefully,
Henry

It didn't really surprise me that Henry was trying to stick with our marriage and make up our differences. He had changed a lot since we were married, but we had a certain bond that had tied us together for all these years.

I remembered our first date. We were going to see a film that had an alcoholic woman in the opening scenes. "Do you mind if we go?" Henry had asked me tensely. I was surprised, but, trying to be charming to this slender, handsome man who was a graduating senior with a marvelous future ahead of him, I said, "Sure. I don't care."

Henry walked along the sidewalk with his hands shoved into his pockets and stared at the air in front of him. I tagged along at his side, wondering what was wrong. "Are you all right?" I asked.

Facing me, Henry stared defiantly into my eyes. "You may not want to go out with me again," he said. "I hate telling you this, but I might as well."

"Oh, that's all right. Don't feel like you have to—"

"No, I will," he said. "Both my parents were alcoholics. My father left us when I was only ten, and then my mother and I lived in a series of flophouses and hotel rooms until she died when I was sixteen. I got a job helping out in a store and the guy that owned the store let me sleep in a room behind the storeroom. I finished high school that way. My mother"—he hesitated and clenched his fists, shaking them as if he would hit me—"my mother was the biggest bitch in the world. She was utterly rotten. I hate her."

"It's all right." I was trying to be soothing. "It's OK. I know what you mean."

"Nobody knows what I mean," he said, the full weight of self-pity darkening his voice. "I lived with two people who couldn't even manage to crap in the toilet most of the time. I spent my first years learning to heat cans of soup and clean up vomit. But she wouldn't let me go. Not her. She'd dress up and go to court and cry and they'd let her have me again. Then we'd move to another town where she didn't have any bar bills yet."

I stood there on the sidewalk in that beautiful college town and felt the tears in my eyes. "I know, I know." I was laughing and he glared at me. "No, I'm not laughing at you." I was laughing harder now and crying too. "I know just what you mean. My father drank all day and all night. I don't know how I would have made it without my Aunt Nell. My God! He even used to bring this goat in the house."

Henry and I fell on each other. He told all. I told all. The stories were not unlike. We ended up going back to my dorm, where I signed in with a flourish and then sneaked out a fire escape. Henry stood under the ladder and caught me when I dropped to the ground. We went back to his apartment and sat drinking coffee and talking until the sun rose. We couldn't bear to leave each other all day. He cut his classes and sat beside me in mine, holding my hand. We walked all over the campus, kicking the leaves out of our path and talking, talking, until we were hoarse about what it had been like. All the terrors came out, all the shame and humiliation and some of the anger.

That night we went back to his apartment and slept together

in his single bed, too afraid to dare make love for fear of messing up what we felt, too tired to talk anymore, just clutching each other in our sleep like drowning swimmers who have finally found dry land.

I remembered what Henry had said the next morning over eggs and juice.

"Orphans. We're orphans both of us," he said. I had nodded. He was right. We had both endured and survived and had been orphaned together. We knew what it had been like. I knew what he had suffered and he knew what I had also suffered. It was not a bond to discard lightly.

THE ORPHANS In 1809 a baby was born in a log cabin in Kentucky and given the name Abraham. He was named for the patriarch, the father of the Israelites, and he was four years old when another baby was born in 1813 and named Jefferson after the brilliant, red-headed author of the Declaration of Independence. The two babies were born in Kentucky, but neither family was content there. The children were moved to other places, one going North and one being taken South, and thereby hangs the issue.

Had both children remained in the state where they were born, had they both been carried North or carried South, then things might have happened differently. But they were divided from their birthplace and were fated to become enemies. Abraham Lincoln remained in the North and became President of the beleaguered Union. Jefferson Davis was made head of the Confederacy of the South, and so the bloodiest period of American history was to be presided over by two men born in Kentucky.

The boy didn't know anything about Abe Lincoln and Jeff Davis. Oh, his father talked a lot about it at the dinner table, but the details weren't interesting to a boy of nine or ten. History wasn't important to him, but at twelve he knew what he had to do. His heart was not in the Union cause. His father talked about the "just cause of the Union," but the boy couldn't feel it. He buttered his bread and drank his milk and said please and thank you and thought about it, but he couldn't *feel* anything for the Yankee cause.

It was the South that had captured his heart and fancy, the South with her cry of freedom and independence, the South which was the underdog already and fighting for her life, the South with the gaiety of spontaneous causes and the opportunity of a new nation being created. He dreamed of this new, foolhardy country rising up unshackled by the deliberations of men like his father. His father and his father's friends were not men of imagination. They tended their stores and clerked in banks and bought and sold and lay snoring in bed beside their fat wives. They were cautious and careful and liked to "go through proper forms." It had no spirit. It rested heavy on a twelve-year-old boy.

They lived on the Ohio River in a town small enough to fit in the bend and crook of the river as it flowed to the Mississippi. People in the town were not for this Southern rebellion. Being townspeople and small farmers, they didn't need slaves in any quantity, and the causes of large landowners in Georgia and Alabama were not their causes. The boy floated on the surface of the town like a waterbug. He darted here, he listened there. It was reported that he hadn't been in school for three weeks, for which he was whipped with a willow switch on his legs until welts came up.

It wasn't the whipping that did it. He always used to tell his children later that the whipping wasn't the thing. He ran off because of his joy, not his pain. There was a dream, a vision of a new country that had captured his soul the same way his great-grandfather had been captivated by the dream of a new republic a century before.

The place to go was Bowling Green. It sat squarely on the Louisville and Nashville railroad lines where the line from Memphis joined the main tracks. Everything that had to pass through Kentucky to the South or to the North passed through the train station at Bowling Green, so this was where he ran. Here the army was forming.

Of course he lied about his age. He claimed to be seventeen, and when this was met with laughter, changed slowly to sixteen.

He was registered a member of the 1st Kentucky Brigade and given the job of drummer boy. Never having played a drum was no handicap. None of the men pouring into Bowling Green had done any soldiering, and his faulty drumbeats only seemed correct in the heat and the dust and the chaos of early drilling.

They lined up and drilled irregularly, some with bare feet and squirrel rifles, most confused by any military terms, laughing and joking all day, roasting fat bacon on sticks at night and eating pans of cornbread, drinking everything and anything, singing, dancing, raising hell in the town, and just generally enjoying themselves.

Having lived on isolated farms, never exposed to any community life, some of the men caught every germ in the camp. There were deaths from measles and mumps, typhoid and chicken pox, but that was to be expected. Other diseases not discussed so openly were passed around between the soldiers and any willing girl in town, but the boy didn't know that. It was in Bowling Green that the traits of the Kentucky Brigades became marked and first observed.

They had a tendency to stay drunk whenever there wasn't anything more interesting going on. They liked to sing, particularly sentimental songs that could bring tears to the eyes of elderly ladies and hardened generals alike. They carried large knives, so large that the officers objected to so much weight being packed unnecessarily, and they were excellent marksmen. They stole everything that wasn't nailed down, but stole with a lightheartedness, a hilarity of spirit that was like children stealing apples. They lied and told stories and played immense practical jokes on each other, and for relaxation they fought. The floors of the tents didn't get swept with regularity, nor was any menial work performed with any interest. Above all, they were gentlemen, and gentlemen didn't take orders or do menial work. There was some thought that these men would never be able to fight as an army, and their cussed individualism was the bane of their officers.

The boy's name was Lionel, so they promptly called him the Cub, and he was taken into their games and follies as one of them. He joined them in everything except their women, even drinking gingerly from their kegs and fighting halfheartedly with some of the smaller of the men. They liked him. He was a thin, short boy with intense black eyes and the dead white skin of his Irish ancestors, and he watched the camp with interest. So far, war was everything he had hoped it would be.

But it couldn't last. On Lincoln's birthday in 1862 the Kentucky Brigade marched away from Bowling Green, which wept for them and then sighed in relief and unlocked their daughters. The campfires down by the river were put out for a last time, and they were gone. No one knew then how long it would be before they could see their homes again.

The men marched singing, happy to be doing something at last, but as the Tennessee state line came nearer, they grew silent and angry. Why should they abandon their state to the infestation of the Yankees? Why not stand and fight?

Seeing their anger, the officers dismounted and led the men on foot over the state line into the South. John Cabell Breckinridge led the 1st Kentucky Brigade on foot into Tennessee, and he was as worried as they were. He had a much better idea of how serious this march was and he also knew what they were walking into.

The boy didn't know anything. He walked with his light pack and his drum and tried faithfully to beat out even measures for the men. By night his hands were numb, and he sat disconsolately on the back of a wagon. His feet were puffy and blistered, and in anger he threw his shoes away. They were the last shoes he would have for over a year.

They marched fast. They were going to their first battle, and the men could sense the noise and action up ahead. They hurried as if they were going to a lover.

The Cub saw the war coming toward him across a field. He had heard the noise for hours, but he first saw war in the shape of a cannonball that bounced and darted in his direction across a field like a rabbit. He just stood and stared and was saved only by an older man who grabbed his pants and pulled him out of its path. The Cub turned and watched it bounce on until it hit a man in the knee and he fell screaming. The men loaded their guns, many of them guns that John Brown had used in Virginia, guns that had been stored in Virginia arsenals and then shipped to Kentucky for Kentucky troops.

They marched in April to a place called Shiloh Church, where one of the loudest and bloodiest services of the war was held. The Cub saw the fighting secondhand as he marched through the battlefields already filled with dead men, dying men, screaming and moaning men, and shrieking, plunging horses whose tongues fell out of their mouths like rope.

They tried to keep the young ones out of the front lines. The Cub spent his days at Shiloh standing in a hospital tent, holding his chloroformed handkerchief over the faces of men while the steady scrape of the saw cut through flesh and bones. He saw legs and arms and feet and fingers and toes chopped and cut and sawn off and thrown in piles on the floor. He didn't flinch but couldn't eat that night. He thought it was a terrible thing and knew that God could do no worse for a man than to shatter his leg with a cannon at Shiloh. This was before he became a man. It was before he learned that chloroform was not inexhaustible in the South. This was before he learned to tie a man to a table so he couldn't move while they sawed away with no chloroformed handkerchief at all. He hadn't learned those knots yet.

Pitying his white face, one of the older men handed him a bucket and told him to go get some water. It was night. The battle was over for now. If they had water, the man would boil up a little tea for the Cub. That'd make him feel better if he couldn't eat the rancid pork and cornbread.

The boy took the bucket and walked through the woods to Shiloh Branch for water. It was black, black as night is after a day of looking at shells exploding and blood running out of bodies. His clothes were black in the night, and he couldn't see the stains of other men's blood. It was nice standing there listening to the creek flow by, standing on a log in the dark when it was so silent and it seemed that no man would dare fire a single bullet to disturb the quiet.

The log shifted softly under his feet and he jumped off with a shriek. The bucket fell and he reached for it, trying not to see that the log he had stood on was a man's body with no head, and the other logs floating by, caught on brush and hanging crazily into the water, the other logs were corpses too.

He got the water, but the tea didn't taste right. Tea made from Shiloh Branch wouldn't ever taste right again, he figured. On April 5 there had been 2400 Kentuckians around him. By April 8 there were only 1600.

At Vicksburg the Kentucky men were put down on the river to move supplies. They were shelled pitilessly by Union gunboats for two weeks, but there was humor too. When they were finally allowed to pitch camp inside the city, which sat on a bluff above the Mississippi, the men decided to have a race.

They caught two wild hogs, hogs turned loose so long ago in the woods that they had no memory of men and swilling troughs and pens. Two men volunteered to be jockeys, and they kicked the pigs into a wild gallop on their improvised racecourse. The enemy floating in the river heard a cheering and promptly began shelling the city. That was enough for the pigs. Being ridden by men and screamed at and kicked was one thing. Loud explosions near their tender sides was another.

The Cub shrieked with the other men and watched in dismay as one of the pigs headed for the edge of the cliffs. "Hold him back!" the men screamed, and then they screamed, "Jump, jump for God's sake!"

The man, determined to win his race, stubborn Kentuckian, ardent horseman that he was, stayed on the pig, not even condescending to jump off when the cliff was at his feet. Riding the pig, kicking it angrily to the last, he went over the cliff on the pig's back. The pig lived, but the soldier broke his neck, and the men killed the pig and ate it that night in anger.

The boy stood on the cliff and watched the pig and the soldier careen out into space, turn one gentle somersault, and land far below in a puff of dust. He waited to see what would happen, but the thing didn't work. No devils or demons were exorcised from the pig or the man on this day. The order came to march on.

They marched the hardest march of the whole war. It was hot, hot like the Cub had never felt, and the mosquitoes were rumored to carry their own whetstone under their wings to sharpen their beaks. It was his first encounter with yellow fever and malaria, and he watched the men die before they could get to Baton Rouge. They fought again when the end of the march came, but then they had to begin all over again. There was no end to it, no reasonable way to see when it would be done.

And it was about now that the name began. They called themselves the Orphans. The Kentuckians were the Orphan Brigade. They had lost officer after officer. Their leaders were shot down and left them or were transferred to lead Alabama men or Tennessee or Georgia men. Their land, their sweet motherland, was dead to them. They couldn't go home. They couldn't pay little visits with kin as the war dragged on. The Kentucky mail was run by the Yankees, and their letters could be delivered only by travelers going that way or by the circuitous path of Washington, D.C., and its enemy labyrinths. They were orphaned and alone. They weren't even true Confederates because their state was in the hands of the Union forces and hadn't properly seceded. Of all the soldiers and brigades in the Union and Confederate armies, only the Kentucky Brigades were completely made up of volunteers. They were lonely and felt that the war had orphaned them as surely as it killed their horses and rotted their coats and ruined their stomachs and filled them with rage and wet their pants with fear.

But their playfulness was never completely broken. The Kentucky troops had a reputation of being the hardest-fighting and hardest to discipline of all the Confederate troops. They had no use for formality and saw no sense to any order at all, except the order with which they flung themselves at the enemy. Rumor in the Yankee camps had it that the Kentucky brigades were at least half made up of wild Indians. Only Indian blood would explain the ferocity of their fighting. But what did they have to lose? They were orphans.

So in September they had a steamboat race as they were moved upriver, and they threw everything burnable into the furnaces of the steamboats, including finely carved doors and furniture and gaming tables, and one man drowned, but it was fun.

They finally got as far north as Knoxville. They were cheerful. Knoxville wasn't home, but Kentucky wasn't far away, and when they began to march north they sang and whistled and played hilarious jokes on each other.

Then it was before them, in their eyes' compass. The mountains that rolled down into the Cumberland Gap like a woman's hips when she lies down in a hammock, those mountains that were blue and hazy in the distance, rose up in front of them. They marched with determination. They would take their home from the enemy.

The Cub vowed privately to steal a horse and ride home, just for a few days, to let them know he was alive, to see his mother again and tell his father that war was not what any man said it was. But he never did it. They were turned back. There were more battles to be fought that couldn't wait on his mother's smile.

He had given up the drum. Drums were fine for drill, but men in battle couldn't hear them anyway. Besides, he had seen too many men lying dead to be contented with only a drumstick for a weapon. He picked up a Union rifle that lay still wet with the blood of a man who stared up at the sky and might have smiled to be out of it but that his face was half shot off. The gun gave the Cub a new purpose, a new life, and he learned to shoot it by aiming at men.

They fought at Stones Creek. They got to Vicksburg after the battle was lost and went on the Chickamauga, bloody Chickamauga. The Indians said that Chickamauga meant River of Death and the Cub agreed with them. At night they slept in the field and listened to the howls of dying men and horses rising up around them, but it was the first battle that was a victory for the Kentuckians.

They paid for their victory. The 2nd and 9th Brigades lost 248 men, half the men they had left alive, and one-third of the Orphans lay crushed after Chickamauga's river of death poured over them.

They played still, joking and entertaining themselves as fiercely as they fought. They stole books whenever they could and pored over anything printed that came to them. They still sang with tears in their eyes of their homes and their women.

They threw their officers into wheelbarrows and had hilarious, disgraceful races that left the officers black and blue and furious but laughing. They staged cockfights and kept pet dogs whom they fed better than they ate themselves, and if there had been a guardhouse, half of them might have been in it.

It wasn't so bad doing guard duty at night now. Since none of the men had shoes in February and March of 1864, they were allowed to leave their tents, look around, and hurry back to the tent. "Tent" was not the correct word. "Tent" meant any sort of shelter you could throw together with old rags and tree limbs. But tents were not their main problem.

It was Sherman. That Devil. That son of a bitch. That great soldier and iron man who cared nothing for weakness and the tender respect of home and family. He knew what he wanted. He wanted to win the war. He wanted to end this stinking, foul, filthy thing that had spawned death as a lecherous woman might spawn children. He would end the war if it cost him his good name in the South forever. And so it did. "Sherman" was never uttered in the South for nearly one hundred years without a shudder or a spit on the ground.

Sherman was marching toward Atlanta, and Joe Johnston was given the job of stopping him, deflecting him, slowing him down, doing anything he could to prevent what everyone saw coming down on the South. The Orphans were going with Joe. It was going to be glorious. True, they were outnumbered three to two by Sherman's forces. True, it would be the hardest overland campaign of the entire war. True, Sherman had a reputation of being a hard man to beat, but there were 1512 of the Orphans left out of nearly 4000 that had started off back in Kentucky, and they were always good men in a fight. Atlanta put her faith in Joe Johnston and prayed.

The Cub ceased being "the Cub" at Chickamauga. He had demanded and received the rank of lieutenant. He had killed and fought and run and thrown himself on the ground with the best of the men, and he had received his red badge of courage, a bullet passing cleanly through the stringy flesh of his left thigh. He was Lieutenant Lionel now, the little lion, and he led men when other officers older than he fell.

Of all 1512 Kentuckians at the beginning of the campaign against Sherman, only 513 were left to surrender when word finally got to them that Lee had given up at Appomattox twelve days before, on April 9. It had been a bloody dance with Sherman. They didn't have the guns. They didn't have the cannons and artillery. They didn't have the wagons and horses and clothes. They didn't even have food for days at a time. But mainly, by April, they didn't have the men. They were dead. Or wounded. Or left behind lying maybe dead, maybe alive, in the woods. The men just weren't there anymore.

Four thousand men walking out of Kentucky and only 513 left to go home. Of those 513, only 50 had never been wounded during the war. And the end was terrible. Constant skirmishes. Retreating. Trying to hold. Retreating again. Walking in circles to come up on more death and more hunger and more cannonballs flying at them from the inexhaustible Union supplies. No chloroform left. No army hospitals. No medicine and no clean bandages. Just the constant marching, marching, firing the gun if you had bullets and then marching again only to see the blue coats coming at you the next day.

They got word that it was over and they cried. If only they had had more guns, more horses. If only their officers were alive and their friends still by their side. If only the war could stop for a while and let them get breath, why they could go on and win this damn war. The war was their mother and father by this time. Home was so long ago, so far beyond Stones River and Vicksburg and Chickamauga and Sherman. The war had folded them to its bloody bosom and they didn't want to leave it. The Orphans had become war's children, and they wept when war was taken away from them. They felt abandoned again.

"I don't want to go home a lieutenant," he told his commanding officer, and the man looked at the boy, ravaged, sixteen-going-on-a-hundred, and he nodded.

"All right. You can go home a colonel. You've fought like a man."

And they sent around the camp until they found a sword that still looked like a sword, and he was knocked lightly on the thin bones of his sixteen-year-old shoulder and made a colonel. It was duly entered in the books two weeks before Appomattox, and he went home a full colonel.

They wandered home. Like men who have been to hell and allowed to return to the world of the living, they arrived on front porches and trailed into backyards. The colonel went home too, but his father was set against him for his stupidity at fighting for the wrong side, the side that had the bad taste to lose the war, so he moved South. He settled in a place called Toms Creek, and he worked for the saloonkeeper.

Old General Joe Johnston went home too. He hated to lose that war, but he was a soldier till the end of his life. Twenty-six years after he heard that Lee, that gray man whom Johnston had loved, had given up the fight, Old Joe went North to New York. He went to attend the funeral of a friend, General Sherman. Standing in a sleety rain, Joe stood bareheaded until a young aide whispered, "Please put your hat on, sir. You'll get sick."

"If I were in his place and he were standing here in mine, he would not put on his hat," Johnston said. Joe died from the severe cold he caught at the funeral, and Sherman had someone to talk to in heaven—or hell, according to some. The two old men walked out of life almost hand in hand, still dancing around each other as they had in the fields of Georgia.

But the Cub—or the Colonel, as he was called all his life— lived longer than Sherman, longer than Joe Johnston. He worked as a bartender and then owned the saloon, and he ran it in good order.

There was no fighting in his saloon. Any man who raised his fist was liable to feel the wiry arms of the Colonel throwing him out onto the dusty street, and no ears bitten off in fights were ever tacked over the Colonel's bar. He ran a clean place, never drank a drop, and lived to see his son, who cut his teeth on beer caps under the bar, become the leading citizen of the county.

His son loved politics and bay horses and lived to raise his own son, who drank too much, and see his own granddaughter go off to college. It was just as well that he never saw a dark-haired girl, his distant kin but with his black hair and dark eyes, give birth to a fatherless child in the hospital in Toms Creek in 1979.

The campaign had been long, and the battles had left the Colonel silent and still angry. He had fought. He had seen most of the men around him die, and they had not won. He often dreamed at night about the blood, the gallons of blood that he had seen spill and gush and trickle and flow from men's bodies, and he wondered if it would have felt different walking home to Kentucky barefoot and hungry if he had known that they had won. The Colonel was no fool. In his heart, he couldn't believe that it would have made all that much difference. Spilled blood was spilled. The fact of the blood changed a man. He didn't think it mattered anymore who had won. It was the blood that was the thing. The blood stayed in his dreams forever.

I was scared of Henry's coming to Toms Creek. Had he come before Dinah and I went to the Hermitage or maybe after the baby is born, I thought, then I might have known what to say to him. I might even have known how I stood. But Henry was coming to see me at exactly the wrong time.

It was this feeling of desperation that led me to go over to Tom's apartment early that morning. Henry had to be picked up in the Nashville airport that afternoon, and I had to settle things with Tom. I had to know where Tom and I stood before Henry started talking to me.

For the first time since I had been in Toms Creek, it became important that I look good. Resenting the feeling of trying to look pretty for two men in one day, I nevertheless spent the night at Aunt Nell's and washed and brushed and ironed like a teenager going out on a date.

And the summer had improved me. I was thinner, and the thinness gave my face an interesting quality. I was tan and in pretty good shape from swimming, and my dull hair was brightly sun-streaked with gold lines. I put on a raspberry-pink silk dress, simply cut but clinging, and my good shoes. Looking the best I could might give me the courage to ask questions, make demands, even to figure out what I wanted.

The cab dropped me at Tom's apartment building, and I knocked on his door with some curiosity and a lot of hopefulness.

I had never been to Tom's apartment before. He opened the door wearing his work pants and a T shirt. I had interrupted him as he was getting ready for a day at the building site.

"You're sure dressed up for breakfast. Come on in, honey."

"Good God, Tom," I said when I stepped into his apartment. "You weren't kidding about not caring what your apartment looks like. This is really amazing."

"Well," Tom said, moving some clothes off a chair so I could sit down, "I never have asked you to come over and clean it, so you can't complain."

I looked at the dishes with rinds of cheese and chicken bones on them, a glass of milk that had hardened to a jelly, newspapers everywhere. It was chaos.

"Well, I'll do a few dishes if you want." I began picking up plates.

"Nope." Tom took them out of my hands and put them back down. "I'm too liberated to let you do that."

I felt like a friendly dog that had invaded a fox's lair. Cleaning up his chicken bones for Tom just made him nervous.

"Are you liberated or do you just want to keep me out of your life?" I asked.

"You're in my life. We've been going out together this summer. It's been fun."

I stood up and looked out the window at the street. Nobody was on the sidewalk. It was quiet.

"You don't want to be a housewife over here. You left all that in California, didn't you?" he asked.

"That's true, Tom. You get tired of doing that stuff for someone who treats you like a cheap servant, but it's nice to be needed sometimes. Do you ever need a woman?"

"You ask me that?"

Tom put his arms around me and felt my breasts under the thin, pink silk. "You know I need you sometimes," he whispered into the back of my neck as he kissed it tenderly and ran his tongue down my shoulder over the silk.

I leaned back into his tall, heavy body and shut my eyes. He was warm and strong and smelled faintly of soap. I liked his hands and that made me sad.

"I like your hands," I said.

"Did you come up here to criticize my housekeeping or to have fun?"

"I don't know, Tom. I just came to see you because Henry is flying into Nashville this afternoon. I have to pick him up. He's staying the night and then going to Louisville on business."

Tom moved away from me. "Well, that's nice, Camille. Maybe you should think about getting back together with him. He dosen't seem like a bad guy."

"But I don't want him here, in Toms Creek, now. I don't know what to tell him."

"Tell him about what?"

"About Dinah. About us. About me, I guess."

"Look, Camille. Dinah is pregnant and going to be fine. You're having a vacation, and you don't have to say anything about me. What good would that do?"

"Do you feel anything for me, Tom? Do you care what I tell Henry?"

"I care about what's best for you," he said, but he didn't look at me when he said it.

I felt my face get hot. "The hell you do. You care about keeping Tom Church's skin safe. You care about making sure you put out for nobody. You don't give a damn about me."

"We had fun together. What more do you want?"

"Is that all it was for you? I was just the visiting fireman who kept you busy?"

"What do you want from me? I never promised anything. I gave you a good time. Fucking women. They always want more than they've got."

"We're just for fucking, aren't we? That's all you care about. Me and Dinah and all of us. Feel up our tits and fuck us."

I put my hands on the kitchen counter next to the window and felt the smooth, wooden handle of a hammer under my fingers. I gripped it in rage with both hands to keep from flying at Tom.

"That's sure all Dinah was good for, and the boys told me she wasn't even much good for that." He grinned.

"You talked to your nephew about Dinah? You talked about that girl like she was a piece of meat?"

"Tits and ass and cunt are meat. What else do you think they are?"

"You fucked me to keep me quiet. You never cared if it was me or anybody else, it was only because you worried that I'd make waves."

"I wanted sex and you were there. Why not take it? The trouble with you, Camille, you think too much."

"And Dinah was there, so they took her."

"She didn't mind that much. Besides, she had sex before with those boys, and she got in the car of her own free will. Nobody made her get in that car. What did she expect? She only got what they thought she wanted."

I raised the handle in my hands and swung it before Tom knew what I intended. The hammer glanced off his arm, which he threw up instinctively, and it grazed his skull hard enough to make him stagger.

I tried another blow, and he caught it on his shoulder. Wrenching the hammer away from me, he got in one good punch that hit my left eye. I shrieked and flew at him, hitting him with my fists, biting his hand when he pushed me away, crying out, *"You bastard, don't you ever say that. Goddamn you, she's just a girl."*

Tom hit back and we slugged it out. The first blow with the hammer had stunned him and made it a fairer fight, and I hit him with my fist squarely in his solar plexus, dropping him to his knees with a grunt.

He fell into me, clutching my thighs as he went down, dragging me down onto the floor. I realized that he was crying, crying the way a boy cries with his eyes tight shut and his mouth twisted in an effort to contain the tears.

We rolled over and over on the rug, my hand in his hair, too close for blows, struggling until we were exhausted. Tom's greater weight finally pressed me down onto the rug. He was saying something over and over.

"I loved him. I loved him. I loved him."

"You bastard," I said, but the rage was gone.

"You don't know. I loved him and he ruined it all. He ruined it. He's just a sheep. A fucking sheep. He's no good."

"Oh Tom," I said. "He was all you had."

"He was all I ever could love, and now I can't stand to sit in the same room with him. He looks at me and I can't meet his eyes. I hate him."

Tom rolled off me and onto his back. "I was just trying to protect him. He was so scared."

I lay against Tom's shoulder and I cried too. "It gets messed up so easy, doesn't it?"

"I didn't mean to make you feel bad, Camille. I did go out to the cemetery to see where you stood, but I didn't mean to sleep with you. That just happened. I'm sorry. Oh Christ, I'm sorry."

Half of me believed Tom and half of me didn't. There was blood in his hair where the hammer had grazed his scalp, and my dress was torn and dirty.

Tom leaned over my face. "Oh shit, I gave you a black eye." He looked carefully at my eye, touching it with his forefinger gently. "I guess nothing ever works out right," he said, and then he bent and kissed my eye as a mother might have.

I felt the eye swelling and cried, and Tom cried, and we kissed and clung together in our desperation at the awfulness of life. I felt warm and tired and sad, and I kissed Tom gently. His mouth tasted salty with blood and I didn't know if it was my blood or his. We made love as if we were two invalids who had been very sick and had to be careful not to make any sudden moves, any difficult gestures, for fear of breaking new bones. We made love delicately, cautiously, with great remove.

Tom drove me back to the cemetery in silence, and I knew we could never go back to night swims in the river and having fun. I wanted what Tom didn't have to give, and Tom wanted what he could get almost anywhere. Seeing Tom hadn't solved any problem of talking to Henry, but I knew where I stood now with Tom Church. I doubted that Tom and I would ever make love again.

I wore sunglasses to the airport. They were large and dark and hid my swollen left eye. I couldn't bear trying to explain that eye to Henry until I had thought of a decent story. Since I lived in a tent, there were no doors to bump into, and Henry knew me too well to believe any lie but the most crafty one. I had changed clothes and washed up. I looked pleasantly tan and relaxed when Henry got into the air-conditioned car that I had rented for my trip to Nashville.

"You're looking great, honey," he said, kissing me tentatively on the cheek. "Have you lost some weight?"

I admitted that I had, received compliments on my tan, and Henry told me all about what had been happening since I'd left San Francisco.

"The brokerage house is undoubtedly the best thing I've ever done for myself," he said. "We're doing great. I can work all day and it's different from before."

"Since you're working for yourself, you can take more time off," I suggested.

"Well, technically you're right, but actually I work even longer hours. Knowing that it's my business and that I get one-third of all the profits means that any hours put in seem less a waste somehow. I work all the time."

Henry sighed contentedly. He leaned back in the car and closed his eyes. I pointed out how pretty the countryside was and how lush everything must look after San Francisco's sun-dried hills, which burned yellow and then brown by July every year. Henry nodded but didn't seem interested.

"There isn't much around here, is there?" he asked.

I looked at the fields and the trees lining the road and had to agree. No, there wasn't much here. Just a lot of land, creeks, rivers, caves, little towns, farms. Not much compared to San Francisco or New York or London.

"Are you really living out at the cemetery?"

"Yep. It's mine. I own it and I'm entitled to live on it."

Henry shook his head. "Oh, come on now, admit it. You really spend most of your time living with your Aunt Nell, don't you?"

I shook my head. "I like living out there. I can see the river through the trees, and the fields are full of corn and tobacco plants behind the cemetery. I'm up on a little hill and I look down on fields and the river and the cemetery. It's real pretty."

"It's real quiet. I can't imagine you stuck in a town the size of Toms Creek for long. You've forgotten how much you love the city."

I thought about that as we drove into Toms Creek. It was true. I had forgotten the city. My days were slipping past so quietly that I might have even forgotten my life. I looked at Henry and touched him on the arm. "I'm glad you're here. You've never seen where I grew up."

Henry smiled and nodded. He stared out at the checkerboard painted on the feed-and-grain store. I smiled at him. If a man like Henry came all the way to Toms Creek to see me, I must still be worth something, I thought. It made me feel uneasy, though. I was resisting the rush of gratitude. I held back and didn't want to throw myself into his arms or run away with him. Maybe I preferred being a nobody all my life.

Aunt Nell was standing on the porch with her best straw hat on. It was huge, even by Aunt Nell's standards, and covered her head like a low umbrella.

"Come in, come in," she cried. It was beautiful. Aunt Nell and Dinah had cleaned the house and set the table with her best crystal and china. On the table was a country ham covered with brown-sugar glaze, a clove centered in each neat diamond pattern. There was salad and summer squash and biscuits and beaten biscuits, and, I was sure, peach pie for dessert. Water in crystal glasses, iced tea, and even a bottle of wine chilled and ready for Henry, now the man of the house, to uncork and serve.

Aunt Nell removed the hat with decorum and hung it on the coat tree in the hall. She stared at my sunglasses and said, "Take those silly things off and we'll eat."

I shook my head and walked into the dining room.

"This is just incredible," Henry said after his fifth piece of country ham. I knew he would be drinking water all night from the salty meat, but he ate on happily.

"Well, I don't get a chance to cook for a man very often." Aunt Nell twinkled and dimpled at Henry until I nearly threw up.

"You could cook for me and Dinah," I said.

"Oh, you're always trying to lose weight, and Dinah shouldn't eat too much rich food now." Aunt Nell smiled at Dinah. "It won't be but a few weeks now," she said.

Henry was flirtatious and charming and pretended much more interest in Dinah than I knew he really felt. Dinah was just a small-town girl, not very bright, who was doomed to a boring life, as far as Henry was concerned.

As we left, I shot an angry look at Aunt Nell. "You sure do know where the butter is on my bread," I said.

"Oh, don't be silly, Camille. It isn't that. I think he is a perfectly nice man, and I'd just love to see you happily married again."

"When was I ever happily married?" I asked petulantly as Henry and I left.

The cemetery was lush and rolling and the graves were neatly clipped and tended. My tent was nearly hidden under the trees on the hill. Henry admired the view of the fields and the glints of river between the trees.

"Do you want to take a swim?" I asked. I wasn't sure that I wanted Henry in my river.

"What I want to do is sit here and talk to you."

Henry put on a pair of shorts and a knit shirt and sat on the grass. He looked at me with satisfaction. "You're looking good," he said.

I was resentful. Everything was at its best for Henry, the food, the hospitality, even me. It was all designed to reflect on him and be there for his delectation. I knew I was being silly. There was nothing wrong with Henry's enjoying himself and enjoying Aunt Nell. What did I want?

I was thinking so hard that I forgot my eye and took off the sunglasses absentmindedly. I chewed on one of the ear pieces and Henry stared at me.

"Oh my God! What happened to your eye? No wonder you kept those glasses on. Good God, have you seen it?"

I went into the tent and got a hand mirror and stared at my face. In the tanned skin a blue stain began near my nose and spread up to engulf the whole eye. My eye showed no white but stared out like a marble buried in a plum. The plum with an eye, I thought gloomily.

Henry was in the tent beside me. He turned me firmly around and stared at the eye. All my lost weight and tan were overwhelmed by the ugliness of my eye. I shut both eyes and felt the tears squeezing out from under my lids. Everything was perfect for Henry except, as usual, me. I was the one jarring note in his little vacation.

"How did it happen?"

I didn't answer. I suddenly wanted to tell all, drop limply on Henry's shoulder, and howl and blubber and hear his indignation. I wanted to hide in him and let him be angry for me.

"I've been dating someone . . ." I began.

"Jesus Christ! Are you telling me that some guy did this? My God, Camille, who in hell are you going around with?"

"He isn't that sort of person at all," I said. I didn't want Henry to think I was dating losers and men of low character. "He is a contractor and builds houses and apartment buildings and things. He isn't so terrible, but we had a fight."

"I never knew a man who was decent who would give a woman an eye like that. I mean, we've fought, but I never hit you, did I?"

"Well, I hit him first, and it just sort of happened. He felt terrible about it." I was crying harder now. In the light of Henry's normal reaction, my bruised eye seemed monstrous, unforgivable, shameful. I sobbed, not knowing whether I should tell how I had fought until Tom quit fighting and then how we made love.

"Well, I can tell it's about time that I got here." Henry's chest swelled in indignation. He was John Wayne and the cavalry saving the helpless lady in distress. His eyes glinted with the honest wrath of a good Indian-killer.

"You poor baby," he said and folded me into his arms. "Don't worry, it's going to be all right. You don't have to date any more monsters. I can take care of you."

Henry was kissing me. "Lie down and let me see. Have you had a doctor look at it yet?"

I lay down and Henry lay beside me on the sleeping bag. He

examined the eye and then began kissing me again. I felt sad and helpless. It was true. I was a beaten woman. I turned to Henry crying and said, "Oh, Henry, oh, Henry—"

And so it was that at eight o'clock in the evening on July 23, I made love for the second time in one day, this time with my husband, a man absolutely noble in his intentions and incorrect in his assumptions. I succumbed to his lovemaking like going under water. I was passive and feminine and shy and let him save me with his ardor. Henry was there. I was safe and secure. He would take care of me and never let another man hit me.

We spent the night together and slept deeply. It was seven when we woke up the next morning, and Henry had to get dressed quickly to get to Louisville on time. He was meeting with the vice president of a company that made paper containers, and he didn't want to be late.

"You just get Dinah through with her little mess, and then you fly back to San Francisco," he said. "It's obvious that you aren't making it here. There isn't anything in Toms Creek to hold your interest anyway. I'll get things set up, and maybe we can buy a new house, travel a little, entertain some."

Kissing me firmly on the mouth, he said over his shoulder as he moved toward the airline terminal, "We are finally going to get what we've wanted, and I'm going to give it to you."

I waved good-bye and watched him disappear into the crowd. He was offering me a new chance, a new life of elegant lunches and ski trips and gambling parties by the shores of Lake Tahoe. I knew what he wanted. I had read about people like that in the columns of the San Francisco papers every Sunday. He was going to give me everything that I couldn't get for myself, plus the security of his presence—his maleness and stability that would keep the wolves of life at bay. No one would ever hit me with Henry as my husband.

I thought about the marriage we had had and the marriage that lay in front of me. It wasn't the sort of thing I had been trained to expect, but there was no reason to think that a marriage in 1979 should be like marriages in 1940 or 1879 or 1840. I didn't know what to think about marriage anymore. There had been times, I had been told, when marriages were enduring and lasted, when families were close and loved each other. I didn't know if that was just one more lie to join all the other lies I had uncovered, or if there was something wrong with me that I couldn't get that glorious state. I drove back to Toms Creek and thought about the marriages I had known and the marriages I had been told about. Marriages and families floated through my head like menus. I had to think about it.

A GOLD THIMBLE
AND EMBROIDERED ROSES

When I was a child, my great-grandmother Georgia lived with Aunt Nell. She had the back bedroom upstairs and spent most of every day reading with the aid of a large magnifying glass. When I was three she taught me to read by sitting me in her lap with a Bible on the table in front of us. "See that word?" she would demand. "That says 'revelation.' Now. You find another 'revelation' on this page." I would pore over the words line by line, find another word, and be rewarded with a peppermint drop. It was my Granny Georgia who told me about the Civil War.

"I was born in 1858," she would begin. "I was a late baby, the only girl, and my six brothers were much older. When the Civil War began there were fights and arguments until my mother wouldn't come to the dinner table.

" 'I can't listen to any more of this from the men I love,' she'd say, and go sit in her room upstairs.

" 'They're not men. They're damn fools,' said Papa.

"What he meant, Camille, was that three of his children were going to fight for the Confederates and three for the Union. Now my papa thought the Confederates were fools. He couldn't stand their bragging or their talking of honor night and day. So he was angry all through the year, even when one son was killed when he fought with Stonewall Jackson. Papa said the boy was a fool and kept on saying it while he held the list of wounded and dead in his hand and tore it to shreds and the tears poured down his face all the time.

"One fell with Jackson. One fell with Grant's army. Two came

211

home safe. One rode with Morgan's raiders and was put in prison and escaped. They dug out with teaspoons and carried the dirt out of the cells in their socks and pockets into the prison courtyard. And one didn't come back when the war ended. That nearly broke my mama's heart, Camille, but it gave me an afternoon I'll never forget.

"Now my mama worked hard. There was an Irish girl to work for us, but Mama got up at dawn and worked until she went to sleep at night. She never just sat down the way we are sitting now. Whenever she sat, she picked up her workbasket and sewed. She did all the sewing for the family. That meant making pants and shirts for seven men and sewing every buttonhole on those shirts by hand. Mama made shirts for my brothers all through the war while they were gone, just as if they were at home, and if she didn't know where to send them, she'd lay them in the cupboard wrapped in paper."

" 'Who's that for?' my papa would say.

" 'Stephen,' Mama would answer, looking up from the buttonhole she was working.

" 'Damn fool,' Papa would say. 'Riding with Morgan. The man's no better than a bandit.'

"But Mama never raised her head. She just kept sewing on all those hundreds of buttonholes like Stephen was upstairs in the boys' loft asleep, where she wanted him to be.

"Since she sewed so much, she was very particular about her sewing basket. It seemed big to me when I was seven and eight. It wasn't one of these flimsy little things that women use nowadays. It was a big, heavy basket lined with cloth and had wooden drawers that stacked up on each other inside. Every needle and button was valuable, particularly during the war, when she couldn't replace things easily, so I was forbidden to touch Mama's workbasket. I had my own little basket and by eight I was hemming tea towels and making my own shifts, but Mama's basket was never to be touched or played with.

"Mama was sitting on a chair on the front porch sewing. Her basket was at her feet, and I sat on the top step sewing too. It was a hot afternoon in July a year after the war ended. I was talking the way children do, when Mama suddenly screamed and leapt up. I was too scared to move, and I stared at her.

"She just stood there with her hand pressed against her mouth. Her gold thimble flew off her finger and was lost in the bushes, and then Mama kicked her workbasket out of her way and ran down the steps, down the walk, out on the dusty street, silent and furious in her determination to get to a thin man who stood in the street.

"He just stood there and watched her come, and I figured, having seen Mama's face, that she was going to kill him, so I hid my face in the shift I was sewing and didn't look. But she didn't kill him. She grabbed him and screamed again and then fainted.

"There I was, Camille, eight years old, my mother's sewing basket broken at the bottom of the stairs, needles and pins and buttons and her darning egg lying all over the walk, or lost, I knew, in the grass, lost like her gold thimble that I was allowed to use myself only if I was sick and in bed, all of it lost and broken and my mother lying out in the dust of the street, her hair falling down around her and lying in the ruts while some strange man stood there and laughed and laughed.

"It was James of course. The brother who hadn't come home. Who had been reported dead. But he had lived, God only knows how, and was put in Andersonville prison camp in Georgia, where they just threw the food over the walls to the men like they were dogs, and some of them got to be a lot like dogs by the end of the war. Not that there was that much to eat in Georgia by 1865. Bread that had straw and sawdust baked in it to make it seem more than it was, food for cattle and horses that gave men dysentery until they bled to death lying in the mud and their own filth! Oh, it was a wicked place to put my brother!

"And he died of it. He died of tuberculosis a year after he finally managed to get home. He'd written, but the mail was not good then. It was always likely to be stolen by renegade soldiers. And that's my second memory of the war.

"The first thing I remember happened when I was about six. It was the last year of the war. After supper every night Papa sat in front of the fire. Mama sewed. The Irish girl sat there too, and I sat on Papa's lap while he read something from the Bible before bed.

"Suddenly the door flew open and a man rushed in. He had on a blue uniform and a handkerchief tied over his face so only his eyes showed. I was so intrigued with the handkerchief, I didn't notice the pistol in his hand.

" 'I want your money,' he said.

" 'So do I,' said Papa, but Mama looked at Papa. 'Andrew,' she said.

" 'So Papa got up and gave the man a little flannel sack that Mama had sewn. It had roses embroidered on it and a heart with *Andrew* and *Catherine* sewn across it in tiny stitches.

"Papa threw the sack to the man, who caught it and poured the money out onto a table. It glittered on the mahogany, and he took a long while picking it up and putting it back in the little sack with only one hand. It was all of Papa's gold pieces that he stole, and we never saw him again.

"It hadn't scared me much, Camille, but that summer when I nearly died of typhoid fever, I cried and cried in the fever and begged the man to give the little flannel bag back to Papa. 'Keep the gold,' I said over and over in the fever. 'Keep all the gold, but please give back the sack with the heart on it. Give it back. Give it back.'

"When I came out of the fever, there was a flannel sack all embroidered with roses and a heart that had *Andrew* and *Catherine* sewn across it lying on my pillow. Mama told me that the man had heard how sick I was and had ridden all the way back from Cincinnati to give me the little sack, but that was a lie. All those long three nights Mama had sat by my bed and sewn another sack for me just like the one the Yankee had stolen, while Papa read the Bible to her, and I lay between them on the bed, tossing and raving with fever."

It doesn't make sense that I would go to sleep feeling so good and have the kind of nightmare that I did. It wasn't a new dream.

I had dreamed this before, about once or twice a year since I was thirteen. It was my ghost, the chain that tied me to the past, my buried childhood.

I woke up in the tent, trying to cry out and not making any sound. It had all been there again. The kitchen. The food on the walls and ceiling, flung on the floor and the counters, and there he was, trying to open a can and crying and screaming, throwing the can away from him. My father. My drunk father who was having his worst time of all.

I remembered the day it happened with the dreadful clarity that we have when events change us. It had been a good day, a day of summer sun and clear skies. I had spent the afternoon down by the river swimming and reading books. I had nailed planks in the crotch of a tree and sat there, hanging over the river, reading for hours by myself.

I walked up the path to the house with no thought of anything terrible that might happen. True, my father had been drinking heavily for years, but I thought that he would just go on like that forever. I didn't know what liquor could do. I didn't know what Aunt Nell had been waiting for and dreading for so long.

I walked up the path, carrying my books and towels, and I heard him screaming before I could see the farmhouse. I thought he had fallen and broken his hip or that someone was trying to kill him.

Dropping everything, I ran up the path, through the yard, and in the back door. The whole house was quivering with his screams. I stopped in the hall and stood there. I knew this was something I couldn't imagine. No one who had just fallen down would scream like that. Scared to move but forced to, I got to the kitchen door.

He stood in the middle of the floor and he was trying to open a can of soup. I didn't recognize the kitchen at first. There were cans lying all over, cereal boxes empty and ripped, the refrigerator door hanging open, and shelves on the floor. There was food on the floor, food spilled on the counters, and dripping from the ceiling. I hadn't known that we had that much food in the house.

My father had no clothes on, and his pants and shirt lay on the linoleum in the middle of spilled tomatoes and beans and beef stew and flour and sugar. He stood naked, holding the can as far away from his body as he could get it, trying to open it with a can opener. He screamed and screamed.

"What is it? What is it?" I was screaming too. "Why have you thrown all the food on the floor?"

He didn't even see me. He wrenched the can top off, cutting his thumb on the jagged metal. Holding the can at arm's length, he stared at the cream soup congealed neatly inside.

"Oh God! Oh God!" he screamed and flung the can away from him, hitting the kitchen window. The window shattered, but he didn't hear it.

I stared at him. He had food all over his legs and chest. He was thinner than I thought he was, and he didn't look human.

"Stop it, stop it, stop it!" I kept screaming, but he didn't hear me.

He just stood there, trying to open another can, howling like a dog that's been hit by a car.

I didn't wait any longer. I ran for Aunt Nell. "Come quick, he's gone crazy and he doesn't have any clothes on. He's thrown all the food at the walls! Oh please, come quick," I cried and felt all my fear pouring out onto Aunt Nell's lap, where I had thrown myself. "Help, help, help," I sobbed.

She called my grandfather and he went over to the house with his hired man. They cleaned my father up a little and got the doctor. After a shot to relax him, they took my father to the hospital, and I didn't see him for a week.

By the time I was taken to visit him, I hated him. Seeing him standing there naked with food all over him, seeing him howling and crazy, understanding now that he thought there were snakes and toads and slimy things in the cans, pouring out of the cereal boxes and hiding in the milk, I couldn't forgive him. Nobody who stood there like that could ever be normal, and I was chained to his craziness forever. I was his daughter, and I wouldn't forgive him for it.

He lay there in the white bed looking clean and thin and with his most pitiful expression. I knew that look well. He used it on all of us when he wanted to convince us that he was really a good man. That he just needed another chance. I looked at him and hated him.

"I wanted to fix some dinner for you, Camille. It was late, and I knew you'd be hungry. I wanted to fix something to eat to surprise you."

I didn't hear his words. I didn't care what he said. Leaning close to him as if I were going to kiss him, I whispered in his ear so that Aunt Nell wouldn't hear, "I hate you. I just hate you. You're a terrible person." Then I kissed his cheek to fool Aunt Nell and didn't say another word.

He talked a little to Aunt Nell, and she said he mustn't get tired, and we went away. I had nothing to say. I wanted to get out of the hospital and out of his life and out of the whole family if I could.

And I dreamed about this for years, sometimes three or four times a year, sometimes just once or twice. I was used to the dream, but it was suddenly new to me. I sat up sobbing and crawled out of the tent into the lighter air of summer night. The stars were bright with almost no glitter and shone straight and hard. I shivered and walked barefoot over the grass to my father's tombstone. Staring down at the ground, I cried as hard as I had cried at thirteen. It might have happened just an hour ago, the whole thing. I was young and small and didn't like it that he howled like that, didn't like the dirty kitchen, didn't like his standing naked with no modesty at all. I felt that he couldn't see me, hadn't ever seen me, would never be able to see me again.

And then it came to me like a blow. I staggered and sat down on the dark grass in my cotton gown. I couldn't bear to think about it, but I had to. Everytime I thought of it now, it was like being beaten.

"I wanted to fix some dinner for you, Camille."

He hadn't wanted to be different. He wanted to be normal. He wanted to have a nice, hot meal ready for me when I came in tired from swimming all day. He went into the kitchen to cook for me, and he kept trying to find some food, even though he could see nothing but snakes and frogs and roaches in our kitchen. He fought the monsters and kept opening all those damn cans so I could eat dinner. His very clothes turned to writhing serpents, and he couldn't even keep them on his body, but he kept opening boxes and jars and cans. He didn't want to have me fixing dinner when it was getting so late and he knew I would be tired. He was trying to feed me.

I lay on the grass there in the dark and howled almost as loudly as my father had howled. We had been lost and damned and doomed living there in that house together. We never had a chance. I hated his drinking and always would, but suddenly I could understand him. I knew who he was. For the first time I had to admit that he had loved me. For the first time I felt that I truly belonged to him.

It had been two weeks since Henry's visit. I was doing nothing during the days except going over to visit Aunt Nell and seeing an occasional movie when the two local theaters changed their bills. It was the middle of August, and I couldn't pretend any longer that winter would never come. Although we were still in the grip of summer heat, and the corn was full-eared in the fields, I knew that this was the tail end of summer. September would be hot, October hot with some cool days, and then November would end my time in the cemetery. I wasn't an Indian, able to live here with no heat and no real protection against the cold and sleet of December.

I sat and tried to make some sort of plans. I even walked over to the shopping center and bought a small black notebook and a new pen, in an effort to be businesslike and sensible. I sat on my folding chair, staring at the tobacco leaves in the field next to the cow pasture, and made lists.

The first list was a list of what I actually had in the world. It was pitiful when you consider that I had worked since I was twenty-three and had helped run a nursery school for fourteen years.

All in all, Lacey and I got about ten thousand dollars each out of the school, maybe twelve thousand on a good year. I could sell my interest in the school to Lacey, but I wouldn't feel right about asking more than whatever she could get a bank to lend her. Maybe thirty or forty thousand, I figured.

I didn't have much furniture or household goods. Henry and I were always waiting to have the perfect house when he got rich, and it hadn't yet happened when I moved out. I wasn't going to haggle over a beaten-up couch and some stainless-steel forks. To hell with it.

Henry and I would sell the house if we divorced, and I would get half of that, maybe fifty thousand if I were lucky. House prices had risen to unbelievable heights around San Francisco since we had bought ours, and I thought that my half should be worth a lot of money. The house plus the interest in the school would be about seventy thousand dollars, a tidy sum.

But at this point my list and notebook and new pen fell to the ground and I forgot them. Lists weren't much good unless you knew what you were going to do. It seemed pointless to get a divorce. Why bother? Prince Charming probably wasn't out there, and if he was, the thrill would last for only a year or two at best. I didn't have children to consider. Henry was going to get rich, and he was offering me part of it.

It was true that Henry didn't make his offer in the most romantic sort of way, but Henry had never been much for romance once we were married. His offer had been straightforward and simple. The question was, did I want to live like that? I could see Henry and me, him in a leather jacket, expensive Levi's, and gold chains, with a thirty-dollar haircut, me wearing a little tennis dress, white shoes, my hair done simply and expensively, and a cashmere sweater tied carelessly over my shoulders. There we would be, eating a perfect, nonfattening lunch with a perfect bottle of wine, surrounded by all the other perfect people who cared so little for money that they could tie a cashmere sweater in knots and be indifferent. I thought darkly of my only cashmere sweater, stored carefully in a plastic box in Henry's house. I didn't bring it to Kentucky because I didn't want to mess it up.

I wasn't sure that I could do it. I would probably relax and go out to lunch in an old sweatshirt from the Army Surplus Store and forget that I had dirt on the knees of my pants from gardening. I would make friends with all the wrong people, as I did at parties. Put me into a room with one hundred people, and I always sit in the corner with the craziest person there. Worse yet, I usually like them.

Poor Henry. I was a stone around his neck, his awkward, peculiar wife who hadn't even given him two sons who could go to Stanford and do well in economics. It didn't matter anymore about the children. With my luck, they would have been girls who married at seventeen and kept coming home to use the washing machine. I just wasn't a person who set styles or kept up appearances.

But what else was there for me? I wasn't part of Toms Creek. Dinah would have her baby, and Aunt Nell would be busy raising the child she never had. Dinah would go back to school and eventually marry someone halfway decent. There was nothing here for me. Tom Church didn't want to do anything but have sex occasionally. He wasn't someone I could plan a life with or even love in the way I wanted to love. There was no one here for me.

I put the notebook in the tent and forgot it. Lists weren't going to help me. I had better reconcile myself to Henry and be grateful that he was there. A lot of women weren't lucky enough to have a Henry on tap. I had better do what he said and wait till Dinah had her baby. Then I could go back to San Francisco and take up the elegant life. It was fated. I was going to be one of the Beautiful People.

August dragged on. The weather was hot but not too humid, and every day was like a gift that opened with the sun and ended in starry nights. The whole county was under a charm of perfect summer weather. It rained gently, so the corn was as high as I'd ever seen it. The days were around us like the perfection of the year unfolding, and it was wasted on us all.

I sat and brooded and worried and wrote evasive letters to Henry, who wrote back quoting the going prices on condominiums in Maui and Tahoe. Tom Church saw me once or twice, and we were not angry but the whole thing was making him uncomfortable. We did not make love again. Aunt Nell didn't pay any attention to anything but Dinah and her lingering pregnancy, and Dinah watched her TV and grew more swollen-bellied and white-faced as the days went on. The baby had been due for six days when Aunt Nell arrived at the cemetery on August 22.

Her old blue Chevy could barely make the hill, and it crept up as quickly as Aunt Nell could make it move, wobbling as she always did over the edges of the grass with total disdain for the middle of the road. Aunt Nell was as likely to drive on the left side as the right, and thought it a sign of excellent driving to allow everyone complete freedom of choice in selecting their half of the road.

Not getting out, she called to me, "Get in quick. It started yesterday but we didn't realize it. I didn't know, and Dinah wouldn't go see her doctor. She kept saying that it must not be labor because it didn't hurt much. She's waiting. She won't go to the hospital until you get there. Hurry up, Camille. Don't worry about what you're wearing. Come on now."

I slowly got into the car, wearing shorts and a T-shirt. My clothes didn't bother me. I was paralyzed. Standing there hearing that it had begun at last was terrifying and exciting at the same time. I felt as shocked and elated as if it were I going to the hospital to deliver a baby. I looked at Aunt Nell, who crouched forward, driving intently all over the road. She too had flushed cheeks and was like a child on Christmas morning. Both of us, I thought with amusement, were suffering birth by proxy. Dinah was having the experience that neither of us would ever have, and we were enjoying every minute of it.

Dinah sat on the porch, and she didn't look very well. There was no flush in her cheeks, and I couldn't really believe that the huge weight in her body could ever get out. There was just too much of her.

"Have you called the doctor?" Aunt Nell asked. "Is your overnight bag ready?"

"I guess that I can call him from the hospital," Dinah said.

"Is that what he told you to do, child?" Aunt Nell was already going upstairs to get the overnight bag. "Did you get your toothbrush and put it in?" she called from the landing.

Dinah didn't say anything. She stared off into space and ignored us.

"How long have you been in labor, Dinah?"

"I don't know. I didn't think it had started, but I had real bad backaches yesterday and the day before. Maybe that meant that it was starting."

"Why don't you let me call your doctor and let him know it's begun. Then he can meet us at the hospital or whatever he wants to do," I finished lamely. I didn't know what the doctor would do. I have never had an obstetrician. "Are you all right? Have you had any pains yet?" I was standing over her, staring in fascination. What did she feel? I was hungry for her to tell me all about it as it happened.

"Are you having contractions?"

"I don't really know, Camille. It just hurts awful. It isn't like just one pain. It just hurts. Sometimes it gets worse and then it just hurts all over again."

"Don't worry, Dinah. We'll be there, and I'm sure it will go fine. Just think! You've started so early in the morning, you'll be sitting up tonight and watching the TV in your room. I'll have them put one in for you, and their reception is probably much better than what you get here. It'll be over soon."

Aunt Nell bustled down with a small suitcase and her purse. We got Dinah into the car and drove outside of town to the county hospital. It was modern and new and I was reassured. Dinah would be in good hands once we turned her over to the nurses and her doctor. Dinah was too shy, I thought. She didn't even want to bother her doctor with the labor.

But when we signed in at the emergency room, as all women in labor sign in, I found out that it hadn't been shyness.

"Who's your doctor, dear?" the nurse asked.

Dinah stared at the floor and crouched lower in the wheelchair she had been seated in.

"Have you called him yet?" the nurse went on.

"I haven't been to a doctor," Dinah whispered.

The nurse glared at Dinah and then at us. "Hasn't she even been taken to a doctor during this pregnancy?" she asked icily.

Aunt Nell and I must have looked stunned. The nurse didn't

know what to do. "Have you a doctor that you want to deliver your baby?"

"Why, she's been going to that new, young doctor," Aunt Nell said. "Dr. Robertson. She went every month and every week for the last month."

Dinah shook her head. "I never went to a doctor," she said.

The nurse and I were totally confused. "Didn't you ever see him?" she asked.

Dinah shook her head.

"But where did you go those afternoons?" Aunt Nell was nearly in tears. "You said you were going to see him, and you went out every month. Where were you going?"

"I just walked around. I never went. I saw two doctors when I got pregnant. I hated it. It was awful. I couldn't stand doing that again. I never want anybody to touch me again. I made an appointment, but I just couldn't do it. I just walked around and sat in the park. I couldn't stand having someone else look at me and poke at me. I didn't do it."

Aunt Nell and I didn't know what to say. The nurse took over smoothly. "I can contact Dr. Robertson or let the doctor on call deliver Dinah's baby. What do you want to do, Dinah?"

Aunt Nell was past speech and Dinah just shrugged. "Call Dr. Robertson and tell him that we would like for him to deliver Dinah," I said. "I'll talk to him when he gets here."

Dinah was wheeled off and I tried to get Aunt Nell to go home. "Don't worry so. She's young and healthy. Women delivered babies for millions of years with no doctors. She'll be all right."

"But, Camille, we didn't know. We didn't know she was doing that."

I finally persuaded her to go home and wait until I called her. There was no point in both of us being at the hospital, and Aunt Nell looked tired already. I was reminded that she was seventy-eight, a fact that she didn't care for and I didn't pay much attention to most of the time.

Dr. Robertson was kind and friendly. I explained how Dinah had gotten pregnant, the filling station and oil can, and her angry family. "They threw her out, and I guess the examinations to determine if she was pregnant weren't very pleasant with her mother and father standing there condemning her all the time. She's scared to be examined and hasn't even seen a doctor since she was about two months' pregnant. We didn't know she wasn't seeing you," I finished guiltily.

He didn't say anything, but just nodded and went off with the nurse to see Dinah.

And so I sat. And sat. And sat.

At three in the afternoon, I begged the nurse to let me see Dinah or Dr. Robertson or someone. He came out looking tired and I began to worry.

"It's going to be a breech birth. She's been in labor for a day or two, but the baby couldn't drop down, so she didn't know. I'm going to try to deliver it without a cesarean section, but you have to be prepared for that as a possibility. I'm not going to let it go on too long. She's too young and has been through too much. It isn't as if we're dealing with a healthy, adult woman. I'll let her try to have it, but the cesarean is a real possibility at this point. I wish to God she'd come to see me before. Then we might have had a better chance of a normal delivery."

I was stunned. It wasn't supposed to be this way. Dinah was going to go in and have eight or nine hours of labor and produce a lovely baby and that would be that. How could such an ordinary thing as childbirth get so complicated?

"Does she know? Can I see her?"

"I explained to her what is happening, but she doesn't act like she really understands. She is in a lot of pain now. I'm keeping it down, but I have to let it go on for a while until I decide if the cesarean is necessary. She's underage. I'll need you to sign a form now so that if I need to operate I can do it with no hesitation. You can see her. Maybe it would help her."

Dinah lay in a bed with railings. Like a deformed infant, she tossed and writhed between the bars, her belly distended, her hair wet. There was an intravenous tube in her arm, and the white skin was already bruising around the tape.

"Oh, honey," I said. "I'm sorry it's taking so long for you. Dr. Robertson is really a good doctor, and he'll take care of you. It's going to be over . . ." I trailed off. I didn't know when it would be

224

over for Dinah. I remembered my glib assurances to her before we got to the hospital. Now I knew there wouldn't be any television for Dinah tonight.

Dinah flung my hand away and rolled into a ball around her stomach. Throwing her head back, she howled and screamed. I hadn't been ready for it, and I nearly fainted. "Oh, please, please don't," I said. "Oh, Dinah! Oh, honey, I wish I could do something . . ."

A nurse came in and felt Dinah's belly. "You'd better wait in the visitors' room," she said, not looking at me. "Dr. Robertson is coming back in now. Dinah needs some coaching. She's a nice, strong girl, and she'll be just fine."

The words were calming, but the intensity with which the nurse stared at Dinah worried me. The words were just there to make me go away.

Dinah wasn't screaming now. Her white cotton gown was up over her shaven pubis, and she lay limp. "I'm scared," she screamed. "I'm scared. I want it to stop. Stop it, stop it."

I looked at her and didn't know what to say. I stood, helpless. It was too much for me, and I nearly ran out of the room.

"Will she die?" I demanded of Dr. Robertson as he came up the hall.

"We won't let that happen," he said. "She's doing all right. It's too bad that it's a breech birth, but there are thousands of breech deliveries every year, and the mother and baby come through just fine. You go home and I'll call you."

I waited in the lobby until five, but I hadn't eaten since breakfast and the air conditioning made my bare legs chill and numb. I asked the nurse if there was any word yet, and she shook her head. "Dinah is doing just fine. We'll deliver that baby before the night is over."

I gave up and went to Aunt Nell's. She was sitting in the living room, not doing anything. She sat in a chair and didn't say a word when I walked in. "She's going to be all right," I said quickly. "The baby isn't here yet, but I signed the form so the doctor can do a cesarean if he has to. She'll be all right."

"It's my fault. I didn't even meet her doctor, Camille. I never took her in for her checkup and saw that she was going to him. I just sent her off as if she were a grown woman. If she dies, it's on my head."

I said all the meaningless, hopeful things, and we both sat there. The house was hot because Aunt Nell hadn't shut the shades against the summer sun, but by ten o'clock the air was cool. I made sandwiches for us and some coffee. Aunt Nell ate only because I had gone to the trouble to fix it. She didn't seem to taste the food or care about it.

The call came at two in the morning. Dr. Robertson was triumphant.

"Well, we did it. The baby is born, and Dinah is doing just great. It was hard, but I'm proud of her. She delivered a beautiful, eight-pound, three-ounce baby girl just an hour ago. The baby is healthy and doing well. That's one reason it was a problem, because it's such a big baby. I thought I was going to have to do a cesarean, but at the last minute the baby took care of the problem and it all went well."

"Can we see her?"

"Not tonight. She's asleep for a while. I knocked her out once the baby came so she can rest. She isn't a particularly strong girl. I asked her about nursing the baby, and she said she didn't want to. I thought it might be best to put the baby on formula, considering how hard a time Dinah has had. I want her to be in the hospital an extra day or two so she can rest before she has to start taking care of the baby. She's going to sleep late tomorrow, and then you can visit her and take a look at the baby. Maybe after lunch."

I got off the phone and was laughing like a lunatic. "It's over, and Dinah and the baby are both doing great! She had it without a cesarean, and the baby weighs eight pounds and three ounces."

Aunt Nell put her head down and wept. "Oh, Camille. That's so nice. I'm so happy for her." Looking up, she began to straighten her hair. "Is it a boy or a girl?"

"A girl," I said. "Another woman in the family."

"We'll raise this one right," Aunt Nell said. "I won't let anything harm this baby."

"No alcoholic fathers," I said laughing.

226

"No dead mothers and no rape and no horrible things ever!"
Aunt Nell was nearly crowing in pride. She was going to have a
baby at last.

THE BLOODIEST BATTLE

General Bragg entered Kentucky and announced his intention of capturing Louisville for the Confederates, rallying the state to the flag of the South and forcing the Kentuckians to secede from the Union. He fully expected the young men of Kentucky to rally to the cry of the Confederacy and join his 30,000 men. The way Bragg figured it, his army would double in size and he would add the state of Kentucky to the Confederacy with one simple campaign.

General Buell of the Union Army was stationed near Nashville, Tennessee. Hearing of Bragg's plan, he marched north to try to prevent Bragg from entering and capturing Louisville. Bragg had a clear road north to Louisville, which sat invitingly on the Ohio river, but Bragg made an error in judgment. Instead of marching north, he turned toward Bardstown and moved off the main road that led to Louisville. Too good a general to ask why, General Buell marched unimpeded to Louisville, where he gathered an army of 100,000 men and took over all the collected stores needed for his campaign.

While Buell was successfully raising and supplying the Union troops, Bragg scattered over the state, managing to spread his troops over six counties. It was October 1862. A brutal drought had dried many of the creeks and watering holes in Kentucky. The rivers were low, and the mud banks, exposed now above the sluggish streams, stank in the sun. So 160,000 men moved over the state of Kentucky in the grip of Indian-summer heat and drought. Sometimes for hours at a time there was no water for the marching men. Scouts rode out to find water, any creek, well, river, that held enough water for the troops. Searching for water up a dry creek bed, a party of Confederates fell on an encampment of Union soldiers whose job was to hold several pools of water along Doctor's Creek. The first skirmishes of cavalry began in the morning as some of the Confederate forces blundered against the Union men. By two in the afternoon, the soldiers were fighting savagely.

Neither army was in a good tactical position, and neither expected a battle. Wandering in search of water, the men were suddenly facing each other and had no choice but to fight. There were cannon and guns, but by late afternoon most of the fighting was hand-to-hand combat. Men were too close to load and fire their guns and so they fought with bayonet and knife. The wounds sustained were worse than any that either side had seen. Men fought in blood-soaked clothes until they fell from loss of blood. They slipped in the softening ground, which drank up the blood and became damp for the first time in months.

And not only was the battle unorganized and bloody. It was the great chance for the Union forces to overcome the entire army of Bragg, capture the general and his officers, and cut off a large part of the Confederate forces.

The chance was missed not because of Buell's lack of determination or his poor military judgment. All of Bragg's men lay defeated right in the palm of Buell's hand, and Buell let the Confederates retreat back to Tennessee. It wasn't really General Buell's fault. It was the fault of a natural phenomenon that can occur at any time in any place and this time happened to occur on the afternoon of October 8, 1862, around the battleground where the battle of Perryville was taking place.

General Buell sat in his headquarters, waiting to see if a battle would begin. If the fighting looked serious, he had 40,000 men who could be quickly pulled into Perryville to subdue the Confederates. Holding the main part of his force back, he committed only 22,000 men to Perryville.

General Buell sat in his headquarters, waiting for reports. He knew there was skirmishing, but it didn't worry him. There couldn't be much real fighting going on, because his headquarters was only two and half miles from Perryville. Any noise of artillery and cannon would be heard immediately. The day dragged on. The reports were odd. The tent of the general lay in silence under the hot sun, and Buell sipped water nervously.

Bragg also sat in his camp. It was quiet. There was no noise of battle. The day lay like a blanket over Bragg and his officers as they waited. All was silent.

After three o'clock in the afternoon, Buell finally heard the sound of guns. They boomed over his tent like fireworks. Startled, Buell sent General Gilbert to the battlefield to find out what was happening. By the time Gilbert returned, the battle was nearly over. Buell was confused. Afraid to act without information, he waited. Instead of following the Confederates and surrounding them with his reserve force of 40,000 men, Buell sat and gathered information.

Buell had first heard the sounds of battle about three o'clock. By five it was over. He couldn't believe that the Confederates would pull out after the short skirmish he had heard. Most of the main shelling was over by three. Buell still thought that he was dealing with a small action, a prelude to the battle he expected would come later.

It was nature that confused General Buell and General Bragg. They should have easily heard the cannon from where their headquarters had been located, but something called "acoustic shadow" had fallen over the countryside. The sound of the battle was refracted out into space to come down far away, perhaps to be thrown out into space forever. The unusually hot weather and the patches of cold and hot air hanging oppressively over the hills near Perryville created a barrier that the sound could not penetrate or penetrated in an unnatural pattern. The noise of cannon and guns went on for hours before either general heard anything except the birds calling in the trees. Buell and Bragg sat two miles from the battlefield as if they were in Eden. No noise of the battle came to them.

This acoustical shadow ruined Bragg's planning. He couldn't believe the reports he received. The shadow of silence lay over Buell, and he never thought to call in his reserve troops. The battle was going on. The men fought desperately with little leadership until they had to slice and tear like mad dogs at each other's throats. The generals were ignorant of it all until too late.

Acoustic shadows drift and float over the earth. There is no way to predict with any certainty how sound waves will behave. The spoken word can leave your mouth and be carried straight upward to disappear forever. There is no certainty in this world that when you speak you will be heard. There is no way of knowing whether the sounds you make will carry and be heard correctly by those listening. Like General Buell and General Bragg, we sometimes sit in our tents straining for sound, leaning into the wind to catch any murmur or articulation that will define for us the shape of events and, like the good generals, we hear nothing, nothing at all, until it is too late.

I slept late at Aunt Nell's house and then walked back to the cemetery to get dressed. I swam in the river and the whole world seemed different. There was a new person alive, a new girl to grow up and see the world the way it lay that morning in front of me. The river water was almost sweet smelling against my skin, and the sandbar was warm. I'll teach her to swim in the river even if I go back to California, I thought. This baby would learn to swim and dive in the green water like an otter. I could always come back for a visit.

Aunt Nell picked me up in her Chevy. I didn't even care about the erratic driving. I just sat smiling, looking out at the town and the countryside near the hospital. The farmers were beginning to bring in their hay, and it lay in piles, fragrant and beautiful in the morning sun. Aunt Nell had bought a large bouquet of roses and a box of chocolates. I felt bad that I hadn't thought of it, but vowed to do something for Dinah later.

The doctor felt Dinah needed a private room for the first day so she could sleep and rest with no one talking to her or interrupting her with other people's visitors. The lunch carts were being wheeled back to the kitchen when we got off the elevator.

Dinah looked so different that I was amazed. She was very pale and looked exhausted, but she was also very flat. She lay in the bed with the covers neatly folded under her arms. The sun came through the windows and made a pattern on the linoleum floor.

"I'm so glad it's over, Dinah," I said, leaning down and kissing her cheek. "You look beautiful. You did a great job, honey."

"I'm glad that it's born. I've been so much trouble to you both," Dinah said. "But now it's different. The baby is my responsibility. I had it, and I'll take care of it. Thank you for the candy and flowers, Aunt Nell."

"Of course it's your baby. Of course it is." Aunt Nell was nearly crying. "But my goodness, you're so young that you need to go on with your life, too. I can take care of the baby so you can go back to school and have a normal life. I'm going to just love helping you."

Dinah looked very empty. "It's up to me to take care of it," she said.

"Well, thank God it's here and out of you," I said laughing. "I sat in the reception hall all day just nearly dying, Dinah. I'm sorry it was so hard for you. It doesn't mean that another baby would be that hard to have. They say the first one is hardest."

Dinah nodded. She wasn't saying much, but I knew she must be tired and still a little in shock after the hard labor.

"A little girl." Aunt Nell looked fondly at Dinah. "A beautiful healthy little girl, the doctor told us. What do you want to call her, dear?"

Dinah shook her head and didn't say anything.

I grinned at Dinah. "Maybe you should name it after Aunt Nell."

"Oh no!" Aunt Nell shook her head. "You certainly don't have to name her after me. Nell isn't such a wonderful name. I'll bet you have a name you'd love to call her that we'd never think of."

We looked at Dinah and she didn't say anything. Opening the box of candy, she stared at the squares and ovals of chocolate but didn't take one out. She put the top back on neatly and said, "I'm not going to name it now. I don't want it to have a name yet. I can name it later, can't I?" She looked at me.

"Sure," I said. "Why don't you just get to know her first. A name will come. She'll get a name when you know who she is."

"I'm not ready yet," Dinah said, "but I'm going to be the one who is responsible for everything."

What is "everything"? my mind immediately thought, and I

opened my mouth to ask when Aunt Nell said, "Of course, Dinah. You are a good, responsible girl. We know that. You will take care of your baby, and we'll be there to babysit and help you. It's all going to be fine." Aunt Nell was nearly crying again. She was happier than I'd ever seen her, and I was a little jealous. I had never been able to have a baby to show Aunt Nell.

Dinah shut her eyes. "I'm so tired."

"Well, I thought you might like to have us push you up in a wheelchair and you could show us the baby. The nursery is open, and we can peek at her through the glass, but you just rest. We'll wait and let you show us your baby tonight or tomorrow. We'll come back soon." Aunt Nell moved to the door.

Without opening her eyes, Dinah said, "Oh, you can go look at it. Go ahead. I'm just so tired."

"Well . . ." Aunt Nell paused. She felt that Dinah should show us the baby, but she was also dying to see it. "If you're sure that you don't mind, we'll go and see her before we go home."

I kissed Dinah's cool cheek again and shivered. Lying so pale and still, she was like a corpse. "Take care of yourself, and be sure to call if you want anything, no matter how small. We'll bring you chocolate malts and cheeseburgers if you want them."

A smile flickered over Dinah's face and she opened her eyes. Putting up her arms like a child being put to sleep at night, she clasped my neck. "Thank you, Camille. I sure do like cheeseburgers." I started to stay and talk to her, but Aunt Nell was already out in the hall. She wanted to see that baby. "Good-bye," I called.

The two of us stood outside the huge window that looked into the newborn nursery. A masked nurse asked which baby we wanted to see, and we said Dinah's. Going to a small wire basket on tall legs, the nurse reached into it and picked up a tiny piece of flesh that curled its fists into the air and wailed as it was lifted.

We stood close to the glass and stared at the baby that was held for our inspection. She was very red and had lots of dark hair, and her eyes were closed in anger. Wailing at being woken up, her fist shook in trembling rage. The child was very small and probably the most beautiful thing I had ever seen.

232

"Gosh," I said. "I feel like a grandmother."

Aunt Nell didn't say anything. She had her handkerchief out and was crying openly. "Another little girl, like you were. New babies are just so perfect."

We drove home dreamily, surrounded by the smell of newly mown hay and the noise of afternoon traffic. Dinah wasn't the same person anymore. She was the mother of a child now, and that changed everything for her. The tiny, perfect thing with red fists and dark hair made Dinah a new person. We were both too glad to talk about it and just sat drinking iced tea through the afternoon heat without saying a word, just smiling.

Dinah came home on the fourth day. I drove the car with Dinah in the front seat, and Aunt Nell sat in back holding the baby. It was still called simply "the baby" because Dinah hadn't decided on a name. I rather liked her caution in picking a name. Having been called "Camille" from birth, a romantic, French, feminine name like a sigh, I objected to this instant naming of babies. If my parents had just gotten to know me for a while they might have given me a more appropriate name, like Rebecca or Molly or Joan. "Camille" always conjured up a picture of a tiny, delicate figure swathed in layers of tulle who sat in a box at the opera. It wasn't such a bad idea to wait and see what the baby was like.

Dinah went inside and was put to bed in the back bedroom downstairs. I had spent a day cleaning out and putting the boxes left there for storage in the attic. The room was just temporary, until Dinah was allowed to walk up stairs again. It was sunny and cheerful, and the baby slept happily in the baby bed which I had dismantled and set up again downstairs in the corner. We would move everything again in a few weeks.

Dinah spent the first week home doing lots of sleeping and just taking it easy. Aunt Nell wouldn't let her raise a finger to do anything except take showers and brush her teeth. Aunt Nell even got in the habit of telling Dinah, "Now dear, why don't you go take a shower and clean up while I give the baby her bottle."

"You don't have to tell her when to shower, Aunt Nell," I said, grinning at her.

"Well, she is so tired and abstracted. That's what having a baby can do sometimes. She's so young, Camille. I just give her little pats in the right direction. She shouldn't lie in bed *all* day."

I agreed. Dinah wasn't interested in going out, but I talked her into sitting on the porch every evening and cooling off after the day. It was still hot with that breathless, end-of-the-summer heat of late August. Dinah sat obediently, but she might not have thought of sitting there in the evening cool if I hadn't arrived every night to help with dinner and talked her into joining me.

The baby was Aunt Nell's darling. She bathed and powdered and oiled and combed her until I feared for the baby's skin. "Don't scrub her raw," I warned, and she sniffed and went right on with it. Since the baby was on bottles, Aunt Nell insisted on getting up for the two- and six-o'clock feedings. I offered to sleep there and take over the night feedings, but Aunt Nell was determined to do them alone.

"I don't sleep that much anyway," she said. "It's real nice sitting there in the night with the baby. I have some company with my insomnia."

I was touched and a little sad. Aunt Nell had taken on a whole new life and was thriving in it, but she was old. I hadn't thought that she might have insomnia and get up at night feeling lonely. God knows, it was wonderful for Dinah.

I must admit, I enjoyed helping out with the baby. I did feel like a grandmother, and I cuddled and fed and diapered like an old pro after the first few days. Sometimes Aunt Nell held the bottle firmly and defensively against her chest, glaring at me as if defying me to take it away from her. I would laugh and hand the baby over. It was lovely, the old face and the bush of white hair bent anxiously over the other face, so much tinier and redder but equally wrinkled and anxious-looking below the straight, silky, dark hair.

Dinah accepted all the royal treatment and didn't say much. She wasn't very talkative anyway, so we just smiled at her and tried to get her to eat. She was too thin, and since the birth she hadn't had much appetite. It seemed as if the more the baby ate, the less Dinah did. The baby grew fatter and slept beautifully between bottles while her mother ate only when urged and watched her interminable television programs all day.

"It's the shock of birth," Aunt Nell assured me. "I've seen it before with young girls. She didn't expect such a hard time, and she's still sort of caught up in it. She'll get better. School starts the end of September. I don't want her to take a full course, but she might take the advanced typing class she's talked about. I could drive her over to the high school, and she could just take the one course. It would get her out of the house and back to some normal activity. She needn't worry about the baby. I have that in hand," she finished proudly.

Hoping to encourage Dinah, I decided what my present to the new mother would be. I bought her a beautiful bright-red typewriter with its own red leather case. Stopping at a jewelry store, I also spent more money than I could believe on a heavy silver cup. I would take it back and have it initialed when the baby was named.

She had to be named soon. Aunt Nell had arranged for her to be christened on September 2nd. That was only a few days away. I asked, "Why the rush?" but Aunt Nell was old-fashioned.

"You can't let a baby stay unchristened," she said firmly to Dinah and me.

"But she's perfectly healthy. Why the hurry?" I asked.

"Well of course she's healthy." Aunt Nell was indignant. "She's a beautiful baby! But it's time for her to be christened."

"Don't you see?" Aunt Nell hissed at me as I left. "September second is right during Labor Day weekend. Most of the people will be out of town, fishing and camping on the lakes around here. The church won't be so full. I thought Dinah might like it better if it's quiet in church that day. She's so quiet and shy herself."

Dinah didn't come up with a name, and I sort of hoped that she would settle on "Nell." It would make the summer complete for my aunt, and God knows she deserved something after helping Dinah and spending her savings on baby beds and diapers and hospital bills. I wandered back and forth from the cemetery to the house and watched the baby sleep and eat and fuss when she was bathed. I could see that things were settling down and becoming routine. I wouldn't be needed for much longer. I could fly back to Henry and my new jet-set existence in another week or two.

It must have been the heat Friday night that made me sleep so badly. I rolled from side to side until nearly dawn and then slept so lightly that I felt exhausted when I woke up at about nine o'clock. The first day of September was going to be just another summer day, not the sign of coming autumn.

I went outside and stood blinking in the sunlight. It was a good day for a swim and then a late breakfast. I had to go to Aunt Nell's later to reassure her that her preparations for the baby's christening were all flawless. Aunt Nell had bought her a white dress, not the long white dress that I had been christened in as a baby, because Dinah had unexpectedly objected to using that dress. Aunt Nell was disappointed but went out and bought a simple white christening dress that Dinah did not object to. Nell had one of her friends see to the arrangement of flowers for the altar in celebration of the baby's becoming a Christian, and she was in a panic that Dinah might refuse at the last minute to go to the church.

There was also the problem of the name. Dinah said that she would tell us the name Sunday. It was irritating and silly and pointlessly mysterious for Aunt Nell to cope with. She had to call the minister and tell him that the baby's name wasn't certain yet, but she would give him a slip of paper with the name written on it before the service. I was annoyed with Dinah for not making up her mind. Twenty-four hours couldn't make that much difference in her choice, and it would have calmed Aunt Nell down.

I took a towel and walked barefoot down through the field to the sandbar where I swam. As the first shade of the trees passed over me, I doubled over and reeled backward into the sunny field. My whole body seemed to turn inside out, and I vomited messily onto the earth. I staggered and dropped to my knees, leaning heavily on my hands, and retched and retched. Nothing much came up. I hadn't eaten breakfast yet, and there was nothing left from last night in my stomach, but my stomach heaved and convulsed on and on. Finally it was over, and I stood up. I was lightheaded. Forgetting the towel, I walked shakily through the trees and into the river. I washed my mouth out with river water but felt too weak to swim.

It was disgusting. Tomorrow I had to stand up in church as one of the sponsors of the baby while it was christened, and I had the flu. I shouldn't go near the baby as long as my stomach was upset or she might catch it.

I went back and sat in my tent, eating some bread. I might throw that up too, but I was hungry and felt empty. I ate bread and drank some canned apple juice that was in my food box. I felt better almost immediately, and didn't know what to do. I would have to sit out here all day and not get near the baby. I could get to church in a cab. Aunt Nell could send one out for me tomorrow morning. Then I could stand well away from the baby so it didn't get sick. The last thing Dinah and Aunt Nell needed was a baby with flu.

I walked to the shopping center and called Aunt Nell. She was sympathetic but agreed that I shouldn't be near the baby. We set up the arrangement for the cab and I told Aunt Nell completely truthfully that I felt all right now, but there was no sense in taking chances and exposing the baby. I bought a sack of food, crackers, and more apple juice in case I couldn't keep anything else down. I hated it. I was never sick, and wasn't interested in having my body betray me during my last weeks in Kentucky.

It was five o'clock in the afternoon when I saw someone walking between the trees near the river. I stared hard at the dark line of trees with the river glinting between them. It was all still, but then I saw movement again, to the left of the house, moving down the small bluff where the house stood toward the lower bank of the river. The person was moving toward my sandbar, where I went to swim.

I was too far away to recognize the face in the shade of the trees, but I saw the flash of a bright blue shirt. It was a funny color blue, sort of a turquoise but with lots of green in it. It was unmistakable. The only time I had seen that color before was in a dress that Dinah had.

I stood up and waved. "Dinah?" I called. I couldn't figure out what she was doing here. She moved faster, heading for the path to the sandbar. Then I saw her moving quickly away from me, and I knew she was going down to the river. It was odd. She carried a large, flat basket on her arm. I didn't remember the basket, but I knew that I had seen it somewhere before.

I got up and walked into the field. If Dinah intended to swim, I was sympathetic. It was a miserably hot day and she must be sick of being cooped up. First she had sat around through the end of the pregnancy, then four days in the hospital, and now, being housebound while she recovered. But I didn't think she should be swimming yet. I wondered if the doctor would allow swimming in the river so soon after having a baby. It had been only ten days.

I walked more quickly and then suddenly stopped in my tracks. I felt the hair rising on my arms. No. I was being melodramatic. She wouldn't kill herself. She was being taken care of, and we weren't giving her a hard time about the baby. She wouldn't want to die. Something nagged at me. It was the basket. The basket.

Then I realized and began to run. "Dinah, Dinah, Dinah!" I screamed. "Wait, for God's sake wait. Don't, don't. Wait! Dinah, Dinah—"

The ground wasn't even and I stumbled. I was running hardout now, with my arms outstretched in front of me. I was trying, even across the field with the trees between us, to catch her back, hold her, grab her.

I felt my cheeks get colder and didn't know that I was crying. "Dinah, she doesn't even have a name. Wait! Wait!"

The trees were silent and I ran through them, ignoring the pain when I stepped on sticks, ignoring the sapling that I careened off with my shoulder. I forgot the path and cut through the bush toward where I knew she must be, where she had headed as surely as if it were her place and not mine, as if she knew where she was going and knew it better than I did from just hearing me talk about it.

The sandbar was liquid gold in the late-afternoon sun. How can it be so beautiful? I wondered. And it was beautiful. The full sweep of the sandbar cutting out from the bank, and then the river flowing green and warm in the light. Even the curve of Dinah's back, doubled up and crouched over herself as she had fallen on the sand, was beautiful, a beautiful curve of turquoise blue against the gold and green.

She lay still and my eyes went beyond her, over the surface of the river. It was there, bobbing and turning gently in the river. The basket floated slowly with the summer current and the handle stood up in a ludicrous curve that turned and became a single line as the basket circled in the current.

I didn't say a word to Dinah but ran past her, probably never having even paused in my running but having taken it in like a picture, a scene that hung in my mind like a photograph. The sandbar. The girl crouched with her face hidden. The river, and on the surface of the river, a basket with a piece of cloth trailing over the edge.

I ran into the water and began swimming only when I couldn't run any farther. At least I could swim. I could swim well. And this thought kept going on as I turned my face into the water and swam furiously, swam violently toward that silent basket that floated ahead of me down the river. I can swim well. I can swim well, my mind kept repeating over and over. I swam and swam. It seemed to me that no one had ever swum so strongly, but something was wrong.

I raised my head and looked up. I should be nearly at the basket. I should look up and see it right in front of my arms, bobbing one or two strokes away. I would grab it gently and tow it back. I would be careful not to tip it or let it go under. It was right in front of me, I knew.

The river was empty. Ahead of me was only the far shore and a log that stuck out into the mud. I was in the center of the river, and the basket was not in front of me. For a second I thought that I had swum in a curved line and missed it. It must be behind me.

Kicking with my feet, I whirled in the water, then whirled in a circle. There was no basket. It was gone, as if it were an imaginary object that had never been.

It's not too late, I thought. I might be able to dive and find it. I heaved up and downward into the river. The current was strong in the middle and I had a hard time swimming directly down, but I managed to hit the bottom. I felt through the shifting mud, which was like heavy water on top and thickened as my hands dug down in it. I kept my eyes open, but at this depth I couldn't see.

I had to surface, but gasped in air and dove again. I dove. I dove. I dove and then went down again and again. I didn't have time to call to Dinah. If I could just find the basket in a minute or two. It might not be too late.

Coming up, I saw someone else on the sandbar. It was Mr. Branch. He must have heard my screams and come down from the house. "Oh, help! Help!" I cried. "Dinah's baby has drowned. Get a boat. Get help. Help!"

I dived back down and was still diving when Mr. Branch rowed up the river in his fishing boat.

"Where did it go down?" he asked.

By that time I was exhausted and confused. I peered back at the sandbar. I had drifted downriver while diving. The basket had probably sunk farther up the river, but the current would have carried it down, I figured. I didn't know where to look. It was like one of those problems in algebra, where you have to gauge the distance traveled in a boat when you know the river's current. If only I had some paper and knew the speed of the current, I thought, I might be able to remember enough algebra to figure it out.

"Do you have some paper?" I cried.

"What?"

It was no good. He didn't understand. I felt a momentary flash of rage at Mr. Branch. He didn't have paper. If I had paper I could find the basket.

"I can't find it," I said, clinging to the side of the rowboat. "I've gone down and gone down. I can't find it." I was crying.

"How long has it been?" he asked gently. He didn't understand the details, but he knew.

"I don't know."

"Well, it took me a while to call the sheriff and get my boat out here. I think it's too late, Camille." He reached out and took me by the shoulders. I fought him off at first, but he made me get into the boat. I wallowed over the edge and lay on the bottom crying. Mr. Branch rowed steadily to the sandbar and I heard the soft shush of sand under the prow.

Then I thought of Dinah. I staggered up and waded onto the dry sand. She was still and silent, curled like a rock. I didn't know what to say to her, but I had to say something.

I was too tired to stand up and sank heavily onto the ground by her.

"Dinah?" She didn't answer or move. I knew what the basket was now. It had held Aunt Nell's kindling by the fireplace. It had been beside the hearth since I had been younger than Dinah.

"Dinah?"

She moaned and rolled over. "They told me I had to be responsible about it," she said.

I couldn't think past the basket. It bothered me that she had used Aunt Nell's basket. "Why did you use the kindling basket?" I demanded. Aunt Nell would miss the basket and wonder where it was. I was still gasping for breath and beginning to shiver when the summer wind hit me.

"The pillow wouldn't work," Dinah said. She was whispering to herself, staring blindly at the sky. "It wiggled so much, Camille. It looked easy, but the pillow wouldn't work."

"Why?" I almost shouted. "Why did you do that? What in God's name were you thinking?"

The shadow of the sheriff's deputy fell over us on the sand. "Is this the mother?" he asked, and another one said, "It's the little girl."

"His mother didn't want him and she put him in a basket and floated him out on the water and a princess found him. I learned that in Sunday school," Dinah was whispering on to herself, ignoring the men and me and the river and everything around her.

"We were taking care of the baby. You didn't have to lift a finger. Why would you—" I sobbed and my voice broke. I couldn't stand to say the word.

"Like Moses," she crooned. "But, Camille"—she clutched my arm with her cold fingers—"there aren't any bulrushes here, are there? Are there bulrushes around here?"

I just stared at her. Another boat scraped on the sandbar and I could hear low tones of men talking. Chains rattled and oars thunked against wood. "Over here, Jim," someone called. I heard a truck being driven through the brush, with crackles and a slap as saplings sprang away from the tires.

"Why didn't you just get an abortion?" I asked.

"There were two of them . . ." she began.

"Two what?" I was tired, and it wasn't making sense.

"Two of them and they looked at me and it was awful. One after the filling station. He cleaned me up inside from the oil cans. Then there was another man. My mother told him I was pregnant. Are there bulrushes here, Camille?"

"Why did you do it?" I said again. I didn't know how long I could sit here saying the same thing. One boat had swung out into the river's current, and long chains hung down from its sides. The men moved it slowly down stream.

"The second one was the one who did abortions. He said yes, he would give me one. Do you think it could be like Moses, Camille?"

"Why didn't you get an abortion? Tell me why, Dinah!" I was determined to pursue this. A dragonfly lit on my leg with a blaze of purple and I watched it move its wings slowly in the sunlight.

"He was right, Camille. I thought about it, and he was right. "He said," she hurried on, seeing that I was going to ask again. " 'I don't know why all you girls go out and get yourselves pregnant and then expect me to kill it for you. You ought to be more responsible.' "

Dinah stared at me, waiting for me to understand. I was so tired. I felt lightheaded and I had swallowed too much water.

"I couldn't expect anyone else to kill it for me, so I waited and then I thought of Moses, and I came here . . ." her voice trailed off and she lay back down on the sand. Her skirt was dark turquoise, and water from the edges dripped slowly into the sand and gravel. She was wet to the waist where she had waded into the river.

"I wanted it to be like in the Bible. I thought about it, and I decided that maybe someone would find it, floating along. I didn't know there weren't any bulrushes here. I just had to be responsible. They all told me so."

She stared at the sky and then suddenly sat up. "You hate me, don't you!" she cried out. "You hate me now because I wanted it to be like that. You'll never like me again!" She turned her strained face to me and I shrank back. I couldn't follow her tortured logic. I didn't want to get lost in the dark woods of her mind. I could still feel the current of the river mud pulling at my hands as I dug blindly down, searching.

"I don't know," I said.

"But don't you see," she said. "I had to do it today. I couldn't do it later. I couldn't do it after it was baptized. Can't you see?"

There were three men around us. They stood in their uniforms and listened quietly, and I was suddenly afraid for Dinah. "She's only fifteen," I said. "I don't know what she was thinking. She brought her baby down here and floated it out in the river in a basket. I tried to stop her and then I tried to find the basket. It wasn't there. It just wasn't there." I was crying again and my body shook as I stood up. One of the men gave me a hand. "I tried." My voice was rising.

The men conferred in whispers with Mr. Branch and one of them started back up the path. Mr. Branch held the rope on his boat and looked sadly at me and Dinah. Dinah was doubled up again and lay on the sand without even breathing, it seemed.

Leaning over her, the deputy put his hand gingerly on her shoulder. "Come on now. I'm not going to hurt you. There's no need for you to sit down here. You just come with me and we'll go to Juvenile Hall. You can rest out there until we figure out what to do about this."

His kindness and firmness seemed to rouse Dinah and she unfolded. "Yes," she said simply, and, standing up awkwardly, she let him take her arm and lead her off.

I sat on the sand and didn't know what to do. "What are they doing?" I asked Mr. Branch.

"The other deputy went up to call for boats and have the river dragged. They'll drag here and upriver and try to find the baby."

I hid my face in my knees and wept.

Mr. Branch patted my shoulder as gently as the deputy had patted Dinah's. "It's all right now. It's all right. You did all you could. There wasn't a thing else you could have done. You're wet and cold. You go up and get some clothes and come down to the house."

I wanted to obey someone. I stood up and stumbled through the trees to my tent on the hill overlooking the pasture. I grabbed whatever lay on the floor and walked back to the house. For the first time in twenty years I lay in the old bathtub and felt the hot water warming me. I knew that I had to talk to the deputies and call Aunt Nell before it got on the news. I had to get out of the hot water and go to Aunt Nell, but I floated and shut my eyes. I couldn't understand it yet. I didn't want to see Aunt Nell until I was calmer. I lay there and thought and cried silently and worried about how to tell her. All I could think was how upset she was going to be that it was her basket that Dinah had used. I hated it that Dinah had used something of Aunt Nell's to kill the baby. I couldn't see how to tell her about the basket.

The bath did warm me up and I didn't feel quite so shaky when I walked to Aunt Nell's house. Mr. Branch offered to drive me, but he looked as shaken as I did, and I didn't want to make him do any more for me.

The fact of death changed the town as I walked through it. The storefronts and the town square were more real, more solid for the fact of death, but I felt distant from the people and stood at one corner waiting for the light to change as if a glass cage were around me. I heard the people on the streets talking, but the words bounced off the glass and didn't touch me.

Aunt Nell came out of the kitchen when I walked into the house. "Camille? Have you seen Dinah? I cannot think what she is doing. She's been gone for over two hours, and she took the baby for a walk. I know she's tired of being so tied down, but I don't know if she should be walking around town carrying the baby so soon after her delivery."

She looked at me, and I stood silent. Out of pity, I gave her another minute of ignorance. She was really very small and frail standing there.

"Well, maybe you should go out and look for her," she went on. "I'd go but I have the ham in. How are you feeling? Do you think it's anything catchable? You don't look well."

"Aunt Nell." I took her hand and pulled her to the sofa. She sat down and watched me in surprise and then in fear. Her face visibly shrank and fell in on her bones.

"Oh God. Something's happened," she said.

"Dinah put the baby in a basket and took it down by the sandbar back of the farmhouse. She took it down there where I swim. She waded in and just floated the basket out in the water."

Aunt Nell was crying. She sat perfectly erect and cried with no sound.

"I ran when I saw her. I knew something was wrong, so I ran down there, but it was too late. I swam out and tried to get it, but the basket went down. I dived and dived."

I was crying too and my voice was shaking. Aunt Nell patted my hand slowly as I talked. Her tears stopped like the sudden drying up of a spring. "I tried. I tried, but the basket went down and then I couldn't find it. Mr. Branch came out. He called the sheriff. They took Dinah out to Juvenile Hall."

"Yes, yes," she said calmly. "It's over now, dear. It's all over now." She looked at me and quietly said, "It is my fault."

"There's no way you could have known. You took care of her and loved her, you couldn't have known she was going to do something so crazy."

"We loved her too well," Aunt Nell said. "We never let her care for her own baby. She hardly held her own child these last ten days. Do you realize that, Camille?"

I thought about it. It was true. "But Dinah needed to rest. She didn't want to take care of the baby."

"That's true."

"Anyone would say that we were doing exactly what she needed. She had a hard labor, and she is so young. Even the doctor was concerned about who would do the work when she came home. Remember how he asked about it?"

"It is my fault. All of it is. Your father is my fault. You are my fault, I sometimes feel, and now Dinah's baby died because of that terrible thing. It died because of the thing I did. It's my fault."

She was in shock. I put my arm around her rigid shoulders and tried to draw her to me. "It's all right. You've never hurt me. I don't know what I would have done without you."

"No, no." She pushed me off angrily. "You just don't know. No one knew except for your grandfather and his wife. She knew too. She should never have known. He should never have told her. She was young and had never hurt him, and he told her. It was weak, weak of him."

"What are you talking about?" I asked.

"It's too late to care. I don't care. I can't care anymore about it. I will tell you what happened.

"When I was a girl I grew up on a farm. We lived far from other farms, and my brother—your grandfather—and I had no other children to play with. We were three years apart and had been playmates from the time I could walk. He taught me to walk and made me talk, and I tried to keep up with him all my childhood. I loved him and he loved me, and it was something that made our parents proud that we got along so well and never had to be punished for fighting.

"But we were growing up. I was thirteen, and we began to spend long hours after chores in the summer wandering all around the farm. We would take a picnic basket and books and a blanket and go off to read all afternoon. He was so brilliant. He would make me read books that interested him so I could talk to him about them. I read all sorts of things I didn't really understand so that he could have someone to listen to him when he needed to talk about the books. We talked about everything. All the things that we couldn't mention to our parents. Religion, history, philosophy, poetry. We talked and talked about them. We would lie on the blanket on the shady side of a haystack and stare at the sky and hold hands and talk.

"I have never loved another person the way I did your grandfather for those three years between thirteen and sixteen. We meant no harm.

"Oh, we knew it was wrong. Neither of us was so silly to think that it was something that was acceptable, but we didn't know it would go any further than us. We thought that we could touch and kiss and no one would know. It was our secret. It wouldn't hurt anyone. It was a secret of ours just like the fact that we didn't really believe in God the way our parents did.

"And, of course, we didn't just hold hands and kiss. One day it was too much for him. It was too much for me too, but I didn't believe that for years. I thought it was he who needed it, but I did too. We were flushed and almost sick with each other, and he made love to me. I didn't like it much at first, but I loved him, and soon I liked it too. I liked it, and then I craved it. We would both race through our chores as if we were crazed so we could slip off and make love. Our parents thought we were reading too much and laughed at us. They had no idea.

"I wasn't a fool. I had grown up on a farm. I knew about pregnancy and babies, but I didn't connect it with me. Isn't that odd? After seeing all those animals give birth, I never thought of my body being able to do that. It was like a magic world that we had made. I couldn't believe somehow that the normal rules of nature would apply to my brother and me.

"I was lucky. I found out that I was pregnant when I was sixteen. God knows why I hadn't gotten pregnant before that. It was lucky because I discovered the pregnancy in October. My parents assumed that I had gotten pregnant by one of the farmhands we had hired in August and September to get in the corn and the hay. There were always traveling farmhands who would drift in about harvest time and then drift on. One of them had flirted with me so openly that my parents assumed it was that man who had gotten me pregnant and then left.

"My brother and I decided to let them believe that. Our world was still intact. We let them think that I had slept with that man, and we were callous and cold to my parents. Neither of us cared about their pain. We were still above all the things that had to do with my parents and the farm and the reality of my pregnancy. We were enchanted. Special.

"My mother arranged for our family doctor to abort me. It wasn't pretty. I went with my mother to visit him at his house. His wife and children were out at a church social. I lay on his wooden table in the kitchen and he scraped me out. I held on to the table legs and my mother held my head so it wouldn't fall over backward. I never cried out, and oh, it was painful. It did something to me. I was changed, but I still loved Jeffrey with the same passion. I was glad for the abortion. If the baby was born, then what would I do? It would have ruined my family. I was proud to have the pain. It was different back then. Thank God for abortion, I thought.

"When it was over, I went home. The day I got home, I lay in bed and my brother sat by me. He read to me. My parents thought he didn't know about the abortion. They didn't want him to know.

"He sat and read, and then we made a pact. We agreed that we would never, ever marry. We would never take another person as a wife or a husband. We could never tell anyone about it, so we could never marry. It would be dishonorable to marry and let them think that we were pure. We would not lie.

"I lay there in that bed with my mother's quilts over me and held Jeffrey's hand and promised to stay single forever, and he made the same promise to me. It was the most beautiful moment of my life. It must have been enough love to last me forever, because I kept the promise. I never married. I was pretty. I had chances. But I would refuse. The love between Jeffrey and me was like a vision, a dream. I would not lessen it by marrying and having sex with another man.

"When I was twenty-four, I was a confirmed old maid. I was happy. I had known a love that was greater than any of the ordinary stuff of marriages and romance. And that was when Jeffrey betrayed me. He announced that he was marrying Rebecca Dunbarton. She was only nineteen and very lovely. I knew he liked her, but I never believed that he would marry. From the day that he announced his marriage, I never spoke to your grandfather unless I had to. I never saw him. I never forgave him.

"But at least I knew that she didn't know. I would have seen it in her eyes. She was too young and too open to hide it. When I met her, she was sweet and natural with me. I knew that Jeffrey and I had something she knew nothing about. It was something to hold on to."

Aunt Nell looked at me. She was like a death's-head in her pallor, and her flesh was fallen and sunken on her skull. I was crying, but she stared unmoved at me. Then she continued to tell her story.

"It happened suddenly. Jeffrey and Rebecca had been married about a year when I heard that your grandmother had left town. She had gotten on the afternoon train north and had run away to her older sister's place in Ohio. Everyone in town was talking. My brother had gone down to the shanties by the river where the men gambled and drank. Jeffrey had been drunk for two days by the time I heard about it.

"I went and found him on the fourth day and took him home and put him to bed. I sat by the bed all afternoon and into the night. He didn't wake up until just before dawn. It was still dark out, but the birds were moving and the chickens were clucking. I sat and watched him sleep off four days of drinking.

"I was still in love with him, you see? I was trying to take care of him. Then he finally came to, and I asked him what had happened. Why had she left? I don't know what I expected to hear. Perhaps I wanted him to say that the marriage was over.

"He told me that Rebecca was pregnant. She had told him about the baby when he got home for lunch, four days before. She was radiant, excited, proud. Jeffrey heard her talk and knew that his child would be born with a cloud over it.

"That's what he said to me, lying there in the bed all unshaven and gray in the face. 'I knew that the child would have a cloud over its life because Rebecca didn't know the truth about me,' he said.

"So he told his wife about us. He told her that his first child had been aborted on a wooden table in a country doctor's kitchen with me bleeding from my mouth where I bit my lips rather than scream. He told her about us and about our baby.

"And I sat there and listened to him smash our whole enchanted world to pieces. Every word was like a blow from his fist. He told me that Rebecca had to know because there mustn't be any barrier between him and his wife while she carried the child.

"There I was, sitting by that bed, feeling that I had been abandoned and exposed, and he only cared about Rebecca and how she had accepted the story.

"I didn't say a word. Something in me was turning to stone, and I couldn't speak until I was stone down to my soul itself. But Jeffrey went on and on about how Rebecca had cried and been upset. How she had packed the pictures of her family and some clothes and run away. He even looked at me, exhausted from his drinking, and asked me if I thought Rebecca would come back.

"Finally he was silent. I was hard and cold all through my body. There is no way to explain what happened to me in that room, but no soft places, no tender corners were left inside me. I was stone through and through."

Aunt Nell paused and ran her hand over her face like she was brushing cobwebs away. I tried to take her hand, but she pushed me back. "Don't touch me," she said. "I can't stand to be touched now." I waited, and then Aunt Nell went on.

"That was the dreadful part, the part I wish I could undo. You see, Camille, I began to curse my brother. I cursed his child and his wife and any children his child might have. Until I ran out of breath and strength, I cursed his life.

"It worked. All those curses took hold. Only Rebecca escaped my curses. She seemed happy with him, and she must have forgiven him. She loved her son. I think she even forgave me, because never by look or word did she hurt me. I came to see that your grandmother was a wise and noble woman. We never talked about any of this, she and I, but I had come to recognize before she died that Rebecca was a noble woman.

"She was so young, and Jeffrey must have shocked her terribly. She ran to her sister's in Ohio and stood on that platform with the lightning over her head and she stared at that great serpent rising up out of the earth. I've seen it. It rises up out of the ground and surprises you. It coils among the trees where you wouldn't ever expect to see such a thing.

"I heard about her trip later from the servant. The lightning striking down from the sky and Rebecca standing on the platform, looking at that snake on the earth below her. I don't know what Rebecca thought while she stood there, but she came home to Jeffrey. Your father was born seven months later. Rebecca came home to love and forgive, and she tried to get away from the snake.

"But your father was never the man he should have been. He was weak. He was a drunk. When I saw that, I was afraid. I prayed at night for God to lift the curse and make it stop with that generation, and then, when you were born, I thought it would be all right."

"But, Aunt Nell," I said gently. "I'm not cursed."

"You are barren. You wanted children and could never have them."

I was stunned and tried to help Aunt Nell. "It's all right," I said. "I'll stay here for now. I'll move in upstairs and be here with you for a few weeks. We'll get out of this."

"No one ever gets out of anything," she said. "I know you are worried about me, but I'll be all right. I need to think, and I want you to go. Let me just sit here and think." Aunt Nell sat completely still and shut her eyes.

She was firm and cold. She meant it. I stood up and walked out the door, feeling like a stranger to myself. I looked at her but knew of no easy thing to say that would help. I left the house and walked back to the cemetery in the twilight of early September. The heat was breaking. The air was heavy and smelled of rain.

I lay in my tent and did not cry but felt sad and old and helpless. Aunt Nell's story explained a lot of things that had never been fully realized before but had lain beneath my consciousness like stones in the water. My grandparents and Aunt Nell had never been together very much. They never had family dinners together or long visits on the porches on hot summer nights. Thinking back on it, the only times I had seen my Aunt Nell speak to my grandfather were when my father was in the hospital recovering from his drunken sprees.

The sadness of it was endless. The sadness seemed to go on from generation to generation, and I was caught in it too.

◇

It began raining during the night, and I woke to hear it on my tent. I was tired and felt the same sickness I had had the day before. My body couldn't have picked a worse time to weaken. I crawled over to the door and out under the sycamore tree. It was wet on the ground, but the branches shielded me while I threw up.

Now I was empty and remembering the death of the baby. I thought of crawling back in my tent and spending the morning crying, but a sheriff's car was winding up the gravel path. I pulled on slacks and a shirt. There was no avoiding the day.

The deputies were polite, although they obviously thought, seeing me in my tent with uncombed hair and pallid face, that the whole family was insane. I thought I would die if I didn't eat.

"I haven't had breakfast yet. Could I get some now?" I asked.

They agreed and stopped at McDonald's, where I ate eggs, sausage, muffin and potatoes, and drank two cups of hot, sugary tea. "I have flu," I explained. "Don't sit too close."

They sat drinking coffee in another booth while I ate, and then we drove to Aunt Nell's house. The deputies were being very patient, considering how crazy they must have thought I was, and they didn't comment on my absentmindedness or the peculiarity of my living conditions.

"Who's the legal guardian of the girl?" they asked on the way to Aunt Nell's.

I thought about it. "I don't really know. I know that Aunt Nell told her parents that Dinah was staying with her, but I don't think Dinah's parents ever wrote her or visited her."

Aunt Nell was fully dressed and composed. She looked about a hundred years old and was acquiring a fragility that worried me. She had been very thorough when the sheriff's deputies had arrived. She produced letters from Dinah's parents saying that they wanted nothing to do with Dinah. They never wanted to see her again. They could forgive the rape, but they would never forgive her for not aborting the baby. Dinah had ruined their chance for a cover-up.

"When I got this letter, I went to see Judge Simpson," Aunt Nell explained. "He had the juvenile authorities talk to Dinah's parents. They were adamant. They never wanted to see the girl again. The judge thought it was best that Dinah be given to me as a ward. She was not made a ward of the court. She was given to me to care for, and I was made her temporary legal guardian. You can see Judge Simpson for the details. There was going to be a hearing after the baby was born, and I assume that her parents would be called to attend. I was willing to have Dinah and her baby live here. I live alone, and it was nice having her."

The deputies asked if Dinah had been treated for any mental problems or if she had been sick. Aunt Nell didn't flinch but looked colder and more ancient as she answered.

"Camille thought of the idea of some sort of counseling. I suppose I am too old-fashioned. I wanted to help her myself. I saw psychiatrists as outsiders. I was too proud to admit that I might need some help with Dinah. I've never had a child myself, and I wanted to be completely responsible for her. As I am. I blame myself for what happened."

"You couldn't have known," I protested. "You did for her more than anyone could have."

"I wonder. A home for unwed mothers might have been better than just sitting here with an old woman. I wonder."

I was frantic. Aunt Nell was the kindest person I had ever known. True, things had worked out disastrously, but I didn't think she should be so hard on herself. I reached over and took her hand.

"The only problem is that you didn't get to Dinah in time. If you had raised her for a year before the pregnancy, or if you had been there right after she was raped, you would have saved her. But Dinah got to you too late. You mustn't give up now. You're all that Dinah has."

"I think I must give up, Camille. I have to admit that I am not equipped to raise a young girl. I am too old. The judge suggested as much to me, but I tossed the idea off. I think now that he was right."

We filled out dozens of papers concerning Dinah. Most of the answers we didn't know. I had no idea when Dinah had had measles if she ever had them at all. They wouldn't let us see her. She was under observation for ten days. Then we could visit. They agreed to let Dr. Robertson talk to her and check her physically.

I spent the next day trying to talk to Aunt Nell and keep her spirits up, but it was useless. She was sunk in her memories. I suggested that Dinah was really pretty distant kin to be included in a curse, but Aunt Nell only said, "She lived in my house. That was enough."

It was in the afternoon paper on Monday. The juvenile authorities did not release Dinah's name because she was underage. They described the drowning of the baby as if it were an accident, a silly girl who was playing with her new baby by the river and floated it out in a basket. The newspapers were quite kind, considering what a sensational story it was. One reporter showed up at Aunt Nell's and hung around on the sidewalk like a vulture. I told him that if he stepped on the property I would have him arrested, and then I pulled all the front blinds and shut the door. I would not have them bothering Aunt Nell.

"I'm going to bed for a nap," she said finally the afternoon of the second day. "I really need a few days alone, Camille. You come back in a few days and we'll talk."

I didn't know what to say. I wanted to comfort her, but she was beyond that. She was so sure that she had caused all of our problems. It was terrible, but my sitting in the living room wasn't having any effect. I kissed her and left. I was tired. I was sleepy. Delayed shock, I thought, and I too slept all afternoon. Sleep was the best part of my days now.

I woke up about six o'clock in the evening. The sun was still high, and I was hungry. I had been sick again that morning for the fourth day in a row, but now I felt lethargic and still sleepy. I dressed to walk over to the shopping center and have a sandwich and salad for dinner. A milkshake, I thought. What I really want is a milkshake. I hadn't had a milkshake in years. My stomach rumbled at the thought of the creamy, cold drink sliding down my throat.

I stood holding my bra, thinking about milkshakes, when it came to me. I froze where I was, holding my bra in one hand and my dress in the other. I stared at the green wall of the tent and my head hurt with thinking.

Throwing the clothes down, I dug out my notebook and flipped unseeingly past my lists. On a blank page I wrote:

JULY 23

I had made love the morning of the 23rd with Tom Church. Then I picked up Henry in Nashville and made love with him that night. Calling either episode lovemaking was stretching the point. One was caused by pity for Tom and the other by a bad case of self-pity. Whatever, I had sex twice on the 23rd.

My last period had been after the Fourth of July. I couldn't remember what day it had started. Closing my eyes, I tried to think, but the early days of July were like a dream. They all slid together into heat and romance with Tom Church. I hadn't seen him or made love for over a week, maybe ten days before the 23rd.

I had missed one period, which should have come about the first week of August, at least by the 10th. It was possible that I was in the process of missing another period. It was September 3rd. My head spun with numbers, added and subracted back and forth.

There is no need for panic, I thought. So many periods had been missed during my life. That was one reason why I had trouble getting pregnant. I wasn't the most fertile woman in the world. But to be pregnant now? At thirty-nine? It didn't make sense. Maybe it's early menopause, I thought gloomily. God knows I felt old enough.

Throwing on my clothes, I nearly ran to the shopping center. I bought a test kit that guaranteed to predict whether you were pregnant, and would have used it in the restaurant bathroom, but the directions said I had to wait till morning. I am probably the only woman in the world who doesn't know if she has the flu, is in shock from a sudden death, or is pregnant, I thought.

I must have read the directions twenty times before morning, even getting up and reading them in the middle of the night. At seven in the morning I crawled out of my tent and vomited. Vomiting every morning was the only dependable element in my life at this point. Opening the test kit carefully, I read the directions for the last time and began.

I peed sloppily into the lid of the test kit, collecting a sample. Then I squeezed the contents of a small vial into a test tube and added a single drop of my own urine. I pressed a rubber stopper securely over the end of the test tube, shook it hard and placed it gently in a holder made for it. A mirror under the bottom of the test tube reflected its liquid contents.

In two hours the test would be complete. If at that time the mirror reflected a dark-brown ring in the bottom of the test tube, a donut of color, then I was not pregnant. But if the whole bottom of my test tube reflected up at me a solid, brownish-yellow overall color, I was pregnant. It was seven o'clock. I had two hours to wait.

I didn't look at the test tube again until the hour hand on my watch moved firmly onto the nine. I went into the tent and stared at the plastic kit. I didn't dare touch it for fear I would tip it over and spoil the test. Under the test tube, which hung suspended in its small box, was the mirror. In the mirror I could see the reflected spot of yellow-brown from across the tent.

There it was, a circle of yellow-brown color, solid, a single overall color, unbroken and decisive. The test wasn't even faintly inconclusive. I was pregnant.

Thirty-nine years old, pregnant with my first baby, and I don't even know who the father is. All those years of faithful marriage and doctors' tests and trying to get pregnant, and it happens to me at the wrong age, at the wrong time, and probably with the wrong man.

Which one was the wrong man? I thought about it. Both of them, I gloomily decided. How on earth could I have managed this? Tom Church had been modern and polite, asking me what sort of contraceptive I used. I had laughed and told him that he needn't worry, "God himself couldn't get this body pregnant."

And Henry. He had never needed to ask, of course. We used contraception the first couple of years, but then we never again needed it. Contraception had never been one of my worries. I couldn't say that I had been taken advantage of. There was absolutely no one to blame.

I went back to the shopping center and ate a thoughtful breakfast. I was becoming one of their best customers. After prolonging my cup of tea and dragging it out with another muffin and a second cup of tea, I had to do it. I called Henry collect. It seemed appropriate. Like a teenager calling from college to tell Dad and Mom that she is knocked up.

"Henry? I need to talk to you." I didn't know where to start.

"It's lucky you caught me. I was just going out. I have to go down the Peninsula today to look at a software firm. What's happening?"

"Oh, Henry, I don't know. It started two days ago. Dinah came down to the river. She had her baby in a basket. I ran down to try and stop her, but I was too late. The basket sank before I could get to it."

"Jesus Christ! What are you saying?"

"The baby is dead. The papers reported it like it was an accident, but the juvenile authorities are protecting her. She did it on purpose."

"Do you mean she killed the baby? Is she crazy? Has she got a lawyer?"

"Well, she's a juvenile. They said we can get her one, but first they're observing her and doing some psychological testing."

"Let's hope she's crazy. Then they can put her away for a while."

I wasn't sure that I wanted that. "Well, I don't know if she is insane. She seems sane enough except for what she did that day."

"I suppose you'd better stay there until they decide what to do with her. Since she's a juvenile, there won't be a real trial, I guess."

"I don't think so. She admits what she did, but she was raped. And then she's so young. I don't know what they'll do. I think she needs a lot of counseling."

"Well," Henry went on, "that'll be best. This way your Aunt Nell doesn't have to worry about raising a baby at her age. Dinah can be taken care of by the juvenile system. If her parents won't help her, she belongs there anyway. There's no reason for your Aunt Nell to take on such a crazy kid at her age."

I was trying to work around to my pregnancy, but it was difficult. Talking about a young girl who was out of control and a murderess was hardly the best introduction for the announcement of the birth of yet another child.

"Not all kids are like Dinah, of course."

Henry laughed. "I'm not so sure. Oh, they don't all kill their babies, but they seem to be crazier and crazier all the time."

This wasn't much of an entrée, but I plunged ahead. It was long distance, after all. It was costing Henry money.

"Henry, I also called to tell you something else. I've been really sick for a few days, throwing up and all." I talked faster. I wanted to get it out before he interrupted me. "I got a test kit and used it this morning. It came out positive. I'm pregnant."

"What?"

"It's true, Henry. The kit. There was this bright yellow-brown circle. That means you're pregnant. I'm really pregnant."

Henry was silent for a moment. "Are you sure those things are certain? Hadn't you better go get some other sort of test from a doctor? Shouldn't you get a rabbit test?"

"I don't want to kill a rabbit just because I'm pregnant, Henry. The test was positive. I got pregnant when you were here. It's the only time I had sex since my last period. July twenty-third. That's the day."

"Well, my God, Camille. I don't know what to say."

I wasn't done. "But there's more, Henry. You see, Tom hit me that morning when I went to see him, remember? I had a black eye."

"Of course I remember."

"Well, we made love too."

"You mean he made love to you and then beat you up! What sort of bastard is he?"

"No, not exactly. We fought and then we made love."

Henry said nothing, for which I was grateful.

258

"You see . . ." I began.

"What I see is that either one of us could be the father."

"Right," I said stonily.

There was a silence that seemed to stretch on and on, then Henry spoke. "Camille, I've got to be at a meeting in an hour. Let me call you after the meeting, say in two hours."

I agreed and sat on a bench near the phone booth. I could have left, gone back to my tent, or shopped, but I sat on the bench and waited. The ring of the phone made me jump. It had been an hour and forty-five minutes.

Henry plunged right in. "Camille, that is one hell of a thing to drop on me right now. I've got this business flying, and I have to travel a lot, entertain, be seen in the right places. I was looking forward to doing it together. How can you do that if you have a baby? Even with a full-time nanny, we'd be tied down, and I know it would be hard to find someone to take care of it."

"It's true," I said. "It would change things."

"It's not as if this happened ten years ago. Even five years ago. This is just the wrong time. I don't think I want a child anymore. I don't know if I ever wanted one the way you did. You don't want it now, do you? At your age? It could be hell having it."

"I don't know."

"Goddamn it, Camille—you don't even know if I'm the father! Why don't we just enjoy life? I'll call your doctor and set up an appointment for an abortion. You can leave Kentucky in a week or two and have a simple abortion the day after you get back. My God. We're too old for this. It's too late. Besides, I may not even be the father."

It was all true. I was too old. I didn't know who the father was. It would mess up Henry's life. Why should he support a baby that might be another man's child? I was tired and sick of thinking about pregnancy and babies. Dinah had burned me out.

"I'll be home in two weeks, Henry. I wouldn't ask you to support a baby that might not even be yours."

"I know it's hard on you, honey, but we'll take a trip when it's over. To Hawaii or someplace relaxing. You'll get things back in perspective when you can rest up. Don't worry. It's a simple operation, hardly an operation at all."

"That's true, Henry. I'll call you again before I leave. It won't be long. They don't take that long to decide what to do with juveniles, I think."

I hung up and felt light and free. I didn't have to have the baby. I could be thin and elegant and sophisticated and ski and eat expensive lunches and be married to a successful, rich man. I was sorry, but this was not the right time for a baby. I'd given my body a chance for fifteen years and it had failed. Now was too late. Somehow, everything was always too late. Even though it was still afternoon, I returned to my tent and went to sleep.

It was early in the morning when I woke up, and I felt disoriented. I vomited on the grass, heaving over my empty stomach. Other than my morning sickness, everything had changed. Dinah was in Juvenile Hall. The baby was dead. Aunt Nell probably wasn't going to raise Dinah. I wasn't needed now, because the baby was dead and Dinah was being taken care of. Aunt Nell had a mysterious past and was living in constant depression over the mythical curse she had put on our family. My grandfather had not been perfect, and my grandmother was more compassionate than I had ever known. I was able to have a baby, but I didn't know if I wanted it now. Worse yet, I didn't know who the father was, and Henry was not interested in raising a child.

It had all worked out in a strange sort of way, and it depressed me. The thought of skiing in winter and Christmasing in Hawaii did not lift my spirits. I had come full circle and was back with Henry, unemployed, would be childless soon and could start again. Everything had changed but everything had somehow stayed the same. I groaned and stared out of the tent flap.

The light was still gray, but the birds were loud in the sycamore over my tent. It was almost time for the migrating flocks that flew into Kentucky and then on south every autumn. I remembered looking out my bedroom window and seeing a thousand yellow finches on the patchy grass in our backyard. They had landed and picked among the gravel and grass for any small bite they could find, moving and fluttering on the green like sunlight filtered through a strainer. I too would migrate soon. The nights were colder. It was time for me to go.

I went down to the sandbar and stood shivering on the edge of the river. The morning was warm, and the sandbar still bore the marks of boots and the scrape of boat hulls that had been dragged up while the deputies conferred. They had found nothing.

I knew that the baby was long gone. Who knows if such a tiny human would even float for long? They had found the basket, wet and broken from the hooks, but the baby had been drowned forever in the green water of Barren River. My arms broke out in goosebumps. The baby had floated and drifted in the river currents, down through the mud and silt, and must be miles from here by now. Every bank and bush had been searched for twenty-four hours by men looking for the tiny body.

I stared at the river, but I couldn't swim. Even that had changed. Even the beautiful river, my river and my swimming place where I had swum as a child, the place of my real baptism, even that had changed for me. I looked at the sun shining coldly in the dawn light on the water, and I didn't believe that I could ever again go into the river. It was not warm and sensual and sweet-smelling for me now. It was a serpent, green and cold and heavy, flowing over the land, past the town, unfeeling and indifferent. Babies, people, houses, branches, leaves. It made no exception. All fell into the river during the year, in summer, in flood time. It swallowed them all, ate them, and killed them.

I began walking up the riverbank. I walked aimlessly along the bank and watched the river. I walked on, climbing through the barbed-wire fences that marked the division of fields, threading my way through cows that lay under the trees by the river's edge, walking upriver.

The river's silence was eternal and terrifying. I tried to think rationally, but I was long past believing in breakfast and facewashing and the mechanics of living. I couldn't pretend. It's all pretending. We wash our faces and brush our teeth and dress and eat our nourishing breakfasts and stay busy all day, but the river doesn't go away. It lies here, green and cold and silent and flows on and on and ignores us. There was no set of rituals that could barricade me from the river. It could swallow me up as readily as the baby. The whole town could march down and walk into the green water, and it would flow on and stay silent still.

It was hotter now. I was lightheaded and saw the rise of ground that lay back of the boarded-up cave. I stared up at the rising sun and it was white and blinding. I forced myself to look into its eye. I will stare it down, I thought. I will stare at it until it goes out and then it will be dark.

Finally, I couldn't see the sun at all, only dazzling spots of light. I stumbled down the bank to the cave's entrance, feeling the rotted boards under my groping fingers. I ripped them off and fled the bright world into the cave, stumbling in the gloom where the small entrance of the tunnel had been boarded up years ago by my grandfather.

The cold breath of the earth drifted out to me, and I smiled. They boarded it up so I wouldn't go down. But I was going to go down now. What right had my grandfather to keep me out of the dark? The blackness of the hole was unseeable, and the cool air soothed my eyes. It didn't matter if I went into caves anymore.

THE CAVE

The tunnel widened until it ended in another wall of boards. These were better preserved but nailed together more loosely to form a barrier to the inner chambers of the cave. I ripped the boards off and was able to stand now as the chamber widened and deepened in the earth. I felt my way around a corner, going on and on until the light from the entrance was gone.

The darkness was complete and I was alone, with no person who knew where I was. I vowed to lie there, on the rock and the dust of the cave floor, and never come out again. I lay down, curled into a ball, and shivered, my mind blank. But how long can any of us lie on a rock floor in the dark and not move? It doesn't matter that our minds are blank. What matters is that our hipbones begin to ache. Our necks stiffen, calves knot. We move, we try to get more comfortable so we can concentrate on our self-pity. We try to be filled with despair, and instead we sneeze ignominiously like dogs with dust up our noses. . . .

I sat up, hugging my knees, and then felt a brief curiosity. Never as a child had I been this far back into the cave. The chamber must be large, larger than I remembered. I had no flashlight, but a lump in my pocket was a pack of matches I used to light my campstove. I would light just one match, look around, and then sit here forever.

The match sparked noisily in the silence and the light blinded me for a second. Holding the match out in front of me, I stood awkwardly and stared into the chamber.

"The baby!" I shrieked, and dropped the match in panic.

"It's the baby. Oh, God . . ."

I was sobbing now and lit another match in fear. It couldn't be the baby. The baby was deep in river mud. Gone. Lost. The baby was forever dead.

But as the second match burned, it showed in front of me, near the side of the chamber, a baby. Not a real baby, I could now tell, but a plastic doll, naked in a basket covered in lace and pink satin like a bassinet, lying there on the rock floor.

The match flickered out before I could see anything else. I was still shaking but no longer frightened, and I lit my matches one by one as I explored the vision they gave me.

The wall back of the doll was covered with pictures, colored spots that were hard to see at first. I held a match close and found a collage of faces, babies' faces. Torn out of magazines, they smiled as they ate, were bathed, were tossed into the air. Pinned into one crack in the wall was a note written in a firm, square hand. The match was hot on my fingers as I read:

June 18.   I miscarried again, Help me, Lord.

The match went out, and I lit another with shaking hands. More pictures of children and babies pinned to the wall and another note in the same handwriting:

I don't care about the cancer. I will have a child before I die.

Tears came to my eyes, and as the match went out I cried silently in the dark. I knew this handwriting. I had seen it in half the books in the house where I was born. I lit another match.

There was a box covered with a cloth in front of the wall of pictures. A vase had once held flowers, but only wisps like hay were left. There had once been candles. A few drops of wax stained the cloth. I held the match near the back wall and read a note pasted to the bottom of a picture of a woman bending over a sleeping child in a crib.

Let me carry just one child. Just one. Please.

I knew this handwriting. The notes had been written by my mother. She had decorated the basket with lace and satin. She had put the doll in and filled the vase with flowers. My mother. Lillian. This was her place.

I was desperate now. I had to read all the notes. I tried to see another before the match burned my fingers.

September.   The first miscarriage. Please let me try again, Lord. Please. Give me a child.

I sat down as the match went out and felt in the dark for the doll. I knelt on the stone floor and held the hard plastic baby to my breast and wept again.

"I'm so sorry," I cried out. "I'm sorry. I didn't know. I thought you were just weak and silly. No one ever talked to me about you. I didn't know who you were."

Still holding the doll, I stood and tried to light a match. I dropped the pack of matches and had to crouch on the cave floor, feeling blindly for it. Holding the matches like a lifeline, I lit another and ran my eyes over the pictures, looking for other notes. There were two pinned high on the right:

I know there must be a child inside me. Please let me get pregnant and carry it. Let me get my baby out.

My child will be good and brave and a decent person. Help me carry it.

I blew the match out and sat sucking my burned fingers, cradling the doll on my arm. I rocked the doll and licked my fingers to make the pain go away and cried. Cried heavily, sobbing not for my mother's miscarriages, not for the blood that poured out of my young mother and probably frightened her so much, but cried in shame.

She thought her child would be good and decent, and, worst of all, brave. I cried in shame as I thought of my summer. Sitting passively at the cemetery. Sloughing Dinah off onto an old woman who tried to get help from me, tried to make me talk to the girl, listen to her. Letting life flow around me and refusing to take hold of it. Too stubborn and weak to do something, anything that might have saved Dinah's baby.

Ignoring my burned fingers, I lit another match and put the doll gently down in the basket. I read a last note:

> *They say I won't live long, but I have a child in me. Let me give life to this one child. Don't let me lose another one.*

I read that note and put out the last match. For a few minutes I stood and felt love coming over me. Love. Powerful and gentle, that angel, love, filling me as I thought of my mother. Love comes to us as a gift, sometimes undeserved, sometimes earned with terrible price. The sudden recognition of who a person is can fill us with joy, with understanding.

So it was that at the age of thirty-nine I fell in love with my own mother in the dark of a cave thirty-seven years after she had died and left me to live in the world without her.

I had no more matches and it was dark, but this time I was moving, moving out of the cave quickly, my mind going faster than my body could. Talking out loud. Stumbling. Trying to sort it out. "I've got to see Aunt Nell. I want to know what she knows about my mother. Lillian. My mother's name. Lillian. I have to talk to her about Lillian. I have to get a psychiatrist for Dinah. My God, I have to go see the poor girl. She is just the age a daughter of mine might have been. My God. I once told someone that Dinah wasn't my daughter. Who was it? When did I say that? She isn't my daughter, but I can claim her.

"Dammit. I've got to get a lawyer. Talk to Henry about a divorce. Money. Some sort of work. Aunt Nell."

It spun around in me. There was so much to do, so much to say and to hear. I felt tears of rage and humiliation in my eyes when I realized how little I had done. How much I had avoided, how much I had turned away. I brushed the tears angrily off my face and ran across the fields. I had to get dressed. Rent a car. Buy a car, dammit.

And first I had to deal with what happened to Dinah. I had to deal with the lies and the evasions. I had to see Tom. I had to move. I had to live.

Aunt Nell was right. You never really get out of anything, but that was all right. I didn't want to get out of things anymore. No other baby would ever die because I tried to get out of life. I was going to live.

*O*F FINE FORM

Thomas Wiley made one mistake when he settled near Walker's Creek in Kentucky. The land was beautiful, his wife and four children were healthy and happy. Nonetheless, it was a mistake that would cost Thomas dearly.

Not far from the Wileys' cabin on Walker's Creek was another cabin, and in this cabin lived Matthias Harman. Harman hated Indians, and that was not unusual for 1789 in Kentucky, but Harman was not rational in his hatred. He was a man filled with rage that God even allowed such dirty, heathen, criminal savages to breathe the same air as he did. Harman killed Indians the same way that other men exterminated rats, and his passion was the doom of the Wileys.

It was a beautiful October afternoon. The trees had turned and the children were collecting red and yellow leaves to decorate the house. Jenny Wiley, a dark Scotswoman who was tall and lean, and, as everyone said, of fine form, was alone at the cabin with the three older children, her fifteen-month-old baby, and a younger brother of hers who was trying his wings in the wilderness. When the eleven Indians broke through the front door of the cabin, Jenny had no time to think. She tried to grab the children and hide them behind her, but two were outside, already lying dead with their skulls bashed in. The third ran as far as the cabin door and was killed, her throat cut from ear to ear, as Jenny watched.

The brother fought, but he too was dead in minutes, leaving Jenny clutching the screaming baby to her chest. And it didn't have to happen at all. Jenny and Thomas Wiley hadn't hurt the Indians. It had all begun when their neighbor, Matthias Harman, had killed the young son of a Cherokee chief some time back. The relentless anger and grief of the boy's relatives hunted Harman down as far as Walker's Creek, and, thinking that the Wiley cabin was where Harman lived, they had attacked. Jenny Wiley was left holding her child, staring at eleven Indians who were ready to kill her too, but that was not to happen.

It's hard to know what Jenny Wiley thought about during the next ten days. Did she think much? Was her shock so complete that she didn't think at all? Could she forget the four bodies lying scalped and bleeding, their eyes open in astonishment outside her cabin door?

The Indians loped on trails through rough forest and swollen creeks for twenty-four hours, stopping only once to eat some venison. Jenny was in the middle, clutching the child, who screamed in hunger and exhaustion until he couldn't make any sound, his mouth opening and shutting with nothing coming out. Jenny was glad when the child grew hoarse. The noise annoyed the Indians, and she was afraid they they would kill the baby. Besides, Jenny was eight and a half months pregnant. It took all her will and concentration to keep going. A howling child only drained her strength.

But it didn't work. For three days she kept up with the Indians, regardless of her pregnancy and her bleeding feet and the slaps and torments of the captors. She forded creeks and climbed hills, all at the unvarying lope of the Indians. Until the fourth day. She could no more. Falling behind, she tried to keep going, but the rocklike weight of a fifteen-month-old baby dragged her down. One of the Indians ripped the child from her and dashed its brains out against a large white oak tree. They let Jenny lie on the ground and rest while they took the scalp to add to the other four scalps on their belts.

Jenny was now alone except for her dog, who had followed at her heels, but she was not to be alone for long. By the ninth day the hard-pressed group reached the Ohio River and divided up. Five of the Indians took Jenny up the Little Sandy River. Jenny was not grieving now. She was in pain. All that day she had felt her labor beginning. It wouldn't do to show pain or fall behind. Jenny kept going. She had to keep moving and not show a tremor of her labor. She had another child to think about now.

The river had steep banks with huge overhangs of rock where the Indians often lived. These overhangs gave a decent roof but did not protect against snow and rain on one side. Jenny was left in one of these rock houses, where she gave birth that night to her son. She delivered him herself and was up the next morning, carrying water and gathering wood. A useful woman is a woman who can be allowed to live.

Winter in a rock house is rough for a woman and a new baby, but Jenny was a strong woman. She had worked in the fields with the men since she had been a little girl, she had hunted and chopped wood and carried buckets of water. She could sew and weave and cook and plant gardens and care for chickens and cows and make candles and soap and slaughter pigs and make cheese and chink a log cabin and mark a trail and swim and run and walk hundreds of miles. This was no Philadelphia lady, spoiled and soft, but the product of a green paradise that demanded all that a woman had to give. Jenny saw the trees begin to turn pink and then get new leaves. It was spring.

Since the baby was a boy, it was necessary to test it. If it passed the test, it would grow up Indian, a man. If it failed, well, it was better off dead. Jenny watched from the shore as the baby was tied to a piece of dry bark. Then he was floated out into the river current. Feeling the bark slip and move under him, the baby threw up his arms in startled horror and howled. The Indians were not surprised. It was only a white man's child. They tapped his skull in with the tomahawk, carefully so as not to damage the scalp. It was exceptionally long and had fine hair for such a small child.

Springtime was the time to move on to the buffalo lick. These huge licks where animals came in herds to get the salt they needed were scattered throughout Kentucky. Jenny was the only woman in the group. She had to do all the skinning, gutting, preparing of hides, corn planting, wood gathering, and cooking. She also had to keep a hot fire roaring for hours so that lead ore could be melted. This was woman's work. The men killed the animals, slept, and played games. That was work for men.

And now comes the question that everyone secretly wanted to know. Did Jenny Wiley sleep with any of those Indians? Did she have a lover? Or, since they were savages after all, many lovers? True, she didn't come home pregnant like so many captive women, but it made a person wonder. The frontier was short on pornography, but the stories of women captives weren't a bad substitute. Was it true that Indian men were different? Stronger? More potent? Jenny may have known. She was a beautiful woman and she was their slave. She may have known things undreamed of by her white friends, but she never told. And perhaps there was in her fierce, unyielding person, her face hard with determination to survive and thereby get the better of these damn Indians, perhaps there was in Jenny not much to tempt the Indians at that point.

A year had gone by. It was October again. The leaves were red and gold and the blood of the people who had died on Kentucky soil was seen in every tree of the forest. It was no surprise that the trees sucked such color from the soil. Dark and bloody ground was well fertilized for the roots of trees. And the time for violence came around again as if it were a seasonal disease.

The Indians had captured a young white man. Tying him to a stake, they slowly burned him to death. In their excitement, they looked at Jenny Wiley. She was stiff-necked. She was proud. They would break her.

Tying Jenny to a tree, they piled wood around her, but they had overshot their mark. What can you do to a woman who has seen her brother and four children twitching in their own blood? What can you scare a woman with who has delivered her own baby after a ten-day forced march and then seen the child killed casually on a spring day? What will shake a woman who has had to pick green twigs and tie them in circles to stretch the scalps of her own children? What else can you do to her?

It could be that the lick of flames seemed almost a Godsend to Jenny. She quietly allowed herself to be tied up and then faced the men contemptuously. It didn't surprise her. They could fetch their own wood and water and cure the skins themselves from now on. She would be free at last.

They released her. Nobody knows why. Shortly afterward, a Cherokee Chief bought her from the Shawnee leader of the band. The Cherokee wanted her. He wanted her to be his. Nowadays we would say that Jenny had the sort of genes that he wanted in his own gene pool. In 1790 he would have said that she was a good worker. Whatever. He bought her and promptly tied her wrists painfully tight with buffalo thongs. They were raw leather, and as they dried, they cut her skin.

Jenny slept restlessly. She dreamed dreams. She woke up. She dreamed more dreams. In her dreams she saw the man who had died the day before by torture. He pointed through the forest. Running ahead of her, he showed her the trail to a fort on a river. He beckoned her on.

The Indians went out hunting the next day and left Jenny tied. It rained and thundered, and lightning flashed. Jenny dropped to her knees and rolled over the ground until she lay in the center of a muddy depression. As the puddle formed around her, she forced her hands into the wet mud. The leather softened. It loosened. She ripped it off and was free.

There was snow on the ground now. It was a damp, early snow but it would leave her tracks plain to see, so Jenny waded downstream in the river. Following her on the bank was her dog, happily trotting along, ready for adventure. Jenny called the dog to her and lifted it off the bank into the water. She held its head under until it was dead. Killing the one living thing she had left from the days on Walker's Creek was the only way Jenny had of escaping. The dog would have given her away.

She waded all night in swift-running water. Her feet and legs were numb, but she kept picking them up and putting them down. She could no longer feel the bruises and cuts on her feet. She looked for the fort that had been in her dream. She followed the path. When there was a decision to be made, she took the path most like the path in her dream.

In twenty-four hours Jenny saw her fort. A family on a raft helped the woman across the river and into the gates of the fort itself. Jenny was silent and cold and almost unable to eat or stand up. She was also alive.

Matthias Harman, the Indian killer, escorted Jenny back to where her husband was living in Virginia. They fought Indians on the way, and Jenny killed her share. She had always been a crack shot with a rifle. Jenny and Thomas Wiley went on to have five more children, to replace the five they had lost. They resettled in Kentucky and lived a long life together.

When Jenny Wiley lay dying at seventy-one, in the year 1831, she was in Kentucky and surrounded by her children and grandchildren. As she stared up at the rough ceiling of the room where she lay, did Jenny think of her lost children? Did she long to join them in another land, or were her living children enough? Had she found life sweet enough to recompense for that one year as a captive? How sweet is life? How sweet?

Once again I faced Tom Church's front door. Several million years ago, it seemed, I had rung his doorbell, and we fought. I had no uneasiness this time, no doubts. This time I knew where I stood with Tom. This time I knew what to say.

The door opened and Tom looked at me in surprise. I couldn't tell if he was really surprised or if he was faking.

"Hello, Tom. I need to talk to you."

"Of course, Camille, come on in. I'm surprised to see you is all. After the last time—"

"It's not about that. It's not about us."

"I just don't think we can work anything out between us."

"I agree. I'm not here to work anything out about our romantic interlude. I'm here about Dinah. You heard that the baby is dead? That Dinah put her in a basket and floated her out in the river?"

"Yeah. I heard some talk."

I knew this was an understatement. Tom would have heard everything about the drowning within hours. Tom knew everyone.

"That's part of what I need to talk to you about."

"Well, if I can help—get the judge to let her off or something. She's a minor . . ."

"I don't want to get her off from anything, Tom, not exactly. I'm really looking for some kind of justice."

"You can't usually get that in this world, Camille. Maybe in the next." Tom smiled.

"That's true. We can't ever make up for her rape or for her abandonment, and she'll always have to bear the guilt over the baby's death. It's really all of our guilt, but Dinah will be the one to deal with it."

"I don't see that her killing a baby should give me any guilt—or you either," Tom said in a spirit of generosity. "You've had a hard time the last few days. You shouldn't try to think about this now, Camille. You look tired, honey. You look twenty years older than you did a month ago."

I felt a twinge of wounded vanity, and it made me laugh. Tom was a clever fighter. He put me off-balance so easily by telling me the very thing that our culture makes women most fearful of. I looked old.

"I probably do look older. Thank God for it, if that's what I need to see my life clearly. Maybe I'll bleach my hair white."

"I didn't mean to upset you."

"You didn't. Let's get down to it, Tom. Dinah was raped. The rape was hushed up, and Dinah was quietly gotten out of town with one old suitcase of clothes and three hundred dollars."

"I still believe that was the kindest thing for the girl."

"Your beliefs are of no importance to me right now."

Tom stood up and watched me warily as I explained to him what I intended to do.

"I've thought about it, Tom, and I'm willing to try to get some justice for Dinah in either one of two ways. I'm perfectly willing to hire lawyers, publicize Dinah's rape, and make her a female rallying point. Going back to court and producing all the evidence, all the results and reasons of the rape, might help Dinah get some feeling of self-esteem back."

"You know what I think about that. It's going to be a crucifixion for Dinah."

"Perhaps. But not if we interest other women in the case. With the right publicity, Dinah's case could be national news."

"You'd exploit her like that?"

"That is one possibility," I said. "There is another."

"Anything would be better than that."

"I'm glad you think so, because the second choice is the one that I prefer too."

"What is it?"

"It's like this. I feel that Dinah has been seriously injured and traumatized, first by the rape and then by the abandonment. It made her nearly crazy, and she never got any serious help."

"And who do you blame for that?"

"Who is to blame is not exactly the point. The point is that she was severely injured by six young men. Now she has a life to get on with."

"And?"

"And she should be paid damages."

"Now you're beginning to sound like a blackmailer."

"It isn't blackmail to claim damages after an assault. The second possibility for getting justice for Dinah is to set up a trust fund for her education and her therapy. A trust fund that will give her an edge on life."

"How much?"

"I've thought about that. I think thirty thousand dollars from each of the boys' families is about right. Thirty thousand won't ruin the parents, but it may force them to realize that rape is a serious assault."

"And just who is going to go around, hat in hand, and collect thirty thousand dollars from all six families?"

"Well, you do know them all, and you are the one who talked to everyone when Dinah was raped. That seems to make you the logical person to collect the damages."

"A couple of them are going to have to mortgage their businesses to get money like that."

"I'm sure they can work it out."

Tom was angry now, but I felt no flash of rage to meet his. I was well beyond my anger now and had settled in a country where Tom couldn't follow.

"There's a second condition besides the money."

"Only two conditions? You can do better than that, Camille."

"The second condition is that all six boys go into some sort of weekly therapy and stay in therapy for at least two years or until the therapist gives consent for them to stop. I think those boys need help as much as Dinah does."

"I'm surprised you even thought of them. I thought this was a woman's crusade."

"I've thought of a lot in the last day or two. All those boys need help or they may grow up even more warped than they are now. They've raped a girl. Indirectly, they are partly responsible for the baby's death. The boys need to think about that or they may become monsters. If they aren't already."

"So we come up with your blackmail money plus sending all the boys to a shrink, or you have a three-ring circus in the courts?"

"Dinah is going to get some sort of justice. It can be in court or out of court. You talk to the families and decide."

"And if we decide to call your bluff and go to court?"

"You might be making the right choice. A public hearing might help Dinah more than money."

"You'd love that. A big trial with noble Camille being the protector of a teenaged slut."

"No. You're wrong. I think getting money for Dinah and therapy for all the kids is a better idea. I want Dinah to get on with her life, not be bogged down in a trial."

"You'd never get a nickel for her in the courts."

"Maybe. But people on Kentucky juries are as fair-minded as people anywhere else. We might get a lot more, and even if we didn't get a cent, the legal fees could be enormous."

"I never thought you'd be a blackmailer, Camille. You know I won't drag my nephew's name through a trial."

"I'm not so sure that the names of rapists are that valuable."

"She'd slept with all of them before, dammit."

"One at a time and willingly. That does not give them the right to force her to do anything. You know that."

"How long do we have to think about it?" Tom asked.

"I'll give you three days. Then I'll go to the press and the lawyers."

274

"That isn't long enough."

"It's longer than it took to get Dinah out of town. You had her on that bus in forty-eight hours."

Tom knew I was serious. There was no flirtation or hesitation in me anymore when I spoke to him. He shrugged. "It may take a while to raise the cash."

"We'll be reasonable. The bank can hold the money in trust."

"I have to think," he said.

I didn't believe that Tom would think very long or very deeply, but I was no longer interested in what he thought. I knew he would raise the money rather than have a court trial. He was sick of it all. Tom was a man of action, and his instinct would be to get on with living. Dinah would have her trust fund.

"Handing some money over to Dinah won't prove to anyone that those boys were in the wrong, that they were criminals," were his final words.

I didn't reply. My knowledge of human nature said that Tom was wrong. Paying a large chunk of cash over because of their sons' actions would make every family think hard about what had happened to Dinah. The boys would have to think too. None of those families would hand over thirty thousand dollars and not mention it to their sons.

It wasn't really justice. Tom was right. Real justice might happen in another world, but it couldn't happen in this one. Still, I had to try. All the kids in therapy and Dinah with her own money paid to her as damages was a good place to start.

I knew that Tom would always be angry about the money. He hadn't pulled off the cover-up as slickly as he had hoped. It didn't depress me, though. Not all men were like Tom Church. There would be other men later. Right now I had a lot to do, a lot to prepare.

"How is she doing?" I asked the policewoman at the county Juvenile Hall.

"She's down. No doubt about that. She won't eat."

"Has she eaten anything?"

"Not a thing. Nice girl, though. She's polite, but I can't talk her into getting out of bed."

Dinah lay under a sheet. The room had bright walls, a linoleum floor, a desk and a chair. It was a room like all the rooms in dormitories and institutions. The only difference was that the door opened only from the outside and a square peephole allowed for no privacy.

"Dinah? I've come to see you. I've been so worried about you."

Dinah shut her eyes. "It's all right, Camille."

"No. It's not all right, Dinah. I want you to know that you don't have to be polite and nice."

"What do you mean?"

"Goddamn it, you were raped and abandoned and then you went to Aunt Nell, but you couldn't talk to her. She didn't know what to say."

"She let me stay with her."

"That's true, Dinah, but you needed more than that." I stopped and looked at the girl. I didn't know if I had a right to step into her life, but I was going to do it. I had to try.

"Dinah, listen to me." I took her hand and it lay limp between my own hands. I was surprised at how cold it was. The coldness of her young flesh was not natural, and I felt tears in my eyes.

"Dinah, I really failed you this summer. Do you know what? I'm thirty-nine years old. You could be my daughter, honey. I don't deserve having you as a daughter because I didn't help you when you needed me. But I am never going to fail you again."

"You were OK, Camille."

"No, I was not OK. But that's over. Now listen. I talked to Tom Church. I am going to get enough money for you so you can get an education and a decent start in life."

"You don't have to give me money, Camille." She closed her eyes again.

"I'm not going to give you money. It is not my money. It is yours, all one hundred and eighty thousand dollars. It is yours and no one else's."

Dinah stared at me. "I don't have any money."

"Yes, you do, or you will very soon. The family of every boy who raped you is putting money into a fund in your name. They owe it to you. That money won't make up for being raped and pregnant. I know it won't make up for the baby's dying but it will let you get on with your life."

"They won't do that, put money out for me."

"Oh, yes, they will. I'll see to that. You don't worry about it. I just wanted you to know that you aren't poor anymore. And all the boys have to go into therapy, Dinah. That won't do you a damn bit of good, but it may stop them from raping again. It may not, but maybe it will help them feel how terrible it was, what they did. I'd like to kill them all, but that wouldn't help you either. Not really."

"Their families must be mad if they have to give up all that money."

"I hope so. I hope we hit them where it's going to hurt the most, Dinah."

Dinah grinned. "You're really mad."

"Damn right I'm mad. I'm mad at Tom and the boys and their families and me. Mad at everybody. Except Aunt Nell. And I'm mad at you too, Dinah."

Dinah's face grew still and closed. "I killed her."

"That's not what I'm talking about. I'm mad at you because you're lying here, not eating, not showering, not taking care of yourself."

"I can't eat."

"Yes, you can. Now listen to me. I sat all summer and just let life slide by me. You are probably sitting here right now partly because of that. I never took you to your doctor and checked with him on how you were doing. I knew you were raped. I knew you just sat in your room all day with that goddamn television set."

"You got it for me, Camille."

"Yes. The sum total of my caring for you was in buying you a TV and taking you on a four-hour trip that neither of us really wanted to go on. But that's over. I want you to think about that."

"What do you mean?"

"I want you to remember that all I did was sit around and live like a vegetable. And you wound up in here. My days of being a vegetable and your days of sitting alone in your room are over. I'm going to start moving. So are you."

"They won't let me out of here."

"They will soon. I'm getting you a lawyer. He'll help you, and I'm sending a psychiatrist to see you. You're going to talk about this. When you get out of here, we're going to decide about your education."

"Camille, you don't have to do this."

"I'm just beginning. You're going to begin too. We'll learn together. Now, for today. You're going to get up, take a shower, and eat a little at every meal."

"I can't eat."

"It's hard for you to eat, but you are going to try. I'm going to be a bossy mother and you're not going to worry. You are going to get up every day and try."

Dinah lay very still and tears trickled slowly down her cheeks. They ran down into her hair and she sniffed twice. "I just want to be dead, I guess."

"Well, you are not going to be dead. I won't allow it. You are going to live."

"There's not much point. I mean, it doesn't seem to matter."

I moved off the chair and sat on the bed. Stroking Dinah's face and hair, I felt tears on my own face. "I know you've been through more in the last year than most grown women have been through in a lifetime. Of course you're suicidal. My God, of course you're tired of it all. But truly, Dinah, you must live. Aunt Nell and I love you very much, and we want to live with you, to get to know you better."

Dinah was sobbing now.

"Honestly, honey, I want you to live so much. And I'm going to help you. We have a lot to do, but we'll do it together. We'll make a whole new life, a new family. I promise you."

Dinah sat up and wrapped her arms around my neck and we sat together crying.

"Now, now," I whispered. "We're all going to be all right. You're going to get through this. I'm right here."

Before I left, I saw Dinah up and on her way to the shower. I made sure that the lawyer and psychiatrist could visit, and I

278

begged the policewoman to call me if Dinah seemed suicidal.

"I'm coming back tomorrow," I told Dinah. "You get cleaned up and try to eat. I'll bring you some French fries tomorrow."

"Camille, I really like French fries."

"I'll bring you a double order." I kissed her and left.

Now I had to see Aunt Nell. There was a lot that I had to say to her. She was overdue for a long talk.

Aunt Nell's front door was locked, but she didn't come when I rang the bell. I went around to the side of the house and pulled the trash can over to a window. Balancing precariously on it, I raised the window into the dining room. The lock on this window had been broken since I was a child, and Aunt Nell had never had it fixed. I had always been able to get into her house whenever I needed to.

I'll have to fix this window, I thought. It really wasn't safe to have the house so open. I was surprised that no one had thought of it before.

"Aunt Nell?" I called. The shades were drawn and the rooms dim. "Are you here?"

"I'm upstairs, Camille."

I ran up the stairs and into her bedroom. She sat propped up in her bed, the scrolls of mahogany in the headboard framing her. I automatically leaned against one of the fluted bedposts and grabbed the acorn that topped it. It was beautifully sculpted and felt good under my fingers, and, as usual, Aunt Nell said in irritation, "Stop swinging on the bedpost, Camille. You'll break it for sure doing that."

I stood up straight. "I just went out and saw Dinah. She hadn't been eating and she was pretty depressed, but I think I got through to her. I tried to tell her that we love her and care about her, and I think she was a little better when I left. She needs help, though. I talked to Tom Church and I think there's going to be a nice trust fund for Dinah."

"That's all very well and good, but I told you that I wanted a few days to be alone." Her querulous tone surprised me. She was suddenly an irritable old woman.

I sat down on the bed and looked at her. "What are you

doing?" I asked. Her sewing basket was on the bedside stand and she had her thimble on. Covering half the bed was a quilt that I had never seen.

"It's not really any of your business. I didn't let you in, you know. I've meant to fix that window for fifty years."

"I'm sorry. I just had to talk to you. Is this one of the quilts you made?"

"No. As a matter of fact it isn't." She was still peevish but seemed resigned to having me in the house. "My mother made beautiful quilts, as you know, and this is one of them."

I looked at the quilt and didn't say anything. It was the oddest quilt I'd ever seen. "What on earth are those things you're sewing on?"

"Coffins."

"What?"

"Well, you may have lived in California, but you don't know everything, I see. This is a graveyard quilt. My mother made it before she died. It was her last quilt. She got to thinking about all her dead relatives, and she made this quilt. She had to make it when my father wasn't in the house. He thought it was morbid and couldn't abide the thought of it."

"Let me look at it." I spread the quilt out so it lay flat on the bed. It was a pattern of stars, but in the middle of the quilt was an open space with an elaborate fence embroidered around it to look like wrought iron. Ivy had been embroidered over the gate, and a path of lace led from the edge of the quilt to the center. Appliquéd onto the border of the quilt were small geometric oblongs that did look like tiny coffins, but most of the cloth coffins were in the center of the quilt. They were neatly stitched to the green center space, and each coffin bore a satin label with a name painstakingly embroidered in satin thread.

Bending closer, I read the names: *Jeffrey*, that was my grandfather. *Daniel*, my great-grandfather, *Rebecca*, that was my grandmother. Then I saw two coffins sewn on side by side in one corner: *Jeff, Jr.* said one and *Lillian* said the other. "My parents," I said.

Aunt Nell nodded. "You won't know all of them. Those are my mother's brothers. They all died before her. That is one of her dearest friends. Those two are her parents. And"—Aunt Nell hesitated—"those are ours."

I shifted my glance to the border and stared in amazement. There was a row of coffins: one said *Nell*, one *Camille*, and another *Dinah*.

"My own coffin!"

"I knew you'd think it was silly, but my mother started it, and all the family we were close to have been moved into the center of the quilt, into the cemetery. My mother kept it up while she was alive, and then I put her coffin in when she died. I know it's a foolish sort of thing. We don't think about death the way people used to. No one minded grieving openly back then. You were supposed to do things in memory of the dead."

She pulled the quilt up to her and began stitching on a tiny coffin that was only halfway attached.

"You're putting on the baby."

"Yes."

"I don't think it's silly. I think it is beautiful to put her with the other kin. I think it's like taking her home."

"I don't know. I just felt like doing it." Aunt Nell began to cry, and I took the quilt and needle out of her hands.

"I'll put this one on. It's about time I started doing some of these things for you."

"I don't know what to do about the name." Aunt Nell blew her nose angrily. "I can't bear to have it there with no name at all."

"She was born in August. It's an awfully imposing name for a baby, but you could call her Augusta."

"Oh, Camille. Do you think Dinah will mind?"

"You could ask her."

"Oh Lord, I think and think about the baby. You know"—she took my hand, nearly stabbing herself with the needle I held—"the morning she died I put her down after a feeding. She had a puddle of milk in the crease between her mouth and her cheek. I didn't clean it out. I didn't want to wake her up, so I thought I'd wash her face later. I never got to do it."

Aunt Nell was crying again and I smoothed her hair gently. "Well, it doesn't matter. You loved her and were good to her."

"I know it's silly. I know that God doesn't care if a baby has a

281

dirty face when it dies, but it just sticks with me. I keep wishing I had wiped her face."

I took her hands firmly in mine and shook her gently. "Listen, Aunt Nell. I have to tell you something. I'm not leaving. I'm going to stay here, in Toms Creek, even though you don't have any decent movie theaters. I'm going to live with you, if you'll have me. I'm going to stay here."

She looked at me and I saw her flash of joy and then she pressed it down and shook her head. "No. That isn't right. You have to think of your husband. He can't work in Toms Creek. His business is in San Francisco."

"Oh, come on! Can you imagine me being a jet-setter? Can you see me spending all morning in I. Magnin and then all afternoon dressing to give an elegant dinner party? Can you see me being chic and sophisticated? Henry needs a woman who would enjoy that and could fly all over the world with him whenever he wanted to go. I don't want that. Besides, there's Dinah, too. She's going to need a home. I've let you take all of the burden, but I want to do that now. I'm going to do all I can for her. I'm going to call psychiatrists today and get a lawyer and see if we can't salvage the girl."

I stared at Aunt Nell. "Do you realize? Dinah is just the right age to be my daughter?"

"Well, I realize it, but I didn't think *you* ever would."

I grinned. She was recovering her tartness. Too many soft answers from Aunt Nell was a bad sign.

"Besides, you are getting old and silly."

"What! I may be a little laid down by this thing with the baby, but I'm certainly not silly, Camille." She ruffled like a chicken on a nest.

"Yes, you are. You have the most ridiculous notions about how you have cursed the family. It's like a soap opera. It's all silly. Look at me, for example. I've only been in this town for three months, and my husband only visited me once, and I'm pregnant for the first time in my life."

She looked at me in surprise and then joy. "Oh, my dear! Are you sure?"

"I am sure. And I am going to have my baby. Henry doesn't

want children now, anyway. I'll raise it, and we'll live together and fight over how to cook and keep house the right way, and I'm going to start a nursery school. That will be perfect with a baby around. I'll start a school, and it will be the best one in three counties, and we'll do just fine."

"You're sure you want this?" Aunt Nell was beaming.

"Yes."

"Have you been to a doctor yet?"

"I'm only about six weeks. I haven't thought of that or had time for it."

Aunt Nell pushed the covers back and edged off the high bed. I tried to help her find her slippers and she brushed me off. "I can find my own slippers, thank you. Don't think you're going to begin bossing me just because you're all fired up about being a mother."

She almost ran to her closet. "What are you doing?" I asked.

"Getting dressed of course. It's late and I'm not dressed. Have you had breakfast?"

I admitted that crackers and apple juice were all I had had.

She sniffed in disgust. "I'll fix something for us while you sew that on the quilt. Do try and take little stitches, Camille. Then I'm driving you to Dr. Robertson. You have to start today."

I picked up the quilt and sewed steadily with stitches about three times as large as Aunt Nell's. The day was going to be busier than I had thought. Aunt Nell was taking charge again.

Dear Henry,

I am writing to tell you that I am not coming back to California. I have decided to stay here in Toms Creek and live with Aunt Nell. She is old and alone, and she hasn't asked me to live here, but I want to do it. When I think back on it, she was like a mother to me, the only mother that I had. I think I should help her out now.

I don't know what the court will decide about Dinah, but the lawyer says that her age and the circumstances of her rape will be powerful arguments for some sort of psychiatric counseling. He may argue that the drowning was accidental, that she didn't understand what she was doing anyway. I don't know. The fact is, Dinah needs me too, and I want to be here for her when it is over. She is just so young, and I think I can give her a home.

You are kind to offer me the sort of life you are planning, and I do think it is nice of you to think that I might be there living it with you. I just don't think it is right for me, though. I don't want to entertain all the time and go to elegant places. I would just be an embarrassment to you. You need another kind of woman, and I don't think it is me. I want to start a new life here, my life, and it would probably bore you to death just thinking about how I am going to live. I want us to go ahead and get the divorce.

As far as money goes, we haven't ever fought over it and I don't see any sense in fighting now. I don't want any of your new company or anything you've made in the last two years since we've been separated. I can't believe that you want our old house, it isn't very good for entertaining. When you sell it, I want my half of the money. How much do you think that will be? I am planning to buy my father's old farm, at least part of it and the house, and I will need some money. I also want to renovate that barn and start a nursery school, and that will be expensive. I may be able to get loans, but a nice chunk of money would be great to get started. Can you write me about this?

As for my being pregnant, well, I don't want an abortion. I think they're fine for women who want them, but this is the only time I've ever been able to become pregnant. Even though the circumstances are odd and not really convenient, I think that this baby will be born. I want it. It will be part of my family, the baby and me and Aunt Nell and Dinah. If it is a boy, it will just have to tough it out with all the honorary aunties. Honestly, Henry, I think you are right. I was always the one who wanted the baby. It seems right that I raise it.

As for the baby's name. I am going to use my maiden name. My family has no heirs, so it will carry on the name, and it seems right. I do intend to tell everyone that you are the father. God willing, the baby won't look like Tom, even if he is the father. It would be best for the child that way. Being illegitimate in Toms Creek would be hard. Do you mind? I hope not. I hope you will allow me this one lie for the baby's sake.

Henry, I don't know how to end this letter. I have spent so much of my life caring about you. I don't want to be your wife, and I can't really believe you would want me now, but I think fondly of you. On the whole, for all of our problems, and lack of real sharing, our marriage wasn't so bad compared to a lot of marriages. We did try.

Take care of yourself and enjoy your new life. I intend to enjoy mine. Please write and tell me about the house and all that.

I hope you are happy and that your company gets very rich. I have to go now. I am moving to Aunt Nell's house until I can talk Mr. Branch into selling me the farm, or part of it anyway. You can address letters in care of Aunt Nell and I will get them.

Love as ever,
Camille

I didn't put it in the letter because I didn't want to wound Henry or make him feel sad over old times, but I couldn't go back to him again. I realized that I just wasn't an orphan anymore. I didn't know if I had been claimed or if I had done the claiming, but I could never be his orphan girl again.

My cemetery plot looked bare with the tent taken down and folded. I pulled up all the metal stakes and put them in their plastic pouch, coiled the ropes, and folded the whole thing into a neat package. The chemical toilet had been emptied and cleaned for the last time. My boxes of food were neatly organized and ready to be carried off. The sleeping bag lay across the top of the backpack, and my clothes were stuffed in the backpack, indifferently but tightly. All my belongings lay on the ground in a pile.

I walked over to the space of grass where my father and mother lay buried. "If it is a girl, I will name it for Aunt Nell," I said, looking at my mother's gravestone, "but Lillian will be her middle name."

I looked at my father's stone for a long while and then said, "Well, dammit! I can't name a boy for you. It might be a bad thing in such a small town to name a boy for a man who was an

alcoholic. I can't take the chance on scarring him that way."
Then I remembered something my father once said: "If I ever
had had a son," he had stated while staring into his glass of amber
bourbon. "If I ever had had a son, I would have named him for
my grandfather, Daniel, because this world is truly a den of
lions." Then he had laughed and tossed off the bourbon in a gulp.

"All right," I said to his gravestone. "If it is a boy, it will be
Daniel Carpenter. Maybe you will get your grandson after all."

I turned and walked toward the farmhouse where I had grown
up. It was hot again. We were in for a long Indian summer. The
cows were lying in the shade of the trees by the river. Grasshop-
pers, shrilling their last cries of summer, flew like sparks of neon
from under my feet, and the crows cawed in the oak trees.

I walked quickly and felt happy when I looked at the fields and
the house. The house I had taken care of and hated. The house
that now opened up on the world and let you watch the river and
the trees turning color in the fall.

Besides, there was the barn. I stopped and craned to see its
roof in the next pasture. It had been built well by my grandfather. It might truly be possible to redo it and make a nursery
school there.

Then there were the fields for gardens. A kitchen garden with
herbs and vegetables for me, I thought dreamily. And lots of
small pieces for the children in the school. They could all have
their own gardens.

I stopped thinking about it. There was too much to do today to
get involved in the possibilities of the barn and the pastures. I
didn't want all the land. I wanted the land from where the cave
was to the field beyond the house. That would be all the land I
cared about, the land I loved. The rest could be sold to other
people who would farm it better than I could.

The house and the stretch of land by the river. My child could
grow up here, as I had. I would have to board up the cave again,
but I would show it to the child when it was old enough. You're
not a Kentuckian until you've been down in a cave, I thought,
and laughed.

Mr. Branch was getting old and didn't want to be bothered
with all this land. He was tired of planting his tobacco, and he

missed his grandchildren. I still had to get in touch with a lawyer for Dinah, and the psychiatrist was calling me back at Aunt Nell's in an hour. I didn't have time to talk prices or details with Mr. Branch.

I just wanted to say it to him. I wanted to walk up on the porch and say, "Mr. Branch, my family built this house and lived on this land for years. I've decided to stay here in Toms Creek, and it seems fitting that I buy back my family's place. If you are interested in selling, I am interested in buying. I want my old home back."

I covered the last of the field at a run and stepped through the barbed wire. As I stood up and faced the house, it suddenly came to me that perhaps I hadn't been such a failure at all. I had tried to be a whale, tried to be a huge animal sinking into the sea and swimming freely. I had not been able to do that, but I had stared at enough pictures of fetuses to know what was inside me. There in my womb, diving and floating and moving through the amniotic fluid was a tiny creature that looked at six weeks almost like a whale, a whale as seen at a distance by the eye of God.

I knew it was there. It was perfect and swam freely in the salt sea locked inside me. I hadn't become a whale, but I had made something like it and released it to swim in that warm, liquid darkness my body had created. I walked up the steps of the porch and smiled as I rang the bell. I didn't care anymore about the things I couldn't do. I cared about the things I would do, the people I would love, and that dark, alive place, the saltwater I had made, the sea within.